THE L

SHADOWS AND CROWS

PETER NEALEN

THE LAND of SHADOWS & CROWS

WARGATE

An imprint of Galaxy's Edge Press
PO BOX 534
Puyallup, Washington 98371

ISBN: 978-1-949731-69-9

www.forgottenruin.com
www.wargatebooks.com

CHAPTER 1

SMOKE rose over the green hills, shrouding the white stone houses around the tall watchtower and the blood red sails that dotted the dark, choppy seas beyond in a veil of gray. Thick, boiling plumes billowed from burning roofs, and figures darted between the white walls of the coastal village, while cries of alarm and war rose over the crackle of the flames.

I glanced to my right and left as Rodeffer, Farrar, and Santos moved up through the trees to either side. Gunny Taylor was just past Santos, falling in at roughly the center of our loose skirmish line, and he stepped up to an ancient, wind-twisted oak, laid his M110 in the fork of a low limb, and took a moment to survey the situation through his scope.

I followed suit, getting behind a mossy rock and laying my own M110 in a slight trough in the stone. The rest of the platoon, along with Mathghaman's small warband, got down and scanned the fishing village.

We'd ridden as fast as some of us could ride horses from the city of Aith an Rih as soon as the smoke had begun to rise from the headland and the bells had sounded the alarm. There hadn't been time to brief the situation in detail, even if the Tuacha da Riamog had had all the details.

They might have. They're a perilous people, and they know things that seem impossible to us mere Recon Marines. But there still hadn't been time.

Now I got a sight picture full of a large man, pale and brown haired, with a spade of a beard and shaved upper lip, wearing quilted armor and a bronze helmet with black wings rising from its rim. The sword in his hand tapered to a wicked point, and his hexagonal shield was faced with hide, painted in a dragon design with a long, twisted tongue.

I watched as he pointed toward the tall, white limestone guard tower that doubled as a lighthouse for the headland, guarding the entrance to the great bay where Aith an Rih sat. Arrows rained down from the tower where most of the fishermen and their families had fled as the corsairs landed, but a knot of fully two dozen men, their shields interlocked above their heads, were moving toward the base of the tower. They were all dressed and armed similarly to the giant with the black wings on his helmet, though to varying degrees of richness.

These weren't the savage Dovos we'd fought up north. They wore more than skins, and they carried considerably finer weapons and equipment. I'd doubted that the Dovos could make the passage across that vast sea between the Land of Ice and Monsters and the Isle of Riamog, anyway.

There were a *lot* of them, though. And while an army of Tuacha was behind us, in glittering armor and carrying swords that could probably cleave through any one of these men from shoulder to crotch without slowing down, we were twenty-one men, counting Mathghaman and his five companions, against probably two hundred reavers who were either besieging the tower or running amok through the village, burning and pillaging.

Gunny's first shot was the signal to open the ball. I watched his bullet tear through the big man's quilted gambeson, and the man staggered, looking down uncomprehendingly at the growing red stain in his side. I followed up Gunny's shot with one of my own, slightly higher and more to the centerline. Gunny had hit him, but the bullet hadn't dropped him. Mine blasted through his sternum, and he dropped.

My rifle wasn't *really* an M110, not technically. It was the closest thing that King Caedmon's *Coira Ansec*, an artifact that looked like a gigantic golden cauldron, had produced from my mental image of one. It was balanced a little differently, and the forearm was something closer to MLOK than the Picatinny rail mine had had on it. It probably functioned a bit better than an actual M110, too.

My original M110 had been left behind on the USS *Makin Island* when we'd inserted, heading to Norway but ultimately bound for this strange, spooky world where we'd found ourselves fighting for our lives with nothing but M4s, knives, and guts against monsters, savages, and sorcery.

I transitioned to another raider, even as an arrow as long as my arm smashed through his shield and into his teeth from above. Those Tuacha bows were nothing to sniff at.

A horn sounded, loud and braying over the roar of the fires, the clash of arrows hammering into shields, and the yells of battle. The raiders reacted quickly, turning to present their shields toward us and falling back down the bank toward the sea and their beached ships.

We paused, and I glanced over at Gunny and Math-ghaman again. Both men were studying the situation with narrowed eyes. Mathghaman, a man of some importance among the Tuacha, or so I'd gathered, had a lot more experience with these corsairs, from what he'd said on the way here. But I didn't think even he'd expected such a quick and disciplined response to the opening fusillade of gunfire that had laid nearly two dozen raiders in the dirt, their lifeblood leaking out into the sand and the turf.

Mathghaman had a rifle of his own, though he was a swordsman by training and tradition. It looked more like an old Hawken than one of our M110s, never mind the Mk 48s that Farrar, Applegate, and Franks were carrying now. It was every bit as deadly as an M110, fired every bit as quickly, and he could use its iron sights every bit as effectively as we used our magnified optics. It just looked more...elegant.

Gunny waved at me, and I jogged over to join him, along with Bailey and Gurke, the other two team leaders who'd escaped the tunnels beneath Taramas's citadel.

Mathghaman was still watching the fishing village, where the fighting and pillaging had momentarily stilled as the corsairs retreated and reformed, his gray eyes narrowed but unblinking.

"I take it this isn't normal for them?" Gunny was watching Mathghaman more than he was the enemy at the moment. Shorter than me by half a head, he barely came to Mathghaman's chin, but Gunny Taylor was as hard as they came, and he was the man that we'd all look to for leadership first, no matter how much we might respect Mathghaman.

"No, it is not." Mathghaman wasn't speaking English, but thanks to a gift of the Tuacha they called the "mind speech," we could understand him perfectly anyway. "They must suspect some Tuacha sorcery." His tone turned wry at that. I could easily understand why. I'd seen the Tuacha do some prodigious things, but "sorcery" wouldn't be the term I'd use. More like "miracle."

Gunny scanned the terrain around us. The corsairs' retreat had put them into the low ground, just above the beach. A line of trees stretched up the headland toward the tower, where the corsairs still hadn't penetrated. He pointed. "Conor, Ross, take your teams and move up to that headland. We'll hold here and establish a base of fire." He grinned wolfishly. "Let's add to the legends about what happens when these bastards raid the Isle of Riamog, shall we?"

Gurke and I nodded, and I turned and hurried back to where Santos, a big, shaved ape of a man, Farrar, lean and hungry, and Rodeffer, wiry and long-limbed, waited in the trees, up on their weapons and looking for targets. The corsairs weren't obliging though. Only the occasional potshot sounded across the coast, and that felt more like probing fire than kill shots.

We had resupply thanks to King Caedmon now, though it had seemed to me that there were limits to what the *Coira Ansec* could or would do. At least it hadn't been stingy with ammo so far. So, we weren't nearly as worried about conserving ammunition as we had been up north.

Still, it was weird. These guys were acting like they'd seen guns before and had some sort of plan to counteract our fire. That wasn't good. Had they heard stories from the

Dovos and the Fohorimans in the north? Mathghaman had said these were a different enemy, but I wondered.

I wondered even more when something flew up from the shore, dark and somehow blurry even when I tracked in on it with my scope. That wasn't good. We'd seen things like that in the north, even if only out of the corner of the eye. The Dovos' shamans and the Fohorimans, the twisted, deformed monstrosities that had once been men and women but had long since sold their souls, had apparently used them the way we'd used drones back in The World. I didn't know what they were, but they were a threat, if only because they appeared to serve as the enemy's eyes and ears.

The thing skimmed through the air toward us. I didn't hear the leathery flapping sound that something similar had made in the north, but a hissing croak echoed over the burning fishing village, strangely loud given the other noise of battle and the fires.

As we hustled past Mathghaman and Gunny, heading for the forested flank on the headland, I saw Mathghaman tracking the dark, blurry thing in the air, his eyes narrowed. He whispered something as he lifted his rifle.

The *boom* of the shot silenced the croak. I glanced up in time to see the vaguely corvine silhouette dissolve into oily black smoke and vanish. I nodded with some satisfaction. The Tuacha were not defenseless on the preternatural battlefield. We kept going, moving quickly through the trees and up toward the tower on the headland.

But though Mathghaman had killed or banished their spying creature, the damage was done. Their sorcerer was doing something new. I could feel it as we slipped through the forest, a growing thunderstorm tension in the air. Despite the sea breeze, it felt like the air under the treetops was getting thick and stuffy. It was getting faintly hard to breathe, and I could smell something raw and metallic on the air.

It wasn't far to the tower, barely a thousand yards, and we were moving light. Our uniforms and equipment had changed a bit since we'd inserted off the USS *Makin Island*, somewhere far away in time and space. We all wore knee-length hauberks of green-enameled mail now, light and supple but proof against a lot of arrows and blades. They had mail hoods we could pull up over our heads, under light metal helms that we'd fitted with NVG mounts. But the armor weighed very little, and we hadn't brought our rucks to fight corsairs on what was friendly territory.

So, it was only a few minutes before we'd reached the edge of the woods on the headland and spread out among the rocks and the oaks, looking for a shot at the mob of corsairs down by the beach. But by then, things had already started happening.

Weird, sonorous chanting rose from the beach. As I got behind a massive, ancient oak and got on my rifle, I saw that the corsairs had formed a shield wall in a great crescent around the largest of the beached ships. The ships themselves were high-prowed, black-painted and carved with snarling beasts. They looked a bit more Mediterranean to my admittedly unpracticed eye than Viking. But neither name had any meaning here, anyway.

The shield wall surrounded a knot of raiders, kneeling and swaying around an emaciated, hunchbacked figure draped in black rags. I couldn't make out his face, as it was hidden beneath a deep, black cowl. But pale, crooked arms reached out from the rags wrapped around the figure's shoulders, fingers like claws grasping at the sky as the figure twitched and spasmed, as it continued that droning, buzzing chant.

I might not have been the best-versed in the magic and monsters stuff, but I knew a threat when I saw one. And we'd all seen enough in the north to know that sorcery was a very real threat. I put my crosshairs on the twitching figure in rags and took up the slack on the trigger.

Two things happened in the next fraction of a second. As my trigger broke, one of the raiders in the circle sprang to his feet. Actually, it looked more like he was yanked to his feet by some irresistible, invisible force. And he stood up, right in front of the shot I'd meant for the sorcerer. I saw him get hit, saw the puff of blood and debris as my bullet punched through his lamellar armor and into his back. It was only about a four-hundred-yard shot.

A 7.62x51 round hits pretty damn hard at four hundred yards. Especially when it goes through a man's heart and lungs, never mind his spine, which I'm pretty sure I'd just severed. And yet he stayed on his feet.

Then the sorcerer let out a ragged shout that buzzed and fritzed like a badly tuned radio, reached far over his head, and pulled down.

And the storm clouds above us suddenly dropped.

CHAPTER 2

IN an eyeblink, we were engulfed in cloud, rain, hail, and howling wind. It didn't faze us that much—Recon likes bad weather—but it dropped visibility to zero.

Which was probably the point.

"Bring it in! On me!" I had to bellow over the roar of the storm, even as the oak groaned and its branches lashed at me, leaves torn loose by the wind and the hail and sent whirling around us, adding more obscurant to the swirling clouds, rain, and hail.

They were coming, I knew it, and the storm was going to not only keep them out of sight, but it was also going to cover any noise they made. I squinted against the battering, peering over my sights and looking for the enemy.

With a roar, the first one was on me a second later, even as Rodeffer reached my tree, struggling against the wind. A small man, clad in scale armor and wearing a helmet crowned with a circular horsehair crest, came out of the storm, his hexagonal shield held out in front of him, his eyes slightly vacant as he launched a javelin at my head.

He missed. I didn't. I snapped my M110 up, put my offset red dot on his chest, and shot him through the shield. He was moving too fast for anything but a center-mass shot, but the bullet smashed straight through his shield and his breastplate. He crashed onto his face as the life went out of him.

Another, similarly armed and armored but with an axe raised behind his head to take a swipe at my neck, loomed out of the clouds a moment later, and I put a bullet between his eyes before the next two were on top of me.

I shot one, double-tapping 7.62 rounds through his chest and throat, and he dropped as blood sprayed from a shredded carotid artery. I ducked the swipe of the second's axe, buttstroked him in the guts, then flipped the muzzle over and shot him through the skull at contact distance. Blood spurted out of the hole in his helmet as he fell, and brain matter oozed from his shattered crown.

Then I was just dumping rounds into bodies as fast as I could get a blurry sight picture and squeeze the trigger. The corsairs had gotten spread out in the storm as they'd rushed us, which was a good thing. If they'd come at us in a coherent formation, we might have killed a dozen of them before they swept us under.

As it was, Rodeffer, Santos, and I kept shooting them down as they came out of the swirling, howling gray, until one after another our bolts locked back on empty mags.

There wasn't time to reload, and since we were well inside fifteen yards when the next one, a towering giant of a man with the same ISIS beard as the first one I'd shot, swinging a massive, spiked club with both hands, came out of the storm, I slung my rifle to my back and drew my sword.

I'd taken that blade off a dead Dovo in the gatehouse of an ancient, abandoned castle carved into the solid rock of a solitary tor, far in the north. He'd had the quillons, grip, and pommel wrapped because the runes set into the blessed blade and its hilts must have made his eyes itch. Gunny had cut the wrappings off, and Mathghaman himself had told me to continue to bear the weapon. It was the only one we'd had that could carve up some of the unnatural things we'd encountered up there.

Now I got it behind the round, bronze-faced shield I'd gotten from the Tuacha, and waded in.

I'd learned a lot from Mathghaman and Bearrac over the weeks since we'd sailed away from Teac Mor Farragah. I smoothly deflected the swing of the axe, then whipped my sword into the opening that the deflected blow had left.

He was fast, though, and danced back as two more corsairs came up to either side of him. I still nicked him, and blood began to flow down his arm as he snatched his axe back to cover his front, standing shoulder to shoulder with the growing rank of corsairs hunched behind their shields.

Then a bullet tore through his eye and splashed blood, brains, bone, and hair into the next man's face. Rodeffer had taken advantage of that momentary pause as I'd stepped forward to reload.

I backed up as Rodeffer continued dumping rounds into the advancing ranks of corsairs. I'll be honest, a part of me just wanted to wade in there and come to grips with them, sword cleaving flesh and bone, hand to hand like nature and Robert E. Howard intended. But when you've got an advantage in a fight, especially when you're outnumbered, you use it. So, I backed up, let the sword dangle from its loop around my wrist, slung my shield to my back again, snatched up my rifle, and reloaded.

For a brief moment, as Rodeffer and Farrar smashed bullets into heads and torsos, the suppressed 7.62 shots still thunderous even amid the howl of the storm, I spared a glance around us. I still couldn't see more than a couple of yards in any direction. The wind-whipped oak above us provided no shelter, as the rain and hail were being slung around almost horizontally by the screaming wind. It was a wonder we could even stand upright, let alone hit anything, even at that range.

All I could see were Farrar and Rodeffer. Farrar, Rodeffer, and the growing circle of corsairs, rushing in out of the storm in the hopes they could close the distance before we could shoot them.

I burned through the next mag in seconds, pumping out a constant staccato rhythm of gunfire that dumped another dozen corsairs onto the muddy, hail-strewn ground. The bolt locked back again, and then it was back to the sword as they rushed us in a tight wedge, trying to drive in and overwhelm us before we could reload again.

I had no idea where Gurke's team or even Santos were. The entire world had shrunk to this little corner of hell and the wild-eyed corsairs trying to cut us to pieces.

Like the Dovos in the north, they had to be more afraid of what was behind them than what we could do with our rifles. No sane man tries to rush a team of riflemen with a sword otherwise. Even with a storm dragged down to ground level to act as a smokescreen.

We probably should have fallen back to keep some distance between us and the enemy, but I didn't know where Santos was, or Gurke's team either, for that matter. I didn't want to accidentally shoot a brother Recon Marine in the back because we couldn't see what we were shooting at past ten yards.

So we stood our ground, Farrar producing an axe and Rodeffer drawing a leaf-bladed Tuacha sword. Both weapons were of considerably higher quality than the crude Dovo weapons most of the platoon had picked up during that nightmare trek across the north.

We had an eyeblink to get our close combat weapons out before they were on us.

It seemed that we'd already killed most of the dumb ones who'd just come roaring at us. The corsairs who advanced on us now were in a tight formation, shields interlocked and weapons held ready over their rims. They still came at us fast, almost dragged along by the big bruiser with the horned helmet who stood in the center. They knew that they had to close the distance and come to grips with us before we could reload.

The front line crashed into us, and only the confined terrain created by the ancient trees kept us from being swept under immediately. The oaks weren't as dense as we might have hoped, but they gave us some choke points that kept the full weight of the shield wall from coming at us at once. We fell back, keeping shoulder to shoulder and hewing at the advancing horde, but against a shield wall, three of us weren't going to do much. I split one shield but barely hauled my sword free before a blade nearly chopped my hand off at the wrist.

This wasn't a tenable position. If we didn't fall back, we were going to get slaughtered. But I knew enough to be sure that if we just turned and ran, we'd get slaughtered anyway.

And then it was too late. Farrar turned to the left as a flanking element came in at us from that direction, and Rodeffer nearly got his head taken off as more came in from the right.

"Back-to-back!" We quickly turned in to form a tight triangle, pressed together behind our shields, as blows rained down on us. I deflected some with my sword, caught more on my shield—which was holding up better than the corsairs' shields, but several more hammered against my helmet and my mail. The armor held, and saved my life, but the impacts were bruising nevertheless, and I ached with the effort and the pain of the blows.

We were going to die. We'd survived all the way through the north, only to die in the woods on the island that had been our safe haven. All three of us were completely on the defensive, too busy trying to keep swords, axes, clubs, and spears away from our vitals to fight back. It couldn't last long.

Then the wind changed.

A battering gust suddenly came from the south and tore at the storm clouds around us. With it came a high, clear trumpet call.

Seconds later, the storm was lifting, blasted out to sea by the wind, as the Tuacha's trumpets sounded again, along with the thunder of hooves as the main force from Aith na Rih arrived.

Our attackers faltered suddenly, and then a shout went up from the shore and they were turning and running, trying to get back to the beach and the ships before they were cut off. And they were about to be, as looking through the trees, I could see the great wedge of Tuacha warriors, armor and weapons gleaming, astride those magnificent warhorses, sweeping down the bank toward the ships. Even as I panted and gasped for breath, every muscle aching from the last few minutes of desperate fighting, I saw half a dozen corsairs run down when they tried to turn and fight.

Gurke and his team stood only a dozen yards away, though we'd been cut off from them by the flanking arm of the corsairs as well as the storm. Santos stood with them, to my great relief.

We'd survived. The corsair ships were already starting to back water, pulling at their oars frantically to get off the beach as the Tuacha set fire to those that were too slow. It was over.

If only I'd known.

CHAPTER 3

"THIS was what they truly wanted." Mathghaman's voice was bitter as we looked down at the ruin below us.

We hadn't had time to rest after the fight for the fishing village, a small settlement under the shelter of the headland tower where ordinary men had settled under the Tuacha's protection. Word had reached Aith an Rih that the headland had not been the only place the corsairs had attacked. King Caedmon, who had personally led the counterattack that had saved our lives, had gathered his personal bodyguard and our platoon—with Mathghaman and his own band of warriors, who had effectively formed our replacement fourth team—and ridden immediately for the southeast of the island.

Now he sat his horse next to Mathghaman and Gunny, looking down at the smoking ruin of what had once been a chapel. White haired but still tall, straight, and broad shouldered, the king stood nearly half a head taller than Mathghaman, and Mathghaman was taller than any of us by a couple of inches at least.

I rode up to join them as Bailey and Gurke closed in as well. Gunny Taylor, lean and hatchet-faced, with a few more crow's feet around his burning eyes than he'd had before we'd come to this strange world, glanced over at us and nodded, then jerked his head to beckon us forward.

King Caedmon looked over as we approached, and I slowed my horse ever so slightly. We hadn't necessarily been invited to join them, and while we'd just fought for the Isle of Riamog, after helping Mathghaman, Nuala, and their companions escape from the Land of Ice and Monsters, that didn't make me all that comfortable with presuming anything around the king. There was something regal and noble about all the Tuacha, and that became far more pronounced with King Caedmon. The man's very existence seemed to demand respect. Mathghaman and his team were all gathered around him, but they were Tuacha. We were outsiders.

Bearrac, barrel-chested and black bearded, had a rifle slung across his back but clearly preferred the leaf-bladed sword at his hip. Fennean, whipcord lean and flaxen-haired, loped along with both rifle and sword, his face composed and slightly eager. Fennean was a lot like us. He was perhaps nobler in his attitude and composure, but a part of him relished a good fight like every Recon Marine ever born. Diarmodh, small and quick with pointed features and a luxuriant golden mustache, had taken to the rifle like he'd been born with one in his hands. He carried his slung in front of him, just like the rest of us.

Three more of Mathghaman's band had joined us since we'd returned to the Isle of Riamog, though all three had been aboard the ship that had taken us away from the ruins of Teac Mar Farragah. Conall was a giant, towering over all of us and built like a classical Greek statue. Black haired and blue-eyed, his rifle seemed small in his massive hands. Eoghain was even broader than Bearrac, his wrists almost as big around as my biceps. His fiery red hair and beard bristled, and his rifle was noticeably bigger than the rest.

I can't say it was a .50 cal, but it was close. And he looked like he could take the recoil of a Barrett standing up.

Cairbre had been the last to join. Sharp-featured and black haired with burning eyes, there was something brooding and grim about him, something that had made me a little wary of him from the beginning. The Tuacha da Riamog, the Tribe of the Ever Young, were not entirely human, and they had a nobility, a *goodness* to them that had resonated from the first moment we'd found them in Taramas's dungeon. But there was something dark about Cairbre. I couldn't put my finger on it, but it was there.

Rifles weren't really the Tuacha's style, but Mathghaman and his men had adopted them because they had attached themselves to us. There was an unspoken bond and sense of debt there that Mathghaman had clearly assumed and none of us had dared to speak of.

Gurke and Bailey noticed my reticence and also slowed. But the king nodded, and I breathed a little easier as I nudged my horse forward to join them.

We had stopped on the high ground above another small village centered on a tiny stone chapel. The village was still in flames, even as the survivors carried buckets from the stream that ran down to the sea and threw water on the fires. But the chapel was in far worse shape. I couldn't see the whole thing from where we stood, but the front half of the roof was clearly cracked and half caved in.

"Come." King Caedmon wasn't inclined to sit our horses up there while we watched and talked things over. He nudged his silver-white destrier down the slope, and the rest of us followed, the platoon spreading out without being told into a loose wedge. We were Recon Marines, infantrymen, not cavalry, but we'd learned to adapt quickly since we'd sailed through that unnatural fog bank that had turned into a gateway to this place. And basic infantry tactics seemed to be useful enough under these circumstances.

King Caedmon led the way around to the front of the chapel. Bailey let out a low whistle as we rounded the corner.

Something had hit the front with catastrophic force. Only a handful of stones still stood. The rest had been blasted deep inside the nave. The carved oak doors had been smashed into splinters and scattered within the rubble.

The Tuacha's faces were grim as the king dismounted. I traded glances with Gunny, but he seemed as uncertain as I felt. We didn't know what exactly this place was, but it was clearly significant. Our friends wouldn't look like they were at a funeral otherwise.

The king looked down at his feet as he stepped out of the stirrup. I followed his gaze and felt my hackles rise.

The grass, in a rough circle about a yard wide, was withered and dead. A trail of dead vegetation led away from it, as if whatever had stood there and killed the ground had spread death with every step.

Mathghaman had followed my gaze and looked over at me. "Some of the fallen are so far gone that the earth itself groans at their very step." He nodded toward the dead space. "It would seem that one of them came here with the corsairs."

"Has that happened often?" Gunny asked.

King Caedmon shook his head. "Never in my lifetime." That was probably for a very long time. "The corsairs must have been offered a great price to do this. Even they are not usually so foolish as to consort directly with the damned."

I caught a raised eyebrow and widened eyes from Bailey. I didn't need to ask what that look meant. Bailey and I could almost read each other's minds. We were both thinking about the Dovos, particularly the shaman we'd called Dragon Mask. We'd been skating closer to the mouth of hell than we'd thought.

The king turned toward the chapel. "I think we already know what happened here." He started toward the rubble anyway.

Mathghaman got down and followed, accompanied by Bearrac and Fennean. Gunny, Gurke, Bailey, and I followed suit.

Footing was treacherous as we moved inside. The shadows deepened, but we could still see that the interior was empty at a glance. That didn't make any of us relax, not after what we'd already seen that day.

The Isle of Riamog was not as safe as we'd hoped.

A scrape sounded in the quiet, and a shadow moved near the sanctuary at the head of the chapel. Rifle muzzles came up, but King Caedmon raised a hand to stay us, even though he had his back turned. "Come out, sirrah."

The man who shuffled out from behind one of the carved stone columns that stood to either side of the sanctuary was bent and wizened, and he bowed his white-haired head as he knelt and wrung his hands before the king. Either he was an ordinary man like the fishermen who had sought sanctuary along the coast, or he was the oldest Tuacha I'd ever seen. "Forgive me, my king."

"What is there to forgive?" King Caedmon's voice was clear and grim but not accusing. "Did you hand over Nechtan's Staff to the invaders?"

"No, sire." The old man still bowed his head, his gnarled hands twisting in anguish. "But I did not seek to stop them, either. I hid, while Sister Sebeal defied them and was taken."

For a moment, the king looked down at him, as still as a statue. Finally, he sighed as he reached out to place a hand on the old man's head. "I know your grief, and I grieve as well. But your fighting days are over, Brother Ardhmaeal. If you had stood and fought, they would only have struck you down and taken her anyway." He bowed his head. "Whatever penance by which you seek to make your peace with Tigharn, I will leave to you. I only forbid it to be too harsh." He lifted Ardhmaeal to his feet. "Now, tell me what you saw. Every detail."

Old Ardhmaeal could only shake and weep for a moment as the king held him up with strong hands on his shoulders. Finally, he calmed himself enough to speak.

"They came from the sea in a rush, like a tide. Dozens of them, near a hundred, in close order, their spears like a forest that glinted in the sun. They were on the village in moments, faster than anyone could react. The guard attempted to hold the line in the street, but they were cut down without mercy."

He shook. "There was something else among them. Something that had shrouded itself in utter darkness. It was as if a black cloud glided across the ground."

For a moment, the old man sagged, as if the terror of the memory were about to make him collapse. "I could feel its eyes, though I could not see them. They carried an infinity of malice. It was as if cold, iron-hard fingers closed about my heart when it looked at me."

King Caedmon pointed back toward the dead spot on the ground. "Was that where it stood?"

"Yes, my king. It would advance no farther." There was still lingering horror in the old man's voice.

The king nodded. "The damned dare not tread on ground consecrated to Tigharn. Go on."

"Whatever that old hate was, it threw something at the doors, and the whole front wall collapsed. Then it waited while the corsairs rushed inside. Sister Sebeal tried to block their way, but they struck her in the head and dragged her off. Then one of them threw a black cloth over the staff and took it, while the rest stripped every bit of gold and silver from the altar." The old man sagged again. "I could only watch and fear."

King Caedmon had said his piece about that. "What sigil did they bear? Did you see?"

"Many of them bore some form of the blackened sun, my king."

With a nod, King Caedmon turned to where we stood with Mathghaman in the ruined aisle. "Mathghaman. I know that your errand in the north still calls to you, but I must ask you to put it aside for a time. Will you pursue these corsairs and bring Sister Sebeal back to us?"

For a brief moment, I thought Mathghaman would object. His face hardened and his eyes flashed. I still hadn't heard the full story of what had brought him and his companions to the frozen north, but he had said that they had been pursuing one of their own, who had committed some terrible crime. If it was bad enough to merit pursuit into that hellish place, then it had to have been heinous, indeed.

He hadn't said anything over the last few weeks about going back, but he'd clearly contemplated it. Been planning on it. It had been understood since we'd sailed away from Teac Mor Farragah. We had unfinished business up there, too.

But finally, he bowed his head. "Your champion's will is your own, my king."

King Caedmon gripped his shoulder. "I know what I ask, Mathghaman. And were it anyone else, I would not have laid such a burden on you."

Mathghaman only nodded. Then, with a furrowed brow and another sigh, he turned to us.

Gunny glanced around at the three of us and got short nods from each. We never would have gotten out of Taramas's citadel without Mathghaman, Fennean, and the others. He looked Mathghaman in the eye.

"We're in."

CHAPTER 4

WE were four days at sea before I ventured to ask Mathghaman more about our mission.

He'd brooded most of the time that we'd been prepping to leave. Gunny had tried to ask questions, but Nuala had intercepted him gently. "He will tell you when he is ready. Sister Sebeal means a great deal to all of us, and not only because she is the guardian of Nechtan's staff. But it pains him to leave unfinished business behind him." She wouldn't say anything more, but I was getting the distinct impression that Mathghaman's errand in the Land of Ice and Monsters was far more personal than he'd let on.

Our own preparation had been far more thorough than the last mission prep we'd done on the *Makin Island*. We didn't know where we were going or what kind of threats we might face, and while the Tuacha could tell us a few things about the corsairs, we didn't have enough of a common frame of reference regarding warfare to communicate what kind of gear, weapons, ammunition, and explosives we might want to take. So, we took as much as we could carry. Or, at least as much as the *Coira Ansec* would give us.

That was still quite a lot. Our rucks had been pretty heavy as we'd boarded the high-prowed ship the day after the corsair's raid.

Once we'd gotten gear stowed and tasks assigned, we'd settled into a regular shipboard routine of watchstanding, sleeping, eating, taking turns on the oars when needed, and learning to sail. It was hardly what we'd gotten used to aboard the *Makin Island*, but we'd had to adjust a lot since we'd arrived in this world.

Now, as the sun dipped toward the west and many of our mariners prepared to sleep, I joined Mathghaman in the bow. He was staring off toward the northeast, where we could still only see blank, empty ocean and a line of clouds turned pink and gold as the sun began to set.

Maybe he could see more than that. He was Tuacha, after all. But he was thinking, his eyes unfocused, staring at nothing. He'd been doing that a lot between chores on the ship the last few days.

I cleared my throat. "So, there's still a lot we haven't been told about all of this."

He glanced over his shoulder at me, as if he'd just noticed that I was there. He must have been very lost in thought. I didn't think I'd ever snuck up on a Tuacha before. Their senses were as preternatural as everything else about them.

"Forgive me." He turned away from the horizon and sat back against a coil of rope in the bow. "There has been much to do and much to think on. And there is still a great deal that *we* do not know or understand."

I nodded as I found a seat in the cramped prow beside him. "Such as why these corsairs would have taken Sister Sebeal? I can kind of imagine why they would have taken a particularly special staff."

"Hmm." He looked thoughtful. "If they believe the staff to be some artifact of sorcerous power, they are doomed to disappointment." He scratched his chin. "Though it is possible. The heathens often mistake such relics that way. *If* that is why they stole it. I do not think so, not given the presence of one of the fallen." He was only half talking to me. In a way, I could tell he was thinking out loud.

"So, what *does* the staff do?" I asked.

He laughed softly. "It has been known to cure the sick or wounded who touch it, though only rarely. It is a relic, not a sorcerous artifact. It was carried by a beloved of Tigharn. That is all."

"So, they stole it because they think it's something it's not? Then why are we sailing across the ocean to get it back?" I was trying to figure it out. I wasn't all that well-versed in this mystical stuff at the time.

"Perhaps they did. Perhaps they stole it to profane it. That, I think, is more likely." He looked over at me, that thoughtful look on his face. "And if it were only the staff, perhaps we would not go to such lengths to get it back."

"Sister Sebeal." I didn't need to ask the question. Mathghaman nodded.

"She is the closest we have to a living saint. A mystic and a healer. She is but a girl by our reckoning, yet she holds greater dignity among us than even King Caedmon and his queen." There was a reverence in his voice, but then his gaze sharpened as he looked me in the eye. "Make no mistake, though. Even were she but the poor daughter of one of those fishermen on the headland, we still would have embarked to get her back."

"No one gets left behind." I nodded. That much I could understand.

"Indeed."

The silence stretched. I could feel him watching me as I stared down at the boards of the deck. It was as if he knew what I was going to say next.

For my part, I was trying to figure out how to ask this without sounding petulant, bitter, or worse. After all, rescuing a girl who's a living saint *would* seem to be more urgent than looking for missing Recon Marines who were far from saints and may or may not have survived five minutes after the last time we'd seen them.

Mathghaman reached out and gripped my shoulder. "I know. I have unfinished business in the north, as well. But consider this. If your friends survived that fight in the tunnels, they will be prisoners. There were too many of Taramas's creatures between us and them when we escaped. If not, then seeking their bodies is less urgent." He sighed deeply, and I could tell I wasn't going to like the next part. "If they are prisoners, then you must prepare yourself to find that they are no longer the men you knew. It may have been a mercy if they were killed."

He could tell that I wasn't happy about it. That wasn't a reason to dawdle, in my mind.

"Consider this as well. To find your friends in the north, even after these few short weeks, will require a great effort to penetrate Taramas's citadel—if they are still there. She has other fastnesses. To catch these corsairs and rescue Sister Sebeal should take considerably less." He glanced at the men in our two ships. "We have the numbers to strike the corsairs. To go to war with Taramas would require months more preparation. Preparation that King Caedmon has begun even as we speak." His grip on my shoulder tightened. "We could not go in search of them immediately even if the corsairs had not taken Sister Sebeal. Patience, my friend."

How many times had Gunny Taylor told me that? It wasn't a lesson that I had ever taken to naturally. I wanted to get in and kill bad guys, regardless of odds or logistics. It was a flaw, and I knew it. And it was one that I still hadn't gotten much more of a handle on since Syria.

Somehow, in this place where the Marine Corps bureaucracy didn't exist, and our ties as a platoon were more out of loyalty and the isolation of being strangers in a strange land than any Marine Corps motivation, I doubted that my impulsiveness was going to get any easier to deal with.

"Patience." I sighed. "That's the hard part."

"It is, indeed, my friend." He looked up as the first stars began to come out. "It is, indeed."

CHAPTER 5

THE coast ahead was a dark line, only occasionally visible through the mists. The sun had vanished in the layers of gray over our heads, but Nachdainn was still sure of where we were.

Our rucks had been left down in the hold, but we were otherwise geared up, weapons in hand, scanning the forested coast ahead. I had my M110 braced against the prow, peering through my scope, while Mathghaman stood next to me, staring through the fog with his unaided eyes.

All I could see, through gaps in the white and gray, were dark evergreens, so close together that the shadows underneath were all but impenetrable. The narrow beach below was empty, the waves breaking softly against the rocks. We had to be in a sheltered cove for the surf to be so gentle, but any headlands to either flank were hidden in the shifting mists.

The only sounds were the faint flap of canvas, the dip of the oars, the lap of the waves against the hull, and the distant croak of ravens.

"You know where we are?" We were far enough offshore that Gunny probably didn't need to whisper, but it seemed appropriate, nevertheless.

Mathghaman nodded. "The closest of the Blackened Sun corsair towns lies only a few miles to the south. Nechdainn and I both thought that it would be best to avoid sailing right into their bay."

"Fair enough." Gunny scanned what we could see of the woods. There was something unsettling about that damp, dripping shadow beneath the trees. "Are we likely to run into patrols up here?"

"It is possible. There are trolls in these forests." It said something about how much we'd adapted to this world that none of us so much as blinked at that. *Trolls? Okay. Bring it.*

Granted, I still wasn't sure exactly what he was referring to. The meaning that the Tuacha's telepathy sort of attached to the word said *troll* to me, but we'd called the sort of fish-man things that had attacked us the first night in this place "sea-trolls," and somehow I didn't think Mathghaman was talking about them. He'd said they were in the woods, after all.

But we'd killed a lot of freaky things here already. What was some forest trolls?

Nechdainn kept the ship gliding forward until the keel scraped on the shingle. The oars came in, and we went over the side.

The water was cold, but not a deathly freezing as the far north had been. It only came up to our knees as we waded ashore, several of Nechdainn's deck hands jumping out with heavy lines to hold the ship on the bank while we spread out into the trees, guns up and scanning.

Moisture dripped from the trees, and the mists still curled between the trunks. The ground was rocky and mossy, with some ferns between the boles but very little undergrowth otherwise. Another croak echoed through the woods.

The platoon spread out into a rough wedge by teams, with mine at the point. We'd had to reorganize a bit since reaching the Isle of Riamog, so each team was about four guys, except for Mathghaman's, which was six. Gunny had fallen in with me. Not that he had placed himself under my leadership. He was Gunny.

We pushed about fifty yards into the trees, struggling a little bit under the weight of our rucks. We'd gotten some rest on the Isle of Riamog, and with some time to PT and the good food the Tuacha served we were well on the way to turning into physical beasts. We were still shrimps next to most of the Tuacha, who were Greek statues by comparison, but we were still in good shape even by Recon standards. But heavy rucks are heavy rucks, especially when you're walking over damp moss on rocks.

Fifty yards in, we halted and took a knee, listening and watching. The Tuacha took their own spot and did the same, going completely still as soon as they stopped. In fact, after a moment, I could barely even see they were there, their cloaks blended so thoroughly with the forest around us.

With a scrape, the ship backed water and pulled off the beach. Nechdainn would wait out there in the fog for us and would pace us down the coast as best he could.

After the ship had vanished into the mists, we still stayed where we were, straining our ears and watching the forest closely.

We probably should have gotten moving earlier.

No one had seen or heard anything by the time Gunny tapped me on the shoulder to indicate that we should get going. But I was peering as deeply into the darkness beneath the hanging, dripping boughs as I could, even as I got back to my feet.

I couldn't put my finger on what was causing it, but I'd started to get uneasy a few minutes before. I hadn't seen anything, smelled anything, or heard anything, but I was getting that feeling that we were being watched.

The fact that I couldn't see anything despite how closely I inspected every shadow, every nook under every tree within sight only made it worse. If something ordinary and natural was watching us in that close, damp forest, I should have been able to see *something*. Which meant whatever it was, it wasn't exactly natural.

Welcome to the reality of this monster-haunted world.

As we got up and started moving, I kept my head on a swivel, watching every direction I could as Rodeffer led out. Rodeffer could feel it, too. He was trying to watch every tree at once.

Still, we paced through the forest, turning to the south and paralleling the coast, and still saw and heard nothing besides the faint scrape of a boot or the equally faint rustle of wet gear. But that oppressive sense of being watched just got stronger.

Mathghaman was suddenly next to me. I hadn't heard him move—the Tuacha could move with preternatural stealth when they wished—but he was there in an eyeblink.

"We are being followed. Call the men in to circle up and prepare to fight."

Gunny didn't need to be told twice. He threw up a hand and circled it over his head, and a moment later we were closing in with Gunny and Mathghaman in the center, weapons outboard as we searched for whatever threat was out there in the dark and the damp.

Nothing. No movement. No sound except for the drip of moisture and another echoing *caw* out in the distance.

Then a deep, rumbling growl sounded, all too close. Or maybe it was a chuckle. It sounded like rocks being rolled together. And it sounded like it was behind us.

It was answered by a similar growl that was most definitely ahead of us. Rodeffer lifted his rifle, looking for a target. But all we could see was rocks, trees, moss, and ferns.

When they came, it was as if they suddenly erupted out of the ground.

The first one lunged for Rodeffer, swinging a club that was little more than a tree branch. It had to be eight feet tall and as green as the moss that grew everywhere here by the shore. Dressed only in a ragged tunic—or maybe that was actually moss—it had no neck, its massive head simply planted atop its massive shoulders. Long, pointed ears framed a flat face with beady eyes sunken above a massive, tusked maw. Its arms were long and heavily muscled, and when Rodeffer ducked beneath the swing of that huge club, it slammed into the tree trunk above his head with enough force that it sent shattered bark flying and cracked the club with an audible *bang*.

I was three paces back from Rodeffer, so while he threw himself flat to avoid the blow, I shot the troll through the teeth.

I'd prevailed to get the M110 because I wanted a 7.62 rifle that would reach out farther and hit harder than my 5.56 M4. Facing some of the monsters we'd faced already, having a rifle that was more of a hammer seemed like a good idea.

When my first shot cracked that thing's tusk and otherwise just annoyed it, I kind of wished that I'd asked for a .50, as heavy as that would have been to carry.

It reared back with a snarl, turning toward me, and then charged like an angry bull, swinging that massive tree branch for my head.

But I hadn't just stared in shock when my first shot didn't kill it. I shifted my aim slightly and shot it in the eye. The bullet smashed through the eyeball, splashing fluids and blood from the socket.

That didn't kill it, either. It roared again, the sound like an avalanche, and reared back slightly, but the bullet clearly hadn't gone into its brainpan. That thing had a skull like a tank.

I dropped my muzzle and dumped the next four rounds into its chest. Rodeffer had rolled onto his side, bringing his own rifle up, and hammered a pair into its stomach.

As tough as that thing was, it wasn't bulletproof where the bullets didn't fetch up against bone. Blood splashed as the bullets tore into its flesh, and it staggered. Bloody froth started to gather at the corners of its wide maw of a mouth as we kept pumping rounds into it. Then, finally, with a rumbling moan and a gasping rattle, it fell on its face, missing Rodeffer by inches.

The impact shook the ground and rattled the branches overhead, showering us with water. Rodeffer shot the troll a couple more times under the arm, just to be sure.

"Save your ammo. We've got a long way to go." Gunny stepped forward and prodded the troll's head with his sword. Sticking his point up under it, he levered it halfway around. It stared sightlessly from its one remaining eye, its jaws agape, blood still oozing across its jagged teeth.

Then a new set of grumbling roars went up all around us. That one hadn't been alone.

"Run!" Mathghaman pointed south. "Get out before they close the circle!"

More gunfire *crack*ed from the flanks as Gurke and Bailey and their teams engaged more of the trolls that were pounding out of the trees. A gray one that looked like it was a head taller than the green troll that Rodeffer and I had killed actually *bent a tree out of the way* as it charged toward Bailey's team.

"*Set! Turn and go!*" I pivoted, brought my M110 up, and shot the charging gray troll in the throat.

I'd meant to shoot it in the chest. For all I knew, that thing had a bone plate in front of its trachea, or worse, its spine was armored. And while blood spurted from the wound, it hardly slowed the big bruiser down. I steadied my aim and shot it again.

Meanwhile, as we'd practiced and drilled, Bailey and his team were turning and burning, swinging wide to get around us and stay out of our field of fire. At first glance, fire and maneuver might not seem to be that useful in a world where most of our enemies carried spears, swords, axes, teeth, and claws. But when you're outnumbered—and Recon is *always* outnumbered—keeping that distance is good, and the more you shoot at people, the less enthusiastic they get to go running after you. So, we took the big gray troll under fire while Bailey's team ran to keep their distance from that thing and its club, never mind its fists, feet, and tusks.

Another roar sounded to my left, though it was not answered by gunfire. Another green one, shorter but broader than the one Rodeffer and I had killed, had burst out of the trees and jumped Mathghaman and his team. Instead of opening fire and falling back, though, the Tuacha drew blades and leapt to meet it.

I couldn't spare the attention to watch them carve it up, though I was sure that was what they were doing. They were fast, strong, and consummate swordsmen, and Tuacha blades were on their own level. But we had our own troll to worry about, and it sounded like there were more coming.

Five shots into its A-zone, and that damned thing kept coming. Bailey and his boys were past us and about to halt when another troll, brown and hairy, burst through the trees and grabbed Baldinus.

Baldinus was technically one of our junior guys, but after the Land of Ice and Monsters, there wasn't any such thing. He twisted in its grip, even though he had to be in a lot of pain as that thing clamped him around the mid-section and lifted him toward its gaping gash of a mouth, then he jammed his M110's suppressor between its snaggle teeth and shot it repeatedly. It dropped him and reached up dumbly toward its torn mouth, but none of those shots had penetrated that thick skull.

Then Bailey, never one to wait around and gape when there was killing to be done, ducked in past Baldinus, jammed his own muzzle into the troll's solar plexus, and dumped five rounds up toward its heart as fast as he could pull the trigger.

The troll grasped at its chest like it was having a heart attack and sagged against the nearest tree, blood trickling from its mouth and nose.

I took that all in at a glance, as Farrar, who no longer had the radio to hump, since we had no one to talk to on

HF or satcom, opened fire on the big gray troll with the Mk 48.

He'd held his fire at first because Bailey and his team were in the way. Now he let rip, stitching the thing from crotch to throat with 7.62. The light machinegun, a heavier, 7.62mm version of the 5.56 Mk 46, itself an adaptation of the venerable M249 SAW, was a most satisfying replacement for the M27 Infantry Automatic Rifles we'd had on insert, which had just become slightly heavier versions of our M4s as the ammunition supply got steadily thinner and thinner. We still couldn't afford to spray and pray out here, but that thing was a buzzsaw in comparison.

The troll staggered as it took a dozen rounds through its vitals. Farrar was still getting used to the heavy weapon and was soon off target, but he'd done some serious damage. The last round that had hit actually skipped off the troll's thick skull, but by then it was leaking from a good twenty holes, and its next step saw its knee fold under it. Then it crashed onto its face, bouncing off a tree and making the whole thing shudder clear to its crown. More water flooded down from the branches, spattering the troll as it died.

Then we were moving, bounding past Bailey's team. Applegate had taken their Mk 48 and was currently set up behind the body of the brown troll and had the bipods braced on its side. He just didn't have a target, and Applegate wouldn't waste ammo on the trees.

Mathghaman and his men were moving now, blood on their blades and the troll in a couple of pieces behind them. None of them were so much as breathing hard.

We got past Bailey's team and Gurke's at the same time. I got a glance at Ross Gurke's face as we went and saw sheer frustration there. I realized that they probably hadn't gotten a shot off, while Mathghaman, Bearrac, and Fennean had carved the troll into dog treats. We all respected the hell out of Mathghaman, but when everyone else got to kill a troll while you sat on overwatch, that had to sting.

Don't worry, Ross. I'm sure we'll find plenty of other monsters to kill. It was just the way this place was.

Team by team, we bounded south through the woods, as a gravelly troll voice rose in a great shout behind us. There was a lot of rage and hate in that voice, even though I couldn't understand the words.

But they didn't follow us. Four dead trolls must have been enough.

For now.

CHAPTER 6

WE hadn't gone a klick before we slowed down and returned to a patrolling pace. The trolls didn't seem to be following us, the rucks were heavy, and most importantly, we were close enough to the nearest corsair settlement that we were all thinking that they had to have heard the fight. Even if the roars of the trolls hadn't carried, the supersonic *crack* of gunfire—even suppressed gunfire—traveled, especially in a quiet wilderness like these woods.

Moving through the forest, as quietly as men with seventy to eighty pounds of supplies, ammunition, and explosives on their backs can, we watched and listened. The silence was broken only by the drip of condensed moisture off the tree branches and the distant calls of ravens and crows.

The sense that we were being watched did not go away, however. I kept looking over my shoulder, halting to turn all the way around and check our six every few paces. Scanning the dark trees surrounding us revealed nothing, but the nagging sense of awareness remained.

Maybe one of the trolls *was* following us but staying hidden. That something that huge could stay invisible was remarkable, but I'd certainly seen weirder stuff already. We kept moving, but I dropped back to join Gunny, beside Santos. "There's still something back there."

He glanced over his shoulder. "Haven't seen or heard anything. You sure?"

I nodded. I'd had to learn to trust certain hunches here, nagging feelings that I might have mostly discounted back in the world. I'd always experienced those sorts of heebie-jeebies in combat zones, some more reliable than others. But here, they seemed sharper, more urgent. And they hadn't steered me wrong yet.

"Whatever it is, it hasn't showed itself. But it's back there. I can feel its eyes on us. Just haven't seen it yet."

Gunny peered at me with narrowed, knowing eyes. "You've got something in mind."

"Santos takes the rest of the team, Farrar and I hold here and wait for it. If it wants to play, Farrar stitches it up." It wasn't the most subtle of plans, but there are limits when you're humping a third of your bodyweight and you've already been compromised by unnatural creatures that could appear out of the ground right in front of you. Maybe over time we'd learn some tricks that would give us an advantage against things with preternatural abilities, but for now we just had Recon toughness and things that go *boom*.

Those two things will go a long way if you use 'em right.

Gunny thought about it for a second. "Fine. But don't fall too far behind."

Farrar had heard his name mentioned and had paused already, hefting the Mk 48 and bracing it against a tree. That sucker was heavy, and while Farrar had always carried the heaviest ruck, being the radioman, there's a difference between humping a heavy ruck and carrying a machine-gun. I beckoned him to join me, and we moved to a pile of mossy, lichen-covered boulders between a couple of the bigger trees. I set up on one side, and Farrar set up on the other, deploying the bipods and getting down behind the gun.

Then we waited.

The rest of the platoon moved past us, dwindling into the shadows under the trees to our rear. We stayed put, even as the uneasiness grew, knowing we were alone and unafraid, out of sight of the rest for the moment. I stayed as still as possible, barely breathing as I watched the woods.

Maybe the troll really hadn't noticed us. Maybe somehow, we'd evaded its senses simply by staying still and low. But I didn't think so.

It was big, even bigger than the gray one we'd killed earlier. Hairier, too. Except for its face, which was as flat and brutish as the others, it was completely covered in black hair. Its pointed ears flicked in different directions like a cat's, and it sniffed the air as it stopped just behind a fir about fifteen yards away.

We hadn't heard it or seen any sign of it until it had just materialized behind that trunk.

It stayed put, standing stock still behind that tree, and while it didn't look directly at us, I could tell it was watching us, nevertheless. The look on its face was still one of bestial hatred, but there was a cunning in its eyes...and maybe a little fear.

After a moment, the troll took a step forward, then stopped again. It seemed to be wrestling with something, conflicting emotions crossing its blunt features. That hatred, that hunger for bloodshed was written all over its face. It wanted us dead. It wanted to grind us up and eat us.

But there was something else that was stopping it. Something that made even that mountain of muscle, hair, and iron-dense bone pause and consider if it *really* wanted to go any farther.

That scared the hell out of me.

I stayed where I was, my rifle rock-steady, pointed right at the troll's heart. Horrific, brutal giant it might be, but I'd kill it in a heartbeat if it twitched wrong. It might be able to tear me apart with its bare hands, but I'd already put down two of its buddies. I knew it could bleed, and I knew I could kill it.

I just had to put enough lead into its heart to drop it before it reached our boulder. But that was also why Farrar had a belt fed.

It looked straight at me, then. I took my eye from my scope and met its beady, vicious eyes. It pointed at me with one massive, clawed finger. It spoke, then, and while I couldn't understand the growling, grunting words, in a voice like a landslide, I could hear the bitterness and anger in it.

Then it turned and vanished into the woods, almost as if it had stepped through a door. Just like that, it was gone.

Farrar and I stayed in place for a few more minutes, just to make sure. But the oppressive sense of watchfulness was gone. The troll had retreated.

I didn't know why. And that was worrisome. But we got up and headed south, hurrying to catch up with the rest of the platoon before they got too far ahead. We didn't know what else might be lurking in these woods, and if we were heading into the teeth of something that was scary enough that forest trolls didn't want to tangle with them, we were going to need every gun we had.

Yet as we hurried over the rocks and roots, moving from tree to tree and keeping our eyes peeled for any movement, whether overt or something shifting in the shadows out of the corner of the eye, all I could think of were the oily black horrors Dragon Mask had summoned in the dark beneath Taramas's citadel.

We might not have enough guns for this.

* * *

Linkup went smoothly. I told Gunny what had happened, watching the wheels turning behind his squint as he took it in without a word. He waved at Bailey, Gurke, and Mathghaman to join us, and I repeated the story. Bailey got that look. The "*I would have just killed it*" look. Except I knew that in reality he probably wouldn't have done anything differently than I had. Expending more ammo and potentially getting our heads ripped off wouldn't have accomplished anything, and the mission came first.

The kill count came later.

Mathghaman looked thoughtful, though. "Whatever fallen came with them, it is potent enough to put the fear into the trolls." He rubbed his chin. "We must tread carefully."

"Would they have come this far north if they were heading for the same settlement we are?" Gunny asked.

"The corsairs might not have, but the fallen are ancient and capricious. All it would have taken would be a whim." The way Mathghaman said it put a shiver up my spine. "We have not seen signs of its passage, but it would not take much, even for trolls." He looked around us as the crows cawed in the distance. "We must step carefully."

He got no argument.

* * *

The sun had nearly set by the time we got close to the settlement. We hadn't seen a soul moving around in the woods, and no sounds of civilization met our ears. Only crows and the faint whisper of the wind in the treetops as the mists cleared off.

The forest ended abruptly, opening up onto what had to be pastures. A few sheep with black wool and five horns each wandered over the open ground, skittish and nervous, cropping grass for a few moments before dashing away like frightened birds to another spot. They never got too close to the trees, I noticed.

Rodeffer had halted at the tree line, sinking to a knee and carefully scanning the pasture and the forest surrounding it. The sun had dipped toward the ocean, just visible through the trees to the west, and the woods seemed even darker and more foreboding than they had before. None of us dropped our NVGs yet, though we all had them on, mounted to the light, green-painted helms we'd donned at a security halt about half an hour before. We were still at that point in the dying light of day where there was just barely too much sunlight. It would wash out our NVGs and make it harder to see.

So, we crouched in the deepening shadows, watching and listening.

A sheep bleated. It was a weird sound, as if it were distorted somehow, but that might just have been because it wasn't a sheep like we were used to. There was something prehistoric about it, somehow.

Gunny took a knee next to me, scanning the open ground. It was our instinct to stick to the shadows and the concealment of the trees, but that might be even riskier here, especially as night fell.

Recon is used to being the ghosts in the darkness, the men who go where no one else wants to, lurking in the shadows, watching and reporting until the time comes to either call hell down on the bad guys' heads or else deliver it personally. But we weren't the only bogeymen in the night anymore. Not here.

Give it time.

"Team leaders. Bring it in." Gunny's whisper was low, but it traveled just far enough. If there was something out there with preternatural hearing, it already knew we were there, anyway.

The shadowy forms of the other TLs converged on our tree. "Ross, I want you to take your team around the east flank of the pasture and get eyes on that house." He pointed at the low, turf-roofed hut barely visible in the distance. "Signal back by IR flash, then we'll move up if it's clear."

Gurke nodded. "Will do, Gunny." Then he faded quietly back to grab his team.

The lurid glow of sunset was fading against the black silhouettes of the trees to the west. The stars were coming out above, as unfamiliar as ever. We still hadn't gotten a handle on the night sky here. And the moon had dwindled to new since we'd arrived in the north, so we still didn't know if we were on another world, or our own in some time far distant from our world of MEUs and computers and intercontinental air travel.

I figured it was finally dark enough for NVGs and dropped my PVS-15s in front of my eyes. The green image was still pale and a little washed out, but I could pick out the strange sheep and Gurke's team, having dropped their rucks, moving carefully along the tree line to the east.

I'd half expected to see eyes gleaming beneath those dark firs and cedars, invisible to the naked eye but glaring balefully on IR. It was a relief to see only the shadows behind Gurke and his team, who also had their 15s down as they picked their way carefully and quietly toward the farmhouse.

They didn't move quite silently enough to keep from being noticed by the sheep. The black shapes darted away from them with more of those weird, unsettling bleats. But nothing else seemed to react to their presence.

It took a few minutes for them to reach the house. I was watching through my offset red dot—unlike most of the rest of the rifle, that was an original that I'd removed from the top of my M4's ACOG and affixed to the mount that the *Coira Ansec* had helpfully provided even without my asking—since I hadn't thought to ask for a clip-on night vision optic to go in front of my scope. Trying to look through magnified optics with helmet-mounted NVGs doesn't tend to work very well. Eye relief gets to be a problem.

They spread out and halted in the trees just short of the house, which had been set back a healthy distance from the woods. There wouldn't be much shelter from the weather that way, but if you were worried about what might come out of the woods in the night, I supposed that was a reasonable precaution.

We were far enough away that I couldn't tell who stayed back at the tree line and who closed on the house. I imagined Gurke was probably one of the two who moved. Recon TLs tend to be that way. It's not even really a conscious thought of "leading from the front." It's more a matter of wanting to get our piece of the action and having the weight of authority to make sure we got it.

Recon Marines are all supposed to be self-starters and individual operators, anyway. We shouldn't need a team leader's "leadership" to do what needed to be done. To improve, to get the commander's intent, sure. But to do the job? If you need a leader to hold your hand to do the basics, then you need to go back to the grunts or wherever you came from, Devil.

Gurke and his number two man, who I *thought* was probably Herrera, moved in toward the door. They stacked up for a brief second, then they went in. They hadn't needed to kick the door in—which would have been a bad call to begin with—but just flowed silently into the darkness.

A moment later, they came out, and Gurke reached up and flashed the IR illuminator on his NVGs twice. *Clear.*

From the point of view of avoiding detection, that might have been a relief. But it wasn't. It was fully dark, the night having descended quickly after the last light of the sun faded in the west. There were still sheep in the pasture, unattended and clearly nervous. Where were the shepherds?

Mathghaman took lead, with Bailey behind, and my team held back while Gurke and his fell back to retrieve their rucks. Much like we had in the north, we had to keep those close. They were our lifeline in a land where there was no easy resupply. Especially not for ammo and munitions.

We crossed paths as they headed back. I wanted to ask Ross what he'd seen, but we were going to get a firsthand look in a few minutes. Waving Rodeffer ahead of me, I moved along the edge of the forest toward the hut.

It was tiny, which was no surprise for a sheepherder. The stone walls sagged a little beneath the turf roof, and tiny windows gaped like dark eye sockets in a dead skull. The silence was downright oppressive. Mathghaman's and Bailey's teams had taken up security positions around it, but no one had gone inside.

I stepped to the doorway and briefly shined my PEQ-16's IR flood inside.

There was nothing all that weird at first glance. A small straw bed, a rude table next to a firepit beneath a smoke hole in the ceiling. Half of the back was divided off by a wattle pen for the sheep in bad weather. There was little in the way of furniture that could have been carried off or disturbed.

There was also no sign of the shepherd. At least, not at first.

It's hard to see some things on night vision. Everything is some shade of black to green. And even some of those colors come through weird. Sometimes what's black looks light green on NVGs. So, it took me a moment to notice the stains splashed across the floor and the bed. They had dried, so there was no glint in my flood. Only a darker color that revealed itself reluctantly on IR.

It might have just been a spilled meal. But with the shepherd's absence and the eerie quiet of that place, I suspected it was something less wholesome.

If it was blood, it was about as much as fit in a human body.

Either way, I didn't really think that I wanted to spend the night in that hut. None of the others seemed to, either.

Under ordinary circumstances, back in The World, we'd just be getting started. But we'd already been in a fight and covered almost six klicks with heavy rucks. And as I said before, we weren't the only bogeyman in the dark anymore. So, we set in security and settled in for the night. Mathghaman and his brethren prayed before anyone went down on rest plan.

As we settled in, the wind seemed to whisper with a voice of its own through the treetops. Trees creaked, sounding almost like grim laughter. An owl—or something that sounded like it—screeched and hooted derisively, the sound echoing through the dark.

We watched the woods and waited for dawn.

No one got much sleep.

CHAPTER 7

THE corsair settlement huddled within a timber palisade, the logs peeled, tarred, and chopped to points, with square, covered watchtowers spaced around it about every hundred yards. The forest had been cleared away from the palisade for about a hundred yards in all directions except the west, where wooden piers and docks extended out into the bay. A small forest of masts, furled red sails hanging from the crossbars, swayed on the early morning waves.

Crows perched atop every roof we could see, cawing in the otherwise dead still grayness of the misty morning.

Rodeffer paced carefully through the trees, placing each boot with care. We were right on the corsairs' doorstep, and though something was clearly amiss—we still hadn't seen a living soul since we'd landed, unless you counted the trolls—that was only reason to step even more carefully.

We slipped through the edge of the forest like wraiths, moving slowly and silently, keeping as many trees between us and the guard towers as we could while still being able to observe. It meant some careful and tricky route selection, but Rodeffer was pretty good at it. We weren't moving fast, but despite the urgency of our rescue mission, this wasn't the time or the place for speed.

The forest opened up just ahead onto what appeared to be another pasture. More of the black, five-horned sheep grazed, still every bit as nervous and skittish as the ones we'd seen the night before.

There was something different here, though. Whereas all we'd found in that pasture and hut the previous evening had been scared sheep and an empty shack, now I could smell more than the damp forest.

I could smell death.

It's a distinctive smell. There's no mistaking the stench of bloated corpses and rotting blood for anything else. And it was rising from that palisade in noxious clouds. I was sure that only the cold and damp was keeping swarms of flies from rising in black billows as the crows hopped and cawed their derision of the dead.

Another turf-roofed hut sat out in the pasture. This one wasn't *entirely* unoccupied.

The sun should be all the way up, but it was on the other side of a wall of trees and shifting, soupy fog that drifted through the treetops. The pasture was still wrapped in dim, gray light, the green of the grass and the dark, bluish green of the firs' needles only just starting to show against the blacks and grays. So, the lump in the doorway that faced the palisade and the closed gates on the east side was little more than a dark, unmoving shape, even through my scope. But I could tell what it was.

I signaled Rodeffer and pointed toward the hut. He didn't look comfortable moving out into the open, but he nodded, his lips thinned behind the curly black beard he'd grown over the last few weeks, and stepped out of the trees, his rifle up as he scanned every angle possible. I pointed to Santos and Farrar and signaled that they needed to stay there on overwatch, then followed Rodeffer.

We moved quickly now, crossing the open pasture at a fast glide, ready to shoot if we had to but trying to get out of the exposed open ground in as little time as possible. So far, nothing had popped out to try to eat our faces, but we'd all learned not to take anything in this world for granted.

Rodeffer reached the corner of the hut, paused for a second, then swept past the door, clearing what he could see of the interior before moving on to the far corner and popping around it with his muzzle to make sure nothing was hiding on the other side. He didn't start shooting, or turn and run, so we were clear.

The lump in the doorway was a body, all right. Or most of it. Its head had been ripped off and was nowhere to be seen. Just the corpse to the shoulders, blood splashed across the doorposts and deep inside.

No weapon was in evidence. This man had never had a chance.

I scanned the inside of the hut. Mostly the same as the last, it was still as death. But not as empty as the previous.

I won't describe what had been done to the woman and the children.

A harsh croak sounded, far too close. I snapped my rifle up, but it was just a raven, perched on the peak of the turf roof, staring at me with one gimlet eye.

Was it "just" a raven, though? This place was already giving me the creeps. What if the thing that had already torn through the corsairs could shapeshift?

Those are not the kind of questions we'd been trained to ask, but when you have passed into a realm of monsters and sorcery, you learn to ask them anyway.

The raven croaked again and seemed to laugh as it hopped from foot to foot. It was probably waiting for me to clear off so it could resume its breakfast.

There wasn't anything we could do for the dead. Not at the moment. I turned aside, though I kept a side eye on the raven, and moved up to join Rodeffer. I spared a look at the gate, which was still shut, the watchtowers silent and empty aside from the crows gathered atop their peaked roofs.

Looking back at Santos and Farrar, I circled my hand above my head. *Bring it in.* We still had the rest of the perimeter to scout.

* * *

It was late morning by the time the rest of the platoon joined us in the woods to the east of the south-facing gate. We'd been in place for a while, watching the crows and trying to breathe through our mouths as the stench of death wafted out of the open gateway.

Gunny gathered the team leaders up. I laid out what we'd found. No movement but the carrion birds. The mutilated corpses in the shepherd's hut. Mathghaman's face got ever grimmer as I made my report. Though he said nothing, I could see the look of dread in his eye, a look that told me he had strong suspicions that he knew what had happened but was afraid to voice it.

Gurke stared at the open gates, looking a little green around the gills. "Do we really need to go in there?"

Mathghaman nodded. "We do. If only to ensure that Sister Sebeal does not lie among the dead."

I could have hung back, having just completed the leader's recon of the perimeter. Instead, I got to my feet, my M110 ready in my hands. "Let's go."

* * *

The bodies strewn in doorways and across the muddy track that served as a street leading toward the town square had clearly been dead for a while. Despite the chill and the damp, flies were still clustered on many of them, and the crows had been at them, too. Most of the black carrion birds that perched on roofs and the tops of the palisade walls had clearly gorged themselves. Half a dozen flapped away from the corpse that lay half in the nearest doorway as we stepped past, muzzles raised to cover the door and the darkened interior.

Much like the bodies in the shepherd's hut, this one had been torn open savagely before the carrion eaters had ever gotten to it. Dried blood spattered the doorposts, where the timber door had been smashed inward with horrific force, splintering the wood and tearing the leather hinges off their nails.

I flicked on my PEQ-16's white light and shone it in the doorway. Under different circumstances I wouldn't have dared to use white light, but it was broad daylight, and it wasn't like we were hiding on the open street.

Playing the light over the interior, I saw two more bodies. I couldn't be sure, but it almost looked as if they'd been huddled in the corner, trying to hide, and had been torn horribly as they'd been violently ripped from their corner and flung halfway across the room.

Whatever had done this, it had to be blindingly fast and incredibly strong.

We continued to work our way up the street. The whole settlement was probably close to half a klick wide, mostly consisting of a half dozen longhouses with smaller huts clustered around them. An even bigger, two-story timber building stood at the center, overlooking the town square. I couldn't tell for sure if it was a temple, a castle, or both.

All we saw as we carefully made our way up the street were bodies. Bodies and crows.

The doors to the big timber building hung open, smashed and splintered just like every other we'd seen so far. One was all but gone, only a couple of planks clinging to the leather hinges. The other swung slightly in the faint sea breeze that had begun to pick up, blowing the tattered shreds of the fog inland. The hinges creaked faintly in the otherwise eerie quiet.

I knew what we were going to find in there. No one had shown their face since we'd set foot on shore. The stench of death from inside that darkened portal was, if anything, worse than outside.

We cleared the doorway, then spread out quickly to cover corners and scan the dimness inside with white lights. Stealth had to take a backseat to not getting ambushed out of the dark.

Most of the massive building was one big room with a vaulted ceiling. Dim gray light spilled down from the smoke hole in the center, above a massive, stone fire pit dug into the packed dirt floor. Trestle tables and benches had encircled the fireplace, but many had been smashed and tossed aside. More torn and bloated bodies were strewn across the wreckage.

Three more corpses lay across the dais at the head of the hall, sprawled beneath a tall, timber seat. Above the dais loomed a stone plinth that had been carved into an idol of a figure with a faceless helmet with six horns and a sword in each hand, crossed over its chest.

There was something different about those three bodies.

As we advanced on the dais, I could see that they weren't twisted and sprawled in attitudes of violent death, unlike the rest of the bodies. They also hadn't been torn apart. They looked almost…peaceful.

That was creepy enough all by itself, given the state of the rest of the settlement.

The man had been dressed in a long tunic of dark red wool, under a vest and a cloak of yellow and blue. The woman wore a dress of similar colors, embroidered and inlaid with silver ornaments. The boy might have grown to be almost his father's twin, but he had been only about twelve when he died.

All three were bone white, except for the faint bloodstains around ragged gashes in their necks.

Mathghaman looked down at the corpses, his face grim, and nodded. "Things become clearer."

The term he used next, *fuil armesha*, I understood as "blood drunk." But at the same time, I got a pretty good idea of what he was talking about. Not that I'd needed the context, given what we were looking at.

Vampire.

Clearly, this thing wasn't like the Hollywood version, either. It had massacred every human being within over a mile, and from the looks of things, none of them had been able to touch it.

"There are vampires in this world?" Rodeffer was scanning the roof above, as if looking for the bat-like form hanging upside down from the rafters.

"They are rare." Mathghaman was still looking down at the bodies. He didn't seem to be worried about the vampire popping up out of the shadows. "It takes a great deal of wickedness and crimes deep and unnatural to create a vampire."

"I had dared to hope that none still cursed the earth with their presence," Bearrac growled nearby. "It would explain the dead ground where it stood, though."

"Indeed." Mathghaman took a deep breath, despite the reek of decomposing corpses in the hall. "And it means we must make haste. If such a thing holds Sister Sebeal in its grasp..." He trailed off. Even without knowing her, I could feel his dread. If I'd known then what I do now about vampires, I would have felt the same dread.

Gunny asked the question we were all thinking. "So, how do we kill it?"

Mathghaman turned away from the exsanguinated headman and his family and strode toward the door. "That, my friend, is the question."

CHAPTER 8

WE put the settlement to the torch before we left. We didn't have the time or the manpower to bury all the bodies, or even move them all inside before we lit the buildings on fire. But there were enough wooden houses in that town that the conflagration should be enough to cremate at least most of them.

Flames and smoke billowed up behind us as we moved into the woods, paralleling the narrow dirt track that formed the only road we'd found so far. I was sure the fire would spread once the walls caught, but hopefully we'd be long gone before it could catch up with us. The climate was damp enough that it should be put out by the weather before too long.

Still, despite the low clouds and the mists, that column of smoke had to be visible for miles. There would be no disguising the fact that we were coming—though if we were following a vampire, that might just be a moot point.

We still stayed off the track and moved carefully through the woods, watching and waiting for whatever horror this place was going to throw at us next.

After all, I don't think any of us expected the vampire to be the only monster in the area.

* * *

The rest of the day passed without incident, however. We covered maybe ten more klicks before it started to get dark, at which point we set security and settled in for the night. Gunny and Bailey both brought up fires. The Dovos in the north had lit them at night, as much to try to keep the creatures of the night at bay as to keep from freezing to death. The latter issue wasn't so much of a problem here, especially not with our Ranger rolls and Tuacha cloaks. But we'd already fought forest trolls who could seemingly appear out of the ground without warning. If fires could keep monsters away, the tradeoff seemed to be worth it.

Mathghaman wasn't sure. Bearrac was solidly against it. Cairbre seemed to be in favor. The other Tuacha were either ambivalent or on Bearrac's side.

"Why not have the fire lays ready, and if security sees anything on NVGs, we can light them?" It seemed like an okay compromise to me.

Bailey shrugged as if to say that he thought it was a good enough idea. Gurke was clearly leaning toward fires—he'd been a little rattled since Mathghaman had first said, "Vampire." Most of Mathghaman's Tuacha seemed to accept it.

Only Cairbre glared at me, as if I'd offended his very soul. I locked eyes with him and stared him down, though he could probably cut me to pieces in an eyeblink. I'd respect Mathghaman and Bearrac, and Fennean and Diarmodh. But I wasn't going to bend the knee to any of them. I was a Recon Marine. I'd fought and killed one of Taramas's hunters. Sure, I'd gotten my ass kicked in the process, but it was dead, and I was still breathing.

So, I wasn't going to back down because a Tuacha who hadn't been there on that desperate run from the caves to the sea, or fought without much hope of relief as Taramas's servants and monsters had swarmed us, got butt-hurt because mere mortal me had come up with a better idea.

Still, I'd keep an eye on him. So far, the Tuacha had all been noble, honorable people, but I'd been around people too long to think that there was any group of folks alive who didn't have at least *some* bad apples.

We set security, built the fire lays, and settled in for the night.

* * *

Rodeffer woke me up for my watch, and I rolled out of my poncho and liner, then carefully stowed them back in my ruck. I hadn't taken my boots off, though usually I might take one off during a long halt like this. Those woods just didn't seem like the right place.

With my ruck packed and ready to move if we needed to break out, I tapped Rodeffer and took his place on the perimeter, lowering my PVS-15s in front of my eyes.

"Thought I saw something moving out there a few minutes ago." Rodeffer had put his face right next to my ear, subvocalizing in a voice even quieter than a whisper. "Couldn't hear anything, though, and if there's something out there, it's pretty good at hiding."

I just nodded. Any breeze that had been coming off the ocean had died away, and the mists were gathering again. The tree boles could barely be seen, even on NVGs, and quickly disappeared into the unremitting blackness.

Rodeffer lay down against his ruck, his rifle by his side with the sling wrapped around his arm. He was asleep in seconds.

I glanced down at the younger man for a moment. I envied him that ability. I had to be completely wiped out to fall asleep that fast. They say that soldiers or Marines can fall asleep at the drop of a hat, and it's true for some. For others, the alertness that's been drummed into us for years makes it difficult.

I was still tired, though, so rather than sit against my ruck with my weapon across my knees, I quietly got up on a knee and scanned the woods around us.

And froze.

Something *was* moving through the trees. Something that showed as a pale shape out in the dark, almost as if it was glowing with its own inner luminescence. I felt the hairs go up with the goosebumps all over my arms.

I raised my head and looked under my NVGs. I couldn't see anything. Lowering them again, I could still see that faintly luminescent figure, gliding from tree to tree toward us.

No, not toward us. Toward the road.

Slowly and quietly, I lifted my M110 and tilted it to pick up the offset red dot. Whatever that thing was, it was hard to track. It seemed almost to flicker from time to time, and not in time with its passage behind tree trunks. It was almost as if it wasn't really there.

A moment later, Bailey joined me with a rustle of movement. "Conor, that you?"

"Yeah." I still didn't take my eyes off the specter in the woods or lower my rifle.

"Are you seeing this?" He stepped carefully between Farrar and Santos and dropped to a knee next to me. "I guess you are."

"Yeah, I see it. Not sure what it is, but I see it."

"Do not look at it more than you must." Bearrac was a big dude, but he moved like a cat. I actually started a little when he spoke, practically at my elbow. I hadn't heard him move at all.

"What is it?" Bailey had his own rifle up, tracking the same thing. If it moved wrong, it was going to get multiple 7.62 rounds through it. Whether that would affect it at all was the other question, as it faded and flickered like a badly tuned video signal.

"Vampires draw certain spirits in their wake. Hungry, evil things." His face was faintly washed out and blurry in my NVGs, but I could still make out his scowl. "They cannot prey on a man's mortal body, but they wish they could. They are mindless entities of hate and malice, and if you give them an opening, they will burrow into your mind and seek to prey on your soul." His voice had taken on a haunted note, and I suspected he was speaking from experience. "In their own way, they are every bit as rapacious as the vampire itself."

Bailey had picked up on his tone, too. "You've run into these before, I guess?"

Bearrac nodded. "Long ago. There was no vampire, but many of these things lurk near places of great pain and death." When I looked over my shoulder at him, his eyes were far away. He turned and met my gaze, though he was looking at the tubes of my NVGs. The Tuacha didn't need them. "Look away. Do not listen if it calls to you. Act as if it were not there. Your mind and your soul depend on it."

Having heard that, it actually got harder *not* to watch the strange, amorphous figure in the dark. Even harder to ignore the faint, moaning song that might or might not have been floating amid the whisper of the wind in the treetops. Especially since we had to maintain security. But we had to try. I remembered the weird, horrifying stuff that Dragon Mask had done, and what that had cost us. Letting something like that get its claws into one of us could be disastrous.

It took some doing, shifting our thinking from purely natural threats, people or things who wanted to spill blood and just kill us, to supernatural threats as well. It still wasn't something we were really used to. I'd seen some weird stuff in combat, stuff that made me wonder. But all of that was turned up to eleven in this place.

Given some of the stuff that had been happening before we'd gone to sea on the *Makin Island*, reported as strange while no one dared come close to examining the implications, maybe this really was our world, far in the future. A future where the spooky stuff had finally caught up with us and overwhelmed the modern world with all its tech and assurance that everything was known and cataloged.

"You'll have to tell us that story." Bailey was clearly struggling to avoid watching the luminescent shadow out there, too, and he was trying to redirect his attention. He was also fishing for intel. That was Bailey. He could be even more impulsive than me, but when he put his mind to it, he was a thinker. Most Recon Marines are. Not all, but most.

"Perhaps someday. Here and now, with such things lurking near, is not the time nor the place." Bearrac shook his head. "Watch for other things. Think of home. Pray. To speak in too much detail of such things is to summon them." He rose quietly. "Guard your minds, my friends." He slipped away into the dark, doubtless to warn the others up on security to avoid watching any flickering, glowing figures in the dark.

The thing had drifted past, out of my sector, and so far, hadn't acted like it was even aware of us. I hoped that it stayed that way, that Bearrac had been right, and that it was mindless enough that we actually had to actively gain its attention to attract it. It had been creepy enough even before Bearrac had told us what it was.

"Man, I'm never going to get used to this spooks and monsters stuff." Bailey hadn't moved yet. He didn't rattle easily. I'd watched him kill an abominable snowman—or whatever that thing had been—while it was choking the life out of him. He was a stone-cold killer, and, in many ways, he was the embodiment of the Recon "Suffer in Silence" motto.

But this place had us all rattled, on some level.

"I mean, I'll kill savages, corsairs, and even trolls all day. But this mystical stuff? Shit, man. As soon as I start to think I've figured out the rules, some ghost or something comes along that changes everything." He sighed. "I mean, why is there stuff that can eat your brain that you can't even shoot?"

"Lots of that back in The World, brother." I hadn't really thought about it much before then, but there had been plenty of threats in the world we'd grown up in that we couldn't shoot. Drones, chemical weapons, IEDs...the list went on.

But even as I said it, I knew that this was different. There are things you can do to spot and avoid IEDs. How do you set countermeasures for evil spirits?

"Yeah, but this is weirder." He gusted a sigh. "Never thought I'd be in the middle of a live-fire fantasy novel. Or a DnD game."

"None of us did." There were certainly times when I wished that I could be worried about normal threats, like ISIS, or Iranians, or Russians. But at the same time, there was something about this place that spoke to me.

The Tuacha had shown that while there were a lot of monsters and a lot of evil here, there was good, too. There was something…transcendent. Something that had been lost a long time ago back in The World. The veil was really thin here, and there was something about that that just felt right to me. There was more to everything than just the bare physical reality, and here that was laid open for all to see.

It was scary as hell sometimes, but we were Recon Marines, and we could be pretty damn scary, ourselves.

"Adapt, improvise, and overcome, though." I was still watching the woods, vaguely aware of the specter as it moved on past us, still moaning that eerie song. But I didn't look at it. Did my damnedest to tune out the distant keening it was making.

"Yeah. There is that. Though you know I've got to give you a ration of shit for saying something *so* motarded now, right?"

"Yeah, I thought of that as soon as the words came out of my mouth."

Bailey chuckled. Sometimes, that's all we need, when things are dark and scary and we don't know if the next moment is going to be our last. Just a chuckle, a little shit-talking between brother Marines, and we can refocus and get ready to keep driving forward, one foot in front of the other, damn the pain, damn the danger.

He got up and headed back to his team. Bearrac was still making his rounds, checking on everyone and warning against giving the ghostly thing out in the tree what it wanted. I glanced at my watch. It still wasn't quite in sync with time here. It was almost as if the day was just a few minutes longer, and it added up over time. But it was still good enough for judging how long we had to stay on watch.

An hour and a half left. Then I could lie down and close my eyes again, even if it did mean facing the dreams and nightmares.

CHAPTER 9

THE next village was much like the first. This one had mostly burned to the ground by the time we got there, though. Only the great hall in the center was mostly untouched, and once again three completely exsanguinated corpses lay in the middle.

"Hey, Conor. Check this out." Rodeffer had paused on the southward road, crouched off to one side and studying the marks in the mud. "There's something weird going on here."

I stepped up to join him. Rodeffer had been through the Combat Tracker course, and I hadn't been, but I'd been hunting long enough that I knew how to read spoor. "Yeah, there is."

One set of prints was clearly made by something that wasn't entirely natural. While the prints were human at first glance, the ground in and around them looked almost scorched—dried, cracked and gray. A weed growing up through the mud of the road was withered and dead where a foot had flattened it. Those had to be our vampire's footprints.

But there were others, following along behind. And while it was difficult to pick out patterns in the mass of spoor along the road—some of which was probably fairly old, given the fact it hadn't rained heavily since we'd landed—there was enough to see something was off. Several of the fresher tracks, new enough that they had to have been made since the massacre, were regular, the sort of tracks you'd expect a formation of men to leave, including the occasional smaller hole punched in the dirt by the butt of a spear. But the others, trailing behind and overlaying those tracks...

I crouched down and took a knee because the load of my ruck made a regular squat more than a little difficult, and tried to get a better look at the spoor. Sometimes you have to put the spoor between you and the sun, so that the shadows stand out better. We couldn't see the sun at the moment, between the trees and the mist and clouds, but it was still a better angle than trying to look straight down at them. I could see more detail.

That print led to that one. Then that one. I frowned. Either whoever had made them was drunk, or...

No. Drunks don't usually leave blood trails behind them. I mean, sometimes they do—the Carlsbad Crawl has seen some dudes leave some blood and skin behind—but the more I looked, the more I saw.

There were at least a couple dozen such trails. Close to thirty people had followed the vampire—I could tell that they'd come after by the drops of blackened blood in its blasted footprints—all of them seriously wounded and bleeding.

Or... I shook off that thought. We'd seen some weird things so far, but we hadn't seen the dead get up and walk. Not yet. So, until I actually saw it, I didn't want to think about it.

I stood up. "Looks like he's got an entourage." That didn't explain the staggering steps or the dripping blood.

Mathghaman had come up to join us, tracing the line of footprints with his eyes. He'd heard what I said, but he didn't say anything at first. Mathghaman was a man of few words.

But I needed to know. As much as I dreaded the answer, I had to ask the question. "Have you ever heard of a vampire bringing the wounded along with the rest of its followers before?" That it had mortal servants was obvious from its pact with the corsairs—a pact that clearly hadn't gone according to the corsairs' plan—but there was something off here.

He shook his head. I could see it in his eyes as he met mine that he didn't want to say it. But he could not withhold the truth, either.

"No. They would not show such compassion." He looked down at the awkward prints and the bloodstains. "Not all of their servants are among the living."

Rodeffer swore quietly. "I was afraid of that."

"Great. Fuckin' zombies." Farrar spat. I didn't know how he had any dip left, but somehow he'd squirreled some away. I'd have to talk to him about that. We were operating in a place where we had to assume that everything we faced that wasn't entirely human had senses that could sniff out dip from ten miles away. "I guess we gotta sharpen up our headshots, huh?"

"Is that the way this works?" I looked over at Mathghaman. "Can we kill them by taking off their heads? I mean, kill them again?"

But Mathghaman was shaking his head. "They are like no living enemy you have ever faced. The vampire has summoned dark spirits to inhabit the bodies, donning them like tattered cloaks. They are husks, puppets dragged along by things that have never been human, that have no link to flesh and blood that might render them vulnerable to such wounds."

For a moment, no one spoke. There was a horror to the silence that stretched out, broken only by the faint drip of moisture off the damp tree branches to either side of the road. A raven chuckled overhead.

"So, how do we kill them?" Nagano asked. The other teams had gathered around, though most of the Marines were still on security, down on a knee in the mud and the ferns to either side of the road, under the dripping trees.

"You must either banish the spirit, or else cut the bodies to pieces." Bearrac was looking around at us, his eyes measuring. As if he wasn't entirely sure we were ready for that. He should have known better after the fight at Teac Mor Farragah.

"Well, boys, looks like we've got a use for all the frags and explosives we got the *Coira Ansec* to give us." Santos hefted his rifle in one hand as he patted the grenade pouch on his chest rig. He grinned wolfishly. "Like to see Mr. Dark Spirit try to puppet-master a corpse after it's been turned into pink mist."

Mathghaman raised an eyebrow, but there was a faint, grim smile behind his mustache. Recon Marines tend to be bloodthirsty at the best of times, and while that wasn't always all that in keeping with the Tuacha's sense of nobility and honor, I couldn't help but think that Mathghaman, the King's Champion, was perfectly all right with this particular bit of bloodlust. After all, the targets we were talking about blowing to bits weren't alive anymore. There's something to be said for respect for the dead, but the vampire had already made that a moot point.

"Who's got the thumpers?" Gunny asked. A few reasonable facsimiles of the LMT M203 standalones were brought out. Santos grinned again and reached back for the M79 he'd asked the *Coira Ansec* for. Every bit as capable as the 203s, the M79 was a relic of the Vietnam War that fired the same 40mm grenades. Santos had simply grinned from ear to ear and called himself a traditionalist when he'd drawn the weapon out of the cauldron.

"All right. Thumpers behind the pointmen. If we see a shambling, bleeding corpse coming for us, it gets pink misted." Gunny, of course, had a thumper of his own. It meant he had more weight than the platoon sergeant usually carried, but Gunny had never been one *not* to carry as much firepower as possible. Now that we weren't worried about the precise mission profile and Marine Corps guidelines, he was free to carry as much boom as he wanted. "Let's move out."

With every eye a little sharper, watching for new shambling horrors to come out of the shadows under the trees, we slipped into the woods to handrail the road, while the crows cawed and mocked in the treetops overhead.

* * *

As we moved south, the cleared pastures and farmland became more frequent. We started to see living people, too, though they were scattered, frightened, and ran and hid whenever we approached, on the rare occasions we showed ourselves in daylight. The black sheep began to be mixed in with dark brown, but they were as skittish as their shepherds.

Smoke rose from the palisade ahead of us when we halted on a low, wooded hill surrounded by more cleared pastures. This time, we could see movement in and around the walled village, and when we got on glass, we could tell these weren't the vampire's undead monstrosities. These were living, breathing, deeply frightened men and women, trying to put out the fires while keeping watch for the next attack.

Rodeffer had spotted the smoke first and had picked a route that kept us in the trees and masked by the terrain until we could reach this vantage point, while the rest of the platoon set in back in the dark, under the trees. Now the four of us were spread out in the prone, watching the palisaded village through our scopes.

The massive corsair who seemed to be directing things was armed and armored, as were the dozen or so who followed him around. Under different circumstances, that might seem to some to be the warrior caste lording it over their inferiors, but they were clearly on alert and watching the road and the woods that half encircled the village. In fact, several more were perched in watchtowers overlooking the enclosed bay, positioned to cover the water and the low, forested headlands that framed the sheltered cove. They'd been hit hard, and they had to be ready to get hit again.

Carefully scanning the palisade and the fields around it, I took in as many details as I could. The grass of the fields and pastures were scorched and withered in places, in ways that looked an awful lot like the spot where the vampire had stood outside the chapel back on the Isle of Riamog. Crumpled, blackened shapes might have been corpses. Dark stains still glistened dark red on the grass. Some of the timbers were blackened, as if a fire had raged along part of the wall.

It was hard to try to reconstruct what had happened from a distance. Clearly, the vampire and its minions had attacked this settlement, like it had the others, but in this case, it appeared to have been repulsed. That was good and bad, I realized. Good in that it meant that it *could* be fought and forced away, at least. Bad, in that we didn't know what they'd done differently from the massacred settlements to the north, and we'd already seen the corsairs use sorcery during the raid. Who knew what new devilry they'd cooked up here to drive the vampire away?

I wouldn't have used a word like "devilry" even a month before. This place was getting into my head. The weird part was, I didn't actually mind all that much.

Gunny crawled up next to us, pulling his binoculars along with him. He had the same 1-10x scope that the rest of us had on our M110s, but binoculars could sometimes see more. He propped his elbows on a fallen tree, braced his hands around the ocular lenses, and carefully scanned the ground below us. After a moment, he lifted his eyes from the binos and squinted. "This is going to get tricky."

No one had to ask why. Not only was there a lot more cleared land around this particular settlement, not only was it considerably larger than the last two, not only were there enough living warriors in evidence to make for a tough fight if it came to it, but this settlement also wasn't just a walled village like the last two.

It was a fortress.

The outer palisade was still timber, but it was higher and stouter than the previous ones we'd seen, and stood atop a steep line of earthworks. The watchtowers were as sturdy as the wall, built of thick, closely fitted timbers and roofed with hides. Murder holes were set along the walls, as well, implying fighting positions all the way around, not just in the watchtowers.

We could see plenty of turf roofs above the walls, but the central hall stood atop a massive motte, an artificial hill heaped up inside the palisade. From up there, the guards—whom we could see standing outside the timber-framed doors with spears held stiffly in front of them—could see for a long way. And if they were worried about another attack, they'd have watchers on all points of the compass.

And that was just the watchers with physical eyes.

"We could move along those woods down there." I pointed to the line of dark firs and cedars that bordered the eastern pastures, disappearing behind a cleared, green hill with a low stone structure atop it, that might have just been a ruin, or it might have been a watchtower. The mist made it hard to tell. "We might have to wait until after dark."

"Presuming we have that kind of time, and that worse doesn't come out after dark." Gunny squinted at the road where it went through the fortress. "But we don't have the numbers to tangle with these guys, even if it wasn't just going to slow us down. Who knows how fast that vampire can move?"

"Can't be all that fast with a bunch of corpse puppets along for the ride." But even as I said it, I realized that I had no idea how fast the dark spirits Mathghaman had spoken of could really make their husks move. We weren't dealing with natural phenomena here.

Then the situation changed again.

About thirty riders came out of the gate and turned toward us, spreading out across the road. They didn't look like cavalry, not the way I'd have expected. They were armored and armed like the corsairs we'd fought on the beach on the Isle of Riamog, who had all been on foot, and their horses were more like horses than the creatures the Dovos and the Fohorimans had ridden in the north. But they were short-legged, barrel-chested horses, more like ponies than warhorses. Something told me that these guys rode to the nearest point to the fight, then got off and fought on foot.

Dragoons. That was the term.

Which wouldn't help us as they started to trot along the edge of the woods, several of them disappearing into the trees, ducking beneath low-hanging branches as they went.

"They're patrolling. Sweeping the forest for anyone or anything lurking nearby." It didn't take a genius to see that, but it made our job considerably harder. Especially since we were already close enough that I could see the patterns and designs embossed on their helmets through my scope at ten power.

"Everybody get low and don't move a muscle." Gunny was already wriggling backward, keeping the fallen tree between him and the riders. He was clearly going back to pass the word. "Maybe we can sneak past if we're patient enough." Timing had just become less of an issue than avoiding compromise.

But before he could get far, a weirdly echoing chant arose from inside the walls. I felt a chill that had nothing to do with the damp and the cold wind whispering in off the ocean. I'd heard sounds like that before, and the strange echoing effect only made it worse.

I shifted my point of aim to bring my scope and rifle to bear on the doors to the main hall atop the motte. Just in time to see the black-robed man with flyaway hair and the longest, scraggliest beard I'd ever seen, slump to his knees as a dark shadow flitted up into the sky from his shoulders.

CHAPTER 10

THE shadow was formless, and I couldn't see it if I looked straight at it. I already had my finger on the trigger, the weapon off safe, as I gauged the distance. It was a seven-hundred-yard shot, but that was entirely doable with an M110. Maybe if I smoked the sorcerer, it might interrupt whatever he was doing.

But before I could break the shot, that shadow passed overhead, whispering through the treetops until it ran smack dab into Mathghaman.

Okay, it didn't actually run into him. All six Tuacha were whispering, a low chant in a language I couldn't understand, but didn't have the sort of skin-crawling strangeness that I'd come to associate with sorcery. In fact, it was almost comforting, even as that dark specter flitted toward us.

The shadow stopped dead overhead as if it had just hit a brick wall, then streaked back to the fortress with a high, thin scream. It seemed to stoop down on the sorcerer, who fell on his face.

One of the guards ran inside. I slipped my finger off the trigger, just watching and waiting. Were we made? Or had the Tuacha blinded the enemy enough that we might be able to slip past?

A shout went up from the hall. A brazen horn sounded. It had a different pitch from the Dovos' hunting horns, or the even more disconcerting Fohoriman trumpets. But it heralded every bit of the threat that those had. The Tuacha might have hit back at the sorcerer, somehow, but that just meant that we were made. They knew *somebody* was out there, somebody with the mojo to make their wizard fall on his face.

And the corsairs acted quickly to answer that horn call.

Archers scrambled into the watchtowers, and more mounted infantry rode out of the gates, spreading out facing our hill. Many were archers, while many more carried spears and long-hafted axes. Their armor was slightly different from the corsairs we'd fought before, but only in markings and coloration. Quilted gambesons, lamellar breastplates, and helmets with either forward sweeping horns or short, crown-shaped horsehair crests, stiffened and painted.

They were obviously more civilized than the Dovos in the north, but that doesn't matter much when they're still trying to put an arrow in your throat or bash in your skull with an axe. And the sorcery was another matter.

I cursed under my breath. "I should have smoked that scraggly son of a bitch."

"Don't get too fired up." Gunny had crawled forward again and was watching the line with his binos. "That might have just told them for sure where we are. I don't think they know exactly where we are or who we are. Or how many. They just know that *someone*, or some*thing*, is out here. Look at 'em. Closely."

I scanned the line as the warlord in segmented bronze armor rode out of the gates. Bigger than any of the rest, he was atop an actual warhorse, a sleek black charger that stood several inches taller than the smaller ponies that the rest were riding. At first glance, I had to guess that the horse had been captured; I hadn't seen any other animals quite like it so far in this misty country.

But as I left the black-bearded warlord and continued to scan the growing formation of mounted corsair fighters, I saw what Gunny was talking about. Just going by body language, none of them looked sure about what they were facing, and in fact there was a fair bit of trepidation among them. The animals were restless, too, often shifting and shying, and their riders kept having to haul them back into line. These men had already faced a supernatural abomination that had clearly done a lot of damage, and now they were worried that they were facing it again, or something like it.

I remembered the moaning specter in the night. Who knew what else might be drawn to a vampire's trail of destruction and horror?

The warlord raised his voice, his booming shout echoing out over the pastures and the fields. His mount reared a little, and he lifted his sword, then swept it forward. Slowly, reluctantly, the corsairs spread out and advanced across the open ground as they swept toward our hill. They might not know what had caused their sorcerer's spell to backlash on him, but they must have known which direction he had sent it. And that meant they were coming our way.

Gunny was moving, staying low and slipping behind a low spruce. "Spread out, get low, and stand by. We might not have any choice. Drop rucks and if you've got camo netting or ghillies, get 'em out. If we can stay concealed, so much the better. Nobody shoots until either I give the word, or we have no other choice."

Then he was gone, as we shrugged out of our rucks and found firing positions.

The hill where we'd burrowed into the forest wasn't tall, and the patch of woods wasn't very big. It was thick enough and rocky enough that I kind of understood why the corsairs hadn't tried to clear it, and the rocks would also provide us with a decent amount of cover and concealment. But it wasn't thick enough that I was confident they *wouldn't* sweep it, especially after what had happened to their wizard.

I glanced over my shoulder and peered through the thick stand of trees. Bailey's team was off to our left. Gurke's was on rear security. And Mathghaman's team had simply faded into the trees to our right. I could barely see Fennean where he'd set in just off to Farrar's right. The Tuacha's cloaks seemed to disappear into the landscape, regardless of where we were. He'd flipped his hood up over his face, and I was suddenly struck by the thought that I could only see him because he *wanted* me to see him.

Satisfied that we had the best position we were going to get, I settled in behind another tree and braced my rifle against the trunk, looking for a target.

There was no roaring charge, no undisciplined rush. This bunch of corsairs didn't seem to go in for the berserker tactics that the Dovos or some of their kinsmen who'd hit the Isle of Riamog did. They advanced slowly, in fairly good order, spreading out online to sweep the woods to our flanks as well as surround our little hill in a rough semicircle. I picked one who looked like he was a section leader, a tall, spare man with a reddish beard and no mustache, wearing a lamellar breastplate and splint greaves, as well as one of those bronze helmets with the stiffened horsehair crown. He was just behind the front rank and just ahead of the second rank, a sword in his hand, looking almost more from side to side than he was to the front, making sure that his ranks were squared away and online.

I flicked my rifle to "semi" and rested my finger on the trigger, just waiting for the "go" order.

There were probably about two hundred corsairs with weapons out there. That was bad odds, regardless of the advantage our rifles and machineguns gave us. There were stories about Recon teams in Vietnam who had gone up against VC or NVA battalions and come out on top, but that was usually with air support bringing the hate from on high while they fell back through the jungle. We didn't have a covered and concealed fallback route. We would have to try to hold this patch of woods unless somebody up above was looking out for us and they either bypassed it or missed us altogether.

If they swept the woods, they *were* going to find us. We were somewhat camouflaged, but not *that* camouflaged.

The invisible guy in the ghillie suit going unspotted from six feet away is something that only happens in movies and video games. And we weren't even all wearing ghillies.

They halted about twenty yards from the base of the hill. The warlord was still hanging back at the rear, pointing and bellowing as his entourage tried to pass his commands by flag waves, drums, and trumpet calls. The units out on the flanks had moved into the woods along the coast, while those more inland were arrayed facing the darkened forest to the east.

Something about those woods always made it seem like dusk beneath the boughs, even without the nearly perpetual mist and clouds.

The warlord barked an order, and the section leader in my sights, my reticle hovering just above his heart, moving ever so slightly with my breathing, shouted at his own men. But he was close enough that I saw him gulp a little before he shouted. And when I took my eye off the scope to watch the rest of the corsairs in front of him, I saw the front rank noticeably hesitate before taking a ragged step forward.

My eyes narrowed. There was something about this hill that they didn't like. Something that scared them.

That might be a good thing, but it also might be a very bad thing. The Dovos had been afraid of the tor where we'd found an ancient castle cut into the solid rock. Looking back on it, while Captain Sorenson hadn't wanted to give it any credence, that had been a sign that we might have been safer there. The Dovos, it had turned out, were monster-worshiping savages who had designs on awakening an even older and worse monstrosity than the one they currently worshiped. The tor, we'd found out later, had been the last stronghold of those men who had refused to worship the monsters, and still bore the fear of all the Dovos and monsters who had dashed themselves against its unyielding rock. This hill might be something similar.

Or it might be something much, much worse.

After all, the Dovos had feared the things they worshiped, too. And these corsairs seemed to have clashed with the vampire, even if that was to their detriment. Something I'd learned in Syria, a universe away but ever-present to me, was that you could never expect every enemy to all be on the same side. And not every ally was necessarily on your "side," either.

But so far, nothing had popped out of the ground and tried to eat us. Which was more than I could say for the lines of armed men advancing on the woods, their weapons held ready. They were barely fifty yards away, now. They'd be too close for the 40mm grenades to arm themselves soon.

Then a raven fluttered down to the warlord's shoulder. I couldn't be sure, but it looked like he was listening to it. A moment later, he spoke, then it flapped into the air and glided toward our woods.

That wasn't normal.

The raven circled overhead, croaking and chuckling. The warlord bellowed an order. The front ranks stopped dead where they were. The archers in the rear ranks drew their bows.

Mathghaman and his team might have stopped the sorcerer's spell cold, but there was some other kind of weirdness going on, too, and now we were made.

Gunny didn't bother with giving the order to open fire. He just dumped a 40mm grenade into the middle of the archers.

His standalone M203 *thump*ed, followed a split second later by the heavy *thud* as the grenade detonated at an archer's feet. The man disappeared in the dirty black cloud, as the men around him were flung down in a welter of flying metal, dust, smoke, and blood. The 40mm ogives had a kill radius of about 5 meters, though any of us who had used grenades of any sort in combat knew that the hard and fast numbers were always variable, based on conditions and Murphy's capricious whims.

But that explosion was all the opening play we needed.

A ragged series of thunderclaps, muted by suppressors but still echoing across the fields as the bullets tore through the sound barrier, stuttered along the line of trees. I'd moved my sights back to the section leader and watched him drop as the reticle settled, a hole blasted through his heart. At fifty yards, from a rock-solid shooting position, I would have had to *try* to miss.

Farrar, Applegate, and Herrera opened fire with alternating, stuttering roars, spitting streams of bullets down into the ranks below us. Men dropped in windrows, armor punctured, flesh shredded, and bone shattered. I shifted targets as fast as I could, dropping archers almost as fast as the machineguns could mow them down.

It was a slaughter. In seconds, almost all of the five ranks that had been arrayed at the base of the hill had been smashed off their feet, those who weren't already dead leaking their lifeblood out onto the grass, shaking and moaning as they died.

You could almost see the shock ripple across the fields. Every eye was suddenly turned toward the carnage at the base of the hill. For a moment, everything was still.

Then the warlord bellowed anew, swinging his horse aside, and the surviving corsairs fell back as he roared and threatened, and more archers started coming out of the woodwork, gathering back by the earthworks. Some of those in the watchtowers started to loose ranging shots, arrows arcing through the air to fall short at the base of the hill, though still between us and the dead and dying warriors we'd just shot to doll rags.

Those were some impressive bows. The walls were close to four hundred yards away. An easy shot for an M110 or even a Mk 48, but those defenses provided some pretty good cover and concealment.

This could turn into a deadly stalemate really quick. I saw splinters blasted away from one of the watchtowers as one of Bailey's teammates took a shot at one of the archers, and had a flashback to a firefight in Ratla, when we'd been pinned down and surrounded for eight hours, shooting at shadows deep in half-ruined houses, as the ISIS fighters and their momentary allies had hit us from murder holes or through multiple rooms, where we could hardly see them, much less hit them.

We had to maneuver. I glanced over at Gunny, but if I'd been worried that he'd gotten sucked into the immediate firefight, I should have known better. He'd initiated when he'd seen that it was necessary but then had disengaged to check the bigger picture.

And the bigger picture was grim, guns or no guns.

Even with the firepower we had at our disposal, we simply didn't have the numbers to take a fortified town like this one. Which meant that we had to break contact. We had a reasonably defensible position where we were, but there were two factors militating against holding it. First, the corsairs clearly weren't Active Stupid, as they'd just demonstrated when the warlord had quickly pulled the survivors back from the ambush. They'd figure out some way to get at us, and we simply didn't have enough bullets to hold our ground, not if we were going to continue the mission.

This place wasn't the mission, either. If we got bogged down here, Sister Sebeal was doomed.

And our own mission in the north was, too.

Gunny was already moving back to check our six, to make sure we still had a fallback route. It was going to be hairy, either way. We hadn't come to this position by crossing open fields, after all, but the arm of forest that had led to this hill was neither wide nor thick. We'd still probably get hit from the flanks as we fell back. There simply wasn't enough concealment there, not when the enemy knew to look for us.

But there wasn't really another option. Recon doesn't do, "Hey diddle-diddle, straight up the middle." We sneak and peak until we know every detail of your life, then, if we need to step in instead of calling in the grunts, we can whittle you down through ambushes, raids, and call for fire. We might not have artillery or air here, but the ambushes and raids were still an option. We just had to break contact so that we could fight this on *our* terms.

I kept my eyes and muzzle on the enemy in front of us. The corsairs weren't just sitting still and staring in shock.

The warlord might not know just what had happened to tear his center to bloody shreds, but he'd faced something every bit as terrifying not long before. He'd pulled the survivors into the ditch surrounding the outer earthworks, and the flankers had also fallen back into the woods. I didn't know if the vampire's sorcery had needed line of sight, but the warlord was acting as if he knew that *something* would be accomplished by hiding his remaining warriors.

"Get some claymores out and set in at the tree line. All but two per team, fall back into the woods." Gunny wasn't wasting time. Rodeffer was already digging into his ruck.

Then a chorus of inhuman screams rose from the eastern wood line, and the entire situation changed.

CHAPTER 11

FOR a brief moment, it was as if everything froze. I had my sights on the warlord for an instant, though he was doing a pretty good job of making himself a hard target. At ten power, even from four hundred yards away, I could see the look of dread flicker across his face. For a fraction of a second, this pirate warlord, who doubtless had a lot of blood on his hands, seemed far more human than a lot of the people we'd encountered since sailing through that mysterious fog bank off the coast of Norway. He'd already been hit twice, and now something else was coming in on his flank before he'd dealt with the most recent threat. And from the look on his face, he had a pretty good idea what was out there screaming in the woods, and he knew it was bad news.

But it wasn't just bad news for the corsairs.

Gurke's team had already started to fall back through that narrow strip of woods, and gunfire suddenly erupted back there. Whatever was coming out of the woods, it was all the way around us. We were already surrounded, right along with the corsairs.

The screaming continued almost unabated despite the gunfire. What had just hit us?

The corsairs clearly weren't eager to turn their backs on us, but as the woods erupted with movement, they didn't have much choice. It was as if a momentary, unspoken truce was in effect. They stopped lobbing arrows at us, and we stopped shooting at them, as a swarm of monsters came howling out of the trees.

Their heads were too big for the rest of their bodies, wide and kind of flat, with long, pointed ears standing almost straight out from the sides of their skulls. Even from that distance, I could see just how unnaturally wide their gaping, toothy mouths were, splitting those pumpkin heads from ear to ear. Their eyes were tiny and gleamed red even from most of a klick away.

They were small. Judging by the trees nearby, the tallest was maybe four feet from clawed feet to flat top of its head. But there were a *lot* of them, and they were all armed, waving hooked swords, knives, stone axes, broken sword blades, and jagged, forked spears.

The corsairs nearest quickly formed up and closed ranks, the front line kneeling behind their shields as the men behind leveled their spears over the shield wall's shoulders. They must have faced these things before, or something like them.

The goblins—there was something about these creatures which immediately brought that word to mind—hit the shield wall like a green-and-brown wave. A lot of them were impaled on the spears, while others were hacked down by the swordsmen behind the first rank. But the rest simply leaped or trampled on the bodies of their fellows, throwing themselves over the shields and at the men behind them.

I caught a glimpse of a corsair going down under a hail of hacking blows, blood flying into the air, before we found ourselves fighting for our lives.

More goblins came pouring through the trees as Gurke and his team quickly fell back, bounding from tree to tree as they dumped rounds into the oncoming, waist-high tide of teeth and claws and jagged, rusty weapons. They were so thick that almost every shot went home, splashing muddy ichor and splitting brown and green flesh.

I pivoted, snapping my rifle to my shoulder, and shot a big one, its head almost the size of a medicine ball. It was close enough, and that head was a big enough target, that I split its skull like a melon. The crude, rusty cap it wore went flying as the goblin immediately behind it got sprayed with muddy blood and brain matter.

Now, I can't necessarily put what happened next down to some flash of warrior brilliance. I'm not that guy. I like to think I'm pretty good at my profession, but what I did was more a matter of desperation, not some deeply thought out tactic.

We had just enough space, and while it was still awfully close, I pulled a frag out of my vest, pulled the pin, let the safety lever fly, and fastballed it at the next biggest goblin while roaring, "Frag out!" because throwing a grenade at an onrushing horde that's barely two dozen yards away without warning your buddies will at the very least get someone wounded in a blue-on-blue. Everyone within a dozen yards of me hit the dirt, myself included.

The frag, which somehow the *Coira Ansec* had produced with even the markings perfectly reproduced from one of our memories, sailed through the air, bounced off a tree to hit another goblin in the chest, and detonated. The goblin disappeared in an ugly black cloud, as a heavy *thud* hammered at everyone's guts and blew bark and needles off the nearby trees, frag pattering through the branches overhead.

When the smoke cleared, there wasn't much left of that goblin's upper half, at least a dozen others were leaking greenish-brown blood onto the ground and the rocks, and the rest were running. Running and screaming.

That was a surprise. Everything else we'd seen in this place that wasn't human seemed to be homicidally insane and would have kept coming. Even the Fohorimans would have looked for a different opening after falling back. But the goblins had just gotten spooked by a single frag.

I'd take it.

With half the goblin force streaming back into the woods, screaming in panic, the dynamics of the fight changed again.

The corsairs were still fighting the goblins to the east, but even there, the onslaught had faltered for a moment, as those beady red eyes turned toward the sound of the explosion, which was still echoing across the rolling, wooded hills.

I found myself and my team currently closest to the fleeing goblins. So, I pressed forward, smoking another one that stopped and turned back, my bullet passing through its sunken chest as if it wasn't there, ripping a fountain of gore out through its back. Another one glanced over its shoulder to see the destruction and let out a screeching yelp, putting on more speed.

Then Santos lobbed a 40mm HE grenade into the middle of them, just to make sure they didn't decide that my frag had been a fluke. The dirty black explosion shook the ground and blasted more needles and bark off the trees, even as two more goblins flew apart in a welter of blood and torn, flying limbs.

Almost in an instant, the woods in front of me were empty and still, except for a few ferns still waving slightly after the goblins swept past them.

The noise of battle continued to the east, though the pitch had changed somehow, as if the goblins were suddenly desperately trying to break contact. We still had to figure out our next move. With the goblins we'd been killing having suddenly vanished, I put up a hand to call a halt, rather than go charging into a potential ambush.

Mathghaman and Gunny moved up, speaking quietly. I dropped back behind Rodeffer and Farrar, so I could engage without dropping security.

Even as I did, with a chorus of shrieks and roars, the goblins to the east broke and ran. The second explosion had apparently done the trick. They scattered like quail. When I glanced through the trees, though I couldn't see much, I could tell that the corsairs were too battered and smoked to try to pursue or kill any more of them as they fled.

They were fast little bastards, too. In seconds, the goblins had vanished altogether.

Gunny looked around at us. "Conor, since your team started running after the little weirdos, lead out. We've got a breather; let's use it. Keep tight, move fast, and heads on a swivel. Let's not get bushwhacked if those little bastards get froggy too soon."

Rodeffer was already moving, and I fell in behind him. That strip of woods was so narrow that a Ranger file was the only way to move, and it was faster than any other formation, anyway. In moments, we were halfway down the back slope of the hill.

But we'd been closer to getting flanked than I'd thought.

As we came out of the shadow of a shoulder of the hill, there were suddenly twenty corsair riders about seventy-five yards away on our right.

They weren't in much of a formation. In fact, they appeared to be milling about in some confusion after the goblins had fled. There were bodies of men and horses on the grass, as well as smaller, darker forms that might have been several chopped-up goblins.

But whoever their captain was, he clearly had a head on his shoulders. While there was no recognizable crest to pick him out as a leader—they were all wearing variations on the horsehair crown or forward-thrusting horns on their helmets—the man with the reddish beard barked an order as he looked up and saw us through the trees. The woods in that narrow strip weren't nearly thick enough to conceal us fully.

Almost as one, we pivoted and dashed to cover, weapons coming up, selectors flicked to "fire," seeking targets. I dropped to a knee behind a twisted old cedar, my red dot settling on Redbeard as my finger settled on the trigger.

But then an echoing shout boomed down out of the sky above us.

The corsairs froze, and I think we all did too, just a little. After all, that wasn't a natural shout. I think by then we'd all sort of figured out what a sorcerously enhanced voice sounded like. Which meant that things were about to get weird.

They did, just not the way I'd expected.

The corsairs hesitated for a moment, then Redbeard faced us, threw his spear on the ground, and spread his hands wide before he flung one leg over his horse's neck and slipped to the ground. Then he went down onto his knees and prostrated himself, his arms still spread.

One by one, the rest did the same, though a few were clearly doing it grudgingly, glancing up at the flickering corvine silhouette that had settled in the treetops on the shoulder of the hill.

To my surprise, nobody fired. Recon Marines learn fire discipline early, particularly in the house. I still remember having to run to the top of the hill above the SOTG range and write my name on the white cross after shooting a flyer. You shot targets and only targets, and if you weren't sure, you held your fire until you were sure. You'd just better *get* sure real fast. But this little encounter had amounted to a near ambush, and the react drill for that generally involved a lot of intense violence.

Maybe it was the need to conserve ammo, something every surviving Marine in the platoon was acutely conscious of after that long, harrowing movement across the Land of Ice and Monsters, ending in going black during a desperate fight to hold until Mathghaman's ship could arrive. Maybe that was it.

Or maybe someone was whispering in our ears to hold our fire and see what developed.

I'd had a dream, in the north, shortly after we'd come across into this world. A dream of a luminous figure in the woods, watching over me and letting me know I was not alone. Even at the time, when I hadn't yet even started to accept, much less get used to, the weirdness and the mystic dimension of this place, I'd known that it had been something more than a dream.

The voice from the silhouette sounded again. Fennean appeared at my elbow, having moved up from his position as Mathghaman's pointman.

I kept my sights on the prostrate captain. "What's he saying?"

"The voice is telling the corsairs not to fight us. That he is coming." Fennean didn't volunteer his opinion of what that might mean, but that was Fennean. None of the Tuacha who had gathered around Mathghaman were especially verbose, but Fennean was a man apart even among them, often moving away to scout without making a sound. He glanced at the corsairs but watched the vaguely birdlike silhouette in the tree closely.

"Guns?" I really didn't want to take my eyes or my muzzle off the corsairs, but I had to. "What do you want to do?"

Gunny was hustling up to join us. Bailey's team was still up on the hill, spreading out to the flank to cover the corsairs and watch our six. Gurke's team was moving past us to watch that flank and make sure we didn't get jumped by the goblins again. None of us were too confident that their panic was going to last.

To say we were in a delicate position was putting it mildly.

I wanted to just break contact and get out of there. But I could see on Gunny's face that there were other concerns. Would we be able to break contact cleanly, or would they follow? Would we be hunted, or would they ride ahead to intercept us? They knew the ground a lot better than we did. Nightmare memories of getting compromised in Syrian irrigation ditch hides flitted through my mind. If it was dark, we might have a better chance. But sorcery changes things, even more than technology.

Gunny looked over at Mathghaman. While the big Tuacha had sort of attached himself to us, in many ways, he was the mission commander here. There wasn't a clear-cut chain of command between us and the Tuacha. We still had a platoon—well, a platoon minus, given the losses we'd taken in the north—but Mathghaman wasn't a Marine, and he *was* the King's Champion. "What do you think?"

Mathghaman's brow was furrowed, and he was watching the phantom crow, same as Fennean. I could see the wheels turning. He was thinking through a lot, probably including a number of dimensions we hadn't even thought of. Ordinarily, he was quick to an answer—not out of haste but simply because his mind worked that fast. That he was taking his time made it clear just how thorny the problems we faced at that moment were.

"Let us wait." He spoke slowly and softly. "These are not the same Eastmen who raided our coasts and allied themselves with the vampire. Those were of the Blackened Sun. These are of the Bull's Head. They are still heathens, but they have ofttimes been enemies of the Blackened Sun. If they wish to talk, we might gain safe passage through their territory, simply by being enemies of the Blackened Sun and the vampire that already slaughtered many of their number."

"We slaughtered a few of their number, too." Santos kept his eyes on the prostrate corsairs, though he didn't have his rifle up. He was covering them with the thumper. He should be able to take about a quarter of them out with one shot.

"Indeed. And many will wish for revenge. But these people live in a world of competing strengths, and the wiser heads among them will take such losses as signs of our strength." Mathghaman's tone took on a bit of distaste, but he shook his head. "Their gods are creatures of appetite and power. These ones live by seeking the fine path between competing powers that would destroy them utterly." He shook his head again, sadly. "Their chieftains and wise men will see what we wrought against them, and against the goblins, and will act as they see necessary for their survival."

As he spoke, more horsemen appeared from around the side of the hill, covered by Bailey's team up in the trees. The warlord still sat astride his black warhorse, while the wild-haired, robed man who had fallen when the Tuacha had smacked that strange shadow back from the trees rode a smaller, stockier pony. He looked a little the worse for wear, his eyes sunken and his skin pale, and he sagged in the saddle as he rode. The warlord sat straight, his eyes hooded, but clearly showed some deference to the scrawny, unkempt black robe, keeping his horse reined in and staying close by the man's side.

The black robe acted as if he didn't notice the warlord or the other corsair on his left, but simply rode toward us slowly. He ignored the fighters who were still prostrate in front of us, too, but just rode about three paces in front of them before he halted his pony and leaned heavily on the saddle pommel. He looked about ready to fall off his mount. The backlash from the Tuacha's rejection of his spell seemed to have beaten him down pretty bad.

"Your magic is strong." His voice was little more than a croak. And he wasn't speaking English, or the staccato, guttural speech of the Dovos. The corsair's language was somewhat singsong, though not in the Scandinavian way that we'd somewhat gotten used to working with the Norwegians. It almost sounded East Asian, though it was still different enough that I couldn't put my finger on exactly *what* it sounded like. Though I'm no linguist.

But I could still understand him, even in his up-down, singsong language. The Tuacha could do that naturally. They called it the "mind speech." The followers of the various "gods" throughout the rest of this strange world had gained a certain spell from their masters that could imitate it, though with considerably less ease and clarity.

"Tigharn is strong," Mathghaman replied. "Those He watches over need no magic."

The unkempt sorcerer, or shaman, or whatever he was, tilted his head as if to acknowledge without wanting to. "You fought the goblins who follow in the abomination's wake. And you can kill many of us with great thunder and power."

I wondered if this statement of the obvious was typical, or just laying the groundwork to make sure everyone was on the same page. But then, I'd never been much of a negotiator. That was why I was a Marine.

"We hunt the abomination that attacked your people." Mathghaman stepped out from the trees and stood tall. Farrar let out a strangled sound but restrained himself. The instinct to maintain cover was strong, but we'd seen Mathghaman move faster than any normal man. He could take care of himself. "It raided our lands, using the Blackened Sun to aid it. We have no quarrel with you under this sun." Meaning that he'd be more than willing to cross blades with them another time, but that just stands to reason when dealing with corsairs, I guess. "You might stop us, but we will reap a high price, and you will only aid your own enemy."

The warlord spat something in that singsong speech. Unlike the shaggy man, I couldn't understand him, reinforcing the fact that sorcery was being used to translate.

"Perhaps we would aid an enemy." The unkempt man in the black robe turned back to Mathghaman with narrowed eyes. He was calculating carefully. "But the oversea men are not our friends, either. And we are still many. Perhaps we might not defeat the abomination. But perhaps we might defeat you who have killed many of ours and regain that small bit of honor."

"This is true," Mathghaman allowed, though he was clearly unruffled by the possibility. "Yet we saw your warriors in disarray as we approached, and many more lie dead at the base of the hill. Can you truly afford to take such losses as it would take to kill even a few of us?" He swept a hand behind him to indicate where we waited in the trees, still mostly concealed and with rifles, machineguns, and thumpers trained on the lot of them. "None of your warriors came close enough to even trade blows with us. And everyone in front of me will die, should I give the word."

Mathghaman did not have to exaggerate. There was a regal presence to the man, which made it clear to any who heard him that he was not threatening or blustering, merely stating fact. And it was a fact that he took no particular pleasure in, either.

"We could fight, and many of yours would die. Perhaps enough to force you to abandon this place as the other tribes move against you. Or you could let us pass. We will do you no harm. And we might do great harm to a far deadlier enemy."

The warlord was clearly pissed, muttering to the unkempt man in the black robe, but the shaman raised a hand placatingly. I studied both of them, though my reticle stayed close to the warlord's chest, just in case. There was more going on here than met the eye.

The warlord was clearly the authority, and he could probably understand Mathghaman, but he was somehow restrained by the wizard. As if the decision wasn't solely his to make. That was interesting.

For a long few moments, the wizard and the warlord spoke in low but urgent tones. The shaman must have turned off his mind speech spell or something, because I couldn't make heads or tails of what either one of them said. They were speaking rapidly, and even if I'd had the remotest understanding of the language, I don't think I could have even picked out discreet words at that point.

Finally, the wild-haired sorcerer turned back to Mathghaman. The warlord still didn't look happy, but his expression was composed and he sat straight in his saddle, his head still held high. There was a lot of pride there, but there was more. This man wasn't a complete savage like the Dovos had been. He might be a heathen, a murderer, and a reaver, but he still had some degree of nobility in him.

"Your words are iron, and they are true. There is no friendship between the men of the Black Bull and the men of Over Sea. But the thing which passed here yesterday is a greater enemy by far. Should you kill it, we will be stronger. If it kills you, yet another foe will be diminished."

"Don't you just love a win-win situation?" Santos's voice was bitter.

Mathghaman, though, hardly reacted to the subtext. He simply inclined his head to acknowledge the point.

"It is the decision of the Great Akhavoth, Warlord of the Black Bull, Reaver of the North and South Coasts, Slayer of the Dragon-Crocodile, Breaker of the Horses of the Far Steppe, Bearer of the Sword of Thagerrug, Rider of the Long Sea Serpent, that you shall have safe passage through the lands of the Black Bull." The shaman's voice had gotten sonorous and pompous, even through the strange magic that let us understand his language. "His own son, Almak, will be your hostage and your escort."

Mathghaman bowed slightly, again without giving the slightest impression of deference. "So let it be."

"So let it be." As the shaman spoke, the warlord pulled off one gauntlet, then drew his sword. I had a good idea what was coming next.

He looked up to the sky, muttering in a slightly different language, while the shaman chanted in the same tongue. Then he cut his thumb on the edge of the sword and squeezed several drops of blood out onto the ground.

Mathghaman watched impassively. This kind of blood ritual wasn't the Tuacha's way. I could see a few Recon Marines getting into the spirit of the thing, but to the Tuacha da Riamog, it was anathema. But he seemed to accept it, if only to ensure that the Black Bull kept their word.

"None of the Black Bull will lift a hand against you now." The shaman's eyes were as dead as a shark's as he watched us. I was pretty sure that there was an unspoken *until you're out of our territory* on the end of that statement. "Come. You must meet Almak."

The warlord turned his horse and started back toward the walls. Reluctantly, weapons still held ready and eyes out, we followed.

CHAPTER 12

ALMAK led the way south, and for the first time we traveled mostly in the open, by day, following the tracks that passed for roads in the corsairs' country. Almak rode another pony, but the rest of us continued on our leather Cadillacs. It felt weird, and more than a little disturbing. Sure, Almak's father had shed his own blood to seal his word that we had safe passage, but Gunny, Bailey, and I had all been around tribal societies before, where one's word to a stranger or an outsider was inviolate right up until the point it was more advantageous to the tribe to break it.

Almak was a friendly enough young man. He rode slowly alongside us, a long blue cloak wrapped over his armor and weapons, his horsehair-crowned helmet at his saddle bow and a hood pulled up over his curly hair. He wore an amulet that apparently gave him the use of the same spell that the shaman, Vogrek, had used to make himself understood. He tried chatting with Rodeffer and me on the first day but got little more than monosyllables back. We were moving along at a pretty good pace, making conversation inconvenient, and none of us trusted him that far. So, while he'd subsided a bit, he was still seemingly eager to get along.

The first day took us about fifteen miles south of the fortress of Sekarak. Almak was clearly a little uncomfortable with our pace. He wanted to get to the next settlement before dark, and after what I'd seen so far, I couldn't entirely blame him. The monsters ruled the night in this place, and even the scariest of raiders and reavers feared what stalked the shadows once the sun went down.

We'd learned that the hard way in the north.

That was also what had led us not to object too much to the idea of lighting fires once we stopped. Hypothermia wasn't as big an issue down here, though it wasn't a non-issue, either. The mist and drizzling rain made for a constant, chill damp, and I'd seen guys hype out in sixty degree weather just because their cammies were always wet. So, warmth was an issue that we had to consider. But keeping the creepy crawlies out there in the night at bay was even more so.

"Gurke's team has first watch." Gunny had adjusted things a little bit since the north. Some of that was just to balance things out since we'd lost almost half the platoon in that icy, wintery hell. Some of it was also based on the fact that the Tuacha didn't really sleep. At least, not the way we do. They just sort of zone out for a little bit while still being aware enough—even though they're not moving a muscle or even noticeably breathing—to join a conversation if they feel like it. So, we had shifted to one team on security with the other two down on rest plan.

I'd shouldered Santos aside to build the fire. None of us were exactly amateurs at building fires, particularly not anymore, but I'd lived off-grid in the mountains for about a year before I'd joined the Marine Corps. I'd gotten it down to an art, especially when it came to placement and building it for a maximum of warmth with a minimum of signature. The Marine Corps doesn't teach you that stuff. That's mountain man knowledge, and while I'd read about it in books growing up, it had taken a lot of practice to get good at it.

So, I built our little fire beneath the boughs of an older spruce so that the smoke would get dispersed by the branches overhead. While the scent would still travel, it wouldn't travel as far, and a lot would get attenuated by the smell of the tree. I'd also picked a sheltered spot where the light wouldn't travel far.

Some of these guys would have built a bonfire to try to keep the monsters away. It might work a little bit, though it sure hadn't kept that abominable snowman off us in the north.

With the fire crackling softly, we set in around it, partially shielding the flames from the deepening darkness under the trees, partially getting close enough to take advantage of the warmth. The temperature was dropping as the sun set, and the mist was closing in again, grasping at us with that damp chill that didn't need to get below freezing to start you shivering uncontrollably. Moisture dripped off the branches all around us and hissed in the fire.

I noticed as we broke out our rations—the MREs we'd brought were long gone, and we were carrying Tuacha travel fare, which was a lot more satisfying and a sight tastier—that none of us were looking at the fire. That hadn't been in most Marine training, either, but you learned really fast when doing night operations not to look directly at any artificial or other light source if you wanted to maintain your night eyes. We still had our PVS-15s, but it helped to let your eyes adapt naturally, too.

But Almak apparently wasn't that woods-wise. He was staring at the fire, his back against his saddle, while his pony cropped at the ferns under the trees. We had set in about fifty yards back from the road, so we were pretty well concealed from anyone passing by that way, but our greater concern was what might be prowling under the trees.

He looked up at me over the fire, as Gurke and his boys got set in. He had only glanced at them while they threw up a perimeter another few yards out from our small harbor site, using the rocks and the trees for cover and concealment, setting their team Mk 48 in on what seemed like the likeliest avenue of approach, putting out trip flares and a few claymores, all of which would be carefully retrieved in the morning, provided they didn't get expended during a midnight firefight.

"You are not like the Over Sea Men." He was trying to be friendly again, though there was an element of probing there, too. I didn't doubt that if he survived to get back to his father and his kin, he'd be repeating everything he learned about the Tuacha and their strange allies with even stranger weapons and equipment.

Of course, we were pretty strange by the standards of where we'd come from by then, too.

"No, we're not." The kid wasn't a friend or an ally, and after what we'd been through with the Dovos nar Uergal in the north, none of us were inclined to be trusting when someone whose buddies we'd shot or turned into pink mist was suddenly trying to be friends. But Almak didn't have quite the same oily, underhanded manner that a lot of us had seen through when Dragon Mask had tried it. He seemed to be genuinely trying to make the best of a situation where he was effectively a hostage.

That still didn't mean I was going to get chatty with him.

"Where are you from?" He wasn't getting the hint from our taciturn responses.

"A long, long way away." Which was true enough, either in time, space, or both. We still weren't all that sure.

Almak gestured toward our weapons. "There must be great magic where you come from."

"Something like that." I really just wanted to sleep. I was in better shape than I probably had been when we'd first inserted, if only because of the combination of the low-tech world we'd found ourselves in, without cars or other powered transportation, along with the excellent Tuacha chow, but we'd also just been through a long movement, a fight, and yet another long movement. "It's complicated."

"How did you come to meet the Over Sea Men?" He wasn't going to give up. Of course, the kid had been on horseback all afternoon, while we'd been humping sixty-five-pound rucks.

"Long story." I leaned back against my ruck and closed my eyes. We had about three hours before Gurke came to wake us up. "Let's just say we owe each other."

He seemed to finally get the hint. Quiet descended as Gurke's team settled in and the rest of us passed out.

* * *

My guardian reappeared that night.

That was how I'd started to think of the luminous figure that had appeared in a dream during the first few nights we'd been in this strange world. There was something familiar about him—I always thought of the figure as a "him," even though I could never make out any detail—though he never spoke. He was simply there with the unspoken promise that I wasn't alone.

This time was a little different. He still didn't speak as he stepped out of the woods and stood over our small fire, looking down at me. He just watched me for a long moment. Then he reached down, put a hand on my shoulder, and vanished.

I woke up suddenly. The mist had thickened, and the fire had died down a little. There was no sign of the shining figure. But I couldn't shake the feeling that had been left when he'd disappeared.

He was watching over us. But things were going to get rough.

* * *

As we continued south, the weather worsened. Squalls blew in off the sea, lashing the coast and battering the trees—and us—with rain. The road turned to a sea of mud, sucking at boots and hooves with every step. It was a lot easier to do what came naturally to Recon and stay in the trees, weaving through the trunks and the rocks, where the mud wasn't nearly as bad.

But we ran into a check we hadn't necessarily considered before. And that was Almak.

He was our hostage, but he was also our guide, and he really didn't like the weather. As soon as the first storm blew up, he got visibly frightened, though he was clearly trying to hide it. He insisted that we had to take shelter.

Now, I could see a seafaring tribe having a healthy respect for storms, though I would have expected that their experience on the waves might have hardened them to what common land mammals might consider horrific gales. But there was something else to Almak's fear, as if he wasn't so much worried about getting wet but about something that might come along with the storm.

"I don't know, Conor." With Captain Sorenson missing, the last of the Marine Corps formality—which had been on life support even when he'd insisted on it—within the platoon had pretty much vanished. We all knew who was in charge, and none of us needed to publicly acknowledge it every moment. We still called Gunny Taylor "Gunny," but that was more out of habit than anything else. Plus, "Gunny" is easier to say than "Staff Sergeant." So, Rodeffer and Farrar had taken to using my first name, and I hadn't objected. "This ain't even close to that little blow-up that had Farrar puking his guts out, and we all know how puny that storm was."

"Shut your whore mouth, Rodeffer." Farrar had had a chip on his shoulder about that incident ever since it happened, which had only made matters worse. Let a brother Recon Marine see that something bothers you, and he's going to pick at it like a bad scab, just for entertainment. "I was hungover."

"I was still drunk. *And* I hadn't slept more than, like, two hours." Rodeffer ducked under a low-hanging tree limb. "Didn't see me tossing my cookies over one little wave."

Farrar cussed under his breath as Santos clapped him on the shoulder with a sadistic grin. Santos had been on the tiller that time, and I'd heard his jeering laugh from the other boat, twenty-five yards away.

I just chuckled a little, despite the cold water running down my collar and soaking the padded gambeson beneath my mail. The chill was only getting worse, and lighting a fire in this was going to suck. But Gunny and Mathghaman seemed to be calling a halt up ahead, as Almak insisted, his voice quiet but his eyes wide and his face pale.

"Security halt here." I pointed at the clump of boulders beneath a close stand of blue-black firs. "Let me go see what's going on."

I threaded my way through the trees, past Gurke's team, and joined Gurke himself as we moved up to join the rest of the platoon leadership. Gurke didn't look too impressed, either. "Big, bad corsair. Scared of storms." He spat. "I wonder if that warlord with all the titles just saddled us with this kid to get rid of him."

"Easier ways to do that," I pointed out. "But I don't think he's scared of the storm, exactly."

That gave Gurke pause. He slowed a little, the frown on his face deepening. "Not more spooks."

"Probably." I raised an eyebrow. "Did you really expect anything else in this place?"

He shook his head. Gurke was about half a head shorter than me, just as dark-haired, with lean, hungry-looking features and dark, sunken eyes. He managed to always look slightly resentful, even when he was simply calmly thinking, though I'd gotten to know him well enough during the workup to know that he really *was* carrying around a certain degree of suspicion and resentment most of the time. He wasn't nearly as bad as Zimmerman had been, but it was there. It had led to some friction within the platoon, especially as Bailey and I had formed something of a bloc in opposition to Captain Sorenson's more bone-headed ideas. But what had happened in the north had changed him.

It had changed all of us. But Gurke had dropped most of his reserve and suspicion toward the other team leaders. Granted, he'd transferred it to everyone outside the platoon, but it was progress.

"Fine. Let's go see what new monstrosities we have to worry about." We slogged forward, rucks still on our backs. Until Gunny made the call, we were going to be ready to keep moving.

"Can you not hear? The voice of Murkal is on the wind. We *must* find shelter!" Almak wasn't panicking, but he was scared stiff.

"Slow down." Gunny was using his calm, almost bored voice, the one he used when one of his Marines was getting too worked up. "Who or what is Murkal?"

"He is one of the Dwellers in the Deep." Almak's voice was haunted, and he was pointedly avoiding looking out toward the sea, which tossed and roared at the bottom of a short, rocky cliff, only a few dozen yards from the road. "He draws men down into the waters, where they must serve him forever, drowned men who cannot die."

There'd been a time when that might have sounded every bit as insane as our Kuwaiti terp in Syria talking about witchcraft done with porcupine droppings—no lie, that conversation went on for two hours—but not here, and not now. I had no doubt that there were some superstitions among these people that were worthy of just that kind of contempt, but this was a world where all the weirdness, all the folklore and fairy tale creatures and monsters were real. And they presented a real threat.

After all, we'd been pursued right off the bat by sea trolls answering the calls of something far, far bigger out in the fog that first night.

Gunny looked to Mathghaman and Bearrac, who stood there with arms folded. "Have you heard of anything like this?"

PETER NEALEN

Bearrac nodded gravely. "The Deep Ones are real. We do not give them names, but then, we do not speak with them or their envoys, either. Some of them came to the Isle of Riamog, in the distant past, demanding we do homage to one of their foul number." He snorted. "We refused. They threatened and tried to force the matter through sorcery. They did not return to the depths from whence they came."

The Tuacha were, by and large, good and noble people. But they could be hardcore when it came down to it.

"This isn't a good place to stop, and there ain't much shelter here." Gunny was leaving the supernatural element to Mathghaman and Bearrac. He was looking at things from a mostly practical standpoint. "If we stop now, the vampire can open the time-distance gap even more, and frankly, I think that we'd be a lot better off if this 'Murkal' really is calling if we keep moving." He squinted at Almak, though some of that squint was because of the rain that was blowing into our faces, even partially sheltered by the trees. "If we're just sitting here, doing nothing but staring at the rain, how much easier do you think it's going to be for him to get inside our heads?"

Almak clearly hadn't really thought of that. My guess was that he'd always just headed for shelter when the storms started. Or maybe there was just something about this particular storm. Like I said, corsairs should be used to storms.

"How well do you know the land around here?" I asked.

"I have been this far south many times." He puffed his chest out a little. How much he was telling the truth, and how much he was just trying not to look like a kid in front of the hardened killers and the Tuacha, I couldn't be sure.

"Then you should know the terrain farther inland, off the road and deeper into the woods." Even as I said it, I saw the trepidation in his eyes, though he was trying pretty hard to hide it. I didn't think it was so much worry about navigating, but the woods were almost as scary as the sea.

I wondered what it must have been like, growing up in such a haunted world. Where every shadow held either a monster or a specter, eager to prey on the unwary or simply those who didn't appease them. We'd all grown up in a world that denied any such things existed, though there were plenty of stories that suggested that those denials were often less than truthful. But Almak didn't know any other way.

The Tuacha did, even though they lived in the same world. They knew the monsters were there, and the specters, but while they tread warily where they had to, they didn't *fear* them the way these people did.

Bearrac saw what I was going for. "Come, young Almak. Better the wolves in the woods than the voices from the sea. Conor is right. Let us move inland, so that the Deep One's howlings become little more than annoying noise in the distance."

Almak wasn't sure what to make of that. He had been raised to fear and hate the Over Sea Men, but he feared the Deep Ones more. He finally nodded, though his uncertainty about the wisdom of this course of action was written all over his face.

So, we turned away from the muddy road and the thundering surf and moved deeper into the dripping shadows under the trees.

* * *

We hadn't gone far before I started to think that I could hear what Almak had been talking about. I hadn't been paying much attention to the sound of the wind in the trees before, being somewhat more focused on threats that I might have to shoot, along with the route and making sure that my team was on the alert and keeping pace with the rest of the platoon, since it was our turn on rear security. But as we turned into the woods, I thought I suddenly heard my name called.

I looked around, searching for any sign of a shadower. We'd seen things like that in the woods up north, including a weird, blurry thing that I'd never been able to get a good look at. Sometimes there was nothing, sometimes there were strangely moving shadows. Sometimes there were even eyes. But a careful scan of the trees, the muddy road just visible a few yards behind, glistening dully in the driving rain, and the cliff top just beyond it, showed me nothing.

Conor. There it was again. And that time, it wasn't in the howling of the wind in the treetops, but it had seemed to come with the crash of the waves against the cliffs. Along with it came a powerful pull, a sort of mental demand that I turn and head toward the ocean. There was no seduction to it, no attraction. It was a pure, raw compulsion, a will bent on dragging me to a horror that would last until the end of time.

I forced myself to face front again, praying, not for the first time, to be released from that compulsion. Slowly, as I forced one foot in front of the other, it ebbed away, until we crossed over a low hill about five hundred yards inland from the road, and the sound of the surf died away, drowned out by the wind and the rain.

CHAPTER 13

THREE days later, we reached the edge of the Black Bull lands.

We'd left the storm behind, but the sun hadn't replaced it. Instead, we continued to slog through the wet and damp, as the overcast continued to drizzle a fine mist over us constantly. Cammies were soaked, and the chafing only worsened.

Finding the vampire's trail in that wet should have been next to impossible. Spoor was wiped away as fast as the rain came down, but fortunately or unfortunately, as the case may be, we didn't have to rely on the creature's footprints, or the rotting blood trails that its corpse puppets left behind them.

No, we just had to follow the trail of death and devastation.

The Black Bull might have managed to drive the vampire off from the walls of the fortress called Galonak, but many of the smaller settlements to the south had not been so lucky. As we'd moved back toward the road in the aftermath of the storm, we'd found the steaming remains of another farmstead burned to the ground. The cattle had been mutilated, some of the pitiful animals still alive despite their horrible wounds, and the farmer's family had been dismembered, the farmer himself exsanguinated. Looking at that nightmare scene, I couldn't help but imagine that he'd been made to watch the deaths before the vampire had fed on him.

The sadism of the thing we were following was getting more evident with every passing mile. It was doing this for fun. For sport. And we could only follow and hope to catch it.

Gunny was pissed. He'd pushed hard since that farm, and we'd passed two more before we reached the border with the Gray Hound tribe. We were all exhausted—well, maybe not Mathghaman and his Tuacha—but a growing, cold rage was keeping us going. Most of us, anyway. I'd heard Nagano quietly bitching about getting stirred up over a bunch of corsair savages.

Now we were at the border, and Almak had halted, reining in his tired pony. We hadn't been going at quite the pace to wear the animal out, but movement had been constant, except for about six to eight hours each night, when we'd halted and set security.

And still, the vampire was ahead of us.

"Well, if this is the border, then I guess you've fulfilled your part." Gunny was looking at Almak, who wasn't meeting his eyes. "You're free to go."

I was studying the kid, myself, my rifle held loosely in my hands but ready to snap it up and shoot him if he got froggy. I didn't know what stories he'd been told about the Tuacha, never mind the strangers with the boom sticks, but I'd seen enough propaganda told to the tools of jihadis to have some suspicions. If he figured we were going to kill him rather than let him go, then he might do all sorts of desperate and stupid stuff.

But that wasn't it. As he stared at the ground, shifting his weight in the saddle, I suddenly saw that he was…*embarrassed* wasn't the term. No, he was uncertain and hesitant, but he wasn't scared, at least not of us. Finally, he took a deep breath and looked up at Gunny, who was watching him with narrowed eyes. Eye contact didn't last long before Almak looked down again.

There have been a lot of Recon Marines who couldn't stand up to Gunny Taylor's stare. He was an intense dude.

"I do not know what my father might say, were he here now." Almak's voice was as hesitant as his manner. "The Over Sea Men have been our foes for all of living memory."

That does tend to happen when you live a pirate's life.

"But I would see our people revenged on this creature. My father may have held us back to defend our lands, but to see it escape offends me." He looked up again, taking a deep breath. "I would come with you if you continue to pursue it."

Well, now. I caught Bailey's eye, and we both raised an eyebrow at the same time. This wasn't a development I thought that either of us had seen coming. Sure, Almak had tried awfully hard to make friends, with a group of guys who had some serious trust issues, but to willingly continue his hostage status just to get revenge on a monster we weren't even sure how we were going to take, that took guts.

It was possible he was playing an angle, but once again, I didn't get the same shifty sense off Almak that I had off Dragon Mask. As I studied him, I got the distinct impression that he was entirely sincere. He wanted that vampire's head, even if he had to tag along with foreigners and enemies to get it.

"You're not going to be able to fight the same way we do." I lifted my rifle slightly to indicate that he didn't have anything like it. And he didn't. He'd come armed, but with only a short sword and a recurve bow. That recurve looked like it could launch an arrow with some pretty blistering force, but it still couldn't hope to reach out half as far as our M110s.

"I know. It matters not to me. I will carry, I will serve as need be. I only wish to have my people's vengeance on this monster." He glanced at Mathghaman with some trepidation. The King's Champion stood to one side, his massive arms folded across his broad chest, his face impassive. "Even if it only means being present at its destruction."

"It might not be that simple." Gunny rubbed his chin with one hand, watching Almak closely. "What if it kills all of us?"

"Then I will die, but I will die while trying to kill it." The kid was stubborn, but I should have expected no less from a people like his.

This was the difference between the Dovos in the north and the corsairs. The Dovos were killers, but they were some of the most base and savage people I'd ever encountered, even compared to some of the jihadis running around Syria and Iraq. The corsairs were pirates and raiders, superstitious to the core, but there was still some thread of honor and civilization among them, thin though it might be. Almak knew what he was asking. And he was asking, anyway.

Gunny looked over at Mathghaman with an inquiring glance. Mathghaman didn't drag things out. He just nodded slightly.

"Fine. You're with us." Gunny pointed to the pony. "But that critter either goes back, or it becomes a pack animal from here on out. We're getting off the beaten track and back into the woods, now that we've hit the edge of our safe passage." He grinned humorlessly. "You're on foot with the rest of us knuckle-draggers now, son."

The threat of the vampire notwithstanding, that was what really made Almak's face fall, as if he was just then beginning to wonder what he'd gotten himself into.

* * *

The terrain changed as we moved south. The mountains that had been hidden in the fog and mist, shrouded by low clouds on the rare occasions that the mists lifted on the coast, extended a long finger out toward the sea. The land got steeper and rougher, especially as we moved away from the coastal road, which all the corsair tribes seemed to use to trade in between tribal wars.

We could still follow the vampire's path, mainly by following the smoke and the flocks of crows and other, darker carrion eaters. Every once in a while, we had to send a team down to check to make sure, lest we take the results of a raid between tribes as evidence of the vampire, but each time, they found more of its signature atrocities.

"How's it keeping Sister Sebeal fed?" Santos asked the uncomfortable question on the fifth night after leaving the Black Bull's territory. The silence that followed was every bit as uncomfortable as the question itself. "I mean, unless we're chasing after a monster just to rescue an animated corpse, it's got to be feeding her. She'd be pretty close to starvation by now, otherwise."

"It will have made arrangements." Bearrac had taken Mathghaman's silence as assent to speak. The barrel-chested Tuacha was a font of knowledge, but he always deferred to the Champion. "Those who have become vampires have grown old and wise in their wickedness. It would not have left its lair without a plan. There appear to be some living corsairs still bound to it, though it may also have turned its dead puppets to carrying food for her. She is no use to it dead, and it will know that."

"What use is she to a vampire, except as…" Chambers faltered suddenly and glanced at the Tuacha as if he was wondering at the wisdom of finishing the thought.

"As food?" Bearrac finished Chambers' sentence with a grim half smile that had all the humor of a man walking through a graveyard. "No, all it can do then is kill her." His expression darkened. "You have seen its cruelty, its malice. It will wish to do far, far worse than drink her blood."

Fortunately, he didn't elaborate. Perhaps because night was coming on quickly. Perhaps simply because he didn't want to dwell on such gruesome possibilities. The Tuacha had shown they were capable of comprehending evil without going into great detail about it.

The silence that followed stretched out as each man scanned the deepening dark around us. The remnant of a solitary farmstead still smoldered in the valley below, and the occasional tang of smoke reached us, not from our own fire. The farms had been more widely spread out lately, and we were now far enough inland that we were out of sight of the tribes' coastal settlements and fortresses, which many of them seemed to cluster around, from what Almak had told us.

We were getting deep into the wilderness, and Almak was getting more and more nervous as we went, though he was trying hard to hide it behind hard-eyed bravado.

Still, he kept making odd gestures toward the trees and the rocks, and some of his mutterings had drawn sharp glares from several of the Tuacha, especially Cairbre. I couldn't make those out, but I suspected they were incantations, given the way Mathghaman and his companions reacted when they heard him.

The thought of Almak made me look around again, searching the shadows from the flickering fire for him. He'd been engaging less the last couple of nights. His eagerness seemed to be fading a little as he found that his little rituals weren't particularly welcome. Bearrac had shut him down when he'd wanted to burn something before setting off over a ridgeline the day before, and he'd been surly ever since.

I spotted him as he stepped out of the shadows and slumped down next to his pack. He looked even surlier than before, and when Mathghaman appeared at the edge of the firelight, I thought I was starting to understand why.

"If this thing is heading out of corsair lands, where is it going?" I'd been wondering that as we'd gotten farther and farther from what passed for civilization in this part of the world. The vampire seemed to be heading into trackless wilderness, and if any of the Tuacha suspected where we were going, they hadn't said anything yet.

Mathghaman was still standing at the edge of the firelight, his head cocked back, looking at the stars through a small rent in the clouds overhead. Almost as if he were waiting for Almak to try to head into the dark again. There was something going on there. But he didn't comment on it. Instead, he just answered my question. "The Land of Shadows and Crows."

"Where's that?" Bailey asked. "It sounds like a real great place." Bailey's sarcasm hadn't made as many appearances since we'd linked up with the Tuacha, but occasionally he couldn't help himself.

"On the other side of this mountain ridge, and far down at the end of the mountains known as The Wall of Scath. It is a place of death and decay."

"You are sure it is him, then?" Diarmodh asked. He'd said little so far on this expedition, but he'd clearly been thinking.

Mathghaman moved back to the fire and nodded as he sat cross-legged on the ground by his pack and his rifle. He hadn't looked at Almak since they'd rejoined us, but he was apparently satisfied that whatever had happened wouldn't be repeated, at least not that night. "Why else would we be going this way?"

"Who?" Gurke was clearly irked at being out in the ignorance fields for this conversation.

"He was once known as Val Teren." Mathghaman leaned back against his pack and watched the patch of stars again, through the gently waving boughs of the fir above the fire. "He was a prince of his people, and a great war leader. Their names are long forgotten, buried in the infamy and the dark sorcery that now wreaths what was once their lands." He paused, as if considering how to continue the story, or if he even should. "His old name is only known because he has occasionally used it when he has appeared throughout the centuries. He is most often known now as Unsterbanak.

"I know that it is him because he is making close to a straight line back to the Land of Shadows and Crows. Vampires are territorial. They do not often stray far from their lairs for long. The very earth groans at their presence. You have seen how the land itself dies where he has set foot. They cannot long stand the land of the living, but must slink back to their holes of corruption and decay. And the Land of Shadows and Crows is Unsterbanak's lair." He sighed. "We have many leagues of trackless wilderness to go before we reach it, and if we have not caught him yet, I doubt we will before he reaches his castle. So, we have many leagues to march, many dangers yet to face." He turned to look around at all of us. "Conserve your ammunition as much as you can from here on. You will need it."

Silence fell after that. I'm not ordinarily loathe to sit quietly. In fact, most Recon Marines have to be able to tolerate extended silence. We can go days at a time without saying anything if the hide is close enough to the objective, and I'd been on a few jungle hides on float that really had been. Nature of the jungle.

But I couldn't just let that one sit. The nightmares in this place were bad enough as it was.

"Do the corsair lands go all the way to this Land of Shadows and Crows?" May as well get as much information as possible, especially if it helped the mission—and got us thinking about the practical problems to be tackled, rather than just the nature of the enemy we were following. And if it drew Almak out a little, and defused some of the tension around the fire that it seemed only Mathghaman and I had noticed, so much the better.

"No." Almak's reply was calm and measured. If he was still resentful over Mathghaman's bringing him back into the circle, he wasn't showing it. He wasn't staring into the fire anymore—he'd learned that from us—but he was staring off into nothing, clearly reconsidering the wisdom of coming along. "The Fendak tribes range through these mountains, occasionally raiding down into the lands of the

Blue Skull." Those must be the corsair tribe whose territory we'd just passed through. "They are small and weak, but savage. Every now and again, the Blue Skull must march into the mountains and burn their villages, leaving their warriors hanging from the trees as a warning." Somehow, from what I'd seen of the corsairs, I doubted they stopped at just hanging the warriors, but Almak had picked up on the sense of honor that we had come to share with the Tuacha. He didn't think that we'd react too well to stories of massacre.

We wouldn't, but we could also see through his omission.

"Beyond…" He scratched at his beard. "There are stories. Tales of beasts, and men more feral still than the Fendak. But I have never gone so far."

"Nor have we." Something about the way Mathghaman said that made me think that he'd seen a fair bit of the world, nevertheless. I had no idea how old he was. He and his brethren seemed somehow timeless. "But you are right. Those lands and what dwells within them are more dangerous by far than the Fendak." He looked around the fire again. "I fear that the easiest part of our pursuit may be at an end."

On that cheerful note, with security set, we called it a night.

CHAPTER 14

THE mountains got steeper and rockier as we climbed the long spur that extended west from the Wall of Scath, thrusting like a finger of stone toward the ocean. The trees changed, too, as the air got drier and colder. We were getting closer to the snow line. We were far south of the Land of Ice and Monsters, nearly on the same latitude as the Isle of Riamog, to the best of my reckoning, but it was still winter, and the higher we got, the colder it got.

It seemed, judging by the massive wall of ice we'd glimpsed in the north, that this world was in the grip of an ice age, at least at some stage. So, long winters and cold high country just made sense.

The woods remained dense and dark, and despite the more arid climate, we still found ourselves in the mists all too often, since the clouds were usually lower than the peaks themselves. Almak was getting more and more withdrawn the farther we got from corsair lands. I didn't think it was because he was scared of being away from home. He had scars on his arms and one on his cheek, along with tattoos that he tried to keep hidden from the Tuacha, but they looked like kill tallies to me. He was broad-shouldered and powerfully built, and he carried his weapons with the ease of a man who was quite familiar with them. So, it wasn't distance that bothered him. This man had been raiding, presumably far afield.

I suspected it had more to do with whatever Mathghaman had interrupted out in the dark. And that was concerning. Almak still didn't give me the same bad feeling that Dragon Mask always had, but there was something going on that was definitely no bueno.

Still, we saw little over the next few days and nights. If those woods were as haunted as the forests around the corsair settlements, whatever haunted them didn't seem interested in coming out to play. We hiked and clambered over boulders and steep mountainsides, sometimes using ropes and trees to pull ourselves up, and if we occasionally felt as if we were being watched, none of us could ever spot anything when we looked. Even Bearrac shook his head when I quietly asked him if he'd seen anything. And if any one of us *would* have seen anything, it was Bearrac.

Even so, the shifting clouds and mists made it hard to tell. The snow flurries we ran into on the second day made things worse. Only the fact that Mathghaman seemed to know at least roughly where we were going kept us on course. We'd have lost the trail long before otherwise, between the difficulty of the terrain and the weather.

We were high enough that I started to wonder about Almak's talk of the Fendak tribes. If we hadn't run into any of them so far, maybe we'd bypassed them. Maybe they were just hunkered down for the winter and were smaller and less of a threat than he'd made out. That the mountains to the south were a source of spook stories and nightmares for the corsairs was pretty obvious.

Not that I could necessarily blame them. This entire world seemed to have come out of a spook-story version of a fantasy novel.

But if I thought we'd slipped past the Fendak without either they or us noticing each other, I was about to be disabused of that notion.

* * *

We heard the drums first. I would have believed, as high as we were, past the snowline, that no one would be living up there. But the drumbeats thundered from somewhere in the rocks above us. Almak had his bow out and an arrow nocked as soon as he heard it, scanning the slopes and the trees around us. We were close to the top of a ridge, and the trees had gotten patchy, leaving several open, rocky slopes between stands of wind-twisted pines. We were keeping to the trees as much as possible and carefully trying to avoid the slides of scree and broken boulders that just didn't look at all stable.

Weapons came up and eyes scanned the slopes through optics, looking for targets. The clouds scudded around the jagged, snowy peaks above, blowing snow only adding to the obscuring mists. And we couldn't see anything. Only hear those drums, thudding and rumbling amid the rocks, all too close and yet out of sight.

Rodeffer had stopped, braced against a massive boulder between two equally huge, lightning-blasted pines, and was scanning the ridgetop of the finger just above us and to our east. That seemed to be where the drums were sounding from, though the echoes across the rocks and the mountain peaks made it difficult to localize any sound.

I moved up to join him, beckoning to Almak as I passed him. My team was taking our turn on point, for the second time in three days. Mathghaman and his Tuacha were immediately behind us with Gunny. Almak struggled up against the steepness of the mountainside, taking a knee awkwardly beside and below me, his bow held sideways over his knee, that arrow still nocked, despite the fact he had no more targets than we did.

"Do they live this high? Or is this a hunting party?" I kept my voice low, though there was no way anyone close to those drums would be able to hear me, anyway.

"I do not know." That amulet of his seemed to be much less efficient than either the Tuacha's mind speech or Dragon Mask's spell. It took a lot of focus to understand him, as if he were mumbling. "The Blue Skulls may have driven them higher since the last raids. Word reached us that they wrought terrible slaughter among the Fendak last spring."

"Which might mean they've got more of a grudge than usual, and we might not look like Blue Skulls, but we sure don't look like Fendak, either." I'd seen some of that in some of the more savage areas of Syria, where IS had done enough damage that the locals were just out for blood.

It took him a moment to respond. "If the stories are true, the Fendak cannot have 'more' of a grudge. They hold all outside their tribes as hated enemies."

Again, not an unfamiliar concept, but I didn't bother to say anything.

"I can't see shit, Conor." Rodeffer was still scanning. "Maybe they're just making noise?"

But before I could ask Almak if that was plausible, Santos hissed, "Movement. By that big rock that looks like a tooth, above and to the ten o'clock."

I had to look for a moment before I picked out which outcrop he was talking about. I brought my rifle up and scanned it through the scope but saw nothing but snow, rocks, and scrubby brush.

"It is said that the Fendak can hide in open ground." Almak seemed to hesitate a little as he said it, his words slow and careful. As if he wasn't sure he believed it himself, but the possibility had to be mentioned.

"Apaches." Farrar's one-word contribution actually surprised me a little. He hadn't ever been the most bookish of the platoon. In fact, I didn't think I'd ever seen him crack a book through the entire workup or even the float. He'd watched movies and tried to find the end of the internet, but he'd never been the studious kind. So that particularly historical parallel was a bit out of left field, coming from him.

But it fit. I'd tried, during some of the rare downtime we'd had during the workup, to work on that kind of microterrain stalking that the Apache and Comanche had made famous, but it had required a lot more practice than we'd had time for. And if the Fendak were usually outnumbered by their enemies...

"How'd you come up with that, Farrar?" Gunny was moving up toward the top of the boulder where we'd halted. "I'm surprised you even know what that name means."

"I watched this movie about Geronimo on the ship." Farrar had never been exactly apologetic about his hatred for reading.

"Figures." Gunny dropped his ruck and started to climb up onto the boulder. "Watch for movement. That's going to be the best warning we get."

A moment later, an arrow whined out of the trees across a snow-blanketed slide and smacked into the tree just beside Rodeffer's head. The fletching was black and red, the shaft stained the same colors.

Rodeffer dropped like a rock, making more noise than he probably should have, but I couldn't exactly blame him. That arrow had come within an inch of his ear.

"What the fuck. I still can't see anything." He hadn't just ducked for cover but had dropped behind his rifle and was scanning the trees, his finger hovering on his trigger. I was watching, too, having stepped behind another tree and braced my rifle against the trunk, looking for targets. But whoever had launched that arrow, they were practically invisible.

Then Bearrac fired, somewhere down the slope.

I honestly didn't know if the Tuacha's rifles worked the same way ours did, or if they were some sort of magic. Hell, for all I knew, given the way we'd received ours, *our* rifles might be some sort of magic artifacts. I didn't think so—they at least *appeared* to operate exactly like an M110 from back in The World, and we even still had to clean them—but there was something about the slender, elegant, muzzleloader look of the Tuacha's weapons that just didn't look like they should be as effective as they were.

Especially since the Tuacha weren't using optics. And yet, Bearrac hit something, as a body flopped with a brief, dying scream.

But if we'd been hoping that the hit would have prompted the rest to charge so that we could cut them down with a hail of gunfire, we were disappointed. The echoes of Bearrac's gunshot died away, and the forested mountainside went perfectly still as we held our positions behind cover and searched in vain for the hidden Fendak.

"Sure wish we'd asked that cauldron for some thermals," Santos whispered.

"If they're hidden well enough, even thermals wouldn't help." I'd seen that firsthand, too. Hell, I'd hidden from thermals in training. They're useful tools, but they still can't see through rock or trees.

Then another arrow whistled down at us from somewhere in the rocks up above and slashed Farrar across the back of the neck.

He started to scream, only biting the wail of agony off with a lot of effort, then collapsed and grabbed the back of his neck as blood welled between his fingers. I frowned as I snapped my weapon up toward the rocks where the arrow had come from, looking for a target.

There. The Fendak hadn't been quite as careful this time. I only had a fraction of a head and shoulder to aim at, behind another nocked arrow, but it was enough, especially at barely two hundred yards, my scope dialed up to eight power. I let out a breath and squeezed off the shot as my lungs emptied. The suppressed M110 *crack*ed and surged back into my shoulder. I only saw the Fendak's head—which looked strangely bear-like—snap back as my bullet went through his skull because I still had the rifle braced against the tree trunk and had used that to control the recoil, just in case I needed to take a follow-up shot.

Farrar was keening softly through clenched teeth and starting to writhe as his eyes rolled back in his head. "What the hell happened?" I couldn't spare more than a glance, my eye still on my sights and looking for more targets, but

Fennean had moved quickly to our stricken teammate. "Was the arrow poisoned?"

Fennean had retrieved the arrow and studied it for a moment, before snapping it in two with a grimace. "No. Worse."

"*Worse?*" Rodeffer's voice had started to rise, and another arrow winged out of the trees to shatter on the rocks above his head. He ducked and dropped his voice to a whisper. "What's worse than poison?"

Fennean was crouched over Farrar, trying to hold him still. "It was cursed."

I grimaced as I looked for the Fendak who had shot at Rodeffer, scanning the stand of trees fruitlessly. I was *really* starting to dislike sorcery in all its forms.

Fennean was holding Farrar's hands tightly in one of his, almost as if he was holding him back from clawing at his own eyes, as he whispered in whatever ancient language the Tuacha seemed to use for prayer, or invocation, or whatever they did to fight sorcery. His long fingers were holding onto both of Farrar's wrists while he dug in a pouch on his belt for something. The whispered words seemed to be having some effect, as Farrar's struggles lessened, but his eyes were still rolled so far back in his head that all you could see was the whites, and he was starting to foam at the mouth.

After a moment, Fennean brought his hand out of the pouch with a tiny crystal vial. The liquid inside appeared clear, but at the same time it seemed to glimmer, as if it was lit from within. After pulling the cap with his teeth, he made a strange gesture over Farrar's forehead with the vial before forcing it between his lips and tipping it up to make him drink, whispering gently the entire time.

Farrar struggled at first, but as the first drops passed his lips, he relaxed. Fennean poured the rest of the shining liquid down his throat, as his twisting and shaking stopped, his jaw unclenched, and his eyes came down to the here and now again. They were bloodshot, but at a glance, I could see that he was looking at the real world again. Fennean put the vial back in his pouch, made a sign with his thumb on Farrar's forehead, and then let go of his wrists and stepped back, taking up his rifle once more.

"The wound will take time to heal, but I think the curse is lifted. If you begin to feel strangely, be sure to say something immediately."

Farrar nodded with a pained gulp and rolled back over to pick up his rifle again. Blood still oozed from the cut on the back of his neck, but now it was just a scratch, rather than the life-threatening—or soul-destroying—wound that it had been a moment before.

I saw Almak move. He'd been watching the entire thing, his face blank and his eyes dark, and he made a strange gesture that I couldn't quite make out before turning back toward the Fendak. Something about what Fennean had just done bothered him, a lot.

Then Mathghaman's rifle thundered. *Behind* us, on the west flank.

The Fendak had us surrounded.

CHAPTER 15

"BRING it in tight and keep to cover!" Gunny had figured out that we were in a hell of a crack even quicker than I had. But even so, we were at something of an impasse, and making sure the Fendak didn't get inside our perimeter was only a temporary solution to a potentially permanent problem.

A hail of arrows hammered into the trees and the rocks, the shafts shattering on the stone, sending splinters tumbling through the air. This time, they really did get a little sloppier, and gunfire roared through the misty afternoon to punish those tribesmen who exposed themselves a little too much.

But then Nagano grabbed Synar and tried to rush the closest outcrop that was raining arrows.

Nagano had been quiet since all but he and Baldinus had been killed or gone missing from Zimmerman's team. Bailey had taken him onto his team but hadn't really warmed to him as assistant team leader. He was senior to Applegate, but Bailey had increasingly leaned on Applegate instead of Nagano. There was a lot going unspoken there—Bailey had never particularly cared for his previous ATL, Gonsalves, and had largely had Applegate filling in where needed already—but it was pretty clear that Nagano not only mildly resented being a strap-hanger, but he was also more than a little disturbed by what had happened to the rest of his team.

Especially given that Zimmerman had disappeared into the artifact chamber with the captain just before everything had gone pear-shaped down in the catacombs beneath Taramas's citadel.

"Nagano! Get your ass back here!" Bailey's roar echoed off the mountainsides. But it was too late.

An arrow smacked into Synar's mail, and he dropped on his belly, firing blindly toward the trees and the rocks. It didn't look like it had penetrated the rings. He was still good, just far too exposed, especially as more arrows began to rain down on his position.

Nagano took one to the neck.

It didn't go through his throat, or even hit anything vital, from where I was watching, between searching for targets in the shadows under the trees on the other side of the rockslide.

It would have been kinder if it had.

Whatever curse had been on the arrow that had cut Farrar, something similar seemed to have been put on the one that hit Nagano. He stopped dead, going up on his toes, as if he was about to fall on his face.

But he didn't fall.

He hung there, as if held up by the arrow that had pierced the muscle on the right of his neck, his face turned toward the cloudy sky. His rifle slipped from nerveless fingers to hang by its sling around his neck. Then he started to twitch and shake. Even from a distance, I could see every muscle and tendon in his neck standing out with tension.

The shaking got worse and worse. Then blood erupted from his mouth and nose, and he collapsed. Even then, he wasn't dead but kept spasming and retching blood, as he tumbled down the rockslide and out of sight.

Synar stayed where he was, as the scree shifted under his weight, and he tried to burrow down behind as many of the rocks as possible, as more arrows skipped off the shale or slammed into cracks between them. Only a miracle had so far kept him from being hit worse than that first strike to his mail-clad shoulder.

I think we were all glad of the supple, lightweight armor at that point. Especially after watching Nagano's end.

I found that I hoped, for his sake, that he was dead. There was no way we were going to reach him before the Fendak did. If they even wanted to go near the victim of one of their curses.

"Covering fire on those trees!" Bailey was taking charge of the situation down there. Almost a dozen rifles opened up, their suppressed but supersonic rounds sending a rolling, echoing *crash* across the hillside, impacts smacking bark off tree trunks, smashing tree limbs down onto the forest floor, and kicking up snow and shattered stone. "Synar! Turn and go!"

Synar probably couldn't hear him over the noise, but sometimes gunfire is still communication. After scrambling to his feet, undoubtedly thankful for the kneepads in his trousers, he turned and burned, sprinting as best he could over the uneven and unstable rockslide toward the rocks and the trees where the rest of the platoon was crouched.

He almost made it unscathed, but just before he reached the trees, an arrow struck him between the shoulder blades and hammered him forward onto his face.

I barely saw what happened, as I'd just seen where that arrow had come from, and though it was hard to spot, I could just make out the vague shape of the man who'd loosed it. Putting my reticle just about at chest height, I squeezed the trigger. The *crack* of the shot was almost immediately followed by the silhouetted form spinning down and out of sight.

Synar's mail had saved him again. He was up and being dragged back into the perimeter and behind the cover of another boulder that had fetched up against an ancient, twisted tree sometime in the past.

"Everybody stay in cover!" Gunny bellowed. He slithered down the rocky promontory where he'd been shooting, and jerked a thumb up to where he'd just been. "Conor, get somebody up there."

"Rodeffer, you're up." I would have taken it, but Gunny was already yelling for Gurke and Bailey. He wanted team leaders.

"Almak, how much do you know, and I mean really *know*, about these Fendak?" Gunny asked as we crouched at the base of the promontory. Everything had gone quiet again as the Fendak weren't wasting arrows on targets they couldn't see, and we, likewise, weren't wasting bullets.

"Only the tales that have reached us from the Blue Skulls." He chewed his lip behind his beard, his forehead creased into a worried frown. "They are said to eat the dead, and that they worship strange creatures that live beneath the mountains."

"How do they feel about the dark? Any stories about that?" Gunny was watching him carefully, and I realized what he was getting at. The Dovos had feared the dark, something that we potentially could have used against them—if Captain Sorenson hadn't been so dead set on making them allies—and if the Fendak were similarly afraid of the night, we'd have an advantage.

But Almak shook his head. "I do not know."

Gunny grimaced, but nodded anyway. "Never mind. Even if they think the nighttime is the right time, they *probably* don't have night vision, at least not like what we've got." He looked around at the team leaders. "We've got a couple ways to do this. Either way, we're staying put until after dark."

* * *

The days seemed to be getting longer, but not by a lot. The shadow of the mountain peaks to the west, and the low overcast atop them, meant that sunset came even earlier, and within another half hour we'd pulled out our PVS-15s and were watching the mountainsides around us in shades of black and green.

We'd cached our rucks for now. At least, the four of us had. Rifles were slung tightly across our backs, along with my sword. All I had in my hand was my Bowie, the big fighting knife that generations of McCalls had carried into battle for a century and a half. Ideally, the blade would be blackened to kill any shine, but if we did this right, kept to cover and concealment carefully, it wouldn't show any shine anyway.

At least, not until I used it.

The clouds were moving in again, and the mist was thickening. This would be our time to move. To slither through the rocks and trees and quietly kill our way through the Fendak's encirclement, carving a path for the rest of the platoon to get clear.

Haunted mountains or not, we'd be moving all night until we were well away from the Fendak's territory. Provided this worked.

I didn't put Rodeffer on point, not this time. I took lead myself, down on my belly and low-crawling up along the low line of wind-battered scrub that lined the low finger we'd clung to for the last few hours, half-buried in snowdrifts. The clouds descended still farther, dropping visibility to only a few yards, even on NVGs.

Crawling over snow-covered rocks, uphill, in the dark is not a pleasant experience. Especially in a place where you don't know what the shadows and the mists might be concealing, but you're pretty sure it's something bad.

You've also got to be extra careful looking for places to put your hands and elbows when you're carrying twelve inches of naked, razor-sharp steel in your fist while you crawl.

Of course, we were expecting to take contact sooner or later. But we were hoping it would be a little bit later than right after leaving the perimeter.

A faint rustle just ahead, on the other side of another rock, made me freeze. I slowly brought my knife around as I gathered my feet under me, trying desperately not to make a sound. I couldn't entirely avoid the faint crunch of the snow under my boots, but my mags were secure in my chest rig—though I couldn't carry quite as many of them, I could still fit two 7.62 mags in a three-mag 5.56 mag pouch—so they didn't clack. I turned my NVGs toward the rock, almost certain that that was where the sound had come from.

Heartbeats later, the Fendak slithered around the side of the rock.

He was small, and despite the cold he appeared to be wearing nothing but buckskin leggings and a white-furred hide over his head and shoulders. He carried a short spear in one hand and a wickedly curved knife in the other.

This was going to get nasty.

I held my position, putting out a gloved fist to tell Rodeffer to freeze behind me. Then I crouched there, in the shadow of a short, stiff pine and the boulder, and waited, motionless, as the Fendak fighter edged down the slope.

We were still all in green—none of us had thought to ask the *Coira Ansec* for overwhites. We hadn't expected to be in the snow again so soon, either, especially considering where we'd been heading and the time of year. From what Mathghaman had told us, snow was rare in the corsair lands. They were used to fog and rain during the winter.

But this guy also didn't have night vision. He probably couldn't see far, even with over half an hour of darkness to let his eyes adjust.

He could smell, though. He suddenly froze, looking around with wide eyes. Eyes that glinted a little too brightly on IR.

It went through my head that the Fendak either already had better night adaptation, or had used sorcery to enhance it, just as he locked gazes with me.

He rolled to his side and started to get up, as I lunged for him, trying to get on top of him and silence him before he could call the alarm.

That spear almost skewered me, tearing part of a mag pouch and the backing of my chest rig before skittering off the mail over my ribs. I clamped down on the haft and grabbed it just above his hand, trying to wrench it out of his grip even as I tried just as hard to bury my Bowie to the hilt in his throat.

He got his own knife in the way, and I slashed at it, almost desperate not to get cut by any of the Fendak's weapons. Not after I'd seen what they'd done to Nagano. Almost done to Farrar. I didn't think that Fennean had a bottomless supply of whatever that clear, shining liquid had been, and Farrar still wasn't quite all right, hours later. He kept kind of fading, as if he was listening to something far away that only he could hear.

I dropped a knee on the little guy's crotch, and he doubled up with a groan. That gave me the opening to twist the spear out of his grip and toss it, thus freeing up my right hand to grab his knife hand. Unfortunately, that maneuver also freed up *his* left to grab my knife hand. Then it became a contest of strength and leverage as I bore into him, pressing him into the mountainside as I leaned on the pommel of my Bowie and tried to keep his knife off me.

He was *strong*. I was a lot bigger than him, but it was still all I could do to keep him pinned, and his arm was locked out, keeping my knife at a distance.

Grunts and impacts all around me told me that the rest of the team was similarly engaged. Our plan hadn't quite worked out as well as we'd hoped.

He was twisting under me, as if he were trying to get his legs around and into the guard. Even if he failed, if he hooked my rifle or my sword, I was in trouble. The leverage could only work against me in that position.

So, I took the risk and dropped my elbow inside his knife hand.

The knife skipped across my mail as about half my bodyweight went into his chest. The air went out of him with a *whuff,* and I thought I heard something crack. He loosened up for a moment, which was all I needed.

Twisting my wrist, I broke my knife hand free and hammered the blade down into his chest.

He grunted and sagged, but he didn't stop fighting. Even as the strength drained out of him, he still kept trying to drive that knife into me, and only my mail kept me from getting cut as I fended it off.

Finally, his struggles slowed, and then stopped. I dragged my knife clear and hauled myself away from the body.

The mountainside above me was a hand-to-hand battleground. And more of the Fendak were coming down out of the trees and the mists, weapons in their hands, moving silently and furtively from tree to rock to tree again. They hadn't been waiting us out once the sun went down. They'd been gathering to try to wipe us out under cover of darkness.

I unslung my rifle, canted it to bring the red dot into my view, and looked for a target, even as Santos twisted free of his opponent, his tomahawk coming up and then down in a vicious and final stroke that impacted with a *thwack* and a grunt. He hacked at his opponent twice more, but it seemed like that fight was over.

Then I shot the one that had just crawled up onto the rock above Santos, ready to drop on him with two of those wickedly curved knives. The *crack* echoed out across the mountainside, announcing that the plan was blown at the same time my bullet tore through the attacker's chest from twenty yards away. He staggered but tried to drop onto Santos anyway.

He met the tomahawk on its upward stroke, and it cleaved through his throat even as Santos battered one knife aside.

Then all hell broke loose.

Ululating cries announced to the Fendak that their plan had failed, just as my rifle shot had announced it to our guys. A dozen of them came howling out of the trees, moving like men who could see in the dark. A crashing volley of rifle fire cut them down, sending a couple of them tumbling down the mountain, while others just fell and lay where they were.

"Go! Push!" Gunny wasn't going to go back to waiting. The Tuacha surged up past us, rifles slung and swords flashing in the dark.

I got a new appreciation for just how much Mathghaman and his fellows were pacing themselves so that we could keep up.

With their rucks on, they were still able to pretty much run up the slope, if not nearly as fast as any Recon Marine could run on the flats. And they went through the front ranks of the Fendak like a scythe through wheat. Blades flashed and men died in the dark.

And aside from that first chorus of warning cries, all in near-total silence.

That silence was broken in the next moment by more gunfire. I'd kept my rifle up, looking for targets, and while Mathghaman, Bearrac, and the others had cut off my field of fire to the front, there were more Fendak coming out of the dark on the flanks, so I pivoted and blasted an axe-wielding man with a wolf's head helmet through the collarbone as he leaped toward Fennean's side, even as Fennean cut down another wiry shape wearing what looked an awful lot like a wolverine's hide. Just if a wolverine had sabertooth fangs.

Then Gunny was beside me as Gurke's team surged up to pass us, dragging my ruck with him. We were breaking out, for better or worse.

I let my rifle hang while I shrugged into my ruck. It took a few more seconds, as Gurke and his boys hammered suppressed rounds at the still weirdly silent killers coming out of the shadows to right and left, and Mathghaman and his men kept cutting more of them down with swords gone dark with gore, for the rest of the team to ruck up.

Then we were moving, bounding up to pass Mathghaman and the rest, heading for the cleft in the peaks above, hoping we didn't get lost in the clouds.

CHAPTER 16

WITHIN a few yards, we were completely wreathed in mist and blowing snow. We'd climbed into the stormcloud, and visibility dropped to a few feet in a heartbeat.

That could work to our advantage. It could also be disastrous. We couldn't see the enemy any more than they could see us, but maintaining unit cohesion was going to be a bastard.

So, we slowed down, weapons up as much as possible on the steep and treacherous ground. The snow and the rocks made footing difficult, and with our rucks making us top heavy, it got even worse. We had to lean forward, almost putting our faces to the slope in front of us, and that made seeing and maintaining situational awareness even more difficult.

Rodeffer had to start moving off to the right when the slope to our front became almost sheer. I almost missed it, as my boot started to slip under me, and I put a hand out to catch myself and grabbed a small, thorny bush just before my foot went out into open space.

A suppressed gunshot *crack*ed off to my left, followed by a choked scream.

I found the slightly more level ground that Rodeffer had turned onto, and followed him, finding as we took more of a switchback route that I could maintain my footing better, and straightened up so that I could shoot.

Just in time, too, as two Fendak came leaping out of the snow, curved knives swinging for Rodeffer's neck.

I shot the first one at about five yards, dumping two rounds into his chest. The 7.62 rifle fires a lot bigger bullet, and first-shot disabling hits are a lot more likely than with the lighter 5.56. My first shot was fast, but if it missed anything vital, the second one tore through his side. He went limp mid-leap and tumbled into Rodeffer's ruck, then bounced on down the hill until he fetched up against a tree a few yards below.

The impact threw Rodeffer's aim off, and his shot missed the second man, who was only a few feet behind the first. Then the Fendak slammed into him, and only the fact that he'd braced his back foot against a boulder kept them both from going off into space and down the mountainside.

I struggled forward, letting my rifle hang as I drew my Bowie. My sword was still strapped to my back, under my ruck, where I couldn't get to it. Time had made that a necessity, though I was cursing it as I thrashed through the deepening snow and over the rocks toward the struggling figures. Rodeffer's rifle was trapped between the two of them, as Rodeffer struggled to keep the curved knife away from his throat.

It took a few moments to get to them. They were about evenly matched, even though Rodeffer was noticeably bigger than the little mountain tribesman. But Rodeffer had thrown himself forward as soon as he'd recovered from the initial blow, and almost had the little man pinned against the mountainside.

I tried to climb above them but slipped and dropped to my knees, almost losing my grip on my knife, then crawled forward, grabbed the Fendak by the hair, hauled his head back, and cut his throat.

Rodeffer reared back with a curse as blood gushed from the gaping second mouth I'd just opened below the man's jaw. The Fendak let go of his knife and grabbed for his throat, but it was far too late. I'd cut almost to the spine, and he died with a gurgle as his lifeblood spurted out, staining the snow red and running down the mountain.

I got my feet under me and hauled Rodeffer up. "Keep moving." He spat, though it didn't look like he'd gotten too much blood on him from what I could see in my NVGs, grabbed hold of his rifle again, and started up the mountain.

More gunshots, muffled by the whirling snow and ice crystals, sounded in the murk. "Keep pushing! Up the mountain!" Gunny was still kicking and keeping us doing the only thing that was going to get us out of this alive— break through the encirclement and get to the high ground. We didn't know what was up there, but staying put right then meant dying, so it was better to push and fight than stay put and get slaughtered.

Possible death is always preferable to certain death.

And if you can take enough of the bad guys with you, so much the better.

Another Fendak came out of the clouds to my left, and I pivoted and shot him, my suppressor almost touching his bare chest under the bearskin he was wearing. My bullet pulped his heart and blew most of it out of a gaping hole in his back, and his feet slid out from under him. He *did* hit the end of my rifle then, but I managed to redirect the impact so that he slid past me instead of taking my own feet out from under me. Rodeffer was still moving, so I followed.

Then, abruptly, we were out of the clouds.

The peaks rose above us, still looming several hundred feet overhead, the snow reflecting the myriad stars brightly in my PVS-15s. The sight was breathtaking—almost as much as the altitude and the exertion of fighting uphill through a storm cloud.

Below, the clouds spread out, flat and white, swirling slightly but strangely—and deceptively—calm. Ahead, the snowfield was open and almost unmarked. We'd not only gotten above the clouds, but we'd passed the tree line.

Farrar and Santos came out of the cottony murk off to my left. A moment later, Herrera and Gurke appeared right behind me. Cairbre, Eoghain, and Conall appeared way off to the right.

We'd gotten spread out and scattered in the clouds, but as we mounted higher up the slope, the platoon started to move back together. Weapons stayed up, scanning above, to either side, and below.

But there was suddenly no sign of the Fendak.

"Conor." Rodeffer's voice was a low, hoarse whisper. He'd stopped at a shoulder of the ridgeline we were following up, and pointed.

I followed the line of his pointing finger and squinted. While the moon was down, there were a lot of stars up there. Starlight reflecting off the snow and the clouds made for plenty of illumination, but the saddle between triangular peaks that we'd been heading for before the clouds had closed in was in deep shadow. After a moment, though,

I saw what he was looking at, and my eyebrows climbed behind my NVGs.

We had to be at least eight thousand feet up. If I was judging distances right, that saddle was closer to nine thousand. And yet there were ruins up there. Someone had gone to the trouble to build a fort, or castle, on that saddle.

I wondered if that was why the Fendak had stopped pursuing. The question was, whose fort was it? And had we just escaped one encirclement to walk into a far harder fight?

Motioning for Rodeffer to wait, I took a knee in the snow next to him and looked down the mountainside to where the rest of the platoon was still working their way up out of the clouds. A quick count reassured me that we hadn't lost anyone else after Nagano. At least, so far. Even Almak, hampered by the fact he didn't have either the Tuacha's night eyes or our NVGs, had kept up.

Gunny had seen that we'd stopped and was hauling himself up to our position, with Mathghaman not far behind. Gunny wasn't the fastest Marine in the world. He had one pace, but he never stopped. We could all outrun him in the short term—even for about five miles or so—but he'd catch us all and pass us eventually. The man was a walking tank. Mathghaman kept pace with him, but the big Tuacha champion still looked like he could trot up the steep mountainside like a goat if he wanted to.

Gunny didn't have to ask why we'd stopped. He saw the fortifications right away. Or, rather, the ruins of fortifications. The more I looked at them, the more I saw how they'd crumbled. They'd presumably been up there a *long* time. And abandoned for almost as long.

Either that, or something or someone had come through and half-demolished them.

"Any ideas?" Gunny looked at Mathghaman. "I know that this is somewhat unknown territory."

Mathghaman was studying the ruins. I could only imagine he could see a lot more detail than I could, though maybe he was filling those details in from his own knowledge.

Gunny glanced over his shoulder. "Our new friends don't seem to want to come any higher." Looking back up at the ruins, he scratched his beard through his helmet's chinstrap. "Not sure if that's a good thing or a bad thing. Mathghaman? We need to make a decision."

The King's Champion shook his head slightly. "I do not know what we might find there. Once, these mountains were the border between two kingdoms, but that was long, long ago. We should step carefully."

"Goes without saying." It was the closest Gunny would get to saying *no shit* to our dignified companion. But Mathghaman clearly knew no more than we did about what lay ahead.

"Let's go, Rod." I saw Rodeffer sigh tiredly, steam billowing from his mouth, but he got up and started trudging up the mountain again, turning his makeshift switchback the other direction. It was just easier that way, even though we were atop the crest of the massive finger that stretched down from the peak on the east side of the saddle. It was just too steep otherwise.

Slowly, painstakingly, we threaded our way up the mountain, as the air got thinner and colder, and the night marched on. We kept stopping every few paces, both to catch our breath and to watch the clouds below us. But the Fendak didn't come out. Whatever was up there, the Fendak didn't want anything to do with it.

Under some circumstances, I might have taken some comfort from that. Not here, though. Most of the things the Dovos had feared had been far, far worse than them, and the Dovos were bloodthirsty savages who'd only made an alliance because Dragon Mask thought that our guns could get him closer to the power he wanted.

Granted, it wasn't always like that. They'd feared the Tuacha as well. Along with any other influence that had gone against their dark gods. There had been a reason that my sword's previous bearer had wrapped the hilts, disguising the runes so that he didn't have to touch or look at them. That blessed blade had been quite a force multiplier against some of the monsters. But from what Mathghaman had said about the way to the Land of Shadows and Crows, I seriously doubted that we'd find anyone or anything like that in these high places.

It was past midnight, judging by the stars, by the time we halted on a shelf just outside the ruins, set security as best we could on the side of the mountain, and scanned the ancient fortifications carefully. The saddle was still in shadow and would be until probably about midday.

The wind wailed through the stones, blowing ghostly flurries of snow through the jagged, fallen structures. Once, a wall had bridged the two peaks, with a gate in the center and four watchtowers spaced along it. Two towers were half fallen in on themselves, and the gateway had collapsed a long time ago. Of the two outer towers, one looked remarkably intact, while the other had fallen down the mountain, leaving a trail of detritus that looked almost indistinguishable from a natural rockslide, if not for the remnants of the battlements still visible in the pile.

Enough stone had fallen and rolled down the slope that it looked like the collapsed gateway was still navigable. That was good, because otherwise I didn't know if we could get over any of that, even with the climbing gear we'd brought.

For a long few minutes, we just stayed in place, scanning the ruined fortress. I forced myself not to listen too closely to the wind. It sounded like voices, even when I tried to ignore it. And in that place, I couldn't be sure that there *weren't* voices mixed in with the moaning of the wind. If there were, I was pretty sure they were voices we really didn't want to listen to.

I suddenly thought of that specter we'd seen and heard trailing the vampire, and I shuddered.

"Well, there's nothing for it." Gunny had brought all the team leaders up to the nearest edge of the ledge to get a leaders' recon of sorts before we decided how to tackle this obstacle. "We can go for it, or we can freeze to death up here."

"Let's go, then." Gurke was shivering despite the warming layers that we'd brought. The Tuacha's wool garments were orders of magnitude better than the Dovos' hides— and smelled considerably better, too, even after days of humping rucks through the wilderness—but it was *cold* up there.

"Okay, then. Gurke's team has point." Gunny might have been a little irked at Gurke's impatient tone, and the other team leader briefly grimaced at the realization that he might have overstepped himself. Gunny Taylor was more of a father figure to the platoon than an appointed leader—

certainly far more than Captain Sorenson ever had been—
but sometimes even Dad gets testy.

Herrera led out, with Gurke right behind him, followed by Franks and Chambers. I nodded for Rodeffer to
fall in behind Chambers. That drew a look from Gunny,
but he didn't say anything about presuming to stick close
to the front after we'd been on point for a while. Instead,
he just fell in with us.

So did Mathghaman. He wasn't what I'd call *nervous*—I
didn't think he knew the meaning of the word—but he
clearly wanted to be farther forward whenever the platoon
entered those ruins.

The passage around the shoulder of the mountain and
along the base of the wall was tricky. The wind had picked
up even more, and despite how thin the air was up there, it
was still howling around the peaks hard enough to threaten
to knock you over if you weren't very sure of your balance.
When you're threading your way along a glorified goat
path, with barely enough footing to put one foot in front
of the other, with a sixty-five to seventy-pound ruck on
your back, that makes things hairy.

I'd just reached the base of the easternmost tower and
started to move along the wall itself when Herrera and
Gurke disappeared into the gateway. I had to resist the urge
to speed up. There was no telling what they'd just climbed
into.

I didn't hear any gunfire or screaming, but the wind
was *kicking*, and the roar of the air past my ears and in my
Peltors' microphones might have drowned any of it out,
anyway.

It took far longer than I wanted to reach the gate. The
snow-and-ice-covered rubble in the gateway remained a

formidable obstacle, and Chambers was still helping Franks over the top of the mound as Rodeffer and I moved to join them. The footing was rough, and while a lot of the stones had frozen together, there was always that one that wasn't nearly as solidly placed as it looked. A few went tumbling down the mountainside below us.

Finally, though, we got over the rubble without mishap and found ourselves in the courtyard. Gurke's team had already spread out and taken a knee, holding security inboard while also taking advantage of the moment's rest.

The entire pass had been turned into a castle, with the keep carved into the mountainside to the east. Doors, windows, and arrow ports stared at us blackly, like eye sockets in a weird, alien skull. The crown of the keep had been broken, leaving a scar down one corner and a pile of more rubble at the base. More, smaller structures, now little more than collapsed stone walls, roofless and half-buried in snow, lined the mountainside to the west.

But the structures weren't what had us all staring in a mix of wonder and fear.

The figures formed up in two squares, facing us across the courtyard, were armored in coats of scales, some that reached only to their waists, others clear past their knees. They wore tall helmets, some with long spikes rising above their crowns, others with the crowns thrust forward. They all bore round or crescent-shaped shields and tall spears.

And we could see through them.

"I think we know why the Fendak don't want to come up here." Gurke's whisper was probably pointless, but I could understand why he didn't want to talk out loud, not facing that.

The spectral figures didn't move, even as the wind blew feathery gusts of snow through them. They were faintly luminous, like every special effects ghost ever. I would almost have suspected a trick, except that I could *see through them.* The stone wall on the far side, along with the mostly intact arch of the gate, was clearly visible through shields, armor, and men.

"Uh, Gunny?" Santos's voice went a little higher than normal. "How are we supposed to fight ghosts?"

"We don't." I remembered all too well Bearrac's warning back in the woods outside the burned wrack of the corsair settlement. "Unfortunately, I don't know what we *can* do, now that we're right in their front yard."

More of the platoon clambered over the ruin of the gate, then stopped and stared at the ghostly tableau before them. The security perimeter at the gate got heavier, though no one really wanted to advance toward those faintly glowing figures, motionless in the night.

"Maybe they're just images." Applegate hadn't talked much since we'd gotten there, but back during the workup, if you wanted a spook story about the paranormal, ghosts, or UFOs, Applegate had been the guy to talk to. Not many of the platoon had been eager for those sorts of stories, so he'd quieted down by the time we'd boarded the *Makin Island* to deploy. And little that we'd run into in this world had *quite* added up to the stuff he'd talked about.

Until now.

"What do you mean?" Bailey had perhaps been the most impatient with Applegate's spook stories back then, but now that he was staring at what looked like at least two companies of ghost warriors, he was willing to listen.

"Well, there are a few possibilities when it comes to ghosts. One of them is that they're sort of a 'snapshot' of a point in time, like the replays of the battles in places like Gettysburg and Antietam." The fear and the cold seemed to be forgotten as Applegate warmed to his subject, though he still kept his voice low as if afraid to disturb the specters in front of us. "That's why nobody's ever interacted with the ghost soldiers in those places. They're not really there. They're just an imprint of the event, a battle so bloody that it left a sort of psychic 'stain' on the world." He nodded toward the ghost army. "Maybe that's what we're looking at here."

Then Mathghaman stepped past him, shaking his head. "I do not think so." He walked forward, his sword sheathed, his rifle hanging from its sling. He made a sign on his forehead, the Sign of Tigharn's Protection, and walked out into the courtyard, lifting one hand.

"Who steps within these walls without leave?" The voice was deep and hollow, and seemed to come from the wind itself, rather than any set of vocal cords. More than a few of us—myself no exception—looked around nervously. It was as if whatever mind had spoken the words had used the wind and the gaps in the stones to form the words.

It was also using the mind speech, because the words were definitely not in English, or the Tenga da Tuacha, but we still all understood it as clearly as we understood our own thoughts.

"Who challenges the right of the King's Champion of the Tuacha da Riamog, Servant of the Servants of Tigharn, to pass unmolested?" Mathghaman's voice rang off the stones, rivaling the ghost voice in power.

"*We are the guardians of this place. Oathsworn to hold it in life, we failed, and so we shall hold it in death, until the breaking of the world.*"

Silence followed. One of the ghosts had stepped forward as the spectral voice reverberated all around us. He stood taller than the others, with a rotting horsehair crest atop his tall helm. His face was that of a desiccated mummy, his skeletal hand wrapped around the haft of a spear as translucent as himself.

"In whose name do you hold this place?" Mathghaman folded his arms over his rifle.

"*Our masters are long in their graves. Their kingdom has fallen into shadows and dust. We hold this place because it is our oath. No names have we any longer, nor do we hold this place in anyone's name but the name of our broken word.*"

"This ain't good." Farrar was starting to shake, as hard as he was trying not to. I could understand why. I had no way of knowing what those few moments of fighting the curse that had been laid on that arrow had been like, but he clearly was not happy about facing the blatantly supernatural again. A lot of the monsters in this world we could shoot, stab, or blow up. Not these. How do you kill ghosts?

But Mathghaman was utterly unflappable. "And have you held it, against all comers?"

There was a pause at that, a silence that stretched uncomfortably. The ghosts remained motionless, which was somewhat encouraging, but the voice did not answer, and the spokesman, or leader, or whatever the specter with the crested helmet was, seemed to look down for a moment.

"*No.*"

The despair in that one word was somehow palpable. It went clear to my soul. I remembered what Bearrac had said about a spirit's ability to get into your head and tried to shut down my emotions altogether. Even if the ghosts weren't trying to fight us yet, they could still do damage just by what they were.

"How have you failed?" Mathghaman asked the question with all the authority of a commander demanding answers of his subordinates. And the ghost answered him.

"*A creature of darkness and old night came to this place. It lives, though it is dead, and its wickedness was greater than our fear.*"

"Well, I guess we're on the right track, then," Santos muttered.

"Shut up," Gunny hissed.

Mathghaman nodded. "That creature is our quarry. We have passed through fire and death in pursuit of it. We shall not be stopped by the shades of the disgraced dead. Yet, while I could command you, in Tigharn's name, to let us pass, I will ask. Will you stand aside and let us pursue this enemy which has passed beyond your grasp?"

Once again, the silence was broken only by the distant wail of the wind through the rocks and around the peaks. As if the ghost was thinking it over.

Then the tall one bowed deeply.

"*Our oath binds us. No vendetta, no other word of honor, may turn us from our task. Except one. His name you have uttered, and against that name only must we bow and turn aside.*

"*Pass.*"

I felt my eyebrows climbing. Gunny stirred beside me, and when I looked over at him, I saw his eyes illuminated by the faint green glow from his NVGs. He'd noticed, too, and he was thinking things over.

Mathghaman nodded. It was not a bow, not really, though the next gesture, seemingly directed toward the sky, was. He turned to the rest of us, as the ghost infantry began to fade away into nothingness.

"Come, my friends. We still have far to go."

CHAPTER 17

GETTING down off that mountain took most of the rest of the night, but none of us wanted to stay there, lest the ghosts change their minds. Mathghaman didn't seem to think that they would, and I could kind of see why. But that fortress gave us all the creeps, and besides, the vampire had come this way.

The weather was clearer on the south side of the mountains, though as the sun began to brighten the horizon on the other side of the peaks of the Wall of Scath on our left, I could see the low line of clouds moving in from the west, off the ocean. We had clear skies for a while, but it probably wouldn't last.

We got down into the trees, and Gunny kept us moving for another couple of hours until we found a shoulder of the mountain that formed a fairly defensible crown of rock just above the trees, overlooking the jumbled, forested foothills below the spur of the Fendak's mountains. There was still snow on the ground, but there wouldn't be for much longer. What was there was old, mostly piled under the trees, and had melted away entirely in the open meadows between. The promontory where we set up our patrol base was bare rock.

Every man was exhausted. Almak was actually stumbling, both from fatigue and the stress of the terror he'd endured up on that mountain. He'd barely been able to force himself to put one foot in front of the other on the way through the fortress.

We set security, and everyone else promptly passed out against their rucks.

* * *

It was midday before everyone had gotten at least three or four hours of sleep. We were still wrung out. But Gunny was prepping to head out anyway, before Mathghaman put a hand on his shoulder.

"The lands ahead, if the stories are true, are far more dangerous than those we have already passed through," he said. "Perhaps it would be better to wait a day and proceed better rested. We *will* have to fight, all too soon."

Gunny didn't look happy about it, but some of that was just that old Marine Corps conditioning setting in again. We had trained to keep going for days at a time on two, three hours of sleep at a time. Of course, the strain had still been immense, and we'd already been moving for leagues and days at a time since we'd stepped off the ship.

So, Gunny finally nodded and turned to Bailey, who was sitting up, then to me. "Well, boys, I guess we'll keep the watch schedule running. Nobody get too comfortable, though."

"Don't worry, Guns." I leaned back on my ruck. "I don't think anybody's in danger of doing *that*. Not here."

* * *

We'd *mostly* recovered, at least enough to move out in the morning, by sundown. It was getting cold again, and the wind was whipping down off the mountains, so we'd sort of burrowed into the rocks at the base of the hilltop, trying to find enough shelter from the wind without sacrificing the view we had all around the promontory. It ultimately meant that we had an OP up top, while the rest were in a patrol base down below, just inside the treeline.

Gunny had put his foot down about fires. From what Almak had hinted at, the locals—or perhaps more accurately, the monsters—in this area would smell woodsmoke from miles away and come looking.

So, we found ourselves sitting in the deepening shadows under the trees as the sun dipped toward the distant sea.

"You know, we could see the corsair settlements up by the coast, even at a distance if we got some elevation." Chambers was musing, poking in the dirt and fallen needles with a stick. "But I've been up on the OP a couple of times now, and I haven't been able to see a single sign of civilization or habitation. No farms, no towns, no villages, no smoke, no nothing." He looked up. "Not even ruins like that fortress up there."

"They would have been torn down long ago." Almak seemed to have recovered somewhat from his terror on the mountain.

"By whom?" Bailey was chewing on a stick, watching Baldinus with a narrowed eye as the younger man cleaned his rifle. Apparently, it hadn't been up to Bailey's standards when he'd spot checked to make sure that everyone was ready to fight and break out if need be.

"That... is a very long story." Almak was getting more comfortable, though as he glanced around at us, I could tell that he still wasn't sure exactly where he stood with these strangers who had accepted him as a hostage. Frankly, I wasn't all that sure about where he stood, either. He'd tried to integrate as an ally, and he certainly knew that if he tried to play stupid games, he was going to win the stupid prize of a bullet in the forehead. But there was still a reserve there, a separateness that might have been inevitable but still seemed a little too calculated, a little too sly. As if he was every bit as bad as Dragon Mask but was better at hiding it. And some of that surliness and furtiveness around the Tuacha was still bothering me.

I didn't really think he *was* as bad as Dragon Mask—that would have taken some doing—but I still wasn't going to entirely trust him.

"We appear to have plenty of time." Santos had his head back against a tree, his helmet on but his chinstrap undone, dangling below his fast-growing, bristling black beard. "Just as long as it doesn't get too melodramatic."

Almak glanced at Mathghaman, and while it was getting dark enough to disguise his expression somewhat, I could tell that he wasn't sure how the Tuacha were going to react to this story. Whether that meant he wasn't confident in its truth, or just feared that the bogeymen from Over Sea would object strenuously, I couldn't tell.

"Long ago, when the Old Gods ruled all the world, seven kingdoms rebelled against them. They were small and weak, breakaway duchies and fiefdoms from the greater empires that ruled the world in the names of the Old Gods. Yet they fought to free themselves from that rule, no matter how much the odds were against them."

Almak was starting to warm to his subject, no longer casting glances at Mathghaman and Bearrac every few words. Despite the strange mumble effect that his amulet created, he was falling into a storyteller's rhythm. He'd clearly heard this story many times, enough times that it had been burned into his brain to the point he could mimic the storytellers who'd recited it around corsair fires.

"The wars that followed lasted for years. Great battles raged across the mountains and plains, and terrible sorceries ravaged entire cities. The loremasters still speak in hushed tones of the madness that lurks around Bachmoora, where the daylight never shines, and the empty city watches and devours any who enter it.

"As the weight of the Old Gods' followers bore down upon them, the rebel kingdoms became desperate. One by one, they fell, they fought amongst themselves, or they found another way. It was in these times that the Younger Gods were born, as the rulers of the rebel kingdoms searched out ancient knowledge and artifacts of power, each trying to touch the power of the Old Gods and turn it against them.

"Two of those kingdoms stood in these lands and fought the Commagan Empire of the plains. They had fallen to fighting amongst themselves as the Commagan slowly crushed their forces and drove them into the mountains.

"As the war dragged on and grew more desperate, the ruler of one of the kingdoms turned to the path of sorcery, the path of power. He ascended to become a Younger God. Many of his lieutenants also became great sorcerers, though he always kept from them the secrets of ascension. His power grew, and soon the war was stalemated.

"For many years, the battles raged, as madness took entire tribes and monsters stalked the land. The wilderness between fortresses and settlements grew wilder and more dangerous, and in some places, men fed upon one another because the farms lay fallow and rotting after some spell had robbed them of life."

I glanced at Bailey, who'd raised an eyebrow. We'd never quite confirmed it, but there had been warning signs that the Dovos in the north had practiced cannibalism. It was *somewhat* good to know that at least the corsairs viewed that particular crime with horror.

"Finally, after many years, the great Thoggudan, the Old God of the Commagan, arose from his chambers beneath Fallen Arsamoth and walked the waking world for the first time in the lives of men."

If there had been a fire, Almak would have been staring into it, thoroughly lost in his tale. The kid was a born storyteller, I've got to give him that. He was really getting into it, his voice hushed as if awed by the thought of what he was describing.

"No man could look on him and live. All who saw his terrible face died or went mad, and those who went mad died soon after. None could withstand his shambling stride across the land and over the mountains—not even his own people, whose souls and minds he devoured along with those of his enemies. Night fell across the land, and the sun did not show his face for many days.

"Thoggudan came to the Younger God's last redoubt, and the battle there broke the face of the land, bringing down a mountain upon the city. Death spread across the lands, engulfing both kingdoms with a strange pestilence, until no one of either rebel kingdom lived.

"So the tale reached our ancestors, long ago. None dare walk these lands any longer. It is said that Thoggudan's curse still lies on these woods, and that only monsters prowl in the darkness under the tangled trees." He looked around as if trying to see if his tale had spooked us, almost like a new storyteller at Scout camp. "We have not spoken the names of those kingdoms ever since, lest we bring the curse upon us. They are forgotten." He fell silent then, and for a while there was only the whisper of the wind in the treetops.

"We remember their names." Mathghaman's voice was low and deep in the growing darkness. "Colcand and Volhin. Of the two, only Volhin was one of the Seven Stalwart Kingdoms, which did not bend the knee before the creatures brought into the world by the Summoner." He shook his head. "The Seven did not 'rebel.' They held the line against unnatural interlopers who sought to usurp the place of Tigharn Himself. But many are those who have forgotten that, as their masters will."

Bearrac chuckled. "And not all of the Seven fell, either."

Almak was clearly stiffening as the Tuacha disassembled part of his tale, but he didn't dare say anything either. He wasn't looking at Mathghaman or Bearrac but appeared to be staring at the ground just past his feet. Maybe he understood that the Tuacha likely knew more than he did. Or maybe he didn't want to reveal that he was fundamentally their enemy.

"Indeed." Mathghaman waved to the south. "In fact, one still stands, some two hundred leagues south of here. Cor Legear has held the line against the corrupted Empire of Ar-Annator for nearly two centuries, and still stands strong."

"So, was the rest of his story true?" Bailey asked.

"Mostly." Mathghaman was leaning back against his pack, his chin propped up on his fist, his elbow on his knee. "Much has been lost, even to our loremasters, but the war he told of did happen, and the last ruler of Colcand did seek godhood, only to be crushed by the abomination that ruled Commagan." I noticed that Mathghaman didn't name the Commagan god. Nor did he call it a god. Interesting. "None I know have ventured into these lands since that time, but a darkness does seem to linger under the trees, and no man knows of any men who live here. At least, none who still *are* men." He looked around at us, and even in the dimness, for a moment, his eyes glinted. "I warned you all that the dangers would only grow greater as we continued south."

"What about the vampire? Is he a leftover from this war?" Gunny asked.

"No. He is even older. Some say he walked the earth when the Summoner first came, bringing his promises of power and pleasure. Perhaps those stories are true. He certainly would not have shrunk from the atrocities and sacrifices the Summoner demanded." The King's Champion sighed. "At any rate, he served the Commagan for a time, before he vanished from history again."

"Are the Commagan still around?" I asked.

"A few. They cling to redoubts in the mountains and on islands in the Cardevelen Sea. The madness of the thing that ruled them in the days of the war with Colcand and Volhin eventually consumed them, and they tore each other apart, splintering their empire and leaving it to the mercy of the nomads of the far grasslands and the growing empire of Ar-Annator to the south." His voice grew grim.

"Some few ventured over the Wall of Scath and into these forests. Only a handful of them ever reached Cor Legear, and they would never speak of what they saw or endured. Few of them lived long after they escaped.

"Steel your hearts and your minds. For tomorrow we venture into that darkness."

CHAPTER 18

THE land sloped downward from the promontory where we'd had our patrol base. It was still rough, rocky, and heavily forested. But if we'd thought that the woods north of that spur of mountains had been thick, we were about to get an education.

The trees got taller, darker, and closer together as we descended. Gnarled oaks—though with darker leaves than I was used to—mixed with sycamores and towering pines and firs. And the deeper we got, the thicker the canopy became, gradually blocking out more and more of the sunlight, until we were struggling through twilight into full night when it was barely halfway through the morning. We had to halt after the first hour of movement to pull out NVGs just so we could see. I hoped we'd brought enough batteries, though the 123s that the *Coira Ansec* produced seemed to be a lot longer-lived than the standard lithium batteries we'd had back in The World.

That forest was *wild*. Blowdowns and giant fallen trees seemed to block our path at every turn, making navigation difficult at best. The forest floor was choked with fallen branches and the detritus of a wood that hadn't been thinned or even burned out in a long, long time. The whole place smelled of mold and dusty, dead wood, and…something else.

I couldn't put my finger on it as the stuffiness got closer and more unpleasant. We were all sweating buckets in a short time, as we struggled through and over the fallen debris. It wasn't hot under there, it was just still and close, downright stifling. There wasn't a breath of wind under those trees, and the exertion was bringing everyone's core temperature up without any breeze to alleviate it.

I was starting to get worried about water. We were going to start going through it fast, and if there were any streams, lakes, or springs in this forest, I wasn't entirely sure what a good idea it might be to drink from them. After all, if the woods were cursed, what was the water like?

I shook the thought off as I clambered over another fallen log that looked like it had stood for two or three centuries before it had fallen, decades ago. It was rotting but was still a good three feet thick. I got up on top as Rodeffer slid down the other side, then I turned and reached down to help Farrar up.

As I did, something caught my eye. It was just a bare flicker of movement in my NVGs, but I froze and slowly turned my head to look for it.

Dark and twisted boles of oaks and sycamores stood between the straighter trunks of firs and pines. A larger mound of fallen branches lay beneath the close stand of pines off to my right, and an opening in that blowdown, a deeper black than the rest of the shadows beneath the forest canopy, seemed almost like an eye, watching me.

But nothing moved. Nothing stirred. I stayed where I was, scanning and listening, but the only noises I could hear were the faintly ominous creaking of the trees and the scrambling and panting of the rest of the platoon working their way across the cluttered forest floor.

"What is it?" Farrar had noticed that I'd stopped moving, and he was scanning the forest where I was looking. "Did you see something?" His voice was a low, hoarse whisper. Anything else seemed out of place in there, as if anything more than the absolute bare minimum, unavoidable noise was going to bring some horror down on us. We hadn't seen a monster or a ghost so far since we'd ventured in here, but this place somehow felt even more ominous than the haunted ruins up in the pass.

"I don't know. Thought I saw movement, but there's nothing there now." I turned back to him and extended my hand again. I'd almost unconsciously brought my rifle up as I'd scanned the woods, and now I let the muzzle down, resting the forearm against my knee as Farrar grasped my gloved hand and I hauled him up. "Keep your eyes peeled and your ears open."

"Believe me, Conor, I've been doing that since we got here. This place gives me the creeps." He turned to help Santos as I slid off the log on the other side.

For a moment, I had to stop and look and listen carefully, trying to ignore the icy fingers of fear that clutched at my chest. The rest had kept moving while I'd been looking for whatever might be out there in the shadows, and now that I was on the ground, I couldn't see Rodeffer.

A sudden flash of memory. Not of woods, but of the basement in the house where I'd grown up. There had been one light switch in that dark, cluttered place, and it had been halfway through the room, at the bottom of the stairs. If you were downstairs and heading back up, you had to turn the lights off and climb the stairs in the dark.

I'd been old enough to take some pride in not being afraid of the dark anymore. Except that somehow, whenever I'd turned the lights off in that basement, I'd known that I wasn't alone. That there was something back in the darkness in the far corner, something watching and waiting for me to be alone in the dark.

It had taken seconds to sprint up the stairs to get out of that dark place and whatever was lurking in the shadows. I knew it was all a figment of my imagination, but I'd never quite been able to shake it, and for those brief seconds before I reached the top of the stairs, I'd been as scared as I'd ever been in my life—at least, until the day my parachute came out snarled and I'd had to cut away and land on my reserve.

Something about that momentary feeling of being lost in those impenetrable black woods, when I couldn't see Rodeffer in front of me, brought that fear back. Only for a moment, but something told me that it wasn't going to be the last time.

There was something wrong with this place, something deeply unsettled in this wild forest that blocked out the light and kept the wind from ever penetrating below the canopy. I understood the stories that it was cursed. It had to be.

Then Rodeffer stepped around a tree, only about ten yards ahead, and I breathed a little easier as I stepped off, even while Farrar tried to lower himself gracefully off the log, slipped—or else put his boot on a crumbling bit of rotten wood that gave way under him—and crashed to the forest floor right behind me.

"Shit." He hauled himself to his feet and felt the muzzle of his suppressor, careful to keep his other hand off the firing control. Cramming a muzzle full of dirt and leaves could be catastrophic if we got jumped. "Sorry, Conor."

"Don't be sorry. Just try to keep it quiet." We'd all fallen down on patrol at one point or another. It's unavoidable when you go where Recon goes, into the terrain and the veg where nobody else wants to because it's just too nasty.

With Farrar back on his feet and Santos following, I moved after Rodeffer, deeper into the dark.

* * *

It was next to impossible to say how far we made it in that first day. The route we took was anything but a straight line, and after a few hours, the best we could say was that we were still going generally south. The detritus that choked the forest floor made straight-line travel impossible, even if the trees hadn't been so thick that we couldn't shoot a straight line through them even without the crumbling vegetation on the ground. The constant struggle to get over and around the tangled branches and fallen logs slowed us down considerably, and it was a weary group of sweat-soaked men with bits of bark, leaves, and needles chafing in every bit of clothing who finally gathered in a tight perimeter at what had to be late afternoon or early evening, though it was impossible to tell from our surroundings. It remained as dark as midnight under those trees.

My team had been the trail element the entire day. The realities of the terrain and the vegetation had made it impractical to try to switch out the order of march along the way. We'd have to work on that, or whichever team was on point was going to burn out.

Herrera had found a stream, and once we had halted, he and Franks headed down with their water bladders.

But Diarmodh stopped them. "Do not fill your water from there."

"We've got filters." Franks held up the camper's micron filter that we all carried.

"No filter will make that water drinkable." Diarmodh wasn't looking at the filter. He was looking at the stream. I wondered what he saw, then decided I probably didn't want to know. Not really.

"We're going to run low pretty soon." Gurke had come up to join them. "We're all sweating like pigs in here, and that means water consumption's going up. And we've only got so many bottles and bladders."

"We carry a drink that will sustain us," Diarmodh said quietly. "Though we must use it sparingly. It is less efficacious than water over the long run, but it will serve until we get clear of these woods." He was digging a flask out of his pack. It was a little bit larger than the vial that Fennean had used to help dispel the curse that had almost killed Farrar. This one was metal, wrapped in leather, and when he uncapped it, there was no strange shimmer from within. He handed it to Gurke. "Only a sip."

Gurke took a sip of it, then handed the flask back, frowning a little. "How is it?" Franks asked as he took the flask from Diarmodh.

"I don't know. Tastes... I don't know what it tastes like." Gurke's mouth was working a little as he tried to analyze whatever it was he'd just drank. "It's not bad. And I don't feel as parched anymore."

"It will not last forever. That is why we must be sparing with it." Bearrac had drawn a similar flask from his own pack as he joined my team, taking a sip of his own before

171

passing it on to me. I handed it to Rodeffer first. I'd drink last, as much as my throat felt like it was closing from thirst.

When the flask finally came around to me again, I took a shallow sip. It *was* hard to say how it tasted. It was cooling and refreshing, but the taste eluded description. I wasn't as thirsty anymore, anyway.

"We can spare three sips per man per day," Mathghaman explained. "Even as hard as we march and fight, it should keep us from dying of thirst for that long. We will still have to drink the water we brought with us, but with the Cordial of Eotha, it will last much longer."

"What's wrong with the water in that stream?" Gurke had gone back to the huge oak we'd put in the center of the perimeter, and lowered himself against his ruck.

"It is cursed, as is all else in this land." Mathghaman's voice was low and grim. "A fortunate man who drank of it would fall into a deep sleep, never to awaken before he died of old age."

"And an unfortunate man?" Gunny didn't sound like he really wanted to hear the answer to that question.

"Far worse would await him." Mathghaman didn't seem to be all that eager to get into the gritty details, not there in that darkness under the woods.

"Hey, Conor?" Santos had settled in next to me, satisfied that the team was set in right and priorities of work were happening. "Maybe this place is making me paranoid, but I could have sworn that we're being followed."

"What could be following us in this murk?" Even as I said it, I felt like smacking myself in the head. That list of suspects, in this world, was a pretty long one.

"I don't know. Never got a good look. Only bits of movement and the occasional noise that didn't sound like one of us, and didn't really sound like an animal." He shook his head. "Like I said, maybe I'm being paranoid. Maybe it was an animal. Maybe a deer or something. I've heard whitetails walking through the woods that sounded like some dude twice their size."

"Except we haven't seen any deer here." That had started to nag at me a while back. I hadn't seen any deer, or any other animals, for that matter. No squirrels, no birds, no nothing, unless you counted the hairy black spiders the size of my hand that I'd seen up in the branches when I'd looked up, their eyes glinting on IR like they really shouldn't have.

"No, we haven't." Santos stared out at the dark, looking more than a little spooked. "I hadn't even thought of that." He ran a hand over his face. "Hell, that makes it worse. That means anything back there *has* to be a monster."

"More than likely." I was so tired at that point that my brain had sort of accepted it with a certain degree of blasé. "Probably something either hunting us or still following the vampire's path of death and destruction."

"You think it came through here?" Santos looked around at the woods surrounding us. "I haven't seen any sign, but then, I can barely see my hand in front of my face without my NVGs so…"

"Hell, Vince, it's a vampire. For all I know, it turned into a giant bat and flew over." I put my head back. As nervous as these woods made me, I was dead tired. I forced my eyes open again. It wasn't time for rest plan yet. "You didn't see *anything* that was identifiable?"

He shook his head. "Nothing. Whatever it was, it was staying out of sight."

I nodded as I stifled a yawn, then shrugged out of my ruck straps and levered myself to my feet. "Well, I'll go tell

Gunny. Make sure the guys on security know to keep their eyes open. Not that that should be hard to get through around here."

CHAPTER 19

THE night—if it *was* night—was long and not exactly restful. Once we'd stopped moving around, the forest noises seemed to get louder. The trees creaked and groaned as if they were in the middle of a gale, even though no wind stirred below. Furtive, skittering sounds seemed to come from every side, both in the fallen branches and trees on the forest floor, as well as up in the branches overhead.

Partway through our rest plan, a spider the size of a man's fist landed on Baldinus' head, and he freaked out. He didn't scream or yell, but the stifled reaction was still far too loud, and Bailey was on him in a second, knocking the massive arachnid away while clapping a hand over his mouth. Quiet probably wasn't going to keep any of the monsters out there from detecting us, but it went against the grain to just yell and scream, particularly in the dark.

Baldinus was still hyperventilating, but he nodded at Bailey that he was all right. Slowly, Bailey got off him, and he gasped for breath. He wasn't clutching his chest, but I could still hear his whispered, "Holy shit," from a couple yards away.

Things settled down after that, for certain values of the term. I think everyone who wasn't on security was struggling to get to sleep. I know I was. Every time I started to relax, it felt like I was suffocating.

Finally, after far too long, I drifted off.

* * *

I came awake fast, sat straight up, and groped for a weapon, knowing that it was far too late. But the encircling horde, visible only as glowing eyes above slavering jaws full of needle teeth, wasn't there. Only the darkness, as impenetrable as if we were underground, met my staring eyes as my breath heaved and my heart pounded like a jackhammer. I grabbed for my helmet and pulled my NVGs down, convinced for a moment that I just couldn't see the monsters because of the dark, but as the tubes lit up with their ghostly green, I saw nothing but the spectral shapes of the trees and the fallen branches between them.

"Bad dream?" Santos was up on watch, leaning on his knees, his rifle held ready as he scanned the darkness.

"Looks that way." I was momentarily proud of the fact that my voice hadn't shaken when I'd said that. It had been so vivid, so real. I'd been sure that we were all about to get eaten.

"Seems to be going around." I heard another stifled gasp behind me. "I had a couple of doozies before Farrar woke me up."

"Think it's something about this place?" I wasn't ready to take my NVGs off and close my eyes again yet.

"I don't think there's any doubt." He jerked a thumb over his shoulder toward the Tuacha's portion of the perimeter. "I don't think Mathghaman and Bearrac do, either. They've been talking since the first one, and they got Gunny up to bring him in on the conversation."

I glanced over my shoulder. Sure enough, the two senior Tuacha were sitting up, talking quietly, too quietly to hear. Gunny was crouched next to them, listening. He had his NVGs down, too. It was the only way to see in this deeply shadowed forest, short of lighting a fire, which *really* didn't feel like a good idea.

"Well, I think our best bet at this point is just to get through the woods as fast as humanly possible." I realized as I said it that that was far more easily said than done. The woods were so thick, and the undergrowth and fallen debris even thicker, that any speed was next to impossible.

And if it was as wide as I suspected it was—after all, if this was an old kingdom that had been cursed by a demon or whatever the Old Gods were, it wasn't going to be a little patch of woods you could traipse through in an afternoon—then we might be in a lot of trouble.

Santos was thinking along similar lines. "Hopefully we don't get lost in this murk."

"Can't get lost. That'd violate Rule Two." My eyes were aching, but I still wasn't ready to face whatever might be lurking behind my eyelids again.

Santos didn't miss a beat though. "That's why we have Rule Three."

The chuckle that we both got from that was still somewhat brittle. The Three Rules of Recon had been a running joke since long before I'd gone to BRC. *Always Look Cool. Never Get Lost. If You Do Get Lost, Make Sure You Still Look Cool.*

I checked my watch as our forced mirth died away. I hadn't slept all that long. I sighed and ran a hand over my face, feeling the grit and grime of the last weeks in the field, as well as the stifling closeness of the woods and the vegetable matter and dirt we'd picked up thrashing through it. I had to sleep. I had to get some rest, or I'd become a liability. Exhaustion is cumulative, and I had plenty of built-up sleep deficit as it was.

Sometimes you've got to force yourself to rest and reset when you can. So, I switched off my NVGs, took off my helmet, and closed my eyes to try to get back to sleep.

It took a long time. And once I finally did drift off, the dreams didn't let me rest much.

* * *

It wasn't any brighter when we rucked up and got ready to move again. The oppressive gloom remained, even though, if I was keeping close enough track of time with a watch that never quite added up to the length of the days, it was mid-morning.

Gunny circled a hand over his head to bring the team leaders in. "Mathghaman and Bearrac have been talking, and while I don't entirely understand, after what they told me, I agree. We need to get the hell away from that creek. There's something about it that seems to be making things weirder."

"The passage of the abomination from Commagan left a curse on the land, the water, and the trees. That curse seems to be stronger in these low areas, and along this stream most strongly." Mathghaman's voice was low and hollow. "The closer we are to the stream, the more the curse will affect our minds and draw the darker denizens of the wood to us."

Gurke looked around at the darkness that surrounded us. "Haven't seen much of any 'denizens' so far."

"That will change." Mathghaman's eyes glinted in the dark as he looked over at Gurke. It was a little unsettling sometimes, the way the Tuacha could see in the pitch black as clearly as we could in broad daylight. And their eyes seemed to shine in our NVGs when they did that, too. "Understand, this wood is watching and listening to everything that happens within it, or under the shadows of its eaves. The forest itself, in a way, has been possessed by a greater consciousness. An old, dark, and malevolent consciousness. It knows we are here. And its minions *will* come to stop us. If only because we have set foot within the wood."

"So, while we don't have any maps—let alone reliable maps—of the forest, we're going to strike out roughly due south, which should take us away from this stream." Gunny pointed, since there was no map to indicate the route he was thinking of. "Provided we can stick to some high ground, that should keep us away from the stream."

None of us had any better ideas. Nor did we have much in the way of suggestions. Land nav and patrolling in the dark and the woods was land nav and patrolling in the dark and the woods. Any of the weird stuff was outside of our experience, even considering our adventures in the north, and had to be dealt with as it came.

We rucked up, moved out, and climbed up the shallow slope to the south.

* * *

Getting out of that creek valley was more easily said than done.

179

We hadn't gotten far before Rodeffer ran into a row of blowdowns and thickets that steadily forced us left, back toward the stream. He managed to find a gap, and we started threading our way through, only to find ourselves faced with a jumble of boulders that, while massive and sheer sided, still didn't manage to break up the trees enough to let sunlight in. That upthrust of rock drove us back downhill again, and before too long—though we'd been moving for a couple of hours already—we were all too close to the slow, sluggish gurgle of the cursed stream.

The spiders were getting thicker, too, and I started to imagine that there were some bigger ones up there in the trees. Big enough that they might need a bullet to put them down. I'm not an arachnophobe, but the thought of spiders the size of dogs lurking in the trees in a place like that forest gave me the creeps.

But it turned out not to be the spiders that we had to worry about the most.

We'd been moving more carefully, switching out the point team so as to avoid burning out the pointman. There was no reason to push things at this point. We were going where we figured the vampire had been headed. Even if it had come through here, I got the distinct impression that it would have had an easier time negotiating this shadowed forest than we were having.

So, my team had fallen back to the number two slot, while Bailey's team moved up to take point, when the low hill just off to our right, surrounded by huge trees that weren't growing on it, but were still tall enough to block out most of the light, started to move.

At first, it was hard not to think that the movement might have been a figment of my imagination, maybe an artifact of staying on NVGs for so long. But when the hill itself stood up, glaring with eyes that were deep pits in the loam and the leaves, with a faint green glimmer far back in their depths, I knew I wasn't imagining things.

There was no time to shout a warning. Even as a long limb that seemed to be made of dirt and moss, bound with tree branches, shot out for Rodeffer's head, I snapped my rifle to my shoulder, put the red dot between those faintly glowing eyes, and fired.

You ever shoot at a berm in the rain? The mud just kind of eats the bullet, and if it's wet enough, you can't tell where the impact was. Shooting that thing in the face had about the same effect. And right then, even with my sword back on my hip, I couldn't help but imagine that the blade would do even less, blessed or not. This wasn't a videogame. That thing didn't have hitpoints.

My gunshot had given Rodeffer just enough warning, though, and he'd ducked behind a tree just as the thing's fist of rock and wood and stone closed with a *snap* where his head had been. The thing swiped at him again but smashed against the tree, making the entire bole shake and shudder, as bits of branches and needles rained down on us.

More gunfire tore at the thing as it heaved itself out of the little grove, but it had about the same effect as spitting into a storm. The creature, whatever it was, just absorbed the bullets without apparently noticing, and kept coming.

At least, until Gunny and the others with the thumpers opened up.

The first grenade launched with a *thunk*, barely having enough space to arm before it hit the hulking thing in the side. The detonation was a heavy *thud*, and black smoke and frag mixed with flying dirt and shredded vegetation, and the thing staggered with a deep, unearthly growl. When the smoke cleared, there was a crater blasted in what served it for a shoulder, though it clearly wasn't enough to stop it, or even slow it down that much.

Two more grenades soared in, even as Gunny roared at the rest of the platoon to fall back, stay out of the thing's reach, and in so doing, give the thumper gunners room to work. But the terrain and the woods were tight and constricted, which was probably why this hulking thing had been hiding where it had been. We were almost backed up against that cursed stream as it was.

I didn't want to think about what might happen to a Marine who fell in that stream while trying to evade this monster's haymaker swings.

It advanced on Rodeffer and took another swipe at him that slammed into the ground and made the earth itself shake. It wasn't that fast, which was good, but its arms were long, and each ground-shaking step seemed to cover way too much distance. It towered above us now, pushing trees aside and out of its way as it came. It bent the trunks so far that a few dim, greenish glimmers of sunlight came down on it, if only for a moment.

I'd let my rifle hang, and now I had a frag in my hand. I just wasn't sure what to do with it. More 40mm grenades detonated against the massive creature, blowing bits of mud and rotting vegetation off it, but they weren't slowing it down. I didn't think my little frag was going to do much more than they were. And I didn't want to waste it.

Rodeffer was almost dancing, dodging from tree to tree and keeping just out of sight of that thing. How he was keeping his feet in the dark and the tangled roots, rocks, and fallen branches was beyond me, but I sure hoped he could maintain it for a couple more minutes. Because he was really pissing the monster off.

It opened its mouth—at least, a big pit just below its eyes gaped open—and let out a faint whisper that might have been a roar in a creature with, you know, actual lungs, as it lifted both misshapen, lumpy fists high above its head. Those two glorified boulders on the ends of tree trunks probably weighed half a ton put together. A man that got hit by that combined mass of rock, dirt, wood, and mold would get turned into a wet smear on the forest floor.

But when it tried to roar, I saw my opening. Whispering a quick prayer that I wouldn't miss, I yanked the pin out of the grenade and chucked it as hard as I could into that gaping maw. "Frag out!"

Ordinarily, a frag gets thrown in more of a lofting motion. It's not a baseball, no matter how close it might be in size, and you want to get that sucker as far away from you as possible as soon as that spoon—I'm sorry, "safety lever"—flies free. But I had a narrow target, and it was far too close, so I fastballed the grenade into the thing's mouth.

I wasn't the only one thinking that way, either. At least two thumpers went off at the same time, and while one detonated on the thing's side, the other grenade went inside its mouth, right in front of my frag.

I think everyone had dropped or gotten behind a tree as soon as I yelled. I know I'd thrown myself flat as soon as the grenade left my fingers, my ruck going over my head and burying my face in the molding loam and rotting leaves and pine needles. I was fortunate I didn't fall on a branch and put a stick through my eye.

The twin detonations were muffled by the mass of organic and inorganic matter that made up the monster's body. But the blast was still big enough that bits of rotting foliage, dirt, mud, and shattered rock rained down on us. A moment later, the creature, its "head" half cratered, slumped down to the forest floor with an impact that shook the ground.

I had to roll over to get my ruck off my head, and levered myself up off the ground. Farrar helped me up. "ACE reports?" I croaked.

"Everybody's up. Minus a few grenades and a few rounds." Santos was right there next to me, his thumper still trained on the ruin that had been the giant, or whatever it was.

"We should keep moving." Mathghaman had seemingly materialized out of the gloom, looking down at the slumped shape, that now just looked like a part of the ground again. "It will pull itself together in time. We should be far away from here by then."

Every part of my body hurt, but I wasn't going to argue. We stepped off again, once again trying to find a way out of that strange, dangerous valley.

CHAPTER 20

WE struggled on for hours, always trying to move away from the stream, but the terrain and the forest itself always seemed to drive us east and downhill, closer to the heart of this haunted, cursed forest. The spiders were getting bigger *and* more aggressive, and a few of them got shot along the way.

Every gunshot seemed to echo deafeningly through the otherwise muffled, stifling atmosphere beneath the wood, and I think most of us started to flinch every time, as the sense that we were being watched by a will that really wanted us dead—or worse—intensified every time. No other noises we made had that effect. Only the gunshots. Which was weird, but weird was getting to be the default.

Not that the weirdness of that forest of perpetual night ever got *normal*. It weighed on us more and more, and every time we stopped to rest, it seemed that the dreams were getting worse and worse, the paranoia more intense. Almak was keeping to himself more and more, muttering quietly and keeping one hand on an amulet on his chest whenever he could. I wasn't the only one keeping a closer eye on him, either. Bearrac wasn't being subtle about the fact that he was watching him.

Some of the dreams came without a man even closing his eyes. Applegate stifled a yell as he snapped his weapon up at nothing in the dark, only then realizing that the shadowy *thing* he'd seen creeping toward him wasn't really there.

But there were other things under those trees, besides spiders and ambulatory hillsides and figments of our imagination. And we started to hear them in the distance shortly after we "killed" the mud monster.

At first, they sounded like wolves. But the calls and cries started to sound like much more than just a pack's howls. There were yips and barks and deeper growls, as if an entire bestial language was being used out there in the dark.

It wasn't like the strange screams and roars that the Fohorimans had used in the north. That had been recognizable as a language, as indecipherable as it might have been. This was something different. As if animals had gained a sort of twisted consciousness but had not developed full speech.

But whatever those howling, animalistic sounds meant, there were a *lot* of creatures out there making them. And they were all around us.

We kept moving, slipping from tree to tree while trying to avoid the big, black spiders and their webs. Weapons were up and ready, as we scanned the gloom around us, muzzles going wherever the lenses of our NVGs went. Every man's rifle was already slightly canted, the easier to pick up an offset red dot.

Then Bailey's team started to slow down. The word was quickly passed back. Synar had seen *something*, but it had slipped away before he could identify it. They were moving more slowly in case there was an ambush ahead. We kept moving, scanning the trees a little more closely.

Gunfire erupted up ahead. A chorus of vicious, howling snarls sounded in the dark, but then the gunfire fell silent, and the creatures stopped making noise again.

"Contact, but whatever it was ran," Rodeffer passed back as soon as Diarmodh told him. "Sounds like Synar put a bullet in it, but that didn't seem to slow it down much."

The whole platoon held position for a moment, spread out in a rough column, but after a few seconds, we started moving again, just as I was starting to wonder if Gunny wanted to call a halt.

We probably should have. Walking deeper into an ambush is usually not a good idea. But we also weren't in what any of us would necessarily have called "defensible terrain." We had fought our way back up onto a higher slope, with the stream below us and to the left, gurgling faintly and malevolently, but there was no cover. The trees had thinned slightly, letting in a faint twilight that seemed weirdly bright after the deep night of the last couple of days, but there was nothing to act as any kind of barrier plan between us and any of the monsters. We had to keep moving, if only to get off the X and get to some sort of defensible position.

Which meant we were still on the move when they came at our flank.

I caught a glimpse of one before any of them moved. It was perched atop a fallen log, uphill and to my right. I almost didn't see it at first. It was too dark, and the creature's fur was black as midnight.

It was roughly man-shaped, but with a wolf's head and covered in black hair. Its eyes gleamed in the green picture in my NVGs as it crouched there, its forepaws hanging between its legs. It was massively built, if I was making the shape of it out accurately. I couldn't quite tell how far away it was.

For a second, I wondered if it wasn't just another of the mind games the forest had been playing on us, but then it moved.

With a low, predatory growl, it came off the log and bounded toward Rodeffer on all fours, moving so fast it was almost a blur. But he'd seen it at the same time I had, and pivoted, bringing his M110 up fast.

He was still almost touching the creature with the muzzle by the time he fired. The suppressor coughed, and then the black-furred thing slammed into him, and they went tumbling down the slope toward the water.

There wasn't time to go after them. Because dozens more had come out of the blackness beneath the trees, loping toward us either on all fours or on their hind legs. Massive, rippling mounds of muscle, covered in fur and with claws on all four limbs and with mouths full of slavering fangs, they rushed us with a roar.

Our Mk 48 gunners had been waiting for something like this. They opened up with a chattering, ripping thunder that drowned out the werewolves' snarls, even suppressed. Easily a dozen wolfmen were smashed off their feet in the first bursts.

But they were moving fast, and they were inside what meager final protective fires we had while spread out in a tactical column shortly after that, and it became knife work.

Well, metaphorically speaking. I shot the first one in the teeth as it came for me, and if you've ever tried to get a shot at a charging dog coming for your throat, you might have an idea what that was like, except that this was far bigger and far faster. My first shot ripped along the side of its head, clipping one of its pointed black ears, and scored a burning, bloody gash down its flank. It howled in rage and pain as it staggered to one side, then it recovered and jumped for me. I dumped two more rounds into its chest, as fast as I could ride the trigger reset, hardly bothering to aim. In fact, I'd retracted the gun as it came at me, just to give it less of a chance of grabbing the weapon and dragging it offline.

Since it was in midair when I shot it—and movies to the contrary, bullets don't have enough energy to stop two hundred pounds moving at a considerable pace—it kept coming. I swung aside as it went past and ducked beneath the swipe of claws as it tried, with the last of its dwindling life, to tear my throat out, or at least hurt me in *some* way. Then it was past and tumbling limply to the dirt down the hill.

But the next one was on me by then, and it grabbed my suppressor with one clawed hand as it tried to lunge for my throat. I kicked it between the legs as I lunged backward and pulled the weapon toward me, trying to get it lined up for a shot. The thing was horrifically strong, but it hadn't been expecting me to pull the weapon straight back, and I got enough of a shot that I blew a chunk of its side across the leaves.

The monster *yelped* like a hurt dog, and jumped backward a good ten feet, letting go of the rifle in the process. It scrambled to regain its footing in the loose leaves and needles, and I *saw* the renewed fury flare in its eyes, even as two more came for me from behind it.

But I'd gotten my footing, and was already engaging. Ten feet isn't far, but if you're fast enough, it can be far enough.

I hadn't shot that fast in a long time. I simply dragged my muzzle from right to left, hardly bothering with more than a momentary sight picture, thumping rounds into furred bodies as fast as I could squeeze the trigger. I leaned into the gun, controlling the recoil with each shot, as all six shots blended together into a single, crackling peal of thunder.

The first one took both rounds to the chest. The second caught one to the chest and another through the collarbone. The third took one to the shoulder, and the last round was a contact shot, my suppressor hitting it in the side of the face just before I pulled the trigger. Blood and brains spattered from the entry and exit wounds, as I splashed the contents of its narrow, triangular skull across the forest floor.

After pivoting back toward the rest of the pack, I had to backstep again as the first one I'd shot almost hooked my ankle with its claws. I dropped my muzzle and shot it in the forehead before transitioning to the middle one, which was still alive but only barely. I might not have gotten as good hits on that one, but from the amount of dark fluid pulsing out of the juncture between its neck and its shoulder, I'd severed an artery.

It looked up at me. Even through my NVGs, I could see no humanity there. Only an animal terror and fury that was losing any strength to assert itself.

I shot it in the skull anyway. Maybe, if it had been as noticeably human as the Fohorimans had been—as twisted and post-human as they might be—I wouldn't have done it. But something told me that these things hadn't ever been *people*. That they had once been animals, that they were only the monsters they were because of something that lurked in this forest.

The monster's skull bounced with the impact, and it went still. And then the rest of the woods did, too.

Farrar was reloading. I'd been so absorbed in my own fight, the snarling and the suppressed gunfire, that I hadn't noticed him dumping most of the rest of his ready pouch. Rodeffer had climbed out from under the corpse of the wolfman he'd killed and was on a knee, his rifle still held at the ready. Santos broke the sudden quiet with one more shot, finishing off another creature that had had its spine severed by gunfire but was still trying to crawl toward him.

Gunny came down the line. "Sitreps."

I glanced at Rodeffer and got a thumbs up as I reloaded, myself. I still had a couple rounds left in the mag, but we'd trained for a long time to keep our weapons in the best condition possible. "We're all up, Gunny."

He jerked a thumb over his shoulder. He'd dropped his ruck. "There's a bit of high ground with some boulders up ahead. Get your team up in there and get set. Mathghaman doesn't think we've seen the last of 'em."

"Roger that." I pointed to Rodeffer, who nodded that he'd heard and turned to follow Diarmodh, who was barely visible on the far side of a big pine.

I wasn't all that keen on digging in, if we're being honest. I could see this going very badly. If there were enough of those things, we'd get overwhelmed eventually. Even though every one of us had brought a blade or an axe on this trip, just in case, if it came down to hand-to-hand with these dogmen, they'd definitely have the advantage.

I wanted to keep moving. But it was Gunny's call. Maybe he was worried about getting forced into a worse position if we tried to run for it. If so, he was probably right.

In fact, he *was* right, as we'd find out before too long.

More howls and barks sounded in the woods around us, and I could occasionally catch a glimpse of a glimmer of eyes on IR in the darkness. Then another sound came from downhill and somewhere off to the southeast. It was distant but loud enough that it was clear even through the thick and stifling forest. A series of deep, coughing grunts gave way to a thunderous roar, trailing off into a low, throbbing, pulsing growl that seemed to shake the very ground.

I'm not sure I want to see what made that noise.

We scrambled through another thicket, following a lone IR strobe that marked where Bailey had set up. The ring of boulders was broken by two more twisted, gnarled trees, but it gave us some decently high ground to defend and would force the monsters to climb at least a little to get at us.

Provided the trees weren't so full of spiders that we all got bitten and poisoned before the dogmen could get to us.

We scrambled in as Bailey pointed to a sector across from the Tuacha, who had all but vanished into the rocks on the nine-o'clock side. We got set in, and I made sure Farrar was well-positioned. With only three Mk 48s, we couldn't do fully overlapping fields of fire, but he was set up where he could sweep almost a hundred eighty degrees in front of our sector, at least where there weren't more trees in his way.

Unfortunately, as wide as that field of fire was, the woods had started to close back in on us, and it was pretty damned shallow. If they rushed us, they'd be on the rocks before Farrar could traverse half that arc.

Then, just as Gunny caught up with Gurke's team, they hit us again.

A wave of black fur, claws, and teeth, lit up like a Christmas tree with gleaming eyes, exploded out of the trees. Some of them came low and fast, scuttling or loping along the forest floor on all fours. Others leapt in great, hungry bounds, while still more ran like men, up on their hind legs, forelimbs swinging like a man sprinting, claws grasping as their toothy maws gaped. A chorus of howls, barks, and feral snarls was suddenly drowned out by the crash of gunfire.

Our suppressors minimized the blast, but the supersonic, ripping tear of the bullets' passage through the air still seemed deafening in that close, dark wood. Rounds tore through fur, hide, muscle and bone, smashing through vital organs and spilling lifeblood out onto the ground. And still they kept coming.

I shot one through the teeth at five yards, then transitioned to the next and blew a hole through its stomach, but had to follow up with another shot through the chest when it didn't even seem to notice. The brief respite we'd gotten when we hit one, just not in the vitals, seemed to be gone. Whatever that enormous, bearlike roar had been, it had put a new fire in these things.

Then I was shooting too fast to even register sight pictures. They were getting closer, undeterred by the gunfire, and along with Rodeffer, Farrar, and Santos, I was just dumping rounds into the wall of dark fur until my bolt locked back on an empty chamber.

Under different circumstances, I should have speed-reloaded, but right then a big bruiser of a wolfman, over six feet tall and three hundred pounds if he was an ounce, came leaping over the last one I'd killed with a roar.

I let my rifle hang on its sling and drew my sword.

I'd practiced this particular transition drill a lot back on the Isle of Riamog. Many of us had, though Gurke had never quite been able to bring himself not to sneer a little at the nerds with their blades. But we'd all gone black on ammo there at the end, before Nachdainn's ship had arrived. And without reliable sources of resupply, the *Coira Ansec* being one of a kind and deep in King Caedmon's citadel, we had to get used to weapons that didn't require ammo.

So, as I dropped my rifle, I dragged the sword out in a tight arc that intersected the leaping wolfman about a foot before his claws reached my throat.

I'd seen that blade do some extraordinary things in the north. It had been the only thing that had cut through a weird sort of frost giant in the pass on the way to Taramas's valley. It had similarly been the only thing that had killed one of Taramas's hunters, presumably a Fohoriman, cursed by his own sorcery to be nigh-on unkillable.

But I wasn't sure what it was going to do here. To my relief, it clove through the wolfman's, or dogman's, ribcage, nearly cutting him in half. He howled in agony as he tumbled past, his guts spilling out as he fell in pretty close to two pieces.

Then the gunfire fell silent as the whole fight turned to sword and axe work.

The team closed in, shoulder to shoulder, as we hacked and stabbed and hewed at the fur-clad limbs reaching for us. Sweat poured down our faces and breath got short in the stifling atmosphere beneath the trees, but we kept at it. A claw sank into my leg, and I lopped the arm that bore it off before prying it loose, trying to ignore the burning pain. A short, skinny dogman jumped on Farrar as he was finishing off another, and he cursed as he went over backward, sticking the horn of his axe into the thing's side, before Santos pivoted, stabbed it through the neck, and then turned back to his own next opponent.

But they just kept coming. That was when Mathghaman roared, "With me!" and plunged through the line of slavering beastmen, hewing one nearly in half with his sword, while he shot another through the throat with his rifle, held straight out in one hand.

CHAPTER 21

IT was probably the messiest and most chaotic breakout I've ever seen. Busting out of the Fendak's encirclement had been easy compared to the next few minutes.

The beastmen were still coming, still throwing themselves into the teeth of our gunfire despite the fact that the animals they'd apparently been mutated from should have run in panic from the noise and the destruction. We were killing them in job lots, but they just kept coming. Which, if I'd had the mental energy for the thought, should have been terrifying. It definitely said something about whatever had made that roar in the distance.

The shock of Mathghaman's charge, backed up fully by Bearrac, Fennean, and the rest, broke the attack on that flank, even if only for a few moments. The beastmen fled, their howls momentarily turning to sounds of terror. Mathghaman and the rest of the Tuacha left scores of brutalized carcasses in their wake as they ran.

We followed, but Gunny roared out, "Peel left!"

He initiated, dropping to a knee behind a tree and firing right past my ear, knocking another black-furred dogman sprawling with a yelp. The snarls and roars behind us as we rushed out of the encirclement had only intensified, as the sight of their prey fleeing sent the beastmen into a frenzy. I knew immediately why Gunny had made the call.

They were faster than we ever could be, especially since we had rucks on.

I rushed past him a few steps before stopping. It was going to take a moment to get the platoon strung out into a column to properly execute the "Australian Peel," and I wanted to add another surprise. "Rod! Claymore!"

Rodeffer checked his own rush with a curse, ran back to me, and opened the Claymore pouch sewn to my ruck's top flap, then hauled out the *Coira Ansec's* version of the directional mine and handed it over my shoulder. I grabbed it as he fired into the onrushing pack, even as Gunny turned and ran past us.

I swore under my breath. There was no time. I flipped out the legs, slammed the claymore down on the ground, twisted the blasting cap into its initiation port, then ripped the coil of wire open as I turned and ran after Gunny, even as Farrar opened up with another blistering torrent of fire over Rodeffer's shoulder.

The claymore's wire only extended so far, and I wasn't going to make it that far in one rush, especially since I was praying hard that I didn't yank the mine out of position or pull the initiation system out. I ducked behind a tree as Santos opened fire and Farrar fell back, just as the onrushing tide of claws and teeth reached the mine. "Fire in the hole!"

There was no time. We got rocked as the claymore detonated with a tooth-rattling *thud* and a cloud of black smoke and flying frag and debris. Seven hundred steel balls tore through fur, flesh, and bone, where the explosion itself hadn't ripped the nearest werewolves to pieces.

Then I was shooting again, dropping two more before turning and burning, sweat soaking my cammies as I gasped for air in the stifling mustiness under the trees, my legs burning and my heart hammering. The claymore had put a dent in them, but it wasn't going to last.

A thumper went off with a *thunk*, followed by another *thud* as the grenade went off in the middle of another clump of beastmen, frag ripping through limbs and throats and spilling blood onto the shadowed leaves. I was still seeing all of this in a narrow circle of green. The forest actually seemed to be getting darker.

We raced through the gap the Tuacha had carved in the swarming horde of feral, unnatural creatures, heading for the front of the column. The peel creates a sort of leapfrog, a little different from a standard bounding break contact drill, but in the close confines of the woods, the peel was going to be a lot more practical.

Provided the end of the column didn't get flanked and devoured.

As I ran, I noticed that we were, once again, being forced east and downhill. I wondered, briefly, as I struggled to keep from hyperventilating, if somehow that was deliberate. I didn't think Mathghaman was doing it on purpose, but that consciousness, that malevolent *presence* that seemed all around us in the forest, might well have thrown its hairy, bloodthirsty minions at us at just the right spot to force us into a particular direction.

Which meant that, as many of them as we were killing, we were still doing exactly what the forest wanted.

The peel wasn't the smoothest I've ever seen. Another claymore *boom*ed in the dark, the flash momentarily lighting the woods up through my NVGs, and more thumper rounds blew holes in the attacking force. But there seemed to be more and more of them pouring out of the dark, no matter how many we slaughtered.

I'd barely reached a spot to set in again before the rippling tide of the peel reached us once more. I shot two more bounding monsters that looked almost less like werewolves and more like big apes with claws and snouts, over Rodeffer's shoulder, before he was up and moving, his head down, panting like an exhausted dog. We'd gotten back into pretty good shape on the Isle of Riamog, and the trek south through corsair lands and beyond hadn't exactly made any of us soft, but even Tuacha rations hardly seemed like enough when the gas tank was getting empty. And there's nothing calculated to drain that tank more than an extended fight with monsters that are faster and stronger than you are.

I kept shooting, running my mag dry before Farrar opened fire again, and then I turned and ran, going against training and instinct and dropping the mag into my dump pouch instead of just letting it fall. Sure, the *Coira Ansec* could just produce more mags along with ammo, but leaving things behind in this place just felt like a bad idea.

We were going to run low on ammo long before we got to the vampire's lair, at this rate. *If* we got to the vampire's lair. The terrain ahead was still sloping down, deeper into the forest and toward that cursed, slow-moving stream.

In fact, a few bounds later, we found ourselves right up against that stream, which almost seemed to be smoking in the dark, paralleling it while the dogmen and their weirder, bulkier cousins kept coming at us.

They *were* starting to get more cautious. We'd left a *lot* of them dead, dying, or simply blown to pieces already. As mindlessly aggressive as they'd appeared to be, it seemed almost as if they were regaining some of their earlier cunning.

Maybe because now we're going exactly where the forest wants us to go.

That wasn't a comforting thought.

We kept moving alongside the stream, hemmed in by the terrain, the trees, and the wolfmen, who were still launching attacks, though it increasingly seemed as if they were just doing it to keep us moving. I was getting a really bad feeling about this.

Then the ground flattened out some and started to get swampy. The trees started to change, with fewer conifers and more twisted oaks, sycamores, and now some willows. All of them were darker and looked somehow more sinister than the trees I was used to back in The World.

We kept up the peel, though it increasingly was turning into team bounding overwatch. The monsters were coming at us all along our right flank now. They'd dash forward, then retreat into the trees as soon as we shot or blew up a couple. The rhythm of suppressed gunfire and the occasional grenade explosion kept going as we went deeper, increasingly slogging through ankle-deep mud and weirdly steaming water, though we kept our remaining claymores for later.

Then the lead elements stopped dead. We almost started to accordion together into what all of our training would have considered a dangerously concentrated clump, even as another big, apelike beastman, his jaws distended and dripping saliva from massive, sabertooth fangs, came roaring out of the trees behind us. Farrar cut him down with a five-round burst just before yelling, "Reloading!" The monster tumbled to the muddy ground, its chest and throat torn open, and landed with a splash in a puddle of swamp off to one side of the stream's bank.

More of the beastmen started to come out of the trees, but they'd stopped rushing us. They just spread out, forming a big ring, their eyes gleaming in the dark.

"Oh, this ain't good." Rodeffer was behind a particularly twisted tree, his rifle laid in the fork of a pair of large branches, watching the surrounding monsters. "Why'd they stop?"

"I'm just glad they stopped." Farrar slapped the ammo tray cover of his Mk 48 down with one fist and hefted the machinegun. He was clearly starting to feel the fatigue setting in. Farrar had always tried to be a bit too much of a weightlifter, and his endurance had suffered for it, back in The World. He'd figured things out better after our long trek through the snow in the north, but the fight we'd just been through would have sapped a marathon runner.

"Team leaders up." Gunny's voice was a hoarse croak in the dark. I took one look around and double checked that my team was up; Gunny would want to know that when I joined him. We were all still breathing, though several of us were bleeding from scratches and punctures that would probably need to be taken care of soon, before they festered. But we were all alive.

In fact, I didn't think I'd seen any friendly bodies on the way down here. We might have actually survived this, so far.

So far.

I worked my way under a gnarled willow that seemed to be reaching for me, and came to where Gunny was standing in the midst of a narrow perimeter, along with Mathghaman and Bailey. And I saw why we'd stopped.

The swampy basin seemed to be the lowest point in that part of the forest. But that wasn't what had everyone's attention.

A massive bear—or what might have started its life as a bear—stood waist-deep in the swamp, facing us. Its limbs were longer than a normal bear's, its eyes glowed a lambent green, and most of its hair was gone, replaced by a boar's crest along its back of spines. It had too many teeth for its mouth, and they seemed to thrust outward as it stood there, flexing long claws and grunting.

But it was what stood behind the werebear that really drew the eye, even as I really didn't want to look at it.

The biggest tree I'd ever seen loomed over the basin. It was impossible to say how tall it stood, but its trunk had to be sixty feet across at the base.

And if I'd thought that the other trees in that forest were twisted and *off*, this was by far the most evil-looking tree I'd ever laid eyes on. Its trunk was as twisted as it could be while still growing somewhat upright, and its lower branches looked like dozens of knobby, grasping arms. I didn't see a leaf on it, but somehow it still blocked out the light. In fact, it was so dark that it almost seemed painful to look at, as if it *glowed* black.

Except for the eyes.

Green, luminous eyes glowed balefully from a dozen spots on the trunk, from a couple feet above the ground to high above, almost out of sight amid the restlessly waving branches. None of which moved with any wind, but only on their own.

The Tuacha had formed a line abreast, their rifles slung, swords in their hands. Cairbre alone seemed to have eased back, looking up at the tree, his face unreadable.

I couldn't see Almak, but I could hear him, muttering charms and invocations.

"Gunny." If it seemed somewhat strange to hear Math-ghaman use that term—he rarely addressed any of us first, but more often replied when one of us had a question or something to ask of him—he didn't seem to care. "The bear-man is yours. Leave the tree to us."

That big, mutant bear with too many teeth roared then, and I knew what had made the call that the dogmen, or wolfmen, or whatever they were, had answered. It was the same roar as before, even louder here in the basin in front of it. Then it charged.

We had spread out, Gurke's team taking rear securi-ty, facing the encircling beastmen, and I'd assigned Farrar to join them. The more belt-feds we had covering those monstrosities, the better. So, it was just Rodeffer, Santos, and me facing the bear-monster on the Tuacha's right flank, while Bailey and Synar moved around on the left.

A normal, earthly grizzly bear can go from zero to thir-ty-five miles per hour in a single bound. I think this thing topped that by a good bit. Its first bound carried it half-way to the Tuacha from a standing start, splashing foul, smoking water as it hit, and then it was in midair, heading right for Mathghaman as he and his brethren chanted, in that even more ancient language they used for prayers and invocations, that I'd never been able to understand despite the mind speech.

Easily a dozen bullets smashed into it, tearing through hide, meat, and bone, but it still kept coming, hitting an-other stride about six feet from Mathghaman, streaming blood, the impact of its taloned paws throwing geysers of mud and foul water into the air. We kept shooting it, right up until the point that we were about to point our rifles at each other.

Mathghaman ducked and sidestepped under its rush, and stabbed it in the side in an eyeblink. I almost didn't notice it, his movement was so fast and so economical. But the creature landed poorly just behind him, staggering and falling on its face in the mud, clutching its side.

Bailey had lifted his muzzle as he pivoted to follow it, flipping it over the Tuacha's heads as they chanted, and dropped down to put a round into the back of the creature's skull.

Blood and worse fluids splashed out through the exit wound in its eye socket. For a moment, it struggled, still trying to get up and come at us, then it slumped into the mud.

The tree above us quivered. I could have sworn I heard a voice, just outside the threshold of hearing, and more of the green, hate-filled eyes opened.

Then the bear thing got up.

CHAPTER 22

I knew immediately that shooting it again wasn't going to do anything. That thing was *dead*. Nothing survives getting half its brains blown out through its eye, no matter how juiced up on rage and sorcery it is. That tree was puppet-mastering it, and unless things got real, fast, no amount of firepower—at least not that the rest of us were going to survive, being that close to it—was going to stop it from tearing us apart.

So, while the Tuacha's chanting intensified, I transitioned to my sword again and waded in.

The thing seemed to be already starting to rot. Whatever power had warped a bear—or a man—into such a shape, it had started to break down as soon as it had been killed. Now that it was an undead marionette, it was only accelerating the decomposition.

My first blow severed its arm at the elbow. The limb fell in the mud with a *splat*, thick, syrupy ichor oozing from the stump. I retracted the sword to get in position for a follow-up swing and hacked at its neck.

Blessed blade or no, while it cleaved through the stinking flesh easily enough, it still felt like hacking through a steel cable to get through that thing's spine. It took about half a dozen blows, while dodging and trying to fend off the wild swipes of its still-intact arm, to sever the head.

And the headless carcass still kept trying to kill me.

I almost lost my own head to a vicious swing of its remaining taloned arm. Those claws were three inches long, at least, and they whistled as they passed my face. I brought the blade up and went to town on the arm, which seemed to be a little more difficult to cut off than the first one. It was as if the longer the sorcery animated this thing, the tougher it got. Like it was drying it out, hardening it, over time.

It took three strokes to get through the arm, and it fell writhing to the mud, its claws still grasping for me.

I would have thought that beheading the thing, and lopping off its claws, might have done it, but it still lunged at me, as if it was going to crush me into the mud with the sheer weight of its massive carcass.

Then Bailey was behind it, his axe out, hacking deeply into the back of one of its legs. The carcass's knee buckled, and he kept going with that brutal energy that only Bailey could summon sometimes.

I took a step back for a brief moment as the creature crashed down onto its stumps in the swamp, took a deep breath redolent of rot and something worse underlying it, something hot and metallic, that didn't belong in a marsh or a forest, and then waded in.

It took a few moments for us to reduce the thing to little more than a heaving torso, its spine severed in a dozen places, all four of its limbs completely hacked away. It was ugly, messy work, though my sword never seemed to pick up a stain, but when it was done, we turned toward the tree, our chests heaving with the exertion of the fight.

It sounds weird to say that a tree can get *agitated*, but this thing wasn't any ordinary tree. Even more eyes had opened, and now there were almost a hundred staring, hate-filled orbs glaring down at us from the trunk and more than a few of the branches. And some of those branches were reaching for us.

"Come together!" Mathghaman's roar brooked no hesitation or argument. "Stay close! Fear no darkness!"

But while the chant continued, growing stronger in the blackness, I couldn't see as it was doing much of anything to the tree, except make it angrier.

A grasping branch darted in toward us, and for a brief fraction of a second, I thought I saw a flash, almost like what I'd seen down in the catacombs when Mathghaman had knelt for a moment, and driven Taramas's minions back into the dark. The grasping branch recoiled, and then two more came crashing down on either side of our small perimeter, bristling with weapons but without being sure that any of them would do us any good.

More branches slithered down around us, as if forming a web or a dome overhead. The darkness deepened, slowly choking off what little illumination our NVGs had to work with, until all I could see was the eerie sparks of those glaring eyes, staring their hate down at us. It was a hate as old as the universe, unchanging and unrelenting.

The Tuacha kept chanting, but I could soon hear the voice anyway.

I can't tell you exactly what it said. It was a voice, and it wasn't. I can't remember any words. I don't *want* to remember any words. Whatever it was saying, or projecting directly into our minds, it was nothing but hatred, contempt, and insanity. Through sounds or thoughts without a meaning we could discern, it bore down on us with its immense power, ancient knowledge, and the utter futility of defying it. We would be bound there, in utter darkness, helpless, motionless, for all eternity, while it fed upon our suffering. Nothing and no one could ever save us, because there was nothing and no one *to* save us. There was only the tree, and its undying malice. It would slowly devour us, without ever letting us die or rest. We had come to the end, and it would never end.

If that sounds creepy, rest assured, it's nothing compared to what that was really like.

But as bad as it was, somehow, I kept ahold of a thread of sanity. That thread was the Tuacha's chant, and for a moment, in the utter, oppressive darkness under that thing's branches, it was almost like I could *see* their song, held out to us like a lifeline. Physically, I didn't move. I don't think I could have just yet. But in my mind and my soul, I reached out, grabbed hold of that lifeline, and held on.

Was the darkness lifting slightly? Maybe. It was hard to tell. It was still desperately dark, and the sheer weight of that malevolent presence was threatening to crush me into the mud. In fact, I suddenly realized that, while I couldn't quite see him, I could feel that Rodeffer had dropped to his knees, shaking. I doubted he was the only one. The pressure was unrelenting, and I could feel cold fingers around my heart.

Then, though he never stopped the chant, I thought I could hear Mathghaman's voice in my head.

Fight it. With Tigharn's help, you can.

I gritted my teeth. I still hadn't figured out if Tigharn was the same as the God I'd grown up praying to, but I hoped He was. But I just prayed the way I'd learned as a kid, as I flexed my fingers around my sword hilt, gulped hard, and, careful not to stumble over any of our guys, took a step toward one of the eyes I could see gleaming vindictively in the blackness.

Another step. Yet another. Each one felt like climbing a mountain all at once. I could *feel* that thing's attention as it bore down on me. As if all hundred or so of those eyes was turning on me and me alone. I faltered and stumbled.

Then Mathghaman was on one side of me, Fennean on the other. They picked me up, and together, we advanced on the tree.

It didn't get easier. It was like climbing steeply uphill into a firestorm. I could feel those ghostly fingers clenching at my insides, as if trying to crush the life out of me, or maybe just crush the will so that I would lie down and let it eat my mind for all time. But Mathghaman and Fennean stood tall, though they leaned forward as if facing into a gale, and held me up.

It might have been an hour before we reached the trunk. It might have been days. Time had no meaning in that dark, lightless place.

Three new eyes opened, each the size of a dinner plate, right in front of me. They all glowed green, but one looked almost human, another was slitted like a cat's, and the third was a milky mass of compound lenses, like a fly's.

I could feel that thing scratching at the inside of my head. It still spoke no words, but the thoughts were there, nevertheless. I was an insect, a worm, not even a man, as small and pathetic as men were. I was little more than a morsel, that dared to try to strike at that which was so far beyond me that it was a wonder just being in its presence hadn't turned me inside out.

In fact, the compulsion to turn that sword on myself, and do just that, began to grow along with that scratching sensation in my brain.

Instead, I said a wordless prayer as I lifted the blessed sword, even though it felt like it weighed a ton, and thrust it deep into the slitted eyeball in front of me.

I'd had no idea if the tree was really physical, or if it was *entirely* physical. But the eye *popped*, and viscous, smoking fluid gushed from the hole it left.

I could suddenly see through my NVGs. Only as the green picture came back did I realize that Mathghaman was standing over me as I knelt in front of the burst eyeball, his arms held high, chanting in a booming voice while Fennean held my arm, keeping me from falling down altogether.

Then Bearrac and Diarmodh hustled Gunny and Gurke forward, each of them carrying a satchel charge with the time fuse already smoking.

I didn't have a chance to ask if explosives would really work against something like that tree. They stuffed the satchels into the wound I'd made, which was whitening and cracking around the edges, and then the Tuacha were pulling us back, sloshing through the mud and the vile water, staggering and limping, even as I realized that the impenetrable web of branches and tendrils wasn't there anymore.

If it ever really had been in the first place. At least, in a physical sense.

"Two minutes!" Gunny was trying to shout, but his voice came out as a loud whisper. I suddenly realized that my own throat was as dry as the Sahara, or whatever deserts lay somewhere in this world. We staggered on, the Tuacha seemingly far less affected by the proximity to the tree, even as the beastmen who surrounded us gave way uncertainly, backing up with faint whines and snarls, rather like a dog that isn't sure what's happening but knows it doesn't like it. We shouldn't have ever come out of that blackness around the tree, and it confused and frightened them.

I barely even noticed that we'd been pulled away, off to one side, heading up out of the basin and out of a direct line with the wound. There was a reason for that.

The satchels went off with a world-ending *boom*, flame, smoke, and frag flying out and up in a boiling, black cloud as we threw ourselves on our faces in the mud and the rotting leaves. The overpressure washed over us like a giant hand smacking us into the hillside.

I lifted my head out of the mud and looked over my shoulder as the smoke began to clear. Bits of leaves, wood, and plant matter were still raining down out of the sky, only partially deflected by the branches overhead. I couldn't see the tree at first.

Remembering the beastmen, I scrambled up onto a knee, dragging my M110 out of the mud underneath me, my sword still dangling from my wrist by the thong I'd tied around the pommel. It hadn't picked up any of the grime that the rifle and the rest of me had. It never seemed to get dirty. Blood, mud, whatever, all of it just slid off the blessed sword.

But the beastmen were gone. Vanished as thoroughly as if they'd never been there. The gunfire and the claymores might not have been enough to spook them, but that blast had done the trick.

As I scanned our surroundings, noticing that things were still awfully dark but looked a *little* lighter, the rest of the platoon picked themselves up, shaking suddenly aching heads and checking weapons while similarly remembering the threats we'd been surrounded by not long before.

Which brought me to the main threat.

I turned back toward the malignant tree at about the same time Mathghaman did. We'd gotten a few others between us and it before the charge had gone, and many of them were now barren skeletons, their dark and poisonous-looking leaves flensed off by the blast. At least one had been knocked almost completely over.

The charge wouldn't have been as effective as it could have been, since it hadn't been tamped. They'd just shoved the two satchels into the hole that the burst eyeball had left and then we'd run.

I wondered if it had been enough.

We stepped carefully through the detritus, much of it already starting to sink into the muck of the swamp, weapons up and wary. I could still feel...*something*. Something evil and enraged. But it seemed much more distant now.

Stepping into the basin, I looked up at the tree. A massive hole had been blasted out of one side of that huge trunk, and where there had been eyeballs, now there were only holes oozing what looked a little like sap, a little like tar. Several of the branches had been blown off, and one was embedded in the mud and the muck, its splintered end sticking up into the air. Others were scattered around the swamp under where the gigantic abomination had spread its canopy.

I stepped toward the wreck of the tree and stopped. Something still wasn't right. It was still dark as night, and while I could still sort of see the tree's bark, and none of its eyes, I could still feel a *presence* there, somewhere either deep within or under the tree. It was alive, it was aware, and it was *angry*.

Mathghaman put his hand on my shoulder. "We have hurt it, but it will take much more than we have here to banish it altogether. We might, though, be able to escape now."

I confess I hesitated. I didn't like leaving this thing at our backs, and frankly, I figured we were probably going to have to come back through here, provided we survived the vampire. Right then, I wanted to dig out all the explosives we'd brought and level that entire basin.

Mathghaman must have sensed some of what I was thinking. His grip tightened. "Do you hear me, Conor? We can do no more here. To remain will only strengthen it."

"Indeed."

Both of us whirled, weapons coming up. Mathghaman lowered his almost immediately, but I kept mine, as filthy as it was, pointed at the figure that had just appeared on the edge of the basin.

CHAPTER 23

THE man was small, short, and skinny, wearing a simple robe, belted at the waist with a knotted rope. His face was partially obscured by a deep cowl, though strangely, there was enough illumination falling on him from the gaps in the partially destroyed canopy overhead that I could see his face from the nose down. He wore a short, neatly trimmed beard, and he appeared human enough.

Not that that allayed my paranoia any. I'd seen too much since we'd gone through that fog bank off the coast of the Land of Ice and Monsters to take *anything* at face value.

But Mathghaman reached out and pushed my muzzle down, giving me a look that told me to trust him. He turned back to the robed and cowled figure, but the little man spoke before he could.

"This is no place to linger. Come. Follow me." Without another word, he turned and started to pace calmly through the trees, heading uphill and off to the east.

Gunny and Bailey had come up to join us. "Who is that?"

"I do not know." Mathghaman's reply was pensive, but there was a strange look on his face as he watched the man in the monk's robe. That's the best way I can describe it. He looked like a skinny version of Friar Tuck. "But there is no evil in him. Be he man or other, I think we should follow him."

Gunny gave him a long stare. I couldn't see much of his expression past his PVS-15s, but I could imagine what was going through his head. Mathghaman himself had warned us that we were heading into dark and dangerous territory, only getting worse after we'd left the corsair lands. So, why would he urge us to follow a complete stranger who'd just appeared in the middle of this cursed and insane forest?

Mathghaman clearly sensed our hesitation, and with one hand still on my shoulder, he sheathed his sword and reached across to grasp Gunny's, looking each of us in the eye, at least as best he could while we had our NVGs down.

"I do not know who he is, or where he comes from, and just as you wonder whether anything in this place is *not* a monster or a tool of darkness, know that he is neither. I cannot explain how I know this, but I do."

It was hard to see much more than his general facial expression, on NVGs and that close. He was a little blurry. But all the same, he didn't seem to be out of it or acting weird. He was still Mathghaman. Still assured, firm, and sure of himself. Still the King's Champion.

Gunny saw it, too. He nodded, though still with some reluctance, and looked toward the little monk, or whatever he was. The robed man had stopped and looked back over his shoulder at us, waiting for us to follow. He didn't seem overly impatient, and he didn't even beckon. He just waited.

With a sigh, Gunny pointed to me. "Well, the monsters don't seem to be eager to get near him. And Mathghaman's got a point. He hasn't steered us wrong so far. Let's see where this guy goes. Especially if it gets us away from here. Conor, your team's got point."

It took a moment to get into a movement formation. We kept an eye on the blasted husk of the tree. It might have been my imagination, but I thought I could almost see a faint, green, glowing mist within the splintered cavity that the charges had blown in the trunk. And I could just about feel the hatred lurking there, wounded but not extinguished.

The little friar guy just stood there calmly, waiting, his hands folded within the sleeves of his robe, watching us and apparently ignoring the shattered tree. I wondered at that for a moment. What would I see if he drew those hands out of his sleeves? Paws, tentacles, claws? His face appeared human enough, what I could see of it, but all sorts of spook stories were coming to mind as I watched him. He just waited, though, calm and still.

The beastmen seemed to have fled for the moment, and aside from the eerie creaking and whispering under the trees, the forest was still and silent. The oppressiveness of the atmosphere hadn't lifted, but that didn't seem to bother the little man, either.

Finally, we were ready to move. He nodded once and stepped off through the trees. Rodeffer gave me one more uncertain look, then followed.

* * *

The short, robed figure seemed able to find pathways through the forest that we hadn't been able to find ourselves the entire trip through. We were making better time than we had since even before we'd entered this cursed place that had once been a kingdom called Colcand. And the little man in the robe seemed to be waiting for us to catch up more often than not.

I kept watching him carefully, whenever I could spare attention from our surroundings and the rest of my team. We were all battered, strung out, and haunted by what we'd just been through. Our rucks might be a lot lighter than they had been before, but they were still heavy enough, and as time went on, I began to suspect that the little man's speed and endurance weren't superhuman, after all. We were just tired.

Still, that grates on a Recon Marine when he's panting and sweating, trying to keep up with a short little guy in a monk's habit. But if the little man noticed, he didn't seem to care.

Steadily, the ground rose as we moved out of the swampy basin at the heart of the cursed woods, and away from the weirdly smoking stream. The shadows remained, but somehow they never quite seemed to touch our guide. He wasn't *glowing*, exactly, but he just didn't seem to ever quite get lost in the darkness.

I didn't know if that was a good sign or a bad one.

He kept going for hours. While we got more tired, he seemed as fresh as a daisy. The terrain kept getting steeper, though if my land nav was remotely on point, we should still be a long way from the Wall of Scath. He'd turned a little way to the south after the first couple hours, but we were still generally heading east.

Then there was light ahead.

Real light, not some eldritch glow from some new horror that didn't belong in the waking world. Sunlight, looking golden and green through the leaves over us. I lifted my head and peered underneath my NVGs to make sure that I wasn't imagining it. There it was, though. All was still darkness to our flanks, but up ahead, there was a hole in the forest that let in the sun.

Our mysterious guide was heading straight for that gap in the darkness, his sandaled feet making almost no noise on the forest floor, his hands now clasped behind him. I caught a glimpse of them then and was gratified to see that instead of claws or anything monstrous, his hands were entirely human, with four fingers and a thumb.

Still doesn't mean he's not a monster in some other way. But why would a monster in this dark place be moving so quickly to get into the light?

Rodeffer slowed abruptly as he stepped out of the trees, and as I caught up, I could kind of see why, even as I flipped up my NVGs to keep from being blinded in the sudden sunlight.

We stood on top of a hill amid the dark forest, almost high enough to see over the canopy. Green grass waved in the breeze. It felt like suddenly being able to breathe again after far too many underwater crossovers. A single apple tree grew next to a small stone chapel atop the very crown of the hill.

The robed man was walking quickly toward that chapel, his hands now raised and a quiet chant rising from his throat.

He was speaking the same language that the Tuacha used for their invocations.

The platoon spread out as we came out of the trees and advanced on the chapel. It was a simple structure, though the closer we got, the bigger it was revealed to be. The stone walls had been raised without mortar, and the roof was turf. But that it was a chapel, not unlike the one that had housed the relic the vampire had stolen when it had taken Sister Sebeal, was pretty obvious.

The little man disappeared inside with a wave, and we moved to stack on the door. Just in case. Because you never know, especially in a place like this.

With a sudden movement, Rodeffer and I made entry. He went left, I went right.

I'd expected the interior of the chapel to be dark and dim, a perfect place for whatever monsters the little man might be in league with to wait in ambush. But to my surprise, it was brilliantly lit by a very out-of-place stained-glass window high in the far wall. The floor was bare flagstones, the roof held up by pillars of stone that looked far smoother and finer than the rough stone of the outer walls. Rooms stood to either side of the nave, and the little man stood in the doorway to the left, beckoning us to join him. More golden light spilled through the doorway behind him.

Almost involuntarily lowering our weapons, we followed. There was something about that place that had all of us in a sort of awe. It was weird. And yet, it wasn't weird in a disturbing sort of way, if you take my meaning. There was a peace there, a peace that was wholly different from the suffocating stillness of the woods below that little hill.

A long trestle table stood inside the single room on the other side of the door, and the little man was laying out loaves of bread and apples on the rough-hewn wood. He had pushed back his cowl, and his neatly trimmed beard matched thinning brown hair. He looked up as we spread out around the room, hands still on rifles but muzzles pointed at the floor. His eyes were dark, but there was a light in them that I hadn't seen anywhere in this world apart from the Tuacha.

"Come." He swept his arm around the table in invitation. "Sit. Eat. The darkness cannot come here."

All eyes momentarily looked to Gunny, then to Mathghaman. Both men nodded slightly. There was one man, and we were all still armed. Even if he turned into something monstrous that was going to try to eat our faces, we should be able to fight back fast enough, if nobody put his rifle too far away. And at that point, nobody was likely to.

So, while we had to drop rucks, we kept our gear on as we sat on the equally rough benches set around the table, rifles leaning against the benches or still hanging from slings around our necks.

Mathghaman sat at the end of the table, while the little man in the robe stood at the other end, broke a loaf of bread, and held it up, his eyes raised toward the sky, whispering in that ancient language again. We all sort of waited, I think out of a combination of an implied respect and the fact that we weren't sure what was about to happen.

Nothing did, at least, nothing that we could see. The little man put the two halves of the loaf down on the trencher in front of him and nodded solemnly to Mathghaman, who returned the nod and began to eat.

He wasn't poisoned, wasn't turned into a frog, or anything, so we all started, hesitantly, to follow suit.

The bread was slightly chewy, but it tasted great. Almost too good; given where we were, I was immediately suspicious. But even that suspicion was somewhat allayed by the feel of that place.

"You are a long way from the Isle of Riamog, Mathghaman Mag Cathal." The little man took a small bite of his own as he looked around at the rest of us. The Marines appeared rather scruffier and dirtier than the Tuacha, though we'd all been through the same fight.

"As you are far from the nearest monastery." Mathghaman studied the man, unblinking. "To find a Brother of the Waclafians in this wilderness was not what we expected."

The robed man inclined his head to acknowledge the King's Champion's point. "To cower behind our walls is to surrender the world to darkness. Some twenty of my brothers and I, with the blessing of the prior, went out many years ago, to build our hermitages in the dark and cursed places of the world, to drive the darkness back, little by little." He looked around, his gaze encompassing the whole hill beyond the chapel's walls. "When I first built this place, the wood hemmed me in all around, and the beasts and monsters snarled at my very door." He smiled benignly. "But the light cannot be hidden forever."

"What is your name, Brother?" Bearrac's voice was filled with respect and almost a kind of awe. The Tuacha were eminent warriors, capable of great feats on the battlefield. We'd all seen it. But there was something about this little man who had, apparently, walked into the cursed wood that had grown around some evil demon tree in the middle of a kingdom utterly destroyed by some other eldritch abomination, set up shop, and calmly gone about driving the curse back. And from the looks of him, without a moment's fear or panic.

"I am Brother Melchorius." He spread his hands slightly. "You are welcome to rest here as long as need be. Though I must wonder, what brings you to this terrible place?" He looked over our accoutrements curiously, his eyes resting on our rifles. He didn't seem afraid of them. Just curious.

I kind of gathered that Brother Melchorius wasn't afraid of much.

Mathghaman proceeded to explain our quest. The vampire. Sister Sebeal. The track of devastation and atrocity we'd followed to the Fendak's mountains. The Tuacha's certainty that we were heading for the Land of Shadows and Crows.

Only the mention of that place seemed to shake Brother Melchorius. He made a sign on his forehead, the same sign that I had seen Mathghaman make. "That is a dire place. No one has returned from there in hundreds of years."

"Yet that is where we must go." Mathghaman's voice was heavy but firm. The corsairs, the Fendak, the haunted wood of Colcand and its horrors… none had yet deterred him. The Land of Shadows and Crows wasn't going to, either.

"I would not dissuade you from such a quest, my son." Brother Melchorius looked around the table again. "I only pray that even if you should not return from that blighted moor, your souls remain safe."

"How far is it from here?" Gunny asked.

Brother Melchorius pointed. "The Land of Shadows and Crows begins nearly a hundred leagues from here. Thirty leagues through Colcand, then another seventy across the broken hills of Tethba, before you reach the moors of the Land of Shadows and Crows. From there, the distance matters less. For the wood of Lost Colcand will seem inviting and cheerful compared to that place."

"That's encouraging," Santos muttered.

Brother Melchorius heard him, though. He looked over at us with his eyebrows slightly raised. "I offer neither false encouragement nor fearful urges not to go. I only tell you what is. Lies do not become us."

"Have you seen any sign of our quarry?" Bearrac asked.

Brother Melchorius narrowed his eyes, thinking. "Some five days past, a shadow flew overhead, momentarily dimming the stars. Even at meditation in the chapel, I felt the cold of its passage. It may have been one of the fell creatures of the mountains that sometimes come down to do homage to the abomination in the swamp, but it was moving fast toward the south. It may have been the creature you seek." He bowed his head. "Forgive me. I did not venture outside to see whether it bore Sister Sebeal with it."

Mathghaman raised a hand. Not dismissively but simply to ease the little man's mind. "You could not have known, Brother."

"You may stay here as long as need be." Brother Melchorius stepped back from the table, which was when I noticed he'd never sat down. "When you are ready, I will guide you to the edge of Colcand. The beasts no longer wish to trifle with me. It will speed your passage."

Without waiting for a reply, he left the room, leaving us to eat and wonder at what had just happened.

CHAPTER 24

WE stayed longer than I would have expected. But there was a peace there on that tiny, isolated hill surrounded by darkness that I can't adequately explain. Not that we were hanging out, too reluctant to leave that peace and move on, but we seemed to wait just long enough to be necessarily rested before we moved on.

Weapons and gear were cleaned. Brother Melchorius resupplied us with food and water. When Gunny asked if he had enough for all of us without starving himself, he had only smiled gently and said that he had every bit as much as he needed, no more, no less.

None of us were all that sure what to make of that, but he didn't seem to be willing to elaborate. Given the other strangenesses of this world, it probably wasn't something we'd understand, anyway.

After all, if King Caedmon had the *Coira Ansec*, what resources might a monk who seemed to be single-handedly lifting the curse on an entire fallen kingdom, one prayer at a time, have?

He didn't offer additional ammunition or explosives, and we didn't ask. It seemed inappropriate, even though it was clear that Brother Melchorius had no qualms whatsoever about us killing monsters. It just didn't quite seem right. Maybe he just didn't understand our weapons, but for whatever reason, nobody brought it up.

He chanted and meditated eight times a day. I always listened, even though I couldn't understand the language. There was something hauntingly beautiful about the sound as he stood in the center of the chapel, his arms outstretched, his face turned toward the sky, his deep voice rolling out the strange syllables so that they echoed from the stones, not discordantly, but creating an almost perfect harmony, as if an entire choir had joined in with him.

The Tuacha stood in a semicircle around him while he chanted, their hands folded on their sword hilts, faces raised toward the sky along with his. I didn't think I heard them join in, but they listened.

None of us tried to join in, even though we'd heard similar rituals among the Tuacha on the Isle of Riamog. It didn't seem like our place. Maybe it would be someday, but for now, most of us still weren't especially religious in the first place, and those of us who kinda were, still weren't sure about what all this stuff was.

"Seems an awful lot like prayer back home," Santos had said once though he'd waited until Brother Melchorius was finished to speak. Anything else seemed like swearing in front of your sainted grandma. "But more serious, some-how. Like it's *real* to these people, the way it never was to a lot of the people going to church when I was growing up."

I hadn't said anything in reply. Mainly because I couldn't think of anything that Santos hadn't just said.

When he wasn't chanting or preparing simple but amazing meals, Brother Melchorius was happy to talk. He didn't talk about himself much. Even when one of us asked, he steered the conversation elsewhere. I couldn't tell if it was just humility, or if there was genuinely something he didn't want to talk about, something in his past.

The second time he'd done it, I'd started to frown. When I leaned forward to press the issue, though, Bearrac's hand landed on my shoulder and pressed me back. I looked into his bearded face and saw the warning there. This wasn't something I should push.

I'd found him later, after the evening meal, and asked him about it.

"The Brothers of the Waclafians are an order that only accepts certain men. You or I might be gently turned away to find another order, should we wish to join. Those men who join the Brothers have left their pasts behind, utterly."

"You mean he doesn't remember it?" I was reaching, but again, lots of weird stuff on this side of the supernatural fog bank portal.

Bearrac laughed grimly. "Oh, he remembers it. All too well." He sobered and glanced toward where Brother Melchorius was cleaning up. He never let anyone help with that, either. "The Brothers of the Waclafians are penitents. They are men who have committed terrible crimes, repented, and devoted the rest of their lives to service and prayer." He glanced up at the ceiling, the gesture somehow encompassing the whole hilltop. "Though I have never seen one who has taken on the lifting of a curse like this as his penance."

That put a whole different dimension on things. I looked at the small, unassuming man in the plain brown robe, wondering what he'd done. And then wondering still more at what he'd done *here*. At the serenity he carried around with him and the sense of *goodness* that seemed to cling to him. "What must he have done?"

"That is why I caution you not to ask. As I said, he has left that behind, devoted himself to the task he has shouldered here." Bearrac scratched his beard with a thumb as he, too, looked at Brother Melchorius with a curious eye. "Whatever it was, he chose this place, and this task, himself. They all do."

I just nodded, thinking, watching the unassuming little monk and wondering.

If he noticed, he paid it no mind.

* * *

I didn't discuss that conversation with any of the rest of the platoon. It had seemed like it was too private, too sensitive. Best to leave Brother Melchorius his privacy.

But *somebody* must have overheard it, because the story was all over the platoon in an hour.

"Dude, I bet our little brother over there's killed more people than cancer." Farrar was cleaning his ammo, some of which had gotten pretty muddy in the swamp, and was watching Brother Melchorius out of the corner of his eye. "Gotta be why he's out here. He's probably got people out looking for his head even now."

"Where the hell do you get that idea?" Santos looked up at him with a glare. Santos's hair was growing out, but it was still little more than black bristles, while his beard was getting long enough that he could fill his fist with it beneath his chin. "Oh, wait, never mind. I know." He shook his head. "You watch too many movies and think they're real life."

"Come on." Farrar nodded toward Brother Melchorius. "Why else would a guy come out into the middle of a cursed forest to be a hermit?"

"You don't know, do you?" Santos rolled his eyes. "But you saw *John Wick* a few too many times, so that's *got* to be the story."

"That's all assuming that any of this is real," Rodeffer muttered.

"Now what are *you* going on about?" Santos swiveled his glare toward Rodeffer. "You think we fell into the Matrix or something?"

Rodeffer looked up, and I saw that he was serious as a heart attack, his eyes far away. "We were just within spitting distance of an eldritch abomination. Something that shouldn't exist. Something that we sure as hell shouldn't have been able to blow up. It was in our *heads*. I felt it. You felt it. Even Synar felt it, and his head's solid bone."

"I heard that, Rod!"

Rodeffer ignored the semi-angry riposte. "What if we didn't get out of that dark place it dragged us into? What if we're still down in that swamp? What if all of this is just to mess with our heads?" He swept his arm around to encompass the chapel, the hillside, and Brother Melchorius.

Santos looked over at me with his eyebrows raised. "He might be right."

Farrar blinked. "What?"

Santos was deadly serious. "I mean, Rodeffer just said 'eldritch abomination.' He's not supposed to even know what those words mean. I think we really *are* losing our minds."

"Oh, for…" Rodeffer cursed quietly as Santos laughed. Then my ATL reached over and grabbed Rodeffer by the arm, making sure he hit the pressure point. "Ow, what the fu—"

"You feel that, bud?" Santos held on for a second before he let go. "That's not a figment of your imagination." He let go and leaned back. "Even the most vivid dream, you can still tell it's a dream. This is weird, but it's no dream."

"No weirder than just about everything else that's happened since we helocasted off the *Makin Island*." I leaned back against my ruck. "Though this is the kind of weird I think I could handle more of."

Even as I said it, I knew this couldn't last. We still had work to do. And there was nowhere to go but forward, not right then.

* * *

If there was a fly in the ointment, a disruption of the peace in that little place, it was Almak.

He'd been subtle about it during that first meal in the chapel, but he hadn't eaten any of the bread that Brother Melchorius had given us. He'd stuck to his own rations, his face blank, his eyes hooded.

But afterward, he stayed out of the chapel altogether. He made few excuses, mostly monosyllables, but he was clearly uneasy at best around the chapel as well as Brother Melchorius. He avoided the little monk as much as he could. In fact, he avoided even looking at him when he was around.

I wasn't the only one who noticed, either. Mathghaman and Bearrac had clearly picked up on it, and so had Gunny. We didn't need to talk about it. An exchange of glances and nods, and we had a quiet watch set on him. The Tuacha took most of it, especially at night, when we slept, while they did their strange waking dreaming.

Almak might have fought the Fendak and the beast-men beside us, but he still bore watching.

* * *

The morning of the third day, we got up early, rucked up, and after Brother Melchorius finished his morning chant, we headed out.

He led the way again, turning due south this time, but keeping out of the low ground, paralleling the Wall of Scath. Or at least, that was the route we appeared to be taking from the azimuth that Rodeffer was keeping track of, since we couldn't see past the trees. The darkness had closed in on us once again as soon as we'd gotten off the hill, and we'd had to drop NVGs in front of our eyes again, just to be able to follow Brother Melchorius without falling over every root and fallen branch.

I more than half expected to run into many of the same obstacles and difficulties we had on the way into the forest. And to some extent we did, but rather than thrashing over or through, Brother Melchorius always seemed to find a way around. Even in the spots where it really seemed as if the forest was trying to force us back down and to the northwest, back toward the basin and the swamp where that massive, evil tree squatted in the mud, he still found a way around. It was rough going sometimes—it wasn't as if he could just float over the debris, and we sure couldn't even if he had—but we were still making better time than we had before.

He didn't stop during the day for prayers but chanted quietly as he walked. I had no idea how he knew what time of day it was. It was black as night in my NVGs.

He couldn't see in the dark the way the Tuacha could, at least I assumed that he couldn't, since he carried a candle with him. Granted, that candle never seemed to burn down or go out as long as he carried it, which was weird, but it was pretty clear that someone was looking out for Brother Melchorius.

Assuming that Mathghaman's instincts were right, and Brother Melchorius wasn't some monster in disguise, or an illusion intended to lead us into a worse place than that swamp.

But if that was the case, the predator that was using him like an anglerfish's lure was sure taking its time.

After what seemed like a remarkably short time, we stopped for the night. As we set in security, movement crackled in the fallen growth around us. I scanned the woods, looking for any sign of the beastmen among the dark tree trunks that surrounded our tight little perimeter. We all did, though Brother Melchorius seemed unconcerned.

There. Eyes glinted in the dark, visible only in IR. I pointed my rifle, slipped the selector to "fire" with a faint *click*, and got ready to fight. It had been too good to be true. The beastmen had bided their time, but now they had regained their confidence and were about to hit us again.

But even as I got ready to ventilate a dogman, Brother Melchorius started to chant softly again. The eyes narrowed, then turned away and vanished into the dark.

* * *

It took somewhere around four days to get to the edge of the forest. I can only guess at that, based on the number of times we stopped to rest. Brother Melchorius seemed to make the call when it was time for a long halt, but since he was our guide and the distrust was starting to settle out the longer we were around him, nobody questioned it after the second time.

Finally, the woods started to thin, the air started to clear, and the oppressive dark began to give way to dappled sunlight, even if it was gray and wan, as if shining through clouds. Finally, as we came to a clearing that was covered in stiff, grayish grass and prickly shrubs, Brother Melchorius stopped and turned to face us.

"I have brought you nearly to the hills of Tethba. The going does not get easier here, but here I must leave you." He bowed his head slightly. "My vows keep me to Colcand until the day I die. My battle is there. Yours lies ahead." He went around to each of us, touching each man on the shoulder before putting a hand on his weapon and whispering softly in that ancient language. Synar had almost jerked his weapon away when Brother Melchorius first reached for it, but Bailey stopped him.

When he was finished, the little hermit raised both hands to the sky, shouted something in that ancient, melodious tongue, and then, without any further farewells, turned and disappeared into the shadows under the trees of Lost Colcand.

We turned toward the dark, jagged shapes of the broken hills of Tethba ahead that loomed above the increasingly scattered, scrubby trees.

Brother Melchorius had warned us of some of the dangers that lay within that maze of sharp, jagged rock. If he'd told us only half, he hadn't been kidding when he said that the going wasn't going to get easier.

We headed up anyway.

CHAPTER 25

THE going got tougher fast. The fallen trees and other debris thinned quickly and soon weren't an issue, but as we came out of the woods, we plunged into steep, rocky terrain that turned into a maze in short order.

The sunlight was wan and thin, filtered through what seemed like a haze of fog, but we soon had the tang of dust in our throats. It wasn't warm, wasn't cold. It was just miserable, and I started to wonder what had happened to turn Tethba into this rocky wasteland.

Given its proximity to Lost Colcand, I had my suspicions.

Gurke's team was on point, but we were soon struggling as hard as they were. The rocks were sharp, and we were soon struggling up the side of a razor-edged ridgeline toward peaks that were only occasionally visible in the haze. The entire hillside was a mass of those ridges, as if the ground had been crumpled and all the dirt and vegetation had been stripped away. It wasn't even that eroded when you got up close—that would have been smoother going than the jagged, sharp-edged rocks that had soon drawn blood from every one of us.

We got about halfway up the slope before everyone stopped. I glanced down behind us as we sort of clung to the side of the stony hill, practically on all fours to maintain balance. We really hadn't risen that high above the forest, and the peaks of the hills weren't all that far ahead, either. The broken hills of Tethba weren't especially tall. They were just rough.

After clinging to the side of the hill for a few moments, Gurke's team came back down, Herrera obviously looking for a different route. We stayed where we were. There wasn't a good way back, and Gurke's team wasn't heading all the way back down to the bottom.

In fact, Gurke and the rest of his team hunkered down on the hillside as Herrera looked around for an alternate route. Meanwhile, the haze came and went, though I still couldn't tell what it was. It acted like fog, but it seemed more like dust or smoke.

Finally, Herrera signaled that he'd found a way, and Gurke and the others heaved themselves to their feet and followed, heading downhill and into a draw that seemed to lead higher up toward the crest of the hill.

The route obviously wasn't all that easy, because it was a good five to ten minutes before they'd moved far enough that we got up and followed.

The reason for the delay became evident as we got moving. Footing was rough, as we had to test each step before putting weight down, either because the rocks were sharp and narrow, or because they weren't sitting all that firmly on the slope. More than once, as quiet as we were trying to be, rocks went tumbling down the slope beneath us, banging and rattling as they took even more with them.

At first, we all stopped, freezing in place and getting low, scanning the jagged ridges and hilltops around us at the noise. Brother Melchorius had told us that there were strange, haunted creatures in these hills, things that had crawled into the jagged, broken rocks after Tethba had fallen, long before the destruction of Colcand and Volhin. We didn't know exactly what they were or what they were capable of, but the noise alone was enough to put every man's nerves on edge. Recon doesn't like noise to begin with—though often the routes we took, through the thickest and nastiest brush we could find, where no one else ever wanted to go, meant a lot of noise, just far from where anyone should be able to hear—and in that hushed, dead place every impact of every stone cracked almost like a gunshot, echoing off the stark, rocky hills.

Yet as we slowly, painstakingly climbed higher, we were met only with silence and drifting haze.

No one relaxed, even so.

It took almost three hours and two more double-backs before we got to the top of that first hill. Only to look down a nearly sheer slope covered in scree that dove down into a narrow, V-shaped draw before the ground sloped sharply upward again.

There was no way down that slope, not without risking a bad fall, and from what I could see through the drifting murk, there wasn't a good way up the opposite hillside, either.

But that wasn't the only problem. We'd barely crested the hill when Gurke and his team dropped flat, getting below the crest as fast and as quietly as possible.

We all followed suit. There was no screwing around that far into haunted and cursed lands. Nobody was going to stand around and ask what was going on before taking cover and getting out of sight.

I wormed my way back up to the crest, not far from where Gurke was peering around one side of a boulder shaped like a shark's fin. Easing my head up so as to avoid skylining myself, I looked down into the valley.

I almost couldn't see them at first. They were gray, nearly the same color as the rocks, and they weren't moving quickly. They tended to kind of disappear when they stood still. And between their natural camouflage and the haze in the air, it was hard to see them at all.

After a while, I gathered that they were roughly man-shaped, though how big or how small they were was hard to say. The distance was difficult to judge. They didn't appear to wear any clothing, but as I watched them, and their strange, halting way of moving, I started to notice that they didn't seem to have any facial features, either.

I'd seen some spooky stuff since we'd come to this world, but that sent chills up my spine more than the weird things under the eaves of Lost Colcand's night-shrouded forest. There was something far more alien about these things than any of the other monsters we'd faced so far.

Well, at least any of the *living* monsters we'd faced. I'd find out just how wrong I was about these things being the most alien denizens of this world soon enough.

They weren't groping as if they were blind, but they weren't moving like they could see all that well, either. They jerked their faceless heads from side to side, erratically, their oversized heads thrust out on skinny necks. They made no sound, even though we were completely still, and should have been close enough to hear *something*.

"Dude, what the hell are those things?" Gurke's whisper was barely a breath, but even that sounded achingly loud right then. The creatures down below, however, questing along the bottom of the canyon as if they were searching for something, gave no sign that they could hear. They

didn't have ears that I could see, even as I carefully reposi-
tioned myself, got on my scope, and watched them at higher magnification. Their leathery skin was almost perfectly
smooth, with no orifices in their egg-shaped heads.

"I'd guess they're the creatures that Brother Melchorius
told us about." He hadn't gone into much detail, clearly
reluctant to dwell on the evil that had crept into these lands
after the sorcerous wars that had laid them waste. I came
off the scope. "Even if we could get down there, I don't
think we want to go that way right now."

"I don't either." Gurke was still looking over the crest of
the ridge. "Those things give me the creeps. Though they
shouldn't be able to see or hear us. Or smell, I guess. I don't
even see noses."

"That doesn't mean they can't." I hardly needed to say
it, and from the look on Gurke's face, he'd been thinking
much the same thing. Things were weird here, and getting
weirder the farther south we went. We had to assume that
anything we ran across might well have preternatural senses
that didn't enter into our experience.

That was how we'd ended up in half the fights we'd
gotten into so far, after all.

Gurke slipped back down below the crest of the hill.
"Well, if they're going that way, I think we need to go the
other way." He pointed east, along the razor-sharp ridgeline. "Herrera, let's get going. Move slow, stay quiet, and
make damned good and sure we're staying below the military crest." The military crest of a hill is the line just below
the crest itself. It's where a patrol can walk without exposing itself by skylining on top of the ridge.

Part of me wanted to stay closer to the actual crest so
that we could see over and keep track of those weird, face-

less, gray monsters. I didn't like not knowing where they were. It gave me the screaming willies. The other monsters we'd encountered had been dangerous, but none quite as deeply unsettling as those things. I was reminded of a platoon doc we'd had years back who had been through firefights, IEDs, and all sorts of bad stuff, but bring up clowns, and he shut down. He'd seen far worse, but something about clowns he found far scarier.

These things were like that. We'd arguably seen far worse, especially in the north. Hell, we'd just confronted a demon tree that either housed or was the manifestation of some unearthly entity that was the source of the curse that covered the ruin of an entire kingdom. These things were just weird, so far as we'd seen. But they made my skin crawl in a way that even that tree hadn't. At least, not in retrospect.

Of course, from what Brother Melchorius had told us, while these things might not be as dangerous as the Fohorimans or the otherworldly monsters that Dragon Mask had summoned down in the depths of the earth, we still didn't want to catch their attention.

So, we crept along the ridgeline as the sun slowly set, aware of the sunset only because the gray around us got steadily darker, until we had to drop our NVGs again. Once more, I was glad that the batteries the *Coira Ansec* made for us seemed to have much longer lives than most of the AAs or 123s that I'd used back in The World.

It had just started to really get dark when we halted suddenly. I could see Herrera up ahead, barely, and I could *almost* hear the hissed curse as he stopped.

A moment later, Gurke's team had turned around and was coming back toward us. I signaled Rodeffer to lean up against the hillside and let them go past.

"Dead end. A crevasse about two hundred feet deep," Gurke murmured as he went past.

That was bad news. Hours had been lost as we'd traced along that ridgeline. And now we were going to have to re-trace our steps, back toward wherever those faceless things had been groping their way in daylight.

That bothered me a lot more than the lost time.

We were also getting tired. Because Gurke should have just sent the signal forward, and then Bailey's team, cur-rently taking up the trail position, would take point. But Gurke had clearly gotten it in his head that his team was the point team, so they were trying to work their way past the rest of the platoon. But this was no place to halt and rest. Somebody would fall off the side of the hill, with all the attendant racket, in their sleep.

So, once Gunny got things sorted out—which resulted in Gurke's team taking up the number three spot, in front of my team—we started back the way we'd come.

It was getting darker, though, and the haze had blocked out the stars. Footing was getting more treacherous, as it got harder to see. It was one thing in the woods in Lost Colcand. As pitch dark and bad as that had been, at least the ground had been fairly level, with fewer opportunities to put a boot on a loose rock and get launched into space.

A sudden rattle and *bang* of falling rock sounded in the dark somewhere up ahead, and we suddenly stopped. A moment later, Chambers worked his way back to Rodeffer, whispered in his ear, then disappeared into the dark ahead again. I moved up to Rodeffer.

"Chambers says that Baldinus almost went over the side of the hill." Rodeffer's voice was hoarse, even though he was whispering. We were all probably cotton mouthed and miserable by then. There was a feeling like a damp chill in the air, yet it was dry as a bone. "Gunny called a halt until dawn." I was sure that Gunny had a bit more to say than that, but he was leaving it to the team leaders to do the right thing.

"Okay. Move up until you've at least got eyes on Chambers, then find a spot to wedge yourself in place." I thought about it for a second. "In fact, once you get in position, drop your ruck and go prone, facing uphill." He could still sleep like that when he needed to, and I didn't like the idea of the whole platoon doing the rucksack flop on the side of the hill, all weapons pointed down toward the forest we'd come from. Some of us needed to face that way, sure, but those faceless monsters had been on the *other* side of that ridge.

Rodeffer nodded, and a few minutes later, we were clumped in a narrow draw, about ten feet below the top of the ridgeline, wedged in as best we could, though it still felt like we could slide off the hillside at any moment. Rodeffer faced uphill, I leaned back and faced down, while Farrar pointed his Mk 48 up at the ridgeline and Santos covered back the way we'd just come.

Then, with Farrar and Santos up on watch, Rodeffer and I tried to go to sleep.

Emphasis on *tried.*

CHAPTER 26

THAT night seemed to take forever. With the sun having set, the wind started to whip across the tops of the hills, and it got *cold*. Since the weird stillness of the air and the exertion of negotiating the rocky slopes with our rucks on had made most of us sweat, that was not good. It took some doing to get Ranger rolls out of rucks and wrap up in them, with the whispered caution not to make it too hard to get out and fight if the things with no faces came out of the dark.

It wasn't a comfortable spot, and I'm not just talking about the sharp rocks, the wind, or the fear of sliding off the hill. There was no cover or concealment out there, aside from the slight depression we'd crawled into. We were exposed as all get out, and if someone or something happened to be moving along the ridgeline, even in the dark, they'd see us easily. Or spot us through whatever weird, freaky senses they were using. That was what was really robbing us of sleep, or at least it was robbing me of sleep. I must have started awake a dozen times just during the first two-hour watch, all but convinced that something was crawling down the hill onto us, only to twist my head around and see nothing but rocks and haze.

So, I was exhausted and felt like I'd bathed in grit by the time the eastern horizon started to get light, what seemed like a lifetime later. Still, I got my Ranger roll packed up, got my ruck on, and got ready to move. Rodeffer stifled a groan as he did the same.

The haze seemed to have gotten thicker. It was hard to tell exactly where we were, at least in relation to where we'd first entered the hills. As we waited for the other teams to start moving, I had a sudden hunch and clambered as quickly and as carefully as I could to the top of the hill. After getting down on my belly, I peeked over.

There they were. Almost exactly where we'd seen them the day before. The same four or five—it was hard to keep track, the way they kept disappearing into the terrain— moving the same direction, at almost the same angle, their heads moving around the same jerky, disturbing way.

I dropped down, suddenly feeling my heart rate sky-rocket. That was too weird. How had we ended up in exactly the same relative position with those freakish creatures?

I looked again, half expecting them to have reset, as if they weren't even real, just some kind of illusion or glitch. But they were still there, having moved farther down the canyon floor. They didn't seem to know I was there, but there was no telling until they came swarming up the hillside toward us.

Or just called in something worse, though I didn't know how they'd do that without mouths to yell.

That was a train of thought that could go a lot of weird and unpleasant places very quickly.

I slid back down the hill, tapping Rodeffer to keep moving, and then started picking my way along the rocky mountainside toward Gunny. He needed to know about this.

It took far too long to reach him. By then I'd started to sort of get my bearings. We had actually passed the spot where we'd initially climbed up to the ridgeline during the night, and now we were probably a quarter mile farther west. But those things were still down there.

Gunny listened as I quietly reported what I'd seen. His eyes narrowed slightly as I told him about the creatures being in exactly the same relative position. He glanced over at Mathghaman, who had seen us talking and had paused, watching us over his shoulder. Gunny waved him over, and, after carefully working his way around Eoghain and Cairbre, he joined us.

"What are these things?" Gunny asked after he'd re-layed what I'd seen.

Mathghaman shrugged as he shook his head, looking up toward the ridgeline. "I do not know. There are stories about these hills but little detail. Men have gone mad in them. Others have simply disappeared."

"Well, that's encouraging." Gunny blew a short breath out, almost a frustrated sigh. "Do you think they're keeping tabs on us, or was it just coincidence?"

"True coincidence is a rare thing," Mathghaman mused. "And the closer we come to the vampire's lair, the rarer it will become."

"Can we avoid them, or do we need to set an ambush and see if we can eliminate them?" Gunny was thinking through contingencies.

Mathghaman spread his hands. "I do not know. I should advise the former. Especially since we do not truly know what lurks deeper in. We might kill these only to find that they are the less formidable scouts for something far, far worse."

Which was a good point. It just sent a shiver crawling up my spine.

"Let's keep moving then. We'll just get eyes on over the ridgeline every so often as we go." Gunny was always willing to listen to input during planning, but once we'd "slapped the table," so to speak, the decision was made, and we were sticking to it.

We kept moving.

* * *

It was mid-morning before Synar and Bailey found a way deeper into the hills that wouldn't require ropes or other climbing equipment. The shoulder of the ridge we'd been following leveled out just enough that we could get over it and down into the forked valley below without too much difficulty, though we didn't actually cross over until Applegate and Franks were set up on the shoulder with their Mk 48s.

We weren't taking any chances.

Within a few dozen yards, we were in a labyrinth of rock and dust. The air still felt damp, yet everything was desert dry. There was no sign of the strange creatures.

It would have been easiest to follow one or another of the valleys. Especially since keeping a southerly course was going to drag us into what we call "cross-compartment" movement. Up and down, giving up hard-gained elevation just to try to gain it again on the other side. But staying in the low ground, while sometimes a viable option when that's where the brush is, isn't a great tactical choice. So, sweating and bleeding, we struggled right back up and onto the high ground again.

Not a moment too soon, either. We'd just gotten into the rocks along the top of another ridge that ran somewhat south, southwest when another group of about five of those weird, faceless things appeared below us and far too close, moving down the valley.

Farrar saw them first, freezing and putting up a fist, but he was second to last in the order of march, so I didn't see it for a moment. I looked over my shoulder, spotted movement and saw the group of them, and then threw up a fist of my own. The signal got passed rapidly after that, until the whole platoon was motionless in the rocks up on the hillside, hardly daring to breathe, watching the strange creatures while all too aware that despite the dust and the grime of all our movement through the wilderness since landing on the corsairs' shores, we were still wearing green in a landscape gone totally gray.

But they shuffled and twitched their way past, hardly even turning the blank emptiness they wore in place of faces up toward the hills around them.

Maybe they weren't really aware of their surroundings. Maybe they were something so alien that they *couldn't* register what was around them the way we could.

Or maybe—and I glanced at Bearrac, who was watching them intently, as I thought this—they were something more like the specter we'd seen outside the first village the vampire had slaughtered. Something not altogether physical, and therefore of only limited ability to interact with the tangible world of flesh and blood, but still deadly. I dreaded the thought of what would happen if we ended up in those things' path.

We waited until they had faded into the haze and the warren of draws and valleys behind us. Only then, taking a deep breath that tasted of ashes and dust, did we keep going.

* * *

While it was a lot easier to observe the passing of days and nights than it had been in Lost Colcand, it still seemed like it was harder to actually measure time. We had to keep doubling back, as we came to a wall of rock or a great crack in the ground that we couldn't get across. Soon it felt like we were just circling around and around in the haze and the rocks, while our water slowly ran out and we got more holes in our gloves and our cammies.

Then, about three days into the broken badlands, after avoiding too many of those faceless creatures to count, we came over a ridgeline and saw the ruins.

It was hard to tell that was what we were looking at, at first. The land had changed and shifted, and many of the ruins had been broken in the process. Walls ended in empty space, and cascades of rubble were all that remained of towers, arches, or flying buttresses. At first glance, it would have seemed to only be even more fantastically broken and eroded stone, but some of the lines were too regular, the shapes too deliberate. At least, until they had been suddenly snapped off by whatever catastrophe had formed this wasteland.

And the ruins were teeming with the faceless ones.

We were a good distance away—the haze seemed to have lifted ever so slightly—and the deepest crevasse we'd passed yet lay between us and the ruins. That was a good thing, because as I laid my rifle across a rock and scanned the broken walls and spires, I could tell there were a *lot* of those things.

I studied them for a little bit. Gunny had called a halt, in part because of how difficult that climb had been and in part because of what had just been revealed. The platoon faded into the rocks, taking cover as much as possible, and set security while several of us scanned the ruins.

After a while, I started to notice that the faceless creatures just seemed to be wandering or climbing on the ruins aimlessly, almost like they really didn't know what they were about. It was as if they were groping around in the dark. It really made them seem even more unearthly.

Santos tapped me urgently on the shoulder. I came off glass and looked where he was pointing.

There was a wave of movement coming over a higher ridge off to the east, on the other side of the ruins. From where we sat, it was hard to see anything but a creeping darkness through the haze.

I got on glass but still couldn't make much out, except that whatever was moving out there, there were a lot of them. A mass of bodies was flowing down the side of the ridge, some of them losing their footing and tumbling, only to be trampled by the rest. And they were heading right for the ruins.

We weren't moving yet, so I kept watching. Something about this situation was off, and I didn't think that mass of bodies was moving across these badlands by accident. This was trackless wilderness, ruled by demons and monsters, and nobody just went traipsing around for the hell of it.

At least, I didn't think so. In retrospect, I suppose it made sense that even the demons and monsters had some politics of their own. The Fohorimans and their disciples sure did. But something about this place felt different. As if the web of curses and malevolent, preternatural influences had somehow twisted this entire region slightly out of reality.

In truth, I'd later find that the north was really no different. We'd just still been figuring things out then, so it only *seemed* different.

The faceless ones paid no attention to the mob swarming over the rocks toward them. Again, it was almost as if they couldn't see or hear anything.

Until the mob reached the first ring of the ruins.

They had been in the low ground until then, so as the first ones came vaulting over the crumbling remains of a fallen wall, I got my first good look at what was coming.

Goblins.

The little pumpkin-headed, green-skinned psychopaths that had attacked both us and the corsairs came rushing over the wreckage of the ancient city, their too-wide mouths gaping in evil grins, their tiny red eyes glittering, waving crude weapons over their heads.

Their rush was uninterrupted until the lead goblin, a big bruiser that probably stood four feet high, got within six feet of one of the faceless ones.

Suddenly the aimlessness and seeming blindness was gone. The faceless thing swiveled like a predator that had just scented its prey, and in a flash, it was on the goblin.

The faceless, scrawny creature tore the goblin limb-from-limb in a matter of seconds. Blood and ichor sprayed into the air and bits of goblin flew left and right. And as it did, every single faceless one in the ruins stopped moving, then swiveled its blank, smooth head toward the oncoming goblins.

The goblins didn't hesitate just because the first one had been torn to pieces. With a chorus of bloodthirsty shrieks that we could hear faintly even from over a mile away, they charged.

They probably should have run.

The faceless things scuttled across the ground and over the ruins like army ants, descending on the goblins in a sudden, vicious bloodbath. Before the goblins could even start swinging their jagged weapons, the first ranks had been torn to shreds.

The noises that drifted across the hazy distance to our crude hide were pretty horrifying. Especially considering that the goblins were making all of them. The faceless ones killed in utter silence, despite the frenzy of their attacks.

But there were enough goblins that the rest of the mob got their act together and started swinging weapons and shooting arrows. Including into some of the other goblins near the front that were panicking and trying to run away from the awful, gray, silent killing machines.

It meant something, the goblins coming out of the wilds like that. But right then and there wasn't the time nor the place to debate it. I looked over at Gunny, who was watching the same gruesome tableau. He felt my gaze, met my eyes, and nodded. We needed to make tracks while the faceless ones were occupied.

With even greater care than before, we got up and started moving again, slipping down below the crest of the hill and putting rock and earth between us and the sprawling, broken ruins. The screams and howls of the killing frenzy and the dying goblins still echoed over the badlands as we went, but no one felt like lingering to watch the show.

We almost became part of the show, anyway. We'd gotten about twenty yards before we had to stop dead, as another six or seven faceless ones flowed over the ridge in front of us, splayed out on all fours as they raced toward the bloodletting.

We moved even more carefully after that.

* * *

The next few hours were the most nerve-wracking game of hide-and-seek I think I've ever been through.

With the faceless ones roused, we had to watch every step. It got darker as the clouds overhead got thicker—they seemed to be especially dark to the south, where we were heading—and that made the little roving packs of gray killers that much harder to spot. Most of the groups we encountered were still heading for the battle with the goblins, but we had to continue to be careful. We knew little more about them than we'd known when we'd entered the badlands, but that they would kill anything that came close enough seemed obvious.

We moved as fast as we could while maintaining security and trying not to trip over any faceless ones. We still didn't make it out of those broken hills by nightfall.

It was a long night.

CHAPTER 27

THE inhuman screaming and howling that echoed across the otherwise silent badlands fell silent shortly before dawn. Whether that meant one side or another had won, or had fled, we had no way of knowing.

I doubted that the faceless monsters had been routed. They didn't seem capable of it. There was a mindless menace to them that made it seem unlikely that they could feel fear. We'd seen the goblins break once.

By the time the first light of dawn started to filter its way through the haze that still sat heavily on the jagged hills, I looked around and saw that everyone was already awake, even those who were supposed to be down. We didn't need to get anyone up for stand to.

No one had gotten much rest.

After carefully scanning our surroundings, making sure that we hadn't been quietly surrounded in the dark, Gunny got my team out on point, and we kept going.

The broken hills were silent and empty as we picked our way along the ridgelines, occasionally dipping into the low ground to cross a valley that we couldn't go around. The haze never seemed to lift, and the clouds to the south seemed almost fixed. That grody feeling of cool damp and bone-dry dust lingered, increasing the discomfort as we went.

But we didn't see any of the faceless ones the entire morning. The whole land seemed empty and dead. I sure wasn't complaining, and I don't think any of the rest of the platoon was, either. We'd seen enough horror the day before.

The wasteland seemed to go on forever, jagged hill after jagged hill. None rose more than a couple hundred feet, but the going was slow and agonizing, made worse by the need to stay quiet and avoid exposing ourselves. It was unlikely that we'd trigger the faceless ones unless we got too close to them, but who knew what other monstrosities were hiding in that labyrinth of lifeless rock?

That day ended in gloom and nearly impenetrable darkness. We were still deep within the maze of sharp-edged hills and steep-sided gullies. We found a notch in one of the ridgelines where we could set security on both sides without exposing ourselves too much.

That night was about as restful as the night before.

When we got moving the next morning, I could see the weight of the place and the increasing restlessness bearing down on everyone. It was starting to feel like we'd never escape from Tethba. Everywhere we looked, there was nothing but marching ridges of gray stone, disappearing into the haze of smoke, or dust, or whatever it was.

The only variation was the wall of dark cloud to the south. The darkness that we were steadily trying to get to.

* * *

We found another ruin that afternoon.

This one was smaller and more intact than the one before. A single tower stood, roofless, over a fallen wall and several structures reduced to little more than broken walls and foundations.

Figures lined the top of that tower and parts of the wall. Rodeffer had dropped into the shadow of a boulder the size of a car as soon as he'd spotted them, and I quickly joined him, trying to get eyes on the figures.

Peering through my scope, I saw that the figures weren't faceless ones, but gargoyles, with glowering, animalistic faces and folded wings, clasping the walls with stony claws. I frowned as I studied one of them.

"Conor…" Rodeffer sounded a little hesitant, as if he wasn't sure how to bring this up. "I might be imagining things, but…"

"They don't look like they were part of the building before," I finished for him. And they didn't. Those claws weren't carved into the stone of the structure, they were *gripping* the stone. And from some of the marks I thought I could see, I didn't think they were necessarily just statues put there for decoration.

"Hell." Rodeffer just sounded tired. "Now there are living gargoyles, too?"

Diarmodh had joined us and was peering over my shoulder. He turned and whispered to Mathghaman, and got a nod in reply. "We should move away quietly and not get too close."

"What's in there? Just gargoyles, or something else?" I asked.

"Not so much *what* as *who*." Diarmodh was watching the ruins with narrowed eyes. "Gargoyles do not live on their own. There is no life in them. Only sorcery." He scowled. "It seems that the faceless ones are not the only denizens of this haunted place. And anyone who creates gargoyles is not one we wish to meet, at least not without dedicating ourselves to his overthrow."

In short, there was a sorcerer of some sort in there, probably evil, but that wasn't the mission.

I just hoped that he or she didn't have some other kind of otherworldly scouts out, like the vaguely crow-like shadows the corsair wizards had used that had compromised us while we'd been hiding in the woods.

Still, there wasn't much we could do about that, except trust in the Tuacha's invocations to keep such things off us. I got Rodeffer's attention and pointed down, onto the other side of the ridge. He nodded, and one by one, we slipped out of sight of the gargoyles perched on the distant ruin, hoping and praying that none of them had noticed us.

* * *

At the next halt, I found Diarmodh again. "Whoever took up residence in that tower back there. Were they human?" Somehow that seemed important.

"Probably." The short, blond man looked up at me from where he was painstakingly wiping the dust off his damasked rifle. Really, the Tuacha weapons were works of art. I hadn't even thought to ask for anything like that when I'd gone to the *Coira Ansec* for a harder-hitting rifle. "The monsters outnumber Men in these times. Unfortunately, that has led many to turn to them, rather than what is good, true, and beautiful. Some have turned more thoroughly than others." He nodded back the way we'd come. "There are always those who will risk life and sanity for power. Even to venture into a place like this in search of it."

He thought for a moment, watching me out of the corner of his eye. As if he were debating whether to tell me more.

I decided to press a little. "Would the faceless ones have something to do with it? Maybe he heard about them and decided to come to see if he could learn anything."

Diarmodh shook his head. "I do not think any would have come for the faceless ones themselves, not after what we have seen of them. What they serve, though…perhaps."

"What they serve?" This was interesting, despite the gruesome nature of the subject. "There's something else here?"

He raised his eyebrows. "You saw the demon tree in the center of Lost Colcand. That was not the creature from the Abyss that cursed that ancient kingdom. It came later, drawn to the evil laid upon that land, and fed upon the curse and the horror of what happened there, further twisting and warping the creatures of this world that dwelt there even after the men of Colcand were wiped out." He waved around at our bleak surroundings. "I am sure something similar came here, to Tethba. There are creatures that delight in such…emotional bloodstains. They are like scavengers, burrowing into the spiritual corpse of a people and reveling in the destruction and the evil that is left behind. Some dwell in the heart of living kingdoms. Such lie in Sumnoth in the north, or in stranger kingdoms still, far to the south and the east. Others delight in darker places, such as here. And where one scavenger has come, others are also drawn. By the darkness of their lair, or by the power of such monsters themselves."

I chewed on that for a moment, looking out at the black outlines of the hills against the slightly lighter darkness of the sky. No stars shone through the clouds and the haze. "And people actively look for things like that?"

Diarmodh nodded grimly in the dark. "The promise of power makes men do things that seem utterly insane. Think. Have you never been tempted by such things?"

I grimaced, knowing he could probably see it. The Tuacha could see in the dark like cats. "Yeah, I guess I have." I remembered the spell that Dragon Mask had unleashed on Taramas's hunters, and the mixed feelings that it had brought out. Whatever he had done, it had been so unnatural as to make your head hurt trying to comprehend what had just happened. It had turned the snow black and the Fohorimans into smears on the ground.

Yet it had nagged at all of us, on some level, that the kind of destructive power it had demonstrated might have been useful, especially against monsters that could move faster and take more punishment than any of us.

"Give a man enough time and he can justify almost anything." Something about Diarmodh's tone told me he wasn't just talking theoretically, either. "He will rewrite history and reality in his head to give himself 'no choice,' or turn those who would turn him aside from such a course into cowards and fools. All the while, blinding himself to the risk to his own soul, never mind his sanity or the costs that those around him will bear." His gaze got distant. "That is why the world is as it is. It was not always thus. Even the greatest of monsters, those that did not come from beyond the borders of the world—of which there are many—were once men. Men gone dark and twisted, forever changed by their own pride and lust for power and gain. Men who have sacrificed their very humanity for a little bit more in this world."

It was an uncomfortable thought, given what we'd already seen, even within the platoon. I thought back to some of the things that Captain Sorenson had done, justifying them as strengthening the alliance with the Dovos, even to the extent of taking part in some of their blood rituals.

Was he still alive? Was he recognizably a man anymore if he was?

I didn't have any answers.

The night seemed even darker after that.

* * *

It took two more days of slogging to get out of the hills. We were out of water, and if it hadn't been for the Tuacha's travel rations, light and compact as they were, we'd be out of food, too. We were subsisting on sips from Bearrac's flask.

I would have asked how we got some of the same stuff, but I gathered that it was extremely rare.

The hills dipped into a shallow valley with a fast-moving river running down out of the Wall of Scath at the bottom of it. The barren rocks of the broken hills had given way to short grass and heather, and while it was still cool, almost chilly, the gritty, grimy feeling to the air in the badlands of Tethba wasn't there anymore. That valley felt downright clean, as silent and lifeless as it was, aside from the faint breeze stirring the scrubby grass.

It was open enough that we stopped in a hollow at the edge of the hills until nightfall, though. No one was comfortable with crossing that open plain in broad daylight, or as close as it was going to come with the nearly ever-present cloud cover to the south, on the other side of the river.

We weren't moving that fast when we finally headed out about an hour after dark. Some of that was simply caution. Some of it was exhaustion and dehydration.

It didn't take long to get to the river, and Mathghaman insisted that we hold back from refilling our canteens and bladders until he could check to make sure we weren't going to be drinking cursed or poisoned water. After a few moments, though, he straightened from the water, held one hand out over it, whispered an invocation, and then nodded, waving an invitation. He clearly wasn't entirely thrilled with the prospect of drinking from a stream so close to the Land of Shadows and Crows, but he was confident that it wouldn't do us too much harm.

We set security, taking a knee in the grass in the dark, as a chill breeze stirred around us and the river gurgled with a strangely comforting sound, and took turns filling our water. Mathghaman and Bearrac went around to murmur their invocations over the bladders and bottles, just in case.

Then we waded out into the icy water, crossed the river, and headed up the opposite bank, toward the dark line of trees in the distance and the lowering clouds above them.

CHAPTER 28

THE land rose steadily, if slowly, and soon we were in dark pine woods. Not nearly as dark as Lost Colcand, but the trees themselves were dark, and the clouds thickened overhead, casting the entire landscape into deep twilight, even as the sun began to rise, hours after we'd entered the woods.

The wind sighed through the trees, which were a lot more widely spaced than in Lost Colcand, but everything else was quiet and still. I hadn't heard a bird or a squirrel, or seen any movement at all, since the sun had risen. It was as if nothing lived there except the trees.

Even with the day having come, the pines looked almost black. I'd noticed that many of the trees in this place had shaded darker than what I remembered from The World, but it was somewhat more pronounced here.

We stepped off carefully, eyes up and weapons tracking wherever they went. Movement was easier in those woods, and so was silence, as we patrolled over rocky but generally level ground, covered in fallen pine needles and little else.

So, we made pretty good progress. And we saw nothing beyond the rocks and the trees. No monsters, no animals, no nothing. It was almost relaxing—which made it all the more eerie and paranoia-inducing. If Mathghaman was right, then we were either close to the Land of Shadows and Crows, or we were already there. And after everything else we'd been through, I think we were all expecting the next group of monsters to leap out of the ground or drop out of the sky at any moment.

The clouds got darker, turning the sky a deep, charcoal gray. The terrain was going slowly but steadily upward, though the trees never seemed to get any thicker, even as the light slowly died to a deep, blue-gray twilight.

The darkness grew until our PVS-15s weren't penetrating it well. Since none of us figured that splashing IR lights around that close to the vampire's lair was a good idea, we decided to halt until some semblance of day returned.

There weren't any great places to put a hide. The forest floor was open and clear, the branches mostly more than eight feet above the ground. But we found a spot, slightly elevated, with some larger boulders nearby and a sheer drop of about ten feet on one side, that would have to do.

As the ATLs set in security, Bearrac prowled around the perimeter. Finally, he murmured to Mathghaman, who beckoned Gunny over.

I joined them, along with Gurke and Bailey. This seemed like a team leader sort of thing.

"We should light a fire." Mathghaman's voice was hushed, but the urgency wasn't lost.

Gunny looked around at the rest of us for a second. We'd lit fires while we'd still been in corsair lands, where we'd ostensibly had some safe passage, but this was different. We were deep in hostile territory. Fires meant light and noise, and if we didn't want to proceed at night while showing IR light to see by, lighting a fire didn't seem to be any better.

But Mathghaman gripped Gunny's shoulder, looking around and meeting each of our eyes. "I know. But Bearrac is right. We are on the borders of the Land of Shadows and Crows, and the creatures of the night that are drawn to that realm of death will be more deterred by fire and light than they will by watchful men with rifles in the dark."

He probably had a point. If we really were getting into undead territory, who knew what kind of unnatural things might be prowling around in the dark. If the cloud was some permanent fixture over the vampire's lair—and it hadn't moved in days, so it very well might have been— then we might not have the advantage in the dark that we were used to.

So, while security got set, we lit a fire.

Then we settled in for the night as utter blackness descended outside the flickering circle of firelight, watching the dark as the temperature dropped.

* * *

Santos woke me up for my watch, and I squinted against the glare of the fire. It wasn't even a big fire, but compared to the utter darkness past the first trees, it sure looked bright. I forced my eyes away as I sat up. I'd need my night eyes, even with NVGs.

Santos waited quietly while I got my Ranger roll stowed and pulled my helmet on, then dropped my PVS-15s in front of my eyes. The firelight brightened against the surrounding trees in the green-shaded image, but even so, I didn't think I could see more than about ten yards through the woods. It was that dark.

"Anything?" I whispered as I sat up and checked my rifle, which I'd had under my hand, the sling wrapped around my arm, as I'd slept.

"I heard what might have been footsteps about an hour ago." Santos's voice was hushed, and he hadn't taken his eyes off the forest around us. "Maybe..." His hesitation was palpable, and I turned my head to look at him directly.

"What?" If he'd seen something, I needed to know. It had to be weird, too, or he wouldn't have hesitated that much.

He sighed. "I thought I heard growling. And I thought I might have seen eyes, just for a second."

"Dude, with everything else we've seen and heard, what makes you think that's too weird to mention?" I scanned the darkened forest, looking for eyes or other shapes that didn't belong.

"I dunno." He shifted slightly. I was up and on NVGs, but he still hadn't gone down for rest plan. "I didn't get a good look, and this place has me so damned jumpy that I didn't want to pass on what might have been a figment of my imagination."

I shook my head as I scanned our sector. "Better to report what turns out to be nothing than to ignore what turns out to be something. Come on, brother. You know that."

He didn't have much of an answer. Santos was a solid dude, but he'd never been the type to get into fantasy or spook stories. He'd always been a "feet firmly planted on the ground" type of guy, which, while it had enabled him to maintain his equilibrium once we'd been hurled into this strange place, as he simply dealt with the problem at hand, over time the strangeness had to be eating at him. It seemed that here, on the borderlands of a kingdom of the dead, the weirdness had caught up with him a little. I knew he'd grown up with stories of brujas and other scary stuff in the dark, but he'd never put much credence in them. Now he had to.

"Get some rest, man. I've got this." I didn't want to push him right then. He'd be fine once things got real again, but the dark and the reality of where we were meant that he just needed some space and some time. We could afford a couple hours.

At least, I hoped so.

With a grunt, Santos leaned back against his ruck. He didn't even bother to take his helmet off.

I watched the dark woods around us, my rifle across my knees, and waited.

* * *

That watch seemed to take a very long time. The fire crackled behind me, sending dancing shadows across the trees in front, shadows that very soon seemed to move on their own, as if strange and alien shapes, black as pitch in the dim green of my NVGs' image, were dancing or peeking around tree trunks. There was enough ambient noise between the fire and the faint whisper of the wind in the treetops—which hadn't started until after we'd stopped, which was a little creepy—that it was easy to imagine that I could hear something moving out beyond the firelight. Or was I imagining it? After all, Mathghaman and Bearrac had insisted on a fire to keep...something away.

You'd think that after weeks in the frozen north, and over a week moving through the haunted and cursed remnants of long-dead kingdoms, I would have been able to figure out the difference between real spooks and my nerves getting the better of me. But it's not that simple. Not when the spooks and monsters can get inside your head.

You have to understand the weirdness of this place. Everything we thought we knew, every naturalistic assurance about what's real and what *can't* be real…none of it applies here. The monsters are real. The ghosts and spirits are real. But there's something else going on in places like Lost Colcand, the ruin of Tethba, and even more so in the Land of Shadows and Crows, which we were right on the border of.

It's as if the curses that lie on those places are actively trying to mess with you. Just when you think you've got things figured out, everything changes. Or at least, that's what it feels like. Which might be a side effect of that sort of weirdness. Maybe the curse doesn't need to actually change things. It just needs to get in your head and make you wonder.

So, I might have seen a giant black dog pacing between the trees, out at the edge of the firelight. I couldn't get a good enough look to even be sure that I'd seen anything.

I might have heard a growl, or it might have been the creak of a tree in the faint wind.

It was a long two hours.

* * *

It took most of the next day to reach the edge of the woods. Toward sunset, we started to hear the first sounds of animal life since we'd crossed the river.

Crows. Cawing and mocking. A lot of them.

We came out of the trees on the edge of a moor, as the rain began to fall, right then little more than a mist, though great, gray curtains were visible in the distance, sweeping across the rolling, rocky hills as the wind stirred the low grass and scrubby heather. And we saw the crows.

An ancient, lighting-blasted pine stood alone, about a hundred yards out on the moor. It was huge, split down the middle by more than a few lightning strikes.

The crows clustered on every twisted branch, cawing and croaking. There had to be at least a hundred of them.

They couldn't all be there for the dozen or so withered corpses that swung gently from nooses dangling beneath the larger branches. But then, maybe those weren't the only bodies around, if this really was a kingdom of death.

We didn't stand there staring. Not our way. We'd spread out to find cover and gotten down on security as soon as the lead team—Bailey's again—had halted. But eyes kept straying to that macabre tree and its gruesome fruit.

Welcome to the Land of Shadows and Crows.

CHAPTER 29

MORE crows circled overhead, despite the rain, as we started moving across the rolling, rocky hills. The rain and mist helped us somewhat, as the drifting curtains of gray obscured us from prying eyes—at least, any natural eyes. We used the dips and folds in the ground as best we could, despite the easier movement that just crossing the moor toward the distant silhouette of a massive tor would have afforded.

We were all tired. It had been a long op already. It would have been understandable, especially given the apparent emptiness of the moors—aside from the crows, that didn't seem that bothered by the wet—if we'd just moved in.

But while I heard some muttering from a couple of the junior guys, like Rodeffer and Baldinus, the rest of us were too on edge to assent to taking shortcuts. We were almost to the objective, and things were going to get far more dangerous.

If we'd only known.

It was a long, meandering route, following folds and gullies and staying mostly below the level of the tops of the rolling hills. None of them were particularly tall, and even the gullies weren't deep. The occasional trees in the low ground added some more concealment, for what it was worth.

That tor looked like it wasn't all that far away, but by nightfall we still hadn't gotten halfway to it.

We lit a fire again. While nobody said anything, everyone had seen what looked like a massive black dog, pacing us at a distance. It was never more than a glimpse, suddenly disappearing into low ground or in a sweep of rain. I don't think anyone got a straight-on look at it, either. I know I didn't. It was always a faint impression out of the corner of your eye.

But it was enough that when we stopped and set security for the night, no one questioned when Chambers and Applegate started gathering wood for a fire.

It wasn't much of a fire, as everything was damp, and it took a lot of careful work to get it started at all. The wood all had to be split to get at the drier fuel inside. It was fully dark by the time the first sputtering flames finally caught, hissing as the rain hit it, but just sheltered enough by the willow we'd set up beneath so as to keep burning.

We tried to sleep between shifts on security as the fire spat and hissed, and the wind moaned over the rocks.

* * *

By midday the next day, we had come close enough to a low, stone village at the base of the tor to start to look for an OP.

Our objective rally point was in a hollow choked with gorse and willows about a klick away from the edge of the village. We didn't have maps to work with, so we had to rely on observation through the rain and the mist to look for some place that we could overlook the village, get eyes on, and start to make a plan. We didn't have a map, but we knew we were in the heart of the Land of Shadows and Crows. There was something about that tor, and the castle that stood atop it, visible in only brief, incomplete glances as the clouds shifted around the top, that told us we were in the right place.

Again, I couldn't quite explain *how* we knew this. It just seemed obvious. Maybe it was just an instinct, some sixth sense we were developing the longer we were in this strange place.

It wasn't, but we wouldn't figure that out until it was far too late.

* * *

Two teams stayed in the ORP. They'd coordinate and act as a quick reaction force if one of the OP teams got into trouble.

We'd spotted two potential covered and concealed observation sites in the limited scouting we'd risked from the ORP. One was a rare stand of trees on the side of a hill that appeared to be a shoulder of the upthrust that formed the tor. That was the riskiest site, since it looked like it was close to a road that switchbacked its way up the tor toward the castle.

The second was a cluster of sharp-pointed granite rocks that thrust up out of the ground about ninety degrees around the village from the trees.

Now, either one would have been a bit obvious if we were up against someone expecting surveillance. But this wasn't Syria. And our options were limited.

Bailey and I played rock-paper-scissors for who got which objective. I ended up with the stand of trees. Which meant we had a lot longer route to get there, and we would be closer to that road.

Except by the time we stepped off into the rain, none of us had observed any movement to or from the castle yet. And we should have, if there had been any traffic.

So far, this entire moor seemed to be abandoned, except by the ever-present black dog that had paced us but never attacked, or even gotten close enough for a good look.

If I was remembering my folklore right, that was a good thing, that it was keeping its distance. I didn't really want to meet Black Shuck. Or was it the Hound of the Basker-villes? Can never remember which was which.

But if this was our target, why was everything so emp-ty? That was what we needed to find out. That was why we were slogging through the mist and the drizzle, assault packs on our backs, rucks left in the ORP, weaving through the maze of little valleys and gulches to get to our OP.

It was dark by the time we reached the last covered and concealed position behind our observation point. This would be our team ORP. I told Rodeffer and Farrar to stay in the ORP with Santos, while I moved up to get eyes on and make sure we weren't going to run into an ambush on the road. Bearrac had embedded himself with my team, so he came with me, his hood up and his cloak spread over his shoulders, making him almost disappear even in NVGs.

The two of us crept up to the crest of the hill, where the stony, cobbled road threaded its way up toward the huge massif—it was far bigger than the tor where we'd taken shelter in the north—before zigzagging its way toward the castle perched at the top of what looked like a sheer cliff several hundred feet high.

While Bearrac hadn't really trained to our SOPs, he still halted without needing to be told, in a fold in the ground just short of the road. We both got down in the gorse and the low, wet grass and scanned the road in both directions.

A good thing, too. Because just then, naturally, the only traffic we'd seen on that road all day decided to go by.

Wheels creaking and squealing, a cart was coming up the hill. Both of us got lower, if that was possible, as I mentally cursed my chest rig for keeping me a couple extra inches off the ground.

It took a long time for the cart to pass us. It wasn't exactly moving quickly. I mean, it was an oxcart. They're not known for breaking ground speed records. But this one was clearly in absolutely no hurry.

And it was every bit as creepy as everything else we'd seen in this otherwise silent, still place.

The creature pulling it looked like an ox. Or, I should say, it looked like the silhouette of an ox. It was so deeply black that I couldn't see any shadows or detail, just an empty black shape that moved and pulled the cart, its head down and its horns curving out in front of it. It was dark, sure, but I should have been able to see *something* in my PVS-15s. I could make out just enough of the cart, and the figure walking slowly beside it.

The cart looked ancient, almost as if it were ready to fall apart. Wicker sides rose above the bed, and it wobbled slightly on its single axle.

The figure walking beside it could have been the Grim Reaper.

No scythe, but it wore a long, ragged robe, and its hood was pulled up so that there was only a black *nothingness* where its face would be. Its hands were completely withdrawn into its voluminous sleeves, and a switch dragged behind one, though it never seemed to move it toward the ox-thing.

The temperature dropped as the cart trundled past us. The ox—or whatever it was—made no sound aside from the *clop* of its hooves on the stones. The wheels creaked and squealed as it went, rocking with every step the ox made. The driver walked beside the cart, just behind the harness, hooded head bowed and making no sound at all.

As it continued up the hill, I got a look into the back. It was stacked with bodies.

I could just make out Bearrac's face as he watched the cart, unblinking. I wondered if he was thinking the same thing I was. *If this is the kingdom of the dead, with cursed and haunted lands all around it, where the hell are they getting all the dead human bodies from?*

It seemed to take hours before the cart was almost out of sight, far up the hill, though it was probably a lot shorter than that. I wasn't going to check my watch when we were that close to the enemy.

Finally, I decided that it was far enough away to risk crossing the road. The driver hadn't looked to either side, or up, or back the entire interminable time we'd been watching it. Maybe he couldn't see. Maybe he could but didn't need eyes. Maybe he was more like the faceless ones in Tethba.

We hadn't been burned yet, that I knew of, so we had to push on with the mission.

A quick dash across the road, and we were down in a shallow draw that pointed toward the stand of trees that was our objective. I slowed as soon as we were across, dropping prone again and pointing my rifle up the road, in the direction the corpse cart had gone. Bearrac split the other direction, making sure nothing had come up behind us.

We waited for a few moments until it was apparent that we weren't about to be eaten by weird things coming out of the dark. Then I got up and headed for the OP, Bearrac smoothly and silently rising to follow.

The trees would do the trick and were more sheltered from the road than I'd thought. No monsters. No bodies hanging from the trees. A few crows, but they seemed inescapable. There had been plenty circling around the ORP down in the hollow, too.

So, we headed back to pick up the rest of the team. It was time to go to work.

* * *

It didn't take nearly as long to get the team into the OP. We didn't have to wait for a ghostly corpse cart to go past this time, so we just bumped across the road and into the draw before continuing down into the stand of trees.

From there, Santos set up rear security while Rodeffer, Bearrac, and I got eyes on the village.

It wasn't large, maybe half a klick to a side. Three main streets crossed in a central square, with the small stone-walled houses with turf roofs huddled close together around it. A few larger houses stood on the outskirts, but for the most part, all the houses looked about the size of one-room cabins. There were no signs, no lanterns, and no indications of commerce of any kind. Just a bunch of houses huddled at the base of the mountain, in the shadow of the castle.

Most of that castle was still shrouded in clouds, all but invisible above. But somehow, from this distance, even though we couldn't see it, we could still *feel* the weight of its presence up there.

With our optics broken out, Rodeffer and I started to scan the village.

I was on the six-power night vision scope, while Rodeffer was on thermals. I picked up the figures first.

"Well, this place has a night life. No lights, but plenty of people out on the street. Looks like a regular meeting in the town square." I had one eye to the scope, which was laid over my pack, snugged up between two tree roots. I had a decent line of sight on the square itself. There was a well or a fountain in the center, and probably two or three dozen people were standing around it, all facing the somewhat larger stone house at one side of the square, as well as the tor and the castle above it.

Rodeffer lifted his head and peered over his thermals. I caught the movement out of the corner of my eye and looked over at him. "Why are you looking *over* the thermals?"

"I don't see anybody down there, Conor." He put his eye to the thermal scope again. "Wait. Maybe. Yeah, I can *kinda* see them. But they're…" He gulped. "They're the same temperature as the rest of the ground around them."

I looked down at the crowd, all standing stock still and staring up at the tor that cast its shadow over the village. For a moment, I wondered if they were statues, though I already knew that wasn't it.

Then one of them turned and faced the others, spreading his arms wide. "Can you see that one that just turned around?"

"Where?" He was struggling. "Wait. Yeah. I can see him." Rodeffer gulped again. "He's as cold as the rest of 'em."

"They are dead." Bearrac's voice was calm, but even the Tuacha warrior could not wholly suppress the note of dread in his voice. "No living men dwell here. It is the Land of Shadows and Crows. It is a kingdom of the dead."

I kept watching the group in the square. Aside from that one, they still hadn't moved. What did the dead have to do, after all?

Why would an entire village still be inhabited by the restless dead? Unless that was the curse of this place, like the way Lost Colcand had turned beasts into monsters, or Tethba had drawn the faceless ones into its haze-shrouded labyrinth of rock?

Or did it have something to do with the vampire? I turned my attention to the larger house at the head of the square. "Could they be the vampire's honor guard? Could it be in there, in the big house with the arched portico?"

Bearrac reached for the night vision scope, and I handed it to him. He didn't need it to see in the dark, but as sharp as the Tuacha's eyes were, he probably still wanted the magnification.

He studied the weird tableau below us while I took the thermals from Rodeffer for a moment. Sure enough, none of the figures below shone white against the shades of gray around them. They were all gray, barely discernable from the rest of the town.

Bearrac came off the scope and handed it back. "I do not think it is in there. Look at where they are all looking."

I studied the crowd again, in their weirdly asymmetrical formation. Except for the one at the head who had turned around, all their faces were turned upward.

"The spirits that animate them are doing homage to their lord." Bearrac pointed toward the castle. "In its lair. Up there."

CHAPTER 30

"SO, the dead come out at night." Gunny scratched his beard with a thumb. "This place is definitely messing with the way we operate."

"There will be daylight sentinels," Mathghaman said grimly. "No vampire would make it so easy to reach them. They are cunning, as evil and unnatural as they are."

"What kind of daylight sentinels?" Bailey sounded a lot more chipper than I felt, probably because his team had made it back to the ORP almost two hours before mine. Not that any of us had gotten much rest so far, so that wasn't actually saying that much.

Mathghaman shrugged. "None of us have faced one of these creatures before. There are only stories. And no two tales are the same. Some have used gargoyles, others similar sorcerous constructs. Some have used enthralled mortals. Others abhumans, beasts raised to a mockery of men, like the creatures we fought in Lost Colcand. Vampires are rare, and from the lore associated with them, each has a terrible pride, and so must make their own mark, in whatever strange and twisted way they can conceive. Their imaginations are...extensive in their depravity."

I suppressed a shudder. I'd seen what some of the Fohorimans in the north had been capable of. And from the way Mathghaman and Bearrac talked, a vampire was worse than any of them. Far worse.

I really didn't want to try to picture just how much worse.

"So, be prepared for anything." Gunny, as was his wont, refused to be stampeded, and just accepted it as another problem to be solved. He squinted at the leaden sky. The rain had stopped for the moment, but the darkness above promised more.

I wondered if this storm ever went away, or if the vampire had drawn it here and somehow kept it lowering over its castle. It sure hadn't moved in days.

"That would be best." Mathghaman looked around the damp hollow that was the ORP. Gurke's team was up on security again, their wet cammies almost invisible in the dimness and against the grass and heather. "We will probably want to take all of our explosives. And any other weapons we might carry." He glanced at me then, and I knew he was most emphatically talking about my sword. Which made plenty of sense, given that it was a blessed weapon.

Gunny sighed, then. "As much as I'd like to get in there and get this done, I think we need to exercise a little operational patience." He glanced around in much the same way Mathghaman had done, but in this case, he was gauging fatigue. We'd covered a *lot* of ground, short on food, water, and sleep. And as urgent as the mission might be, he was trying to judge whether the prudent course would be to push through, or wait, rest, and be ready when the sun came up again, hidden as it might be by the storm.

Finally, with a grimace that told me that he really wasn't comfortable with either decision, Gunny said, "We'll hold position here for the rest of today and tonight. Then we'll start up the hill in the morning, hopefully after the dead have gone down for the day. We'll just have to move carefully and avoid exposing ourselves to whatever daylight guardians the vamp's got set in. And be ready to blow the whole thing up if things go pear-shaped."

There were nods of assent. A couple of our Marines looked visibly relieved. Almak was blank and quiet, as he had been since we'd left Brother Melchorius's chapel.

I'd expected the Tuacha to react somewhat harshly to the thought of leaving Sister Sebeal in the vampire's clutches, unrescued, for longer than absolutely necessary, but all of them—except maybe Cairbre, who scowled—seemed at peace with the decision.

I supposed that made some sense. She'd already been a prisoner for weeks. One more day shouldn't make much difference one way or the other.

Provided the vampire wasn't aware of our presence, and decided to finish her off.

That was the thought that weighed on my mind as I settled in to wait out the day. I had never met Sister Sebeal. Didn't even know what she looked like. But she was the mission. And the way the Tuacha spoke about her—though never in great detail, communicating more by tone than words—she was greatly respected and revered. Enough so that the thought of her coming to harm caused them a great deal of pain.

Despite our differences, despite the fact that the Tuacha were clearly something more than human, Mathghaman, Bearrac, Fennean, and Diarmodh were our brothers, bonded through shared hardship and battle. The other three, Conall, Eoghain, and Cairbre, might be less so—especially Cairbre, whom I didn't think had said more than a couple dozen words to any of us since we'd left—but they were loyal to Mathghaman and had developed some of the same bond as we'd fought through corsairs, goblins, Fendak, beastmen, and worse.

So, in a real way, their fears and worries had become ours.

I dreamed about her that day. I was sure she didn't actually look like the kindly nun I pictured, menaced by something that seemed to shift fluidly from a giant, deformed bat into a skeletal man with long fangs and demonic red eyes. But that was how I had her in my head, having never seen her.

I awoke from one scene in which she was ripped to pieces, only to go back to sleep and see her bitten and turned.

It was a long day, and a longer night.

* * *

It was raining again as we climbed the hill.

We'd taken the risk and left most of our rucks in the ORP, careful to memorize its location as best we could, without maps or GPS. We'd need to move fast once things got started, so we just took assault packs carrying some water, survival chow, explosives, extra ammo, and not much else.

Despite the unlikelihood that the ghostly corpse wagon was going to be making its trip to the castle in daylight, we still avoided the cobbled road, moving well around to the east before finding a narrow draw, choked with thorns and brambles that dripped with the ever-present rain, that would give us some cover and concealment on the way up.

Part of the way up, anyway. The mass of rock where the castle perched turned almost sheer after a certain distance, and after several hours of searching, we couldn't find a good way up that wouldn't put us at risk of falling off, never mind being as exposed as bugs on a plate if the vampire sent something out. It wouldn't even need to be anything unnatural. A single man could go to the top of the cliff and just start rolling rocks over and we'd all be dead.

So, despite the tactical unsoundness of it sticking in most of our craws, we had to shift to the road. Which was every bit as exposed, but at least gave us options to get out of the way if rocks started falling on our heads, as opposed to trying to free-climb a sheer cliff.

It still felt wrong, even as we approached it much like climbing a stairwell in close quarters battle. Stairwells are CQB nightmares. That switchback road was very close to just that.

We sort of leapfrogged up, with one team holding security on each switchback as the next team moved up. That way we could keep muzzles on the high ground as well as the village below, still and silent as the rain started again, a steady, depressing drizzle that soaked you to the bone without a hard, honest shower. The stones were slick underfoot, and some of them seemed loose, but fortunately the road was wide enough to make it less of an issue.

Finally, about midday, we reached the top.

The castle didn't cover the entire top of the tor. It stood at the edge, before a wide field of rocks and moss. The road wended its way through boulders and pools of stagnant water toward the gates. The clouds swirled around the castle's towers, lowering only a few dozen feet above our heads.

Thunder rumbled somewhere, and more than a few of us flinched a bit and got low among the boulders as we examined our objective.

If we were expecting some gothic monstrosity, like you'd expect Dracula to live in, that wasn't what we found. There was no outer wall, no intricate crown of pointed spires. The castle was a brutish block of stone, about five stories tall, with windows and murder holes staring darkly like the eye sockets of a monstrous skull, starting about three stories up. There were no gates visible from where we'd come out, but after a moment I could see the beginning of stairs on the far side, one of the three that didn't face the sheer cliff.

Getting in there was going to be interesting, if it was being defended from inside.

We had spread out into a rough wedge, with three teams facing the castle and the fourth watching down the road, the way we'd come. Bailey had drawn the short straw on that duty. But he and his team turned toward the castle as we started to carefully pick our way through the stones and boulders, weapons up and scanning, looking for the daylight guardians that the Tuacha had warned us about.

That field was a lot wider than it looked. It was treacherous, too, with deep holes sunk into the rock that you couldn't see until you almost put a boot down and snapped an ankle. There wasn't a level spot on that field aside from the road. But we really didn't want to go traipsing up to a vampire's front porch on the road.

Soon enough, though, just as before, we didn't have much choice. Baldinus put a foot wrong and went down, breaking his nose on a rock. Herrera got his foot caught, and we had to free him carefully to keep from breaking his ankle, which took far too long while the rest of the platoon held security and watched the curtains of rain and the swirling mist.

That entire time, the castle remained still, the windows dark and empty. The entire place seemed dead and abandoned, except for the creepy sense of watchfulness that lay over all of it. There was *something* in that castle, and it knew we were there.

The fact that it wasn't trying to drive us away only made it creepier.

While he clearly didn't like it, Gunny ordered us all back onto the road. We formed up in a column, alternating to either side of the road, and wended our way toward the stairs and the gate.

I'd started to see more of the steps as we'd moved closer. There was a single, narrow stairway leading up the side of the castle, or keep, just wide enough for only one man to go up at a time. That made sense from a defensive point of view. If you're holding the gate against men with swords and axes, that means you've only got one attacker to deal with at a time.

Against a Recon platoon with rifles, machineguns, and thumpers, things get a little more complicated.

While we'd made better time on the road, once Gurke's team reached the base of the steps, I pushed out into the rocks with my team and carefully clambered over ridges and boulders, trying to avoid the holes, cracks, and scummy ponds that were almost invariably deeper than they looked, until we had a good shot at the arched gateway and the windows above it. We settled in and covered the rest of the platoon as they started up the steps.

The gate was open, I noticed. Given the state of the rest of the castle, I'd almost expected the gate itself to be gone, rotted away by the rain and the years. After all, if a vampire is as powerful and fear-inspiring as the Tuacha suggested, why would one really need a physical barrier? Sure, there's daylight, but that's what they've got their daylight guardians for, right?

That bothered me, though. We hadn't seen any such guardians. Nothing and no one on the road, nothing on watch on the roof, nothing peering through the windows or murder holes. The gateway itself was an empty hole in the stone wall, without motion or light coming through it.

Gurke got about halfway up the steps and tripped, sprawling on the stairs and only catching himself by grabbing the slick stone with one gloved hand, his M110 held muzzle up, still roughly trained on the gateway. I guessed, from the looks of that stairway, the steps weren't all the same height. That might have been because of their age, or it might have been deliberate. One more obstacle to slow an attacker trying to get to the gate.

Gurke and Herrera finally reached the top, though there wasn't room for both. Herrera had to stay a couple of steps below. Gurke also didn't have a lot of space to clear the doorway from the outside, either. He still did the best he could with the considerably longer M110. We were used to doing CQB with M4s, and hadn't trained a lot with the bigger 7.62 rifles. So, his entry was a little awkward.

Herrera followed as quickly as he could, disappearing into the dark inside.

No gunfire, no screaming. Nothing. Chambers and Franks followed, while the Tuacha mounted the stairs.

"Conor, stay on overwatch for the moment." Gunny wasn't yelling, but his voice carried. He was right behind Cairbre.

"Oh, shit." Farrar sounded about as close to panic as I'd ever heard him. "Conor…"

I tore my gaze and my muzzle away from the castle gate. It didn't take long to see what had Farrar leaning into his machinegun, his finger already resting on the trigger.

All around the edge of the field at the top of the tor, massive black dogs, so black that they seemed more silhouettes than three-dimensional animals, with fiery red eyes, had climbed up onto the rocks. They seemed to have come out of thin air—or else they'd clambered straight up the sheer cliffs on all sides.

With low, earth-shaking growls, the creatures padded toward us.

CHAPTER 31

FARRAR didn't wait for me to tell him but opened fire in a moment, the Mk 48 spitting flame with a staccato roar, reaching out through the gloom at the nearest black dog with a stream of red tracers.

The bullets smacked into the beast without slowing it down, let alone dropping it. The deep growl got louder, and that dog opened its maw, showing glistening fangs dripping with what looked like smoking tar.

Santos lobbed a 40mm grenade at another one. The "egg" went off with a *krump* at the creature's feet, but it walked through the ugly black cloud of smoke, dirt, and frag as if it wasn't even there. "Conor! We can't touch these things!"

"Fall back to the steps!" Bearrac beat Mathghaman to the call, his rifle thundering as he took an equally fruitless shot at yet another of the sepulchral beasts. Even the elegant Tuacha rifles weren't doing anything.

"Cease fire and go!" That kind of went against the grain. We'd all trained to break contact by fire and maneuver. But the whole point of the fire was to suppress or kill the pursuing enemy, and if we weren't even going to scratch these things, then it made no sense to waste the ammo. We might need it later.

So, as hard as it was to force ourselves to do it, we turned and ran, scrambling over the rocks toward the steps.

"Ah, shit!" I was halfway over a boulder when I heard Rodeffer yell. Looking back, I saw that he'd slipped, and his leg was pinned in a crack in the rocks, as one of the big black dogs leered and padded closer.

"Don't let them touch you!" Mathghaman had leaped off the stairs and was coming closer, his sword in his hand and his rifle slung at his back. I wondered if my blessed sword might hurt these things, but right then it was more important to get Rodeffer loose and away from that snarling apparition that was getting closer with every languid step.

They didn't seem to be in a hurry, just slowly sauntering toward us, growling, tightening the noose bit by bit. It's hard to explain how you can see an expression in a ghost dog's glowing red eyes, but they seemed to be enjoying every moment of fear and terror.

Mathghaman was moving a lot faster than I was, leaping from rock to rock with each stride, while I had to scramble over each boulder. I *might* have been able to mimic his performance, but I'd probably slip and break my neck.

We reached Rodeffer at the same time. Santos and Farrar had closed in to join him, both still pointing their weapons at the oncoming monsters, though that wasn't going to do any of us much good.

Mathghaman looked down at where Rodeffer's boot was pinched between a boulder and the solid rock beneath it. He grimaced behind his mustache, then simply grasped the boulder and heaved.

It didn't move at first. Every muscle fiber, every vein in his arms and neck stood out as he strained to haul the stone off Rodeffer's leg. I threw my shoulder against it from the other side, and it rocked, ever so slightly.

That deep, vibrating growl rumbled closer, laden with sadistic anticipation.

Tucking my legs, I braced my boots against the bedrock and pushed with every fiber of my being, while Mathghaman pulled. The boulder shifted, and Rodeffer choked off a scream. Then it gave way and rolled off him, and he pulled his bruised leg out.

"Go!" Mathghaman turned to face the oncoming horror, putting up a sign of rejection as he murmured another invocation in that ancient tongue.

I caught a glimpse of the creature's reaction when I grabbed Rodeffer by his pack strap and started pulling him toward the steps. It actually slowed, its eyes squinting almost painfully while it turned its face aside from Mathghaman.

Then we were up on the road and running for the stairs, Mathghaman right behind us. Bearrac was at the top, bellowing in that same ancient language, though it only seemed to be slowing those things down.

I got to experience just how uneven those steps were as we tried to run up toward the gate. No two steps were exactly the same height or depth, and several were asynchronous enough that it was almost impossible not to trip on them. That stair had either been built by a defensive genius or the laziest architect who ever lived.

Given some of the stairways I'd climbed in the Middle East, in another life, on another world, the latter was definitely a possibility.

But we reached the top, even as the closest of the dark hounds reached the base of the stairs, putting one massive paw up on the first step. It had been hard to gauge their size before, but that paw was the size of a dinner plate. These things looked like dogs, but they were as big as grizzly bears.

"Inside!" Bearrac had to duck through the gateway as he shouted. There wasn't enough room on the landing to get past him. So we followed him through, spreading out into the gatehouse as best we could, weapons trained on the gateway itself, even though they wouldn't do much good. Sometimes you just have to do what you trained to do, if only to keep hold of your own sanity.

For a moment, I could just see the lowering clouds and the edge of the rocky field through the gateway. The spectral dogs had closed to where they were out of sight from the gate.

Then the gate slammed shut.

For a moment, the gatehouse went completely black. I cursed quietly as I reached up for my PVS-15s, thankful that we'd decided to wear them on our helmets, just in case it was dark on the objective. But before I could lower them, the sconces along the wall flared to life.

Everyone froze. At least I could see that my whole team, plus Mathghaman, had made it inside. But how had those sconces—which appeared to be regular candles in iron fixtures—just lit themselves?

And what had slammed that gate? It wasn't a portcullis or other falling gate. It was a thick, metal-bound, wooden door. That had apparently swung itself shut with a *boom*. And I couldn't see any machinery that might have done it.

Given where we were, I probably shouldn't have been surprised that weird stuff was already happening, but it creeped me out that much more.

"Uh, guys?" Gurke sounded even more spooked than I felt.

Without every entirely taking our eyes off that door, we turned toward the main room off the gatehouse. Flickering, golden firelight spilled out through the door, warm and inviting. Too inviting in that place. I was immediately paranoid as all hell.

A short, narrow passage, lined with dark, empty alcoves, led into that room. I could only imagine that the alcoves were for more defenders, in case an attacker forced the gate. Unlike the gatehouse and the main room beyond, there were no candles there, making the alcoves look like endless black chasms in the stone walls.

Coming out into the main room, we were confronted with a sight that really didn't look like it belonged in the kingdom of the dead.

Three big trestle tables had been set end-to-end in a U-shape, with ancient-looking chairs, carved from wood and with cushions on their seats, set around the outside. A fire roared and crackled in the fireplace against one wall, that probably was linked into a chimney that went the full height of the castle.

Red, woven cloths lay across the tabletops, matching the cushions on the chairs. Candlesticks held brightly burning tapers, and silver and gold dishes were laid out beneath them, laden with food and drink. It was a feast fit for a king, and I have to admit, after leagues upon leagues and days and weeks on field chow—even Tuacha travel rations—it looked awfully inviting.

"Nobody touch anything." Gunny wasn't taking chances. And with good reason. There was no way that the dead would have any use for any of this, and the fact that everything had lit up as soon as we'd entered was suspicious as hell.

This thing wasn't even trying that hard. This was straight out of every Hammer horror movie I'd ever seen.

Santos was clearly thinking along similar lines. "Not just no, but *hell* no. I've seen this movie before. I know what happens next."

Mathghaman traded a glance with Bearrac, and stepped into the middle of the room, at the opening between the tables, looking around with narrowed eyes. "Santos is right."

"What?" Gunny looked over at him sharply, sensing that there was something more going on.

Mathghaman nodded thoughtfully as he looked carefully around the room at the various bait laid out. "Vampires are subtle creatures. Yet this is a trap for a simpleton." His eyes narrowed. "Vampires wield powerful sorcery, and I would think that this would only be window dressing for a powerful spell of suggestion."

"So, why is it not?" Bearrac was fingering his own weapon as he scanned the shadows beyond the candlelight and firelight.

"That is the question, isn't it?" Mathghaman asked darkly. "Be on your guard."

For a long moment, the only sound was the crackle of the fire and the faint rumble of thunder outside. Eyes searched the darkness beyond the wavering light, waiting for the next wave of monsters to appear.

Nothing did. The feast remained, steaming faintly on the tables, filling the room with a far more appetizing smell than I'd encountered since leaving the Isle of Riamog. Yet it wasn't enough to actually tempt any of us. Not after what we'd seen.

"We've still got to clear this place." Gunny looked up at the ceiling. "Mathghaman, how many floors above us do you figure there are?"

"Two, possibly three." Mathghaman pointed toward the corner. "There is a staircase there." He didn't advise caution. He didn't need to. Stairways are nightmares, remember? And that's without vampires and giant black ghost dogs and the walking dead in the mix.

My team was actually closest, and Santos took lead, pulling his rifle back under his arm as he approached the narrow door leading into the stairwell that went up the corner of the keep. He leaned back as he carefully cleared the entryway and the landing, then brought the weapon up to his shoulder, aiming up as Farrar stepped in behind him, pointing his Mk 48 down the stairwell below, where the creaking wood stairs vanished into blackness.

I stepped in behind Santos and gave his shoulder a squeeze, just before dropping my own weapon over his shoulder and putting two muzzles on the upward sweep of the steps.

I just hoped that anything that popped out died when we shot it. Even if it meant it died *again*.

After all, we hadn't actually fought the undead yet, aside from that bear-thing that the demon tree in Lost Colcand had brought back. We didn't know if it was like *Dawn of the Dead*, where you could just shoot 'em in the head and be done with it, or if it was more like *Evil Dead*, and we'd have to carve them up into chunks so they couldn't move under their own power anymore.

I was really, really hoping for the former. But after that fight in Lost Colcand, I wasn't sure I wasn't about to be terribly disappointed.

Step by creaking step, we mounted the stairs toward the next floor. The ancient wooden beams stood out amid the dripping stone, and when we came to the open door, Santos covered it while I covered up the steps, until I got close enough to take the door while he switched to high security.

With Rodeffer, Synar, and Bailey on my heels, I made entry.

I found myself in a narrow hallway that seemed to go around the outside wall of the keep. Two doors led into rooms on the inside, and I stepped carefully toward the first, while Rodeffer took security around the corner.

The door stood open. In fact, as I got closer, I was pretty sure that any door that had stood in that entry was long gone. The floorboards groaned under my every step, and thunder rumbled outside again, almost immediately after the flash that barely made it through the narrow exterior window on the outer wall.

I paused just long enough for Synar to take the long hallway, covering the next door and the far corner, while Bailey stepped in behind me. We went in almost at the same time, his muzzle dropping past my ear just before he darted to cover the corner that I'd just turned my back to as I cleared mine.

The room had been a bedroom, once upon a time. At least, I thought so. Every bit of furniture was rotting and crumbling. Cobwebs and mold covered everything.

Including the corpse on the bed.

No, it wasn't a corpse. Not anymore. A few shreds of flesh still clung to the bones and the skull, but not enough to call the bones a "corpse."

I still didn't want to turn my back on it. I covered it with my rifle as we swept the rest of the room.

Nothing. No movement, no vampire rising out of the shadows or hanging from the ceiling. No Sister Sebeal.

Unless...

I hoped sincerely that those weren't her bones on the bed, but I didn't think it had been long enough.

It's hard to leave a room without turning your back on the inside of the room. But Bailey and I somehow managed it. "Coming out." Bailey led the way, making sure he wasn't about to get jumped in the hallway before turning back to cover my back as I came out. I think both of us were half expecting that skeleton to get up and come after us. After all, we'd watched the dead standing in a meeting just two nights before.

That particular dead body stayed dead, though. At least, for the moment.

Gunny came out of the next room with Conall and Eoghain. "Floor's clear. Let's head up."

By the luck of the draw, Bailey and I were closest to the stairs again. We entered, finding Santos and Farrar still positioned to cover up and down the stairwell. I bumped Santos, and we headed for the top floor.

This time Santos went first, though I was half a step behind him. We swept into a darkened room, only to be nearly blinded as the vampire pulled his little self-lighting fire and candles trick.

Only this time, he was there to greet us.

CHAPTER 32

THE Fohorimans in the north had all looked inhuman, in some way, shape, or form. Gray skin, too many teeth, red eyes, things like that. This vampire, however, didn't. He looked like the picture of an aristocrat, or at least some sort of Eastern one, wearing a long, red, silk robe with deep sleeves and golden embroidered slippers. His hair was white and long, cascading over his shoulders, and he wore a small, pointed, white beard. High cheekbones and an aquiline nose framed deep-set, coal-black eyes.

He wasn't even as pale as I'd expected. I'd gotten used to the corpse-pale vampire image, but this guy looked perfectly human, perfectly alive. He smiled a little as he watched us make entry, leaning sideways in the massive chair with the carved dragon heads on either side, his chin resting on his fist.

Of course, if he'd had some sort of soliloquy in mind, the fact that it was Marines making entry kind of ruined his grand plan.

Now, we'd only ever trained to shoot on "Hostile Act, Hostile Intent." By the book, the richly dressed man sitting languidly in a chair big enough to be considered a throne wasn't doing anything hostile.

But after long enough in this place, I think we were developing an instinctive sense for the monsters. And we knew this was a monster sitting in front of us. We didn't even have to ask Mathghaman. We just knew.

So, before he could even open his mouth to speak, we were already shooting.

The suppressors kept the muzzle blast down, but the supersonic *crack*s of the big 7.62 rounds were still earsplittingly loud in that enclosed, stone-walled space, despite the tapestries on the walls. I hadn't even given them a look, aside from just enough to make sure they weren't concealing an immediate threat. I'd spotted the vampire in his seat, seen no weapon, quickly cleared my corner, and then pivoted back and opened fire.

For a brief moment, the throne room was a storm of flying metal and crackling noise. Bullets chipped bits of ancient wood off the throne and punched smoking holes through woven upholstery.

But not one of them seemed to touch the vampire.

His face clouded and he stood abruptly. "*Enough!*"

The gunfire ceased, though not because any of us wanted to stop shooting. My rifle stopped with a *chunk* that I could feel as I got a double feed. I could only imagine that everyone else's had just malfed the same or similar way.

I let go of the M110 and grabbed my sword. Just in time, too, because he came off the dais like a whirlwind, and he was right in my face by the time I got the blade out. If I'd been a split second slower, he'd have had me by the throat.

As it was, he snatched his hand back as I got the sword out of its scabbard. I wasn't in a position to stab him or otherwise hit him with it—I'd just barely cleared the sheath and still had the pommel high, the blade across my body and just barely between him and me—but that he didn't want to touch it was obvious.

He hissed, baring a mouthful of needle teeth that looked more like an anglerfish's jaws than a movie vampire's fangs. Then he was gone, back to his throne in an eyeblink.

Standing with his arms folded, he was suddenly the picture of offended aristocracy again, his predator's fangs disguised behind his lips and his beard. "I had hoped that we could treat together, like civilized men." His voice was deep and resonant, and while he wasn't speaking English, he clearly had use of some form of the "mind speech." His meaning was much clearer than, say, Almak's.

"Yet here you come into my house as invaders and trespassers. You attack me without even so much as a word. So be it." He snarled, the inhuman fangs showing themselves again, glistening behind his lips. He pointed a suddenly too-long finger at me and the blade that I now held at the ready. "You may have brought such cursed artifacts into my home, but they will avail you nothing! She is mine, as is her charge!"

Then he was gone, vanished in a dark blur as all the candles went out. It took a second to process the fact that he'd sprouted wings and suddenly flitted through one of the narrow windows, which *should* have been too narrow for him to fit through.

"What the hell just happened?" Bailey cleared his malfunction as he asked the question, stripping the magazine out and racking the bolt several times. He must have had a double feed, too.

"The next step in his game." Bearrac had beaten Mathghaman to the answer, but Mathghaman seemed to be brooding over something. "Make no mistake, this is a game to him. Believe nothing he says. Believe none of his outrage. He has planned all of this in detail."

"So, if he's already that far ahead of us, what the hell are we going to do?" Gurke had barely made entry himself, with the rest of his team, plus Almak, still holding security on the stairs behind us. "I'm not that big on walking into a known ambush."

"He still has his limitations. He is not a god, no matter how much he might fancy himself so." Mathghaman looked over at me and indicated my sword with a nod of his head. "Likely he truly could not touch Conor's blade. It is blessed, and such things burn the likes of a vampire. Remember the ground where he stood, *outside* the chapel. The world itself groans at his step. The holy will only be worse for him. Hence why he called it 'accursed.'"

"So, he really was trying to rip my head off." I sheathed my sword and cleared my own double feed before slinging my rifle to my back and drawing the blade again. If we couldn't shoot him, there wasn't much point in toting the rifle as the primary, unless something we *could* shoot came up. "That's comforting."

"I'm sure he was." Mathghaman wasn't interested in comfort, not right then. We needed to be on the ball, and in his mind, that meant being truly prepared for the threats that we faced. "I suspect he intended to draw this out, however. It is fitting a vampire's pride and sadism." He turned back to the steps. "He likely wished to kill one of us and then flee, daring the rest of us to follow."

"And if we didn't?" Gunny asked.

Mathghaman looked over his shoulder as he stepped to the stairwell. "We would have little choice. Or do you imagine that the gate will open for anything until this is finished?"

He took the lead as we descended to clear the lower floors.

* * *

We re-cleared the floors below as we went. Particularly given the fact that we were facing something ancient and cunning enough to have laid a trap that even paranoid Recon Marines had effectively walked into, we had to expect that anything we'd already cleared had probably spawned all sorts of new horrors as soon as our backs were turned.

The floor below the throne room was just as dark, silent, and still as before. We swept each room, and I still kept a close eye on that tattered skeleton lying on the rotting bed, but it didn't move.

When we descended to the banquet hall, though, everything changed.

The room was dark, the sconces and the fireplace unlit and cold. The tables remained where they'd been, along with the benches, but the feast upon them was rotting and covered in cobwebs.

And the benches weren't unoccupied anymore.

About two dozen figures sat around the tables, stock still and ramrod straight. At first, they were little more than dark shapes in the gloom, but as they turned, almost as one, to look at us as we made entry, our IR weapon lights lit them up starkly in our PVS-15s.

At first glance, I'd thought they were animated corpses wearing crowns, but when their empty eye sockets turned toward us, I saw that wasn't the case at all.

They were human-shaped, but their heads were more like gargoyles'. None had a nose to speak of, their mouths either beaks or some other bestial snout full of teeth. The "crowns" were just horns, short and curved slightly backward.

Their flesh looked like dried clay. They had no eyeballs in their eye sockets. And as they turned and rose from their seats, their maws gaped far too wide in silent roars before they started coming over the tables and benches at us.

They were met with a crash of gunfire. No one had slowed down on the way in, and most of the platoon was now spread out in an L-shape around the room, with only Almak and Cairbre covering the main gatehouse, just in case. And Almak had only turned his back on the horned creatures because Cairbre—who hadn't shown a great deal of respect for Marine tactics before—had grabbed him by the shoulder and turned him to face the gate by main force.

Suppressors spat and bullets crisscrossed the room with a harsh crackle of supersonic shockwaves, smashing through clay-like bodies and heads at over 2700 feet per second.

Body shots didn't do much, just punching holes through and sending sprays of dust and clumps of...stuff out their backs. Headshots, on the other hand, shattered their horned skulls and sent fragments flying, leaving the rest of the bodies to fall to dust and gravel.

All of that came together in a frantic, violent few seconds. I tracked my muzzle across the room, hardly waiting for a sight picture, just dumping rounds into every pale, demonic form that was clambering over tables and benches. I saw two for sure go down to my shots, one with a bullet through the neck that shattered it and sent its head tumbling to the floorboards to shatter on a moldy rug. The other I shot through the mouth as it lunged at me, my muzzle almost all the way inside its maw as I blew chunks of it halfway across the room. Its crumbling body hit me and forced me back a step, fetching my back up against the cold stone wall.

Then the gunfire fell silent. There were no more targets.

The banquet hall was scattered with chunks of the gargoyle things. The whole place smelled of mold, burnt gunpowder, and something else, something vaguely metallic. Which wasn't the odor I would have associated with smashed crockery.

"I'm hit." Herrera's voice was low and pained.

Doc Hartsock crossed the room quickly. Herrera had slumped to the floor against the wall, clutching his guts, and Chambers and Gurke were trying to treat him. "Get out of my way." Hartsock shoved them aside as he pulled his aid bag off his back and turned on his helmet-mounted light. Then he swore.

I couldn't see what he was looking at, and he bit back the curse real quick, but I'd heard that tone before. Herrera was in a bad way.

"We need to keep moving. To stay here will only allow the next act to play out more quickly." Mathghaman wasn't unsympathetic, but he was appealing to a principle that most of us were familiar with. *The best medicine is lead downrange.* In this case, the best way to save Herrera was going to be to fight through and kill the vampire.

Somehow.

"I've got him. Go." Hartsock was already digging his bloodied hands into his aid bag, having pulled Herrera's chest rig out of the way. Herrera was starting to shake, and despite his gritted teeth, moans of pain were escaping his lips. Something fell to the floor with a slithery sound, and Hartsock swore again, as Herrera screamed in a combination of agony and near-panic.

"I'll stay with 'em." Chambers was standing over the two of them, his rifle in his own bloodstained hands.

"And if those things get back up? Or something worse comes through one of those doors?" Gurke demanded. "No, the whole team's staying."

Eyes turned to Gunny, who was thinking about it. "Fine. We need somebody to secure our exit, anyway." I could tell he wasn't convinced that was going to work in this case, but he wasn't wrong, either. And leaving Chambers alone to fight anything that came after Herrera and Hartsock by himself wasn't going to be a good call, either.

"Almak, stay with them." Gunny pointed to our corsair strap-hanger.

Hearing his name called, the younger man snapped his head around from the gatehouse. "No, I should come with you."

"You got to come along. After that, *I* decide where you fit in." Gunny was as unyielding as granite. "And while you've done okay, you're not one of us. That could be a liability down there."

"But I must see this thing destroyed! It is a point of honor! It is *why* I came!" Almak was getting heated.

"And you're helping." Gunny put up a hand. "By holding the way out." He sighed. Mathghaman hadn't said anything, but was standing with his arms crossed over the butt of his rifle, watching. "Look, kid. What's important is putting this thing down. And when it comes down to it, I know my guys will key off each other. I don't know that about you." He pointed at the floor. "So, you're staying with Gurke." He looked over at Gurke himself. "If he gives you any guff, do what you have to."

Then we were turning away from a visibly frustrated and angry Almak and heading down the stairs to the next level.

We probably should have taken him along. If only to prevent what happened next. But we wouldn't know about that until later.

With Mathghaman and the other Tuacha in the lead, we descended into the dark.

CHAPTER 33

IF we were expecting the next floor down to be only one story below, we were in for a surprise.

The stairs kept going down and down, deep into the tor. The wooden steps gave way to wet, slick stone, and we had to watch our footing even more carefully. The temperature dropped, and moisture dripped from the walls.

A strange smell got stronger as we went, as well. It was hard to describe, being somehow both rotting and coppery, metallic. It was similar to the stench of the fallen gargoyle things, but at the same time different. Worse. It seemed to catch at the back of my throat, and I felt a mounting dread, the deeper we went.

The Tuacha seemed unruffled as we went deeper, but I sort of expected that. Even Cairbre was calm and focused, though he seemed almost eager, the deeper we got.

I resolved to keep an eye on him. While the rest of us were feeling the weight of the evil down there, he seemed to be getting excited. That didn't feel right.

But we kept going, IR lights the only source of illumination on that treacherous, winding stairway twisting its way down into the dark.

The Tuacha didn't stop when they reached the next level and saw what awaited us. They made entry, their rifles up just like we did, and vanished into the faint, sickly glow on the other side of the doorway.

The rest of us flowed in after them, spreading out as we found ourselves in a massive, arched cistern, far below the castle. That vague corpse-light was everywhere, coming from no real source that I could see. We spread out on a stone lip that ran around the bottom of the cistern.

The entire bottom below that lip was filled with bones.

Not just scattered bones, either, but a mound that rose almost halfway to the ceiling, which we could barely see with IR floods. None of the skeletons appeared intact, but there were enough ribcages, spines, femurs, skulls, and all the rest that there had to be at least a small town's worth of dead bodies gone into that pile.

Then the pile started to move.

At first, it looked almost as if the pile of bones was just settling, starting to fall apart, as if it had been held in place and in shape by a delicate equilibrium that we'd disturbed when we'd entered. But then, as the cascade continued, some of the bones started to stick together, and not because they were just getting hooked on other bones.

A long, many-fingered limb, made up of dozens of leg and arm bones, held together by nothing that I could see, reached out and slammed its clawed hand down on the stone ledge, mere feet from Fennean. He didn't even flinch but kept his rifle pointed up at the mound, even as more of the abomination began to pull itself together.

Three more limbs shot out of the pile, and then the head arose.

By that time, I'd more than halfway started to expect some cluster of skulls and ribcages, befitting the horror of the thing that was taking shape. But a single, massive skull, easily three feet from jaw to crown, rose above the mass of the mound, a flickering ghost light in its huge eye sockets.

We were in trouble.

Everyone opened fire at once, the suppressed gunfire echoing painfully in the cistern, but all we really managed to do was chip the bone a little. And piss it off.

Two of those long, unnatural limbs swept the ledge with vicious blows that smacked mold and moisture off and scarred the stone itself. Only the Tuacha's preternatural quickness kept Diarmodh and Conall from being turned into red stains on the stone.

Santos let loose a 40mm egg with a *thump*. It was a good shot, hitting the skull in the forehead with a heavy *boom*, but while the massive thing reared back from the impact as frag pattered against the stone above—we were just outside of the frag radius—it didn't seem to have done much.

"Hold your fire with the 40 Mike Mike!" Gunny was clearly worried about friendly fire in that enclosed space, and I couldn't blame him. But what else were we going to do about this thing?

More blows rained down on us as the flickering lights in the place of the thing's eyes glared its hatred. Fortunately, it wasn't that fast, so we were able to stay out of the way, but we didn't have much room to maneuver.

Eventually, it was going to get lucky.

It gaped its jaw in a silent roar, not unlike the gargoyle things upstairs, and I ducked another blow like a falling axe. "Gunny! Do we really need to fight this thing? The door's still open!" I took a shot at one of those viciously glowing eyes, but I may as well have been throwing spitballs.

Almost. It did rear back as the bullet punched into the bone behind the corpse-light eye and put one massive, clawed hand up to shield the socket.

I think Gunny was about to agree with me about pulling back, though. Until a terrified, and very human, shriek arose from the far side of the cistern, behind the bony behemoth.

Mathghaman was suddenly beside me, sending another shot thundering at the other eye. He chipped bone at the edge of the socket, but the creature put up another hand to shield that eye, peering between its clawed, bone-construct fingers as it brought its other two limbs plummeting down to crack the stone beneath our feet as we leaped aside. I could feel the wind as the blow landed, never mind the *boom* as it hit.

Then it swept those two hands to either side, and smacked both of us off our feet.

I don't think I've ever been hit that hard. I was airborne for a second. It's a minor miracle that I didn't break any bones when I landed, but some of that was because I landed on Farrar. We both went sprawling, falling off the ledge and onto the pile of bones. Farrar lost the Mk 48 in the process. He hadn't had it slung, and it went flying into the mound some distance away.

Lying there stunned was about all I could do for a moment, but that moment was cut short when I realized that the bones were shifting, moving under their own power beneath me. A skeletal hand came up and grabbed my boot, then another one grabbed hold of my arm. A forest of them sprang out of the mound, and suddenly I was fighting not to get swept under. Farrar was cussing a blue streak, yelling at the top of his lungs as he bashed at them with his tomahawk, trying to fight his way to his Mk 48.

On my back, I was at a distinct disadvantage. The grasping hands were getting a better grip, and I felt the pressure dragging me down. I tried to rip my arms free at least, but I was pinioned. Two skulls, also showing that weird ghost light in their eye sockets, rose up on separate spines to either side of me like snakes. One had no lower jaw; the other was gaping a leering grin at me.

Mathghaman was fighting his way toward me, even as one of those massive, clawed hands loomed over my head, ready to strike down and end me. My mail had kept me from getting perforated by those claws when it had hit me the first time, but if that sucker came down on my head, I was done.

Diarmodh came leaping down onto the mound, his own sword in his hand, and lopped one of the leering skulls off its slithering spine. Deftly reversing his swing, he sent the second flying with a graceful stroke, and then he was reaching down for me, that blade passing alarmingly close to my arms and legs as he chopped at the hands gripping me, trying to pull me down into the pile of bones.

He hauled me up, even as Mathghaman's voice boomed out through the cistern. "Concentrate fire on its eyes!" He was bounding across the bones underfoot, even as more hands tried to reach up and trip him or grab him to drag him down into oblivion, and ducking beneath another swipe of that massive, too-supple limb of the amalgamated bones of dead men, taking a swipe of his own with his sword.

That leaf-bladed weapon had been blessed, in many ways just like mine had been. I gathered that mine was older and of greater significance and potency, but Mathghaman was King's Champion. He wasn't wielding anything that could be considered *weak*, if that's the right word when talking about blessings and curses.

The monster's arm was moving far faster than it looked, and so his counterstroke merely nicked it. Yet the effect was immediate.

Two bones, what looked like a femur and maybe part of a humerus, fell away, chipped and blackened, and the monster snatched the limb back, though it was long enough that it still seemed to be moving in slow motion.

Mathghaman reached us as Diarmodh clipped off enough of the grasping hands to haul me to my feet. "Draw your sword, Conor, and come with me. We must pierce its heart."

I looked up at the heaving mountain of bones, my heart pounding, as I slung my rifle to my back and drew my sword. "Where does something like that even keep a heart?"

"I did not say it would be easy." Without another word, he started to climb the pile, even as bullets *crack*ed overhead, slamming into the enormous skull, or else into the clawed hands held before it, trying to shield its eye sockets.

Gunny shouted, and the fire intensified. We suddenly had a bit of an opening, as the monster tightened its shield in front of its face, its other two limbs flailing dangerously, but without covering quite as much ground as all four.

Climbing that pile was miserable. Despite whatever eldritch being had made its body out of the dead bones, and the force that was binding them together, many of them rolled out from under hands and feet as we scrambled up, bouncing and tumbling down behind us, occasionally slipping out from under a boot and opening a gap into which a leg plunged. Twice, I half expected to get hauled the rest of the way down, as I dropped a leg up to the knee in the pile of bones.

Then, just below where the four bone tentacles had risen out of the mound, Mathghaman started hacking and digging.

Bones and bits of bones flew. And the thing knew what we were about.

We got hit again, though this time it slammed us down face-first into the pile. I felt a jagged edge gouge my cheek as I got the wind knocked out of me. I lay there, trying to suck wind back into my lungs, wondering why I wasn't dead, when Mathghaman heaved himself back up and turned to meet the next blow, this time with his sword held high.

The monster impaled its bony limb on the point of Mathghaman's sword. And for the first time, I heard a sound beyond the rattle and scrape of bones moving and rubbing against each other.

A deep, dry, otherworldly moan echoed across the cistern as the thing snatched the tentacle back. "Dig, Conor!" Mathghaman stood, buried to his knees in bones, and prepared to hold the thing's claws off. "Find the heart!"

So, I dug. I flung vertebrae, pelvises, whole spinal cords, ribs, jawbones, shoulder blades, and more femurs, tibias, fibulas, humeri, radii, and ulnas than I could count. I dug like a frantic dog, despite the sword in my weapon hand. Soon I'd plunged almost up to my neck in the bone pile, and still there were only more bones, as Mathghaman ducked and stabbed and chopped and blocked, trying to keep those flailing limbs of sorcerously bound bones off me.

My hands and arms ached, and still I kept digging. Gunfire still *crack*ed and thundered overhead, so the rest of the platoon was still in the fight. More cries of fear sounded thinly through the din. There was someone behind this monstrosity, someone begging for help. Possibly Sister Sebeal. I hadn't seen any sign of any other living prisoners in that place. Unless the skeleton upstairs had been one once, but unless she'd been eaten entirely, those bones had been there too long to be her.

Then I saw it.

An entire ribcage came loose in my hand, still attached to a spinal cord. In fact, there was still flesh on it, though long since withered and dried to the consistency of old shoe leather. And there it was. The monster's heart. If you could call it that.

A setting like black iron claws, bound with something like smoking barbed wire, held a blood-red gem about the size of my head. It glowed malignantly, flickering with an ugly light that shaded from red to purple as it pulsed.

"Strike it!" Mathghaman's voice seemed muffled from down in that hole in the mass of bones. I could smell grave dirt and rotting flesh, but there was something different about that gem and its dark setting. Something that stank of sulfur and that weird, metallic smell I'd caught earlier. "Stab the phylactery!"

There was something mesmerizing about the way that thing was pulsating, but fortunately, I'm not easily mesmerized. I lifted the sword, even as the bones started to close in around me, jagged points of broken ribs reaching for my throat, and jabbed it down at the gem.

If it had been an ordinary blade, like my old Bowie, I might not have done it. That thing would probably have broken the tip off my Bowie, if not shattered the blade entirely. It looked pretty hard. But I'd carved up an ice giant—or whatever that thing had been—that nothing else had been able to scratch, with that sword. So I put my back into it, both hands on the pommel, and hammered the point down onto the phylactery.

For a brief moment, I didn't think it had done anything. The tip hit the gem with a *tink*, that was somehow audible over the noise of the gunfire. The bones kept closing in, even as Mathghaman kept swinging his sword, trying to keep me unburied while also trying to fend off the increasingly brutal strikes of the flailing limbs.

Then the phylactery cracked.

I almost didn't notice it, as I was trying not to get stabbed in the neck by the bone pile healing itself. But the pulses had suddenly gotten quicker, almost frantic, like a heart beating under severe stress.

A moment later, the gem shattered.

And then the mound collapsed.

Whatever spirit or magic had been animating that mass of dead men's—and dead monsters'—remains, its departure made the entire mound tumble in on itself, almost as if it had been partially inflated. I found myself falling, pelted by bones and bits of long-dead flesh, until I hit with a jarring impact and was promptly half-buried.

Mathghaman reached down and hauled me up, bones cascading around me. We were now only a few feet above the ledge. He'd apparently kept his feet all the way down.

I looked around, my sword still in my hand. The rest of the platoon was still on their feet, mostly. It looked like

Applegate had been knocked out, but Conall was bringing him around. Applegate had never been pretty, but from the flap of skin hanging down off his cheek and the blood soaking his front, he'd be even uglier now.

All eyes turned toward where we'd heard the frightened cries, now silent.

The vampire stood in a small alcove, lit by two more candles that had appeared in sconces in the wall to either side. He was clapping. Slowly. Mockingly.

"I wondered why you were brought through the mists, across the gulf between worlds. Perhaps I begin to see. But our dance is not over yet."

The candles went out, and he was gone, with no sound but a whisper of wind.

CHAPTER 34

IT took a few minutes to sort ourselves out. We hadn't lost anyone else, though there were more than a few bruises, borderline concussions, and lacerations. The alcove where the vampire had appeared was just that, an alcove. It did not appear to lead into any passage leading anywhere.

"If this is a cistern for the castle, then where is he hiding her?" Gunny scowled around at the wreckage of the bone monster. "Shouldn't this be the bottom level?"

"Were this any normal castle, I would say yes." Mathghaman was already heading for the stairs we'd descended to the cistern in the first place. "But the steps continue down. This thing will have the entire mountain honeycombed with catacombs, traps, and torture chambers." He glanced over his shoulder, and even in the darkness I could see the grim sort of amusement in his eyes. "An ancient keep atop a mountain is not nearly grandiose enough for such a creature as this."

I glanced across at Bailey, who'd looked over at me. It's hard to make out facial expressions in the dark, past PVS-15s, but I knew him well enough to see that he was feeling the same sort of déjà vu that I was.

Back underground. Deeper and deeper beneath the citadel of our enemy. Deep into tunnels and caves filled with monsters and sorcerous traps.

We'd been there before. And we'd barely gotten out with our lives. And even then, not all of us had.

But we had a mission, and we were there because Mathghaman was our brother, and he'd committed to go into the darkness to rescue Sister Sebeal and retrieve the stolen relic. So, as he went down, deeper into the dark, we followed.

* * *

The stairs spiraled down into the dark, but after about two or three stories, a new glow began to come up from a door to one side of the stairwell. Mathghaman paused just long enough for Bearrac to touch his shoulder, and they made entry, as smoothly and quickly as if they'd been doing CQB with rifles their entire lives.

We flowed in behind them, weapons up and searching for targets. By that time, I'm pretty sure we all expected light to mean we were in for another ambush.

The stairs had stopped at that level, and we found ourselves in a sort of antechamber, once again lit by flickering candles set in iron sconces driven into the stone walls. These walls were lined with cut stones, as if we were in a castle, rather than deep underground.

There was only one other exit from the antechamber, leading into a long, high-ceilinged hall, lined with stone statues standing between square columns, lit by even more candles. An ancient rug, crimson and gold, began at the entrance to the hall and rolled out the entire length, disappearing into the candlelit gloom at the end.

Somewhere, deeper in, someone was weeping.

Mathghaman stayed in the lead, moving carefully into the hall. My team mingled with the Tuacha as we watched not only the darkened alcoves along the walls, but also the statues themselves. Anything was possible down there, and we had to expect *everything* to be dangerous.

Each statue looked like some version of the vampire himself. The clothing changed, the hair and the beard changed, but the features remained essentially the same. The entire hallway was a monument to the vampire's ego.

There was the immense pride that Mathghaman had spoken of.

We spread out along one side of the room, trying to avoid closing off anyone's field of fire, as we moved down the hall. Every step, I know I was expecting those statues to suddenly come to life and turn on us, ready to rend and tear. There were enough of them that if that happened, we were in a lot of trouble.

But none of them stirred. The candles flickered and smoked. The only sounds as we paced carefully down the hall were the rustle of our gear and clothing and the distant sound of weeping. A sound of deep and haunting despair.

At the end of the hall, we found ourselves in a great, circular room, easily as high-ceilinged as the cistern had been. Torches blazed along the walls, far brighter than the earlier candles. Flagstones lined the floor, and four more passages led off in other directions.

There was also resistance there.

I'd wondered where the vampire's undead minions had gone, though it was conceivably possible that we'd seen all of them in the village below. But now we faced easily a couple dozen corsairs and other armored warriors, holding a shield wall with spears and swords ready to fight.

And all of them were dead.

It was easy enough to see, even in the iffy light. Some had had their throats ripped out. Others had gaping holes punched in their armor, right through their vitals. Still others didn't show *quite* so obviously fatal wounds, but they were all pale, bloodless, their eyes milky and glazed, and not a single one of them seemed to be breathing.

The place stank of death.

Mathghaman didn't go charging in but stepped up and barricaded on the doorway. The rest of us followed suit, with Bailey's team and several of the Tuacha taking up rear security, just in case the statues decided to come to life—or *un*life—while our backs were turned.

I had moved up as Mathghaman halted, and I crossed the hallway to barricade on the opposite side of the massive, arched door. I'd kept my rifle leveled as I moved, even though I was pretty sure that it wouldn't do much against these things, not after that bear-monster had gotten back up in Lost Colcand. From what I'd seen, to kill an undead, you pretty much had to take it apart, and while the 7.62 M110 packed quite a bit more punch than our M4s had, it still wasn't going to blast these things to pieces. Especially if it had to punch through armor to do it.

But I didn't think we were going to be in a good spot to fight these things hand to hand. Not in those numbers.

As I braced my rifle against the column at the side of the doorway, I got ready to fight, knowing that this was probably going to quickly turn into a break contact drill. And one that wasn't going to slow the enemy down much with just gunfire.

But Gunny had seen what we were up against, and had already made his own plans.

"Get clear of the door." He didn't shout. He didn't need to, down there. Not right then. But when I glanced over my shoulder, even as I moved—waiting around to wonder why Gunny had said to do something usually wasn't a great idea—I saw him lifting that thumper of his. He must still have had a few grenades for it.

I rolled out of the doorway, flattened my back against the cold stone, and dug one of my last two frags out of my chest rig. I pulled the pin as Gunny let fly with a *thunk*, followed a moment later by Santos and Bailey as they saw what Gunny was doing and hurried to follow suit. I didn't bother to cook the grenade but underhanded it into the big circular chamber a split second before the three 40mm grenades went off with a thunderous triple *boom*, sending black smoke and frag boiling through the big chamber, shrapnel pattering off the stone walls. My frag went off a moment later, adding its own *boom* to the echoes.

None of the undead had made a sound.

Letting my rifle hang and drawing my sword, I swung out into the doorway again once the frag had stopped flying. It took a second to see through the still-drifting smoke.

The explosives had done a number on bodies that were already starting to decompose. The front ranks had been blasted to pieces by direct hits, the shockwaves having ripped quite a few of the walking corpses limb from limb. My frag had contributed, though it was hard to see exactly where in the pile of torn, dead flesh and shattered bone.

That barrage of explosives and flying metal, however, had still left about half the force of undead monstrosities shambling toward us.

"Claymore up!"

That should do it.

While it was dangerous, we'd taken a page out of the old MACV-SOG book, and since Lost Colcand, we'd been carrying our remaining claymores already primed and ready to go. All we had to do was plant them, unspool the wire, and mash the clacker. So, it only took a couple of seconds for Baldinus to slam the directional mine down and bend the legs to hold it upright as best he could on the stone floor, and then we were falling back, quickly dashing toward the antechamber and taking cover in the alcoves and behind the pillars.

Nobody hid behind any of the statues. Probably for good reason.

The shambling dead were moving almost as fast. Once they'd started moving, they weren't the shambling zombies we might have hoped, but were advancing at a trot, shields held up and weapons leveled. There were only about half of their number left, but that would still be enough to make it a really bad day. Or night. Whichever it was.

They were already in the doorway when Baldinus hit the clacker three times.

That's the way we always trained to use them, just because you couldn't always rely on the electric ignition system. But in this case, the clacker was from the *Coira Ansec*, and it worked flawlessly with the first squeeze.

The overpressure in that enclosed hall, as towering as the ceiling was above us, was excruciating. It felt like getting hit by that massive bone construct in the cistern above all over again, and my head was splitting by the time the black cloud of dust and smoke dispersed.

Only two of them were still on their feet. Several more had been knocked down by the blast and the wave of ball bearings, but they weren't moving that well, as the claymore had done some considerable damage.

Blades were drawn as we advanced on them, Marine shoulder to shoulder with Tuacha, to finish the job.

* * *

Mathghaman and Fennean had dispatched the two still standing in an eyeblink, their swords moving almost too fast for the eye to track. Heads rolled, though they were quickly replaced by what looked like dark, oily smoke. But with a handful of fast, brutal swings, both bodies quickly lost their legs and then their arms.

Meanwhile, the rest of us were doing much the same to the mangled remnants of other undead that were still moving. I saw the same dark clouds writhing around the severed limbs and half-blasted away head of the one I stood over, until I'd hacked enough of it away with my sword that the darkness suddenly fled.

I imagined I heard a faint, despairing, hate-filled wail as the shadow disappeared. Or maybe I didn't imagine it. We were on this side of the mists, after all.

"Impressive." The vampire's voice echoed grandly through the massive chamber, as if he were standing there with a megaphone, though he was nowhere to be seen. "I begin to see why someone drew you through the mists. Your power is considerable. Most men would have fled screaming from my bodyguard rather than fight them, let alone destroy them so thoroughly." The mellifluous voice grew slightly cross. "I will have to find my servants new vessels, of course. Perhaps you will suffice, once I have learned what I wish to know from your flailings." His voice lowered, becoming even more menacing. "Rest assured, my interest lies with the power behind your coming. You are formidable, but your little magic tricks are of little consequence in the long run. Particularly as your spell components, or whatever they are, get used up." A vile laugh that put my hackles all the way up reverberated through the stone passages. "Oh, yes, I noticed that. What will you do when the power of your weapons no longer suffices? You may have wreaked greater destruction than any other ill-advised adventurer who has invaded my house over the centuries, but your power is not unlimited. Even now, I can smell the blood of one of your fellows. I can taste his fear as his life ebbs. He is nearly mine already. So shall you all be.

"So shall *she* be."

T I felt a surge of revulsion at those words, a desire to see this thing utterly destroyed. It was a better reaction than fear and terror, but at the same time, even as I gritted my teeth and clenched my fingers around my weapons, I glanced at Mathghaman.

The King's Champion, the man who had led us here on King Caedmon's request, who clearly had some personal connection with Sister Sebeal, no matter how quiet he had been about it, stood, calm and collected, and checked his weapons, wiping the rotting gore of the undead off his blade. Then he sheathed the sword, took up his rifle again, and looked around at us.

"Whatever this thing says, do not listen. Stop your ears if its words of despair and defeat have begun to seep into your souls. Pray that Tigharn preserves Herrera and then put his fate from your minds." He hefted his rifle in one hand, muzzle up, as he met each man's eyes in turn, even of his own team. "It will continue to try to kill our bodies, but that is only part of what it wants. A vampire does not only kill. It wishes to corrupt, *before* it kills. It wants to draw out suffering and despair. It feeds on them as surely as it feeds on blood.

"It will only get more difficult from here. For now, it will attack our minds as much as our lives. Be ready."

His jaw set, Mathghaman turned toward the nearest passage.

The rest of us followed, muzzles up to cover every opening, every entryway. Because we'd come that far. What else were we going to do?

CHAPTER 35

THE next passage was a dead end. Some shift in the tor long before had brought the ceiling down in a cascade of broken rock that we wouldn't move in a decade without explosives.

And we weren't exactly willing to use what we had left on just rock.

Retracing our steps, expecting some new nightmare to come out of the shadows at any moment, we made our way back to the central chamber.

Only to find it utterly changed.

The other entrances were all shut, blocked by heavy, iron-bound wooden doors, not unlike the main gate above. A massive fire burned in a fireplace at the center of the room, and the woolgathering part of my mind wondered where the smoke was going, since we were easily a couple hundred feet underground.

More torches blazed on the walls, between tapestries that hung limply, the better to display the richly embroidered scenes of violence, torture, and depravity that glittered in gold and silk thread.

The room was packed with richly clad and richly armored aristocracy, all gathered in a great semicircle around a massive throne that made the one on the top floor of the castle look puny. A pair of enormous dragons, seemingly carved from black stone, with rubies set in their eye sockets, upheld the upholstered seat where the vampire lounged, a golden goblet set with onyx stones in one pale hand.

At the feet of the dais stood a stone altar with human skulls holding black candles at either corner. Dark stains that could only be blood covered the slab of stone that formed the altar top.

Sister Sebeal stood at the foot of the altar, held by two corsairs, massive bruisers in padded aketons, carrying spears and vicious-looking axes. A phalanx of more of them stood around the altar, spears at the ready.

Sister Sebeal was a young woman, or at least so she appeared. I'd learned that age was hard to judge with the Tuacha, and she was clearly a Tuacha, despite the bedraggled and stained appearance of her blue robes and white veil. Her heart-shaped face, bruised and smudged, was still calm, her eyes bright as she looked across the mass of men at Mathghaman, her head held high.

"You came for her, did you not?" The vampire gestured at Sister Sebeal with his goblet. "So, since I am magnanimous, I shall let you see her one last time." He smiled, showing those translucent, anglerfish teeth again. They were stained red. I wondered how many of those corsairs had come south with him, and how many were left.

He stood. "You see, my friends, that we have new guests!" He spread his hands expansively, a few drops of crimson splashing from the goblet. "While they have graciously accepted my invitation to our ceremony, their behavior since arriving has been atrocious. They have comported themselves as defilers and invaders, striking down my servants and even daring to destroy my father's own phylactery." The inherent horror in that statement took a second to sink in. "What shall we do with such boorish guests?" He glared down at us even as he smiled that predatory, nightmare smile. "What *shall* we do?"

The great crowd of aristocrats turned toward us then. And I saw what they really were.

Drawn, desiccated, dead faces glared at us from beneath helms and headdresses. Glowing red smoke drifted in their eye sockets in place of physical eyes. "Bring your servants, my kinsmen!" the vampire roared. "Teach them the folly of their defiance!"

More skeletal hands were raised, and a hissing, susurrating chorus went up. As it did, the three passages we hadn't explored opened, and an army of skeletons poured out, bound together by dark, misty shadows and bearing ancient, rusting weapons and shields.

Fortunately, nobody just stared. "Sister Sebeal! Get down if you can!" Gunny bellowed, just before three thumpers, two M203s and Santos's M79, went off with a series of *thunk*s, sending their 40mm projectiles sailing toward the newly opened passages.

In the meantime, the rest of us opened up on the richly appointed wights, if only to do some damage before it got to hand-to-hand.

I shot one through its gaping, silently roaring mouth, which trailed more of the glowing red smoke, and to my surprise, it actually worked. The helm was blown off as the skull shattered, and with an earsplitting shriek that seemed somehow louder than the suppressed but still supersonic gunshot itself, the red mist flowed out of the dead thing before plunging into the floor and disappearing. The body collapsed the floor like a puppet with its strings cut.

Farrar opened up with his Mk 48, keeping his fire away from the altar and Sister Sebeal but otherwise raking the crowd of wights and the skeletons that were still pouring through the openings behind them. Body shots did nothing, but when bullets struck and shattered skulls, more of that glowing red smoke poured out and descended into the floor with more of those harrowing screams.

Another wight, backed up by a dozen skeletons and armored from head to toe in engraved, rectangular plates, sewed together with iron rings, lunged for me. I had to back up a step, and Mozambiqued the undead by instinct, dumping a hammer pair into its chest as I walked my sights up to its head. The third round was a little low, but still blew through its mouth, gaping hellfire behind a mask of mail, and it collapsed, the spirit howling its despair and rage as it descended again.

The skeletons it had commanded fell to pieces as it hit the floor.

"Concentrate on the wights! If they go down, the skeletons go down!" I shifted aim as I shouted, stroking the trigger as my red dot passed another snarling wight's face, this one in a panoply of overlapping bronze plates. My first shot was a little too fast, blowing a chunk out of its cheek and what had once been an ear, but my follow up blasted through a smoking eye socket, and it dropped with a screech.

We had spread out as we'd come through the entryway, but now we had our backs to the wall, and we had attackers on both flanks as more of the skeletons poured across the floor, rattling slightly but making no other sound.

It was a weird fight. The only sounds were the echoing crackle of suppressed gunfire and the screams, howls, and shrieks of the damned, but those were deafening enough. Long-dead bodies and ancient weapons clattered to the stone floor, the sounds hardly noticeable in the din.

We were killing them faster than they could close the distance, especially with the last few thumper rounds and the two Mk 48s, but as soon as we started to lock back on empty mags, that was going to change.

Even before that. One of the wights darted in as a massive specimen in what looked like a suit of armor out of *Excalibur* fell, and seized Synar by the throat.

He froze immediately, his arms going limp and his rifle falling to hang on its sling as it slipped from nerveless fingers. His eyes rolled back in his head as the wight lifted him, his feet coming off the floor.

Then Bailey pivoted and put a bullet through the wight's skull at point-blank range before twisting back to his right and dropping yet another, wearing armor of overlapping circular plates engraved with snakes, with a round right through the T-box.

Synar fell with the wight and lay on the floor like a dead man. But none of us could stop fighting to check him out.

The best medicine is lead downrange.

I shot two more wights and two more skeletons that got too close before my bolt locked back on an empty mag. There was no time to reload. I let the weapon hang and went for my sword.

I was a little surprised by what happened next.

The wight in front of me, armored like a cataphract, suddenly stopped dead at the sight of that blade, and sent up a keening wail that just about split my eardrums, Peltors or no.

I didn't wait around to try to figure out why. I just lunged forward, much like Mathghaman had taught me during the short weeks we'd had on the Isle of Riamog before the corsair raid, and jabbed the blade through its eye.

There was no scream, no howling dive by the red smoke into the stones of the floor this time. The wight simply collapsed.

And a couple dozen skeletons behind it collapsed into clattering, disconnected bones at the same moment.

I suddenly found myself in a bubble as the undead decided they didn't want to get too close to the sword in my hand. And that meant I had a brief moment to take in what was happening.

Gunfire still crackled and roared, suppressed or not, the echoes reverberating off the millions of tons of stone all around us. The screams and howls just seemed to get louder. But I suddenly had an opening, and that was probably the only reason that I saw the fight around the altar.

The corsairs had turned on each other. Half a dozen of them were clustered around Sister Sebeal, their weapons out, fending off the rest of their fellows while the vampire screamed his hatred and demanded that they all be slaughtered so she could be sacrificed.

She, however, stood tall, her head high, a simple shepherd's staff in her hands, facing the vampire without a bit of fear anywhere in her body language. I couldn't see her face, but even from across the room, I could see the peace in her. She wasn't afraid, even if she was about to be torn limb from limb.

Then she started to advance on the vampire.

The corsairs who had turned into her bodyguard advanced with her, though none of them were showing nearly the fearlessness she was. They edged out to the sides, trying to avoid the vampire, which only put her directly in front of him.

But he didn't attack her. In fact, while he held his ground, baring his mouthful of fangs, he didn't advance at all. His wings, cloudy things that almost didn't seem to be there, unfurled from his back as he hissed at her.

"Mathghaman!" Her voice rang out clearly over the noise of battle. "I need you!"

I looked around, having lost track of exactly where Mathghaman was in all this chaos, to see him hemmed in by wights and skeletons as the vampire waved his suddenly claw-like hand toward the King's Champion. Despite Mathghaman's own blessed sword having come hissing out of its scabbard as his magazine went empty, they were still trying to fight, though they hemmed him in with spears rather than trying to close to tear at him with their bony hands.

But I had an opening.

"Moving!" Training had taken over. If we left a point of domination in the house, we always called it out, just to make sure we didn't get shot by one of our own guys. And I was leaving my position, all right. Cutting right across half the platoon's line of fire.

I hoped this worked.

I lopped off a wight's head as it tried to grapple Santos while he shot down two more skeletons that had gotten too close. Once again, it simply dropped, and then I was past, even as Santos fell in beside me, his bolt locked back, drawing his axe and swinging it into an attacking skeleton's collarbone hard enough to shear through not only the clavicle but half the ribcage.

Farrar was on my other flank, still pouring 7.62 machinegun fire into the undead horde, shattering skulls and bones with every long, staccato burst. Together, we drove through the press as the wights tried to obey their master without coming within reach of my sword.

Several of them didn't make it. One jabbed a spear at me, but I got my gloved hand inside the thrust, grabbed the haft—which felt deathly cold even through my shooter glove—and stabbed the wight through its shrunken, unarmored throat. The second came in swinging and almost took my head off, it was so quick, but I got my sword up just fast enough to deflect the blow and twist my blade just as Mathghaman had taught me, then I pivoted around the other's sword to deliver a lightning riposte that slid right into its gaping, glowing maw.

Stepping over the ruin that had been the wight's body, I continued to advance toward the altar.

The confrontation at the throne seemed to have settled down into a standoff. The bulk of the corsairs were still trying to get to Sister Sebeal, but their former comrades were doing a pretty good job of holding them off. Several of the vampire's corsairs had gone down to the undead, too, it looked like. It seemed that the skeletons weren't all that great at target discrimination.

Sister Sebeal stood at the foot of the throne, that staff held high now, pointed at the vampire. It wasn't quite touching it, but the vampire, snarling and hissing as he was, seemed either mesmerized or trapped, his back up against the throne, pressing himself hard against the stone to avoid being touched by the staff.

We drove into the ranks of the corsairs, Santos and I swinging our weapons while Farrar kept cutting down the undead at our backs with long bursts. I hamstrung one, stabbed him through the clavicle as he fell, then lopped off the head of the next one beside him as he turned and tried to stab me with his spear. Santos went to town on the one to my left, his axe biting deep into the man's un-armored neck with an audible *crunch*. Blood spurted, and more flowed as the corsairs defending Sister Sebeal went on the offensive, driving the hole we'd cut wider.

Then I was bounding up the steps at the vampire, having met the eyes of one of the corsairs for a brief moment. It wasn't much, but we exchanged a nod. We didn't know each other, we'd been enemies until only a few moments before, but right then, we were brothers. He'd watch my back. I'd do what needed to be done.

The vampire, still seemingly frozen in place by either the staff or Sister Sebeal herself, looked at me. And I made an almost fatal mistake.

I looked back into its eyes.

Now, I'd thought of the vampire as "him" for most of the time we'd been fighting our way into those stygian depths, because it had seemed much more human than the Fohorimans we'd fought in the north. But when I looked into those black pits of hell, I knew that whatever or whoever this thing had been before, there was nothing human left, despite its airs of culture and decadence. This was a creature of pure evil. It knew nothing but hunger, hatred, and a deep desire to ruin whatever it could. It was a force of destruction, an unnatural *thing* that should not have ever walked the earth.

But it was still powerful. It still had abilities I hadn't guessed at. And the worst one was that, for a moment, it let me see just how bad it really was.

I don't even want to think about what I saw in those depths. I shudder at the memory of even getting close to that thing.

My knees buckled at the sheer horror and despair of it, as those coal-black eyes seemed to swell and grow and swallow the whole world around me. I felt the darkness closing in, cold and unyielding, and knew, down to the deepest fiber of my being, that there was no hope.

But then Sister Sebeal touched my shoulder.

"Get up, Conor. Tigharn watches over you. You can do what must be done."

Her lilting voice was like the breath of spring, and for a brief moment, as the darkness fled, I thought I saw her actually glow a brilliant white. And then, because she told me to, I acted.

I lunged forward, driving the point of that sword into the vampire's midsection, just below the sternum, even as it shrieked and started to blur.

It writhed around the point, its screams of rage and agony and despair almost enough to overpower my Peltors. But it wasn't done yet. It slapped me, and I went down, almost tumbling head over heels down the dais.

But Santos had driven forward with me, and he caught me before I could fall. "Do it, Conor!" He shoved me back into the fight, as Sister Sebeal stepped aside.

I knew what I had to do. Don't ask me how. It just seemed logical.

I yanked the sword free, brought it back, and swept the vampire's head off its shoulders, the blessed blade going through its cursed flesh like a hot knife through butter.

It died without a sound, crumbling to ash in front of me.

And, in the same moment, the rest of the undead in the great chamber fell, inert, to the floor.

It was over.

Almost.

CHAPTER 36

FOR a moment, the throne room was still. The fires flickered and began to die. The tapestries on the wall started to mold and unravel.

Then the corsairs who had fought on the vampire's side went berserk.

Howling and screaming like men who had lost their minds, they attacked us with reckless abandon, even as the three of us up there with Sister Sebeal turned to join her corsair bodyguard.

Our corsairs had closed in to form a tight formation around us, spears held outward, and their former comrades threw themselves, screaming, onto their spearpoints. One took a spearhead through the throat, while another was stopped dead by another spear that didn't penetrate his breastplate, but just kept trying to shove himself forward, foaming at the mouth.

Finding ourselves behind the wall of spearmen, Santos and I had a chance to reload. We didn't have much left. Only a couple mags apiece. But it would do. Sheathing my sword, I swapped mags and sent the bolt home, then lifted my rifle past a corsair's shoulder to put a round between one of the attackers' too-wide eyes. His head snapped back, spraying blood and brains out the back of his skull as his helmet flew off, and he crashed onto his back.

But then the scrum was too close, and I had to let the rifle hang on its sling and drew my sword again, stepping forward into the slight gap between two of Sister Sebeal's bodyguards.

At almost the same time, the Tuacha waded into the brawl, freed from the press of undead, swinging their swords and axes with a ferocity only offset by their precision.

It was all over very quickly. The vampire's disciples made no attempt to surrender, asked for no quarter. And none was given. They were cut down quickly, caught between the hammer and the anvil, as those who had sided with Sister Sebeal stood their ground and the Tuacha, assisted by Gunny and Bailey's team, carved the frothing madmen to pieces.

Fortunately, unlike the undead, these guys went down when stabbed or cut in a perfectly natural and human way.

Sister Sebeal stepped forward, her hand on my shoulder, and I stepped aside for her, as Mathghaman approached, wiping the gore from his blade on a corsair's tunic. He knelt, bowing to her, as she held out her hand to him. He took it in both of his and touched it to his forehead. "Sister."

"Mathghaman. I had no doubt you would come." She looked around at us. "Though in some ways I wish that you had not. For while you have been victorious, the forces of darkness have learned from this confrontation. I fear that was the vampire's entire purpose."

"But it's dead." Bailey was watching the passages off the sides, his rifle in hand, just in case, as were most of his team. "It can't tell anybody anything anymore."

"If only that were so." There was a sadness in Sister Sebeal's voice. "But while what remained of Val Teren fancied himself a god, he was no less a slave to darker and more powerful forces. And even now, all his secrets and his knowledge are being torn from the tattered, blackened remnants of his soul." She shook her head. "There is no permanent victory here. Not yet."

"Well, with that in mind, I think we should get out of here." Gunny was looking around as the fires and torches continued to gutter and die, the rot spreading across the tapestries and the rugs. The throne behind us seemed to be aging as we spoke, even though it was falling deeper into shadow as the flames receded. "With the way everything else is falling apart, I don't want to be down here when the mountain collapses."

Sister Sebeal didn't look like she thought that was all that likely, but she simply nodded. I don't think anyone really wanted to linger in that place. The vampire and its undead minions might be gone, but there was still something deeply unsettling about it. Too much evil had happened there.

It took a moment to get sorted out. The corsairs didn't speak our language, and none of them had Almak's amulet. Sister Sebeal spoke to them in a low voice, after tending to their wounded, and the man who seemed to be their leader, a short, wiry man who nevertheless had the presence of a seasoned warrior about him, nodded his understanding, issuing his own orders to his men. They eyed us warily, but kept close to Sister Sebeal.

We had our own wounded, too. Synar was still breathing but was otherwise unresponsive. We didn't know what that wight had done to him, but Sister Sebeal had put her hand on his forehead and closed her eyes, whispering softly.

"He hovers on the edge of the dark." She drew her hand back, looking tired. "I have tried to call him back, but now he must find his way out of the shadows himself."

Bailey nodded to her appreciatively, handed Synar's rifle off to Baldinus, and hoisted Synar over his shoulders in a fireman's carry. Bailey's team was now effectively out of action. So, my team and the Tuacha had to split front and rear security, with Bailey's team and Sister Sebeal, surrounded by her bodyguard of converted corsairs, in the center.

I really wondered about that bodyguard, but that question would have to wait until we were somewhere more secure.

Figuring out just which passage would lead us back to the steps was more difficult than it should have been. It was as if something was still warped about that lair, and we had to double back twice. By then, the fires and the torches in the main hall had died completely.

Then I heard something. It was faint at first, but I'd heard it earlier, just before all hell had broken loose. Someone, somewhere down another side passage, was crying softly.

Gooseflesh rose on my arms. The death of the vampire *should* have eliminated its minions, from what we'd seen, but there was still someone or something stirring in this place. As soon as I heard it, however, Sister Sebeal raised her head, cocked to one side to listen. Then she was almost leading the way, hustling down that passage fast enough that Rodeffer had to hurry up to make sure she didn't outpace him.

With white lights on for the sake of the corsairs, we moved down the short tunnel to another round room, not unlike the cistern above, only smaller. There was a deep pit in the center of the floor.

Sister Sebeal stood at the edge of the pit, bending down toward that darkness. The sobbing was coming from the pit.

When we shone our lights down, we saw a couple dozen ragged, filthy, emaciated people, men and women both, huddled in the bottom, squinting painfully up at the light. We'd found the vampire's larder.

"We have to get them out." Sister Sebeal clearly wasn't going to brook any argument, despite how battered we all were. And the Tuacha clearly weren't going to argue, anyway.

"Who has sling ropes?" Fortunately, most of us had decided that if we were going to be fighting through a vampire's castle, ropes might have been a good idea. Only Synar hadn't brought his, and Bailey, who had set him down to check his pack, promised the unconscious man that he'd be doing many eight-count body builders for it.

It took a while to get the people out. We didn't have much in the way of clothes for them, but circling back to the main hall, we found enough of the padded aketons among the dead corsairs to fit them, if poorly. Some of them were pretty bloodstained, and a couple of the women shied away from the bloodied clothing, but Sister Sebeal spoke softly to them, and in time, they calmed down enough to get dressed.

Then, with my team in the lead and the Tuacha in the rear and on the flanks again, we turned back to the statue-lined hall. The reason we hadn't recognized it before was that all the statues had fallen, crumbled away to gravel and sand.

We paced through it, boots almost soundless on the rotting carpet, which was strewn with the statues' debris, cones of white light moving from alcove to shadow as we went.

But we finally found the stairs and headed back up. We were still on alert, weapons at the ready, scanning every opening we passed, never letting security drop, as desperately tired as we were, and as tempting as it might be to assume that with the vampire's fall—and Sister Sebeal's words concerning its fate—there was no more threat.

So, we were still ready for a fight when we reached the banquet hall where we'd left Gurke and his team. And a good thing, too.

As we got close to the doorway, Rodeffer called out, "Friendlies coming in!" The response wasn't encouraging.

"Come ahead, but watch yourselves." Gurke didn't sound too good. "Almak's still on the loose, and he's gone nuts."

We made entry quickly. Gurke, Franks, and Chambers were barricaded behind one of the tables, which had been flipped onto its side.

Doc lay nearby, a terrible wound in the back of his neck. Herrera lay not far from where he'd been wounded, obviously dead. But the gut wound hadn't been what had killed him. His body lay several feet from his head on the floor, still sluggishly leaking blood onto the ancient timbers.

"What the hell happened?" Gunny pointed toward the opposite stairwell, which was the only other way Almak could get in, if he really had gone axe-crazy.

Gurke stood up, obviously hurting. Blood soaked his side where he'd been either stabbed or shot. "Well, first Herrera died. Doc did his best, but he was bleeding out at the same time he was trying to hold his guts in. Then, well…" Gurke swallowed. He wasn't what I'd call squeamish, but as he looked down at his pointman's decapitated body, I could tell that he really didn't want to describe what had happened next. "Then he got back up. And tried to kill Doc."

When Gunny glanced at Hartsock's body, Gurke shook his head. "He didn't manage it. We took his head off first. No, that was Almak, a few minutes later." He was staring at nothing, clearly reliving the events in his head. "He was fine, then he just started screaming and turned on us, swinging his sword. He got to Doc before we could do anything." He looked down at his rifle. "I winged him, and then he ran."

I looked around at the darkened banquet hall, though more light was starting to filter through the outside windows, as the permanent storm above the castle began to disperse. "Which stairwell did he go into?"

"Do we need to hunt him down, or should we just get out of here?" Bailey wasn't usually the one who wondered if we really should kill anyone. But we *were* pretty beat up. And we had a long way to go to get back to the coast, where we *hoped* Nachdainn could pick us up.

But it was precisely because we were so beat up that I knew we had to deal with him. I didn't see Almak's bow anywhere, which meant we could get an arrow in the back as soon as we set foot outside, if he was watching for us.

"Just tell me where he went." I looked Gurke in the eye. He nodded slightly, tight-lipped, and pointed toward the far staircase. Nodding to Santos and Rodeffer, I started toward the stairs. Farrar started to join us, but I waved him back. That Mk 48 wasn't going to be a great choice in the close quarters of the stairwell.

As soon as we started into the stairwell, I could hear Almak. He was groaning and gibbering, occasionally screaming.

And he was above us. Either in the throne room or on the roof. With Santos covering down the stairs, just in case, Rodeffer and I headed up.

We had to clear the throne room at the top first. And that was where we found him.

Gurke had winged him, alright. More than that. He had sagged into the vampire's throne, his sword held loosely in one hand, while the other tried to staunch the blood flowing from his upper chest. More red spittle had spilled into his beard. A wan ray of sunlight spilled in from one of the windows and across the throne, lighting the blood a bright crimson. He didn't have long, from the looks of it.

He turned to look at us as we moved around the throne, muzzles trained on him. I didn't see the fevered vacancy in his eyes that I'd seen in the others down below. He wasn't quite all there, but he wasn't as berserk as the others.

"So, what was the deal, Almak?" I lowered my rifle. "Lead us to the vampire so it could have its way with us? Or did it have its hand up your ass the whole time, and when it went down, you lost your mind?"

He coughed and spat blood again. He really was fading fast. "To let servants of...the Over Sea Men...take the triumph...of the true gods..." Bloody froth bubbled from his mouth. Gurke had gotten him in the lung.

I eyed him coldly. "Should have known. You couldn't take the win for what it was." I stepped in and took the sword away from him, even as he tried to bring it up to stab me. I tossed it with a clatter into the far end of the room. "Or did your 'god' tell you to kill us?"

He looked up at me, a mix of fear and hate in his eyes. "You will learn. You will…learn. They will come…for you. The powers behind you…cannot protect you…forever."

Then he was gone.

I looked down at his corpse only for a moment. What had he meant by all that?

We'd find out. For the moment, we needed to go.

* * *

It was slow going, with our new charges, getting down the road off the tor. There was no sign of the black dogs, though I did see some awfully big paw prints in the mud, suggesting that they hadn't been entirely sepulchral.

Weaving down the switchbacks toward the town, we kept our eye on the turf-roofed houses. The rain was easing up, though some of the vampire's prisoners were still starting to shiver. They'd been huddled together for warmth in that pit, and now they had only the aketons we'd taken off the dead corsairs and their own body heat.

Nothing moved in the village except the crows. They were cawing and croaking, and as we got lower, I saw that they were already feasting on some of the bodies lying in the streets and doorways. The undead here hadn't outlasted their master, either.

But as we reached the bottom of the long hill that stretched out to shelter the village at the base of the tor, I saw that we weren't out of the woods yet.

They'd taken serious losses to the faceless ones. But easily fifty goblins were gathered on or near the road, twitching and bouncing, clutching their crooked weapons, their toothy maws hanging open as they quivered and muttered amongst themselves.

The one standing in the middle of the road stood a little taller than the rest, with a much bigger head, topped with some animal skull. It was carrying a spear, which it stabbed toward us with a nonsensical gibber.

"The vampire is dead." Mathghaman stepped up next to me, staring the goblin down. "We have killed it." He swept his cold eyes over the mass of little monsters. "What hope do you have?"

The goblin was clearly nervous, hopping from one foot to the other, though not quite as visibly scared as the mass of them behind it. But it couldn't back down, either. It let out a screech and jumped forward, shaking its spear.

Rodeffer shot it through the chest.

It tumbled backward, spilling muddy blood from the wound, its spear clattering to the wet cobblestones. Its vacant, red eyes stared sightlessly at the clouds above, which seemed to be dispersing without the vampire holding them over its fortress.

That was the last straw for the goblins, which had followed us from corsair lands, that big-headed one apparently hoping for some revenge—or maybe just a chance to get its hands on our weapons. With panicked shrieks, they vanished into the moors, disappearing in an eyeblink.

Mathghaman put his hand on Rodeffer's shoulder. "Now we can go."

EPILOGUE

DAYS later, we neared the open grasslands of the northern marches of the Empire of Ar-Annator. We hadn't seen a living soul since we'd left the vampire's castle—or an un-living one, either, for that matter. Some deer and other wildlife—which was fortunate, since we were running low on food—but no monsters. It seemed that not all of this part of the world was haunted and infested.

Some of that might have been because of Sister Sebeal and the staff she carried, too.

She'd held it by the fire one night when Bailey had asked about it. "It was carried by Saint Nechtan over two hundred years ago. Since then, it has brought several miracles when touched. Healing, mostly."

"So, why did the vampire want it?" Gunny asked.

She looked at him somberly. "It did not want it. It wanted me."

No one asked her to elaborate. We'd gathered the subtext from what Mathghaman had said.

"What I still don't get, though, is how *they* ended up on our side." Gurke was healing, but his wound was still making him grumpy, and the look he shot the corsairs who had clustered around their own fire, still not far from Sister Sebeal, wasn't exactly friendly. "And why we're trusting them after the way Almak turned out."

Sister Sebeal only smiled sadly. "I did not know him, but from what Mathghaman has told me, he set out with his own darkness in his heart." She glanced at our new friends, who didn't seem all that interested in going back north. "So did they, but I showed them a different path. They defended me out of love, while he came here for the sake of hate."

There was something about Sister Sebeal that made me believe her. Made me believe that she hadn't employed any tricks or mind games but had simply been herself, gentle yet inexorable.

"They will be welcome among us, provided they can put their old ways fully behind them." Mathghaman had said something like this before, but it bore repeating. "Our numbers are few, and our enemies are many."

I looked across the fire at him. He seemed pensive, though even then, he wasn't looking into the fire itself. We had a long way to go yet, but he was confident that he could find a route that would keep us mostly out of trouble until we reached the coast. There would still be monsters, still be dangers, but we'd rescued Sister Sebeal and killed a vampire, and for right then, we were doing okay.

He met my eyes and nodded, as if he could read my mind. Maybe he could. But the look in his eye was reassuring.

We still had unfinished business in the north. And from what hints we'd gotten in the Land of Shadows and Crows, there was a bigger war going on in the background, one we'd only just begun to glimpse. There were terrors aplenty still ahead of us. But while the platoon had been battered and cut nearly in half, we had new brothers among the

Tuacha. Whatever role we had in this strange world, we'd fill it next to them.

And the forces of darkness better look out.

Peter Nealen is a former United States Marine who now writes full time for a living.

https://www.americanpraetorians.com/

Other WarGate Titles Available now:

Forgotten Ruin
Tier 1000

For Updates, New Releases, and Other Titles, visit
www.WarGateBooks.com